TRUE NORTH

JENNIFER G. EDELSON

True North
Copyright ©2022 by Jennifer G. Edelson. All rights reserved.
Published and distributed by Bad Apple Books
Santa Fe, NM 87505

For information regarding book club appearances, bulk buys, or educational, promotional, or business inquiries, please contact BadAppleBooksinfo@gmail.com

Publisher's Cataloging-in-Publication Data

Names: Edelson, Jennifer G., author.
Title: True north / Jennifer G. Edelson.
Description: Santa Fe, NM : Bad Apple Books, 2022. | Summary: After drowning and being miraculously 'resurrected,' Indy starts channeling UFO coordinates. | Also available in ebook format.
Identifiers: ISBN 978-1-7335140-2-6 (paperback)
Subjects: LCSH: Science fiction. | CYAC: Extraterrestrial beings--Fiction. | High school students--Fiction. | Unidentified flying objects--Fiction. | Young adult fiction. | Romance fiction. | BISAC: YOUNG ADULT FICTION / Science Fiction / Alien Contact. | YOUNG ADULT FICTION / Romance / General.
Classification: LCC PZ7.1.E34 Tr 2022 (print) | LCC PZ7.1.E34 (ebook) | DDC [Fic]--dc23.

Cover design by Estella Vukovic
Interior design by Allusion Publishing (http://www.allusionpublishing.com)

PHONE HOME

INDY STARED AT the glowing computer monitor, wavering as she tapped a neon blue nail against her worn wooden desk. Typing in her passcode, her finger lingered over the *return* button for a moment before going live. "Hello, and welcome," she crooned into the microphone, smiling at a green alien GIF dancing on the computer screen.

As soon as the words left her mouth, True North's dedicated line rang. She answered it, jumping in with her usual call to arms. "Disobedience is the real foundation of liberty, so which are you this fine evening, warrior or lemming?"

"You summon UFOs," a male groused. "Does that mean *you're* an alien?"

Indy sighed into the microphone, and the sound came out distorted, disguised by the equipment she'd picked up at Bee's Electronics when she first had the idea to start broadcasting last summer. "Do you have a point, Caller?"

She gave the phone a dirty look for good measure. The cheap plastic burner wasn't really a conduit for the devil. Obvi. But she'd heard some variation of that same question at least once a week since she started True North eight months ago, and it was beginning to blister her nerves.

"Come on," the caller mocked, "you think anyone believes you can predict UFOs and shit?"

The caller's aggressive voice didn't surprise Indy. It sounded like most of True North's hecklers. Dull and a little bit lacking in the brains department. Frustrated, she gave her burner the bird. Dropping her chin in her hands, she pressed her fingertips against her eyelids under her purple-rimmed glasses, silently counting to three. "You're either new to the show or stupid, and I'm leaning toward stupid because I've said it before; I don't *summon* anything. The numbers tell me where the sightings are going to be." Not for the first time, Indy wished she could kick the caller's testicles into oblivion. People like that shouldn't be reproducing anyway.

"Gonna put it out there," the boy snickered, "you're a nut job, Orion."

True North's online chat room lit up. Indy stopped talking, pausing to read the chatter scrolling down her computer screen.

SLIM: Hey, Asshat, Orion's explained it a zillion times. He sees numbers, coordinates. He shares them here. We all go out and confirm.

Annie: Orion's a dude?

TREKKESTER2: Bullshit government propaganda. Orion? Please. True North's a cover. Total disinformation.

SaffronRD: Nah, dude. I've seen it myself. Two weeks ago. Just like Orion predicted, 40.3428° N, 105.6836° W. Right here in Colorado. She's always right.

Annie: Orion's a girl?

TREKKESTER2: Pics, or it didn't happen.

SLIM: Get a life, Trekkester2.

As more posts popped up, a grainy picture that may or may not be someone's tricked-out, oversized, rainbow-hued hubcap spilled into the left side of Indy's screen.

Indy grimaced at the microphone drooping near her coffee cup. Cheap shit. The only gear her minimum-wage, book-shelving gig at the local library afforded.

"You still there?" the caller asked.

"Totally," Indy sighed. "You know, I guess I get why you judge things you haven't seen for yourself. I mean, I've never met you, and I *know* you're an idiot."

"You wear tinfoil on your head?" the caller snickered. "Because it's messing with your brainwaves."

"All the time. To keep dumbasses out." She double-flipped her fingers at the phone, thrusting at the air for good measure. "Obviously, it doesn't always work."

Indy still wasn't sure how to feel about her coordinates. She already believed UFOs existed; what she didn't know was what to make of the inexplicable connection between the numbers in her head and what other people on True North's boards claimed to see in the skies after she posted them. Or even how, other than that she'd seen a UFO hovering above the Holy Ghost River just before she drowned in fifth grade, she might be connected to those sightings.

"As for the rest of you, I'm not a bot. Or an alien. Pretty sure I'm human. Otherwise . . . male, female, or somewhere in between . . . doesn't really matter, does it?"

"Reeeeetaaaarrrd!" a girl screeched in the background.

Indy hung up, ending the call with a canned recording of bleating sheep. As she started to upload another video, the burner lit up again, flashing at her furiously in her otherwise dark bedroom. Hesitating, she primed another round of sound effects, hitting return to send them out into the ether before answering.

"Hello, disobedience is the true foundation of liberty. Rebel or lackey, and how can I help tonight?" she asked, rolling her eyes at the ceiling.

"Why do you hide?" another male voice asked her. "Your voice, I mean?"

"Um, I guess because my identity isn't as important as what I'm doing."

"And what are you doing?"

Good question.

What. Am. I. Doing?

Shrugging, Indy tipped back in her chair and stared up at her egg-carton-paneled, bedroom-slash-attic ceiling. A gift from her mom, shabby chic decorating to the extreme so Indy could amp up her music to near-deafening levels without disturbing her artist father and writer mother's delicate sensibilities.

Indy bit her bottom lip. She'd started posting the numbers to True North's boards the second time they ambushed her, to record them before she forgot, or worse, they split her open. Because when she didn't get rid of them, she felt sick, as in barfing up her intestines sick, like the numbers were parasites chomping on her insides. Still, no one forced her to start an internet radio show. She could have just jotted down the numbers and stuck them in her desk along with all the other obscure things she'd hoarded over the years.

"Rebelling?" she finally breathed into the microphone. "Connecting? Staying sane on the down-low?"

"You call talking to a bunch of dicks who make fun of you connecting?"

"I do when I know a few of you are actually listening—people who feel the same as me. Humans are sheep, Caller. Life is confusing. At least here, we're all honest about it. Dicks and all."

Indy waited for some not-so-witty comeback, but instead, the line went dead.

Fishsticks. Good riddance.

Last thing she was in the mood for was another jock on a mission to prove her wrong. As it was, jocks were the bane of her existence. Or, more specifically, one jock—Sawyer Reyes.

Fiddling with a desktop file marked 'interviews,' Indy booted up a short soundbite from a guy in Utah who claimed he saw a UFO hovering over Salt Lake City's Capitol building last week. As she lined up a few more clips, a message popped open in the upper corner of her computer screen.

LiLi: Stupid caller. Want me to find out who he is and tap his ass?

Indy giggled. Her best friend, Lior, never minced words. Though she did sometimes have a habit of mixing them up. *Trust me,* Indy wrote back. *You don't want to tap his ass. Unless you're into that. Anyway, I'd miss you when you went to jail. Plus, orange looks like butt on you.* The soundbite ended, and Indy grabbed the mic, reminding people she had an open line before switching to an interview with an officer claiming to have evidence proving a secret alien base existed under the mountains in Dulce, New Mexico.

LiLi: What'd I say wrong?

Cap. Not tap. Indy wrote back.

LiLi: LOL!

A GIF of uber-pop-god Jason Leaver being held hostage by a rapping cat 'tapping' his backside popped up on Indy's screen. Indy typed out *barf*, then paused when her True North instant message box flashed, posting an incoming message just below Lior's lovely gift. VISITOR, the handle she'd chosen to announce True North IMs, blinked at her.

VISITOR: They're not random coordinates.

Indy glowered at the message, in no mood for games after the last two callers.

Orion: What do you mean?

VISITOR: Your numbers, they're not random. They are searching for something.

Indy's stomach turned. True North attracted people on the fringes, and as much as she loved talking about UFOs, what she didn't love were the hardcore conspiracy freaks and loonies who pretty much just sabotaged everything.

Orion: Maybe explain who 'they' are?

VISITOR: They need you, Orion.

Orion: Once again . . .

VISITOR: I need you.

Orion: I'm about to block you.

VISITOR: Why?

Orion: It's called trolling.

VISITOR: You hung up on me. I'm just finishing what I started.

Sitting back, Indy tapped one long blue fingernail furiously on her desktop.

Orion: Last caller? That was you?

VISITOR: The coordinates are getting closer to you. How come you haven't gone to see for yourself?

Visitor's question sent a chill down Indy's spine. She never shared personal information on the show. In fact, she used a voice-modifying mic and ran her IP address and internet program through Tor and a bunch of proxy servers. In theory, only she and Lior knew she had anything to do with True North. She'd never even shared the show's home state. And as far as she knew, more people listened to True North in Sydney, Australia, than anywhere near Santa Fe, New Mexico.

Inhaling, Indy tried to imagine Corazon High's student body discovering she was Orion — or at least the kids who listened, like all three of them.

Orion: Hold on a sec, Visitor.

She signed off the show, ending the live part of True North like always, with a Nietzsche quote she hoped made her sound older than her almost seventeen years. "Until next time," she added. "Deuces Losers." To Lior, she wrote. **Gotta go. Sorry. Tomorrow a.m. in front of Calc?**

LiLi: Okay. See ya, wouldn't want to be ya. Lior added a million smiley faces for good measure.

Turning her attention back to Visitor, Indy typed quickly, grimacing at the monitor as though it might leap off the desk and bite her.

Orion: You still there?

VISITOR: Waiting.

Orion: What makes you think I live close to any of the coordinates?

VISITOR: Call it a hunch.

Orion: Do we know each other?

VISITOR: Not exactly.

That Visitor didn't write 'no' outright bothered her. What if someone from Corazon knew she was masquerading as Orion? Even now, six years after drowning, people sometimes still gossiped about how she'd died and been miraculously resurrected. About how she pretended to drown for attention or how she had, in fact, died and came back to life, possessed by demons. That one especially was a Corazon High student body favorite. And she had no desire to ever poke at that hornet's nest again.

Orion: Then what do you want?

VISITOR: It's your fault I'm here, Orion.

Indy sat back, away from the monitor. *My fault? Really?*

Orion: No one twisted your arm and made you listen to the show.

VISITOR: That's not what I meant.

Orion: This is getting old. Tell me what you want, or I'm out of here.

VISITOR: I want to meet you.

Orion: And I want to eat an entire box of Cheez-Its and make out with Dean Winchester. But it's not gonna happen. So sad. Oh, well. She held a finger over the 'return' button. Going now.

VISITOR: Wait!

Orion: What?

VISITOR: I want to go home. I want to find my people.

*Orion: *Snorts* Don't we all.*

VISITOR: I'm serious.

Orion: And you want me to help you how?

Indy sniffed at her cats Kepler and Hubble, lounging on her purple comforter. Like half the people who called in, she was pretty sure Visitor ate bologna on the regular. He was talking her in circles, and for some stupid reason, she was letting him. Why wasn't she in bed already, reading a bad romance while she finished off her smuggled can of Pringles?

Indy waited for an answer, feeling a little uneasy. *Delusional much, Visitor?*

The empty, glowing IM box glared at Indy before winking out entirely. She shook her head at it. Visitor's words, *I want to go home* rang in her ears like he'd said them out loud. And damn. He should know, calling Uber, or 911 even was probably a better option.

Exasperated, Indy closed her laptop. She almost felt sorry for Visitor. Everyone wanted to feel special; some people were just better at carving out pockets of denial and making crap up. Plus, after drowning, she'd spent many nights contemplating her own place in the universe. First, the way kids do, wondering about things like whether God exists and wanted to smite her for sneaking peanut butter and chocolate out of the kitchen after midnight, then later, more philosophically; like whether there were other resurrected girls out there, and if so, whether it meant there was more to life than just a physical presence on Earth.

Indy even sort of understood Visitor. In a way, she wanted to go home too. Because ever since fifth grade, she'd felt abstract, like part of her had vanished underwater. Half of her *was* home. But her other half was still on some weird as hell journey.

MI CORAZON

INDY JUMPED BACK, tripping into a clique of gawking girls as she stepped out of the way of Corazon High's bad-boy track star, Sawyer Reyes. Sawyer sauntered down the crowded hall, completely ignoring the other humans in his path—like always. As Sawyer passed her, he shot her a sideways glance, grimacing or maybe grinning (she could never tell), before rolling his eyes at the jock-heavy entourage that flanked him.

For whatever reason, Sawyer had been giving Indy that sideways eye roll daily since the first time he walked into her tenth-grade American History class, mid-semester. For a year now, it'd been his thing, as though she amused him for the worst possible reasons.

Counting to three, Indy took a deep breath and smoothed her purple Anarchy Now! t-shirt down over her stomach, more to calm her nerves than anything. Two extra steps, and she would have been roadkill beneath Sawyer's feet, as well as fodder for the school's hyperactive gossip mill. It wouldn't be the first time. Whenever she did more than just blend with the crowd, she somehow became the subject of other people's fantastical stories. High schools were the worst kind of breeding grounds for bad gossip and internet memes, especially when you defied the odds and started breathing again after twenty minutes of swimming with the fishes.

Grumbling an apology to the group of girls she bumped into, Indy shimmied sideways through the crowd toward her best friends, Lior and Cora, standing near her locker. Mortified, Indy purposely smacked her forehead into her yellow locker door. "Kill me now," she groaned woefully.

Cora tugged at Indy's high ponytail, grinning good-naturedly. "Smooth," she snorted. "I swear, India, it's like you're pavement. Sawyer's constantly almost running you over."

Indy sighed pathetically, opened her locker, and rubbed her forehead against the cool mirror hanging inside, her real nose smashed up against her reflective one. "He hates me," she moaned. "What did I ever do to him?"

"You bested him at the physics fair," Cora said, smiling at the thought.

Indy laughed. Sawyer's middle name may as well be *Jock*. And he was definitely a rebel. But he also shared almost every AP class Indy had. She was sure he'd never admit it, but Sawyer hated losing anything, merit scholarships and math tournaments included. Still, he'd started giving her those exaggerated eye rolls months before placing second to her first.

"I doubt he even noticed," Indy muttered. "He barely knows anyone exists outside his little bubble."

Cora raised an eyebrow. "Do you care?"

"Not really."

Embarrassed that she even thought about Sawyer, Indy linked arms with Lior and Cora, maneuvering them outside to escape the crowded hallway. Plunking down at the top of a concrete stairwell just off the quad, she opened her Wonder Woman lunchbox—a gift from Cora and Lior on her sixteenth birthday—and pulled out a bagel, surreptitiously staring at Sawyer off tossing a football in the distance. While Lior obsessively braided her long black hair into mini plaits over and over, fidgeting over her lunch, Cora told them about her new crush. Indy ignored them both, daydreaming about Sawyer's lips as she stared at the newly snowcapped Sangre de Cristo Mountains.

"Lior!" Cora suddenly shrieked, pausing to grab Lior's hand mid-braid.

Cora's yelp startled Indy back to reality. She grabbed Lior's sketchpad off the step and handed it to Lior, trying to read her mind. Sometimes she thought she could, especially when Lior raised one perfect black eyebrow at Cora as if to say, *how am I supposed to sit still when you talk so freaking much?*

Nodding at the sketchpad, Cora barked, "Doodle or something. You're driving me crazy."

Lior's dark brown eyes narrowed, focusing on Cora. More interested in blending with the steps than mediating Cora and Lior's dispute, Indy stared down at her black Docs, tugging at a shiny gold lace. Lior could be squirmy, and unless she had a sketchpad in hand, her constant movement sometimes drove people crazy. But Cora especially had little patience for it.

"Sorry," Lior grumped. "I was just thinking about . . ."

Out of nowhere, a soaring football bashed into Indy's travel mug. It knocked the top off, sending streams of brown liquid into the air, showering all three of them with coffee.

Indy jumped up, wiping coffee off her shirt as a swarm of red and brown letterman jackets converged on the steps. They reminded her of clotted blood. That's what most of Corazon High's jocks were, anyway, generic cells clinging together as they floated through the same artery.

"God, Li, I'm sorry!" August Márquez, one of Corazon's star football players and Sawyer's best friend, grabbed Lior's hand, pulling her forward as if to save her. "It was supposed to go that way." He pointed toward the football field.

Lior yanked her hand away, glaring at him. She'd been pining after August since the day August's family moved in next door to her in first grade. And though Lior denied it, Indy was pretty sure August felt the same way. Then high school came around. August grew six inches up and out, and girls with short cheerleading skirts who didn't wear Doc Martens and homemade clothing started paying attention to him.

"It's fine," Lior grumbled.

Indy scanned the crowd on the steps. Six jocks came running after the football, including Sawyer. He stood there staring at her; his head cocked the same way Indy's had been moments earlier, one raven eyebrow angled just enough to make him look arrogant.

"You okay?" he asked her.

Indy balked, resisting the urge to poke a finger in her ear. Sawyer just spoke to her. Like two whole words that didn't include *get* or *out* or *of my way.*

"Yeah, I think so." She chewed on the corner of her bottom lip, trying to think of some witty response. Whenever Sawyer got close, her head spun.

"You sure?"

"Did you throw the ball?" Sawyer's confident grin irked her. Why couldn't she just act normal around him? Why did Sawyer make her feel like he strapped her into a thousand-volt crazy chair and pulled the switch?

"Yeah, but I didn't mean to hit you, India." He smiled innocently. "It wasn't on purpose."

Indy leaned down and snatched the football up, holding it against her chest. She pursed her lips and flared her nostrils at him, waiting for some flash of inspiration.

Sawyer held his hand out, exposing long, graceful fingers. "Can I have it?'

"Sure." Without thinking, she chucked it across the quad, watching it sail past the flagpole.

Sawyer cranked his neck, following the ball as it landed on someone's lunch tray. He snorted, turning to cock an eye at her. A Sawyer expression if there ever was one.

"Okay, then." In a flash, he bounded down the steps, pausing briefly to look back over his shoulder at her with feisty green eyes as he motioned for his minions to follow.

"Yikes," Cora said. "Did you have to chuck it?"

"Sorry." Indy frowned. "It sorta chucked itself."

Lior laughed. "You know you keep giving him more reasons to shun you."

"Me?" Indy screeched. "*He* hit *us* with the stupid ball."

"On accident," Lior and Cora said in unison.

Indy watched Sawyer and the rest of Corazon's finest run off, their heads bobbing. She felt a little bad and started rationalizing her knee-jerk reaction out loud, but her skull split open, violently spilling its contents in a bright stream of pulsating numbers. They hung in the air, hogging up her sight as if they existed for real.

Indy doubled over, smashing her palms against her temples.

"Indy!" Lior yelped, leaning in to catch her.

"Sketchpad," Indy gulped, blindly reaching out to feel around her backpack for a pen.

Lior handed Indy the sketchpad. Squeezing her eyes shut, Indy tried focusing on the swirl of numbers churning through a miasma of colors. 32, 38, 24, 106, 49, 07. She started scribbling, writing them out before projectile vomiting across the steps.

"Jesus!" Lior jumped sideways. Grabbing Indy's forearm, she quickly helped Cora steer Indy back inside the main building, steadying her against a row of dingy yellow lockers. "Are you okay?"

Indy wiped her mouth with her wrist and shook her head, tipping it back against a cool metal door. Peeking out at the hall through pinched lashes, she pretended the kids around them weren't milling around staring. She was aces at pretending. She'd had six long years to perfect it.

"Your nose, babe," Cora said, reaching out with a tissue. "It's bleeding."

Indy took the wad Cora thrust at her and dabbed at her nose, wiping away a trickle of blood. Averting her eyes, she pretended she didn't see Lior gaping.

"Dude, you just puked on the quad steps!" Cora said gleefully. "You're freaking awesome!"

Lior shot Cora a look before gently removing the sketchpad still latched between Indy's tightly gripped fingers. She shielded the pad from Cora's stare, looking down at Indy's numbers before signaling with a nod that they'd talk later.

"Oh my God!" Indy cringed. "Cora's right. I just threw up in front of everyone!"

Humiliation burned through Indy's limbs, turning her into a flushed mess of nerves. If she could sink into the ground or blend into the wall, she would. But her arms refused to work, and her legs wouldn't drop her. Instead, they held her in place against the row of lockers, wobbling like a newborn giraffe. *Great.* She closed her eyes. No doubt she'd go down in Corazon's weekly annals as Friday's lunchtime freak show.

The idea made Indy's stomach turn. People already loved gossiping about her. Because she blurted out what she thought despite her best efforts to keep her mouth shut—usually at the most awkward moments. Because she had an, *I Heart Camus* bumper sticker on her locker door and worked in a library by choice instead of Hot Topic at the mall. Because back in second grade, in the middle of a school assembly, she'd stood up and announced that her imaginary best friend, Günther the Hedgehog, had the same rights as people (and they never got over that shit). But most of all, because after falling into the Holy Ghost River and drowning in fifth grade, she'd told everyone at school that a UFO had saved her.

"Everyone's looking at us, right?" she mumbled.

Lior shook her head, trying to assure Indy that her vomit fest would live in infamy for all of an hour. And Lior meant well, but an hour at Corazon was like a lifetime.

3

RESURRECTION

AFTER A RESTLESS nap, Indy dragged herself out of bed and headed to the kitchen. Her parents were still out schmoozing at some downtown art gallery opening, which meant frozen burritos and a bag of Ruffles again for dinner—not that she was complaining.

Armed with an array of junk food, she went outside to the patio in time to watch night descending over the Jemez Mountains. Above her, turquoise and ruby-hued clouds seeped over golden hills lining the arroyo behind her house, cascading into a cacti-spotted gully. Comforted by the view, she planted herself on her favorite ratty lawn chair and sat cross-legged while she ate, feeling calmer in her secluded backyard.

Nature was Indy's thing. Being outside cleared her mind, and as she inhaled smoke from her neighbor's mesquite fire, she tried to imagine merging with the burgeoning star-speckled night. The great outdoors had been her first love from birth practically, and dying on a high desert mountain in the Sangre de Cristo Pass just strengthened her connection to the landscape. Only hearty things withstood the desert, and she liked to think she was one of them. She liked to imagine that the night she was resurrected, her connection to the land brought her back to life.

Drowning in fifth grade—the figures hovering over the river and the strange lights and rainbow clouds above the water—was still as fresh in Indy's mind as her newly opened bag of Ruffles. Despite temperatures that bottomed out at thirty degrees that night, she'd heard a strange humming noise near their campsite and wandered out of her tent, thinking that maybe her parents were working on some mad-scientist-meets-nature art project down near the river-bank. Barefoot and clad only in a thermal nightgown, she'd dragged along her bear, Boo, who incidentally had not survived. Boo was still one of that night's great mysteries. While paramedics found Indy's body in the river, Boo had vanished into thin air. To this day, Indy liked imagining that he traveled off across the universe with the craft she saw hovering in the sky.

Smiling at the thought that Boo might be out there among the stars, Indy stuffed the last of her burrito into her mouth. Aiming for the fire pit across the patio, she crinkled her napkin into a ball and tossed it over a stack of hewn logs. Laying back in the chair, she kicked her feet up, feeling almost morose as she contemplated whether to post the numbers that split her head open earlier. What if Visitor was right? Or worse, what if Visitor knew who she was and leaked it to all of Corazon High? Just the idea—that she'd be exposed—freaked her out.

Indy sighed. She stood up and stretched, reminding herself to be braver.

What if, indeed. Her life was one big what-if anyway. She lived with it daily. Why stop taking chances now?

Resolute, Indy ran upstairs and woke her computer. Nervous about where the numbers might lead, she tapped the 'live' button and switched on the mic, waking the little green alien on the screen. "Hello," she crooned, "how are you all tonight?" Pausing, she took a deep breath before rushing out, "So, listeners, I've had a really weird day. Are you ready? I've got a new set. Y'all want to know what they are?"

As soon as the words left her mouth, the chatroom lit up.

Matty70: Spill, Orion.

SLIM: Weird is normative for this show.

EVA6969: Hehe. Slim said 'normative.'

AcerRacer: Tool.

Indy unfolded the paper she'd ripped from Lior's sketchbook earlier and entered the numbers into Google's search function, reciting them out loud as she nervously typed them in. "32, 38, 24, 106, 49, 07. Definitely not lottery numbers," she joked. "This time it's . . ." she waited for Google to pull up a map, learning the location along with her listeners like she had since the first time someone on the boards suggested they might be coordinates, "White Rock, New Mexico!"

White Rock, New Mexico.

About thirty miles away.

Close … just like Visitor promised.

HIGHER GROUND

A SATURDAY MORNING rush of motivated students kept Indy glued to the library's reference desk. Around ten, after all the early birders cleared out, she finally found a moment to breathe. Happy to take a break from actual people, Indy coded and shelved the books left in the library's *donations* bin, then made her way to Circulation, ready to make friends with a quiet counter and a seat.

Checking to make sure no one saw her, she pulled a sheet of scribbled numbers out of her jeans pocket, wavering before reluctantly typing them into Google maps again. Yep. Still coordinates. Still White Rock, New Mexico. If she wanted to, she could hop in her Jeep after work and be there in less than an hour.

The new coordinates provoked a mix of horror and excitement. She didn't doubt that the numbers themselves were legit, but she sometimes wondered if the way she interpreted them might be more psyche-driven than celestial, like a fucked-up Rorschach test. Maybe the part where True North's listeners claimed to see disturbances in the sky was an elaborate hoax, or her listeners made the sightings up because they wanted to believe—because sometimes, fantasy was easier to get behind than real life. Or maybe they were all letting themselves get entangled in some weird mass hysteria. Though her gut told her none of that was true. *Something* was unfolding in the southwestern skies, and it would be good to finally know what that *something* was for certain.

Indy abused the library's official stamp seal, power-stamping the circulation counter while she tried to think more rationally about what that something could be. The only other option was to hyperventilate, and crappy though the library pay was, she needed the job. It covered the equipment that kept True North going.

Indy's head throbbed; her imagination stuck in overdrive. What if she drove up to White Rock and something did materialize? What if that something abducted her? Or worse, nothing happened, and she really was delusional?

Finally, she texted Lior.

Want 2 drive 2 White Rock with me when I'm off?

Lior texted back almost immediately. **Why?**

Umm . . . The #'s

Indy waited, watching an ellipsis bounce on her screen.

You sure that's a good idea?

She bit her lip. In the six years since Holy Ghost, Lior never once questioned Indy's crazy story. She'd even championed Indy's decision to start True North last summer, arguing that an online community, where Indy felt comfortable talking about what she'd seen with other people, might do her good. But since the numbers thing started, Lior had also given Indy more than a few well-meaning, equally annoying speeches. *You have a near-photographic memory, Indy. How do you know they aren't last month's NASDAQ returns or lotto numbers? Or the product of sleep deprivation from too much studying* (and true enough, Indy studied a lot, but seriously?) *Or, like, a brain tumor?* For real, Lior had nagged Indy to make a doctor's appointment more than a few times.

Indy sighed. Finally, she typed out, *Guess I'm going to go up there and find out. If nothing happens, moving on. Come or don't. Though I'd love ur company.*

K. Can I bring August?

Seriously? (!!!!!!!!!!)

**Blushes* He's helping my dad fix a hinge on the garage. Asked if I want to grab coffee afterward.*

LIOR! Yes. Bring him. Just don't tell him y.

Duh. I'll say we're going for a drive and maybe some food.

GR8. C U close to 1. Ur house. I'll drive.

Indy shoved her phone in her pocket and grabbed a pile of books from the still half-full overnight bin (because, *hello*, lazy co-workers). Lost in a stack, she absently placed them on the shelves while she obsessed about White Rock. Until Sawyer Reyes's voice echoed in the lobby.

Startled, Indy peeked around a bookshelf to find Sawyer waiting at the front desk carrying two paperbacks under his right arm. When no one came to help him, he called out again, then rang the desk bell—over, and over, and over.

Nervous at the sight of Sawyer tapping one black Converse impatiently against the check-in counter, not to mention his stupid perfect face and somehow messy but still perfectly coiffed pompadour, Indy tossed the book she was holding back onto the cart and smoothed her black-and-white checkered t-shirt, pulling it down flat around her waist. She took teeny, tiny breaths, trying to avoid a mini freak-out as she walked to the counter.

"India," Sawyer said, cocking his head, "I've got two returns."

Oddly enough, Sawyer spent a lot of time at the library, though they never said much more to each other than 'book' 'over there' and 'hello.' Not that it mattered. Sawyer *always* made her nervous, which is partly why she kept the small talk to a minimum. But after barfing on the quad yesterday, she felt jittery just looking at him.

Sawyer handed her two novels. Wielding the scanner, Indy swiped each of the book's barcodes, too aware of the flush spreading across her cheeks. She stared at their book jackets, losing it over the fact that he'd checked out *On the Road* and *The Fountainhead* from the local library just because. No one she knew did that anymore. Most kids either downloaded books from Amazon or Apple or just didn't read. Sawyer, though—over the last year, he'd checked out so many books she'd lost count. His evident love for the Santa Fe library was part of the reason she'd secretly started crushing on him despite his jock attitude. She liked imagining he had these deeper layers buried beneath all that swagger.

Sawyer tilted his head sideways, simultaneously dipping his head lower to meet hers and raising both eyebrows. He managed to say a lot with his eyebrows. They were dark and thick as tar and framed a pair of intense, army-green, often guarded eyeballs.

"What?" Indy murmured, blushing.

"You're glaring at those books like you want to do them harm."

Indy recoiled, surprised by Sawyer's comment. Surprised he just spoke to her at all. She nodded down at the counter. "I was just wondering what you thought of them. The books," she clarified.

Sawyer ran a hand through the shock of dark chocolate waves breaking ranks over his forehead. "You've never asked before."

Indy swallowed, then shrugged. "I love *The Fountainhead*," she said shyly. "I remember when you checked out *The Stranger*. Camus is my favorite. But no one else I know reads him."

"Yeah?"

Sawyer did that thing with his eyebrows again, and India got the distinct impression he had less than a clue how cute he was when he was being contemplative. "Yeah," she said softly.

"*The Stranger* wasn't my thing."

"No?"

"It was too cold." He shrugged. "Too inhuman."

Indy smile-grimaced, nodding her agreement. If it were physically possible, she'd swoon.

"So, are you like, sick?" he asked.

She frowned, flushing with embarrassment. Did she look sick? Did she smell bad? Was she pale?

"You barfed on the quad yesterday, remember? Right after you chucked the ball."

"Oh, oh God," she gasped. "You actually saw?"

"Riley caught it on video." He grinned. "Everyone saw."

Indy opened her mouth. It hung there unhinged, growing stiffer by the moment.

"Right." Sawyer squinted at her. "Well, I'll assume you're okay then. I'm gonna go grab a new book. Guess I'll see you in a few hours."

Indy nodded, then flinched. "Wait, what?"

"White Rock." He shrugged.

She stared at him, mortified. What had Lior done? "I . . . you're going?"

For a moment, Sawyer paled. But it was more like a tic that he quickly caught, morphing from a grimace to an exasperated eye roll. "I thought you knew. August invited me. I won't, though, if you have a problem with it."

"Uh, no," she choked out, one-hundred percent lying. "I mean, it's just, no one told me. We're just going to grab a bite or something. Of course you're welcome to join us."

Fishsticks! How in the world was she supposed to drive straight with Sawyer in her car? They'd just talked more in the last five minutes than they had since he transferred to Corazon a little over a year ago, and she already felt like dying.

"Great. See you soon then."

Rapping his knuckles on the counter, Sawyer walked off, heading for the sci-fi section near the library's entrance. Staring at his backside, Indy sighed and pulled out the library slip from *On the Road*. She dropped it on the counter and typed her employee code into the computer, grumbling when the front door opened, whipping up a breeze that flipped the card over. She went to flip it rightside up but handwriting on the backside of the otherwise clean sheet caught her eye. Someone had written, *I thought I was lost. But all roads lead here. There are no wrong turns, after all.*

Indy grimaced. Lovely sentiment. Too bad having Sawyer join them on the drive up to White Rock felt like the wrongest turn ever.

Since fifth grade, Indy hadn't let herself trust anyone except Lior. And later, for the most part, Cora. After the first couple years of sustained teasing, she'd shut everyone out and powered down. And maybe it *was* all in the past like mama-bear Lior kept reminding her. But old habits were hard to break, especially when they involved ungodly gorgeous boys like Sawyer.

Back safely hidden between two metal shelves, Indy closed her eyes and inhaled, holding her breath for a second. Sawyer made her weak in the knees, no doubt. He earned serious cred in the looks department without even trying. And he *was* smart, racking up bonus points galore. But she'd also convinced herself her crush on him was just physical. That she would never, in a million years, let herself be *that girl*, the one who fawned over the popular boy who basically just ignored her.

Indy puttered around the library obsessing about Sawyer and White Rock until her shift ended. Then she drove straight to Lior's. She pulled into Lior's driveway and immediately spotted August, Sawyer, and Lior one house over, leaning against August's Pontiac GTO—an old thing August had managed to tinker and polish into a beautiful, shiny monster. And dammit. She wasn't going to get the chance she wanted to freshen up, or like, breathe, after all. Instead, Indy parked and mumbled *you can do this* under her breath, waving at them through the windshield manically.

Gleeful, Lior almost floated to Indy's Jeep. She hopped into the front seat sporting an enormous grin. Grateful, Indy got out to let August and Sawyer climb in behind her. No way would she have survived the drive with Sawyer looming in her periphery. When they were settled, she backed out onto the narrow, adobe-dotted street, inhaling deeply again for a different reason. Maybe Sawyer joining them would be a good thing. At least she'd have a distraction until something—fingers crossed—happened.

On the way to White Rock, Lior gossiped about the Prom Committee's plans to hold an eighties-themed junior prom. Indy listened, nodding at the ochre hills surrounding the highway that morphed into red-rock mesas as she drove while simultaneously trying to tune out August and Sawyer, heatedly arguing behind her about which was better, track or football.

Nearer to White Rock, Lior jostled her arm. "So, do you want to go?"

"To prom?" Indy asked, surprised Lior forgot she'd sworn off prom after watching *Carrie.*

"No." Lior rolled her eyes. "August just asked if we wanted to catch Corazon's basketball playoffs in a couple weeks."

Indy's mouth dropped. Because basketball? That would be a hard *no.*

Sawyer caught Indy's eyes in the rearview mirror, shooting her an epic *where do you come from, really?* look. "You don't like basketball?" he asked, leaning over the seatback near her right shoulder.

Indy shrugged.

"Football?"

Indy shook her head *no*.

"Track?"

I like track when I can watch you.

Ugh. She just barely stopped herself from smacking her own forehead. Mumbling, *get a grip* under her breath, she inhaled hard and grasped the steering wheel.

Pitching closer, Sawyer rested his chin near Indy's right shoulder. "What'd you just say?"

"Nothing," she nearly stuttered. "Just humming."

"Huh. What kind of music do you like?"

"Everything, I guess," she answered stiffly. "I mean, I have eclectic tastes."

"Eclectic tastes . . ." he echoed, his warm breath tickling her ear.

If Indy turned just an inch to her right, she was sure she'd find Sawyer staring at her with his signature hooked eyebrow. She heard it in his voice. It permeated the air. And oh, how she hated its effect on her. "At least that's what my parents say," she added.

"Are you close to your parents?"

Indy gave Lior a look, shrugging as they exchanged glances. She loved her parents fiercely, Lior could attest, but they erred on the highly eccentric side of everything, and trying to sum up how *that* affected her would take hours. "Yeah, I am," she answered, and it wasn't a lie. It just didn't speak to the wall she'd built around herself after stewing for too long about all the ways they managed to discount her opinions—including when it came to the night she drowned. "You?"

"Definitely," he answered. "They've always had my back."

"Lucky you."

"Yours don't?"

"No," Indy stumbled. "I mean, that's not it. I was just thinking about all the trouble you get in at school." She snickered before she could stop herself. "They must *really* have your back."

Next to her, Lior squirmed in the seat, giving Indy stink eye.

"No doubt!" August laughed from the backseat, clapping Sawyer on the shoulder. "Dude's a walking menace. But I've never heard anyone complain about it except you."

Embarrassed by her bad behavior, Indy tipped the rearview mirror, lining it up with Sawyer's lowered eyes. "Sawyer, I didn't mean it to sound . . . I mean . . . I just meant, you know. You like . . . you like things on the wild side. And I have a big mouth," she added for good measure.

Sawyer peeked up at her from under dark lashes that reminded Indy of the fans Vegas showgirls used. Even perturbed, his eyes glowed. "You do." He frowned.

"Oh, Sizzle!" Lior exhaled.

"Shizzle," Indy and Sawyer said in unison.

Lior giggled. "Whatever."

From lighting the north quad's garbage dumpster on fire to dating almost every cheerleader on Corazon's squad, Sawyer had a well-earned reputation. But it was also true that nearly everyone adored him. And Indy had seen him do as many nice things for people as she'd seen him act like a jackass. Like when he sent Tommy Parsons packing after Tommy mistook Janelle Tan's 'no' for 'take me now' at Homecoming last year. If Indy were being honest, Sawyer wasn't 'bad' as much as he was rebellious. Unwilling to answer to just anyone. And to that, she related entirely.

Indy tried to hold Sawyer's stare. "I'm sorry," she mouthed at the mirror.

Sawyer sat back, crossing his arms over his chest. Turning to look out at the pocked rockface whizzing by, he pulled a set of earbuds from the denim pocket over his heart and tucked them into his ears, ignoring her entirely until they reached White Rock.

DARK SKIES

INDY BUZZED WITH nervous energy. Sitting in a worn booth across the table from Sawyer, she fidgeted while she alternated between staring at him and peeking out the front window. Until Lior kicked her under the table.

What? she mouthed at Lior.

Lior pursed her lips and nodded at the window, then back at the pizza on the table, shaking her head disapprovingly. Indy got the message. She was acting like a caffeinated honeybee.

"You guys been up to the overlook?" August asked, polishing off his last slice.

Indy nodded vigorously. White Rock sat on a mesa above the Rio Grande, just below the Jemez Mountains. The lookout was one of her favorite places and where she'd been planning to head when she decided to drive up here all along. The site scored mega points for its beauty, and at the tip of the lookout, where the concrete walkway gave way to sheered, red-orange cliffs, mountains framed the Rio Grande's switchbacks down in a sweeping valley.

"I haven't been there," Sawyer answered.

"We should go, then," Lior nodded.

August threw a wad of bills on the table. He grinned, rubbing his stomach over his letterman's jacket. "Let's do it. I need to walk anyway. I'm stuffed to the freaking gills."

Indy held back a snort. Because yeah, August had somehow managed to polish off two sausage and mushroom pizzas on his own. And if that wasn't a sign of high strangeness right there, she didn't know what was.

Only slightly less spastic, Indy drove them to the overlook, excited to see if anything happened *and* eager to share the view with Sawyer. Not that she'd tell him that. Or that they were *sharing it*, sharing it. Just that, she was bursting with curiosity over how he'd feel about the scenery.

She stole a peek at him in the rearview mirror. Sawyer could be a cool cucumber. He never got particularly ruffled. In fact, other than that infernal smirk and eye roll, he seemed pretty chill most of the time, as if his face never mastered more than a few expressions. Though, lucky for him, even blank, it was pretty damned spectacular.

"Wow," he said as they pulled into Overlook Park, "it's awesome."

"Just wait," August promised, crawling out of Indy's Jeep first. Indy barely had the car in park before he climbed over Lior's seat, tugging at the lever and hauling Lior out behind him.

Indy pulled her keys out of the ignition. She flipped her seat forward, watching Sawyer fold himself in half to climb out. Standing in front of her Jeep, he reached for the sky, drawing his runner's body up to what she guessed was his full six feet. He stretched, looking at her curiously before meandering off toward the end of the causeway.

Following behind him, Indy searched the sky. At the end of the walkway, she stopped and hung over the railing, looking down at the Rio Grande in wonder.

"It's how I think of you," Sawyer said, moving closer to stand beside her.

"Huh?" Indy tucked her chin, dropping her head sideways to see him better as she hunched over the railing.

"Mystifying," he said. "Rocky. Beautiful."

Indy stared down at the river valley, tongue tied. Was he serious?

"It's not an insult, India."

She squinted at him, stopping just short of a frown. "I guess I don't know what you mean by *mystifying*."

He shrugged, scrunching his strong shoulders. "I've just never been able to figure you out."

"When have you ever tried?" she sniffed, making a face she instantly regretted.

"Indy's a little tone deaf," Lior cut in. "It's partly why we love her."

Sawyer shook his head, still staring at her. "I try all the time. You just never pay attention."

Sawyer might be messing with her. Messing with her would totally be his thing. But he sounded sincere and maybe even a little bummed about it. "Running me down in the hall every day doesn't count."

Nearly simultaneously, August and Lior burst out laughing.

"Sawyer, you've said like two words to me all year." She frowned.

August scrubbed Indy's crown playfully. "You're so dense you're like a wall, Indy."

Indy swatted his fist away. August might be one of the few people at Corazon, other than Lior and Cora, she actually liked. But she wasn't at all okay with being mocked, even if it was well-meaning.

Peeved, she started to give August a piece of her mind, but the sky rumbled.

Above them, an enormous cloudbank full of high-definition cotton ball clouds formed. It churned, rotating into a shallow funnel. As they watched it, the inside of the funnel flickered, flittering from gray, to yellow, to indigo, then back to white.

"What the . . .?" Lior shielded her eyes.

Indy did the same, mesmerized. "Do you see that?" she whispered. Something metallic-looking with hard edges that peeked through before blending seamlessly back into the cloudbank flickered near the miasma's center. The cloud rumbled again like a storm, though Indy felt sure that the rumbling came from the object inside it. The noise wasn't thunder.

"Nasty storm brewing," August told them.

"It's not a storm," Indy said to the sky.

"Come on," Lior grabbed Indy's arm, "let's get outta here before we get pummeled!"

"By what?" Indy yanked her arm away.

"Lightning," August answered, as though it should be obvious. "Didn't you get the whole 'when thunder roars go indoors' lecture when you were a kid?"

Indy had. But not from her family. Her parents would never let something as mundane as a storm stand in the way of communing with nature. Indy couldn't remember the last time they'd been caught out around lightning when they hadn't just found a slab of rock to hunker down under. Besides, this was different, and Lior knew it. Indy could tell by the look in her eyes.

Indy shot Lior a fiercely serious frown, telepathically reminding her they'd come out to White Rock for just this thing. But Lior shook her head. *Come on, Indy,* she mouthed.

Indy stepped back. "Take my keys." She yanked them from her pocket. "I'm staying."

Exasperated, Lior dropped her arms to her sides. "You stay, I stay."

The clouds above them continued to churn, and Indy stole a peek at Sawyer. He stood beside her, face tilted up, glued to his spot as if paralyzed by the commotion.

"Do *you* see it?" she asked him quietly.

Sawyer nodded. But he didn't look away from the disturbance.

Indy stood beside him expectantly. She watched the clouds roil, rigidly waiting for another glimpse of whatever lurked inside the funnel, her head vibrating like the inside of a ringing bell. Without thinking, she reached for Sawyer's hand.

Sawyer didn't hesitate. He grasped Indy's palm, wrapping his long fingers around hers tightly. Rapt, they watched the cloudbank glow until it vanished as quickly as it appeared, leaving a hole in her heart *and* the sky.

"What *was* that?" she asked reverently.

"India," Sawyer said, releasing her hand, "your nose."

Dazed, she met Sawyer's eyes. They were soft and focused on her face like they had been just seconds ago on the clouds. "Oh, oh God." Frantically, she dug through her jacket, locating an old Starbucks napkin.

"Are you okay?" he asked.

Indy held the napkin to her bleeding nose just as Sawyer pulled a strand of hair off her face. "Of . . . of course."

"Was that even a storm?" August clapped Sawyer on the back. "I've never seen anything like it."

Behind the napkin, Indy shook her head. It wasn't a storm. She felt it in her bones. But damned if she knew how to describe it any better.

"We should go," Lior said softly.

Indy shivered. Staring at Sawyer, what she truly wanted to say was, *you saw what I saw inside the cloud, right?* But the uncomfortable tension that bounced between them all gave her pause. Grimacing, she took a step back. Her head felt like it might burst, and her nose was still full of blood.

"You sure you're okay, India?" Sawyer asked again.

"Yes." She pulled the napkin away and tried to fake a smile. "That was wild, right?"

Sawyer's left eyebrow hooked even higher than usual, almost meeting his hairline. He opened his mouth, but Lior grabbed Indy's arm before he could say anything, pulling her toward the parking lot. "This isn't okay," she growled under her breath, maneuvering Indy to the Jeep. "In fact, it's really wrong."

Indy took a deep breath and let it out slowly, both terrified and elated. Visitor was right. Her numbers *were* legit coordinates. And maybe she had been the only person in her group who noticed the object inside the cloud, but she knew something was in that funnel for certain. She knew it in her gut the way she knew her heart was still seated inside her body. And she was determined to find out what it was.

NIGHTSTALKER

CORA PULLED HER Starbucks apron over her head and dumped it on the coffee house table next to Lior's latte. She clamped her bottom lip between braces-straight teeth as she dipped her head forward, loosening a caramel lock of crimped bang that fell over her peacock blue eyes before she brushed it away, pulling Indy into a soulful hug.

"No one's gossiping about you anymore. I promise."

Indy nodded vigorously. Cora meant well, but they'd all heard the same bathroom talk all week. *Ask Jamie*, Corazon's very own online gossip page, posted that Indy barfed on the quad last Friday because she was pregnant. According to Jamie, after being attacked on a hike up in the Santa Fe Forest, Indy was carrying Bigfoot's child. Because duh. All week long, even Sawyer's eye rolls had been stained with sympathy.

"It's fine, Cor. I mean, really," Indy threw her hands up, "in the grand scheme of things, none of it matters, right?" She shoved a croissant into her mouth and crossed her eyes, but her heart wasn't in it. Visitor still hadn't called back. And his silence, combined with Indy's unanswered questions after White Rock, was crazymaking.

"Oh!" Cora exclaimed, snapping Indy back to attention. "Have you guys heard about that UFO show yet? It's like this pirate radio internet thing. Some girls were talking about it in chemistry yesterday. The show's host, Orion, supposedly gets these visions and tells people where to go to see UFOs."

Lior's eyes popped. She choked on her drink, sending iced coffee shooting out her nose.

"Lior!" Cora screamed. "Gross!"

Indy covered her mouth, feigning a cough. "Seriously, Cor? The internet's full of shows like that. One crazier than the next."

"Seriously. I looked it up. There's a website, too—True North. And it is kind of crazy, but it's also pretty cool. I tried catching the show last night, but I guess there's no schedule. Like the live part just comes on when it comes on."

Lior shot Indy a special kind of expression. It wasn't a secret that she disapproved of keeping Cora in the dark. If Lior had her way, she'd make Indy confess to being Orion right there in the middle of Starbucks.

Avoiding Lior's death stare, Indy glanced at her phone. "Thanks for the coffee, Cor," she spit out awkwardly. "I have to run. Got to stop at the drugstore for tampons before work." She jumped up, sucking down her iced coffee as she grabbed her backpack. "See you guys at the bonfire tomorrow night."

In the parking lot, Indy climbed into her Jeep, hiding behind the silvery sunshade papering the windshield for a moment. Her library shift didn't start for another hour, but spending an extra half hour shelving books would be better than Lior's silent judgment or sitting there obsessing about what a bad friend she was to Cora. Staring at the reflective material, she thought about what she'd seen in the funnel at White Rock and how she'd tried sketching it several times. She hadn't uploaded those sketches to True North's boards yet; she didn't want her listeners to know Orion lived close enough to visit the site. And after hearing Cora's news—that students at Corazon were gossiping about True North—she felt better about that decision.

Indy touched the radiant sunshade, absorbing its warmth. At seventy-five hundred feet, even on a snowy day, the winter sun could still turn the inside of a car into an inferno. But for a few seconds, she felt safe and tucked away, concealed in her little heat bubble. She closed her eyes and dropped her forehead against the steering wheel just as a wave of nausea trucked up her throat.

Abruptly, Indy's head exploded, leaking numbers across the dashboard. Reaching blindly for the glove compartment, she grabbed a pen and tried scribbling them on her arm. 32, 95, 73, 105, 74, 25. Gasping, she squeezed her eyes shut and lay down over the parking brake, leaning her head sideways on the passenger seat. Rubbing her cheek against the edge of the worn leather cover calmed the thumping in her brain; the shaded square was still gratefully cool, and she stayed glued to it, watching the numbers shimmer behind her eyelids while they faded. When she opened her eyes again, the clock on the dash read three thirty. Three thirty! Somehow, she'd drifted off.

Still unsteady, Indy latched onto the steering wheel and yanked herself upright. She pulled the sunshade off the window, started the Jeep, and groggily threw it in gear, heading slowly for downtown. Luck be with her, Rose, the most distracted librarian Indy ever met, would be too busy cataloging to notice she was late for work.

At the library, Indy parked behind the deco building in an employee space and snuck in through the back entrance. Her head still hurt, so she brewed an extra strong pot of coffee in the back room, then cleared all the returns her lazy-ass coworkers hadn't managed to shelve yet, before heading to Circulation. Except for the children's section, the library was deader than a morgue. No one seemed to notice she was late. Which, gratefully, also meant no one was around to look over her shoulder when she pulled up Google on the library's search engine.

Staring down at her arm, she typed out 32, 95, 73, 105, 74, 25 and hit enter, nervously waiting when the bar in the address field stalled, taking what felt like hours to load her results. Frowning at the outdated computer monitor, she chewed on a thumbnail, then nearly fell off her stool when the page finally displayed her new co-ordinates—Cloudcroft, New Mexico. Just a couple of hours south of Santa Fe.

At five, Indy found herself standing at the Circulation desk, staring out at the lobby. Confused as ever, she grabbed her coffee cup and moved to the check-out counter to riffle through her secret stash of UFO and paranormal-related reading materials. Perched on a stool, she settled on *Life Beyond: True Death Encounters,* zoning out before she even got halfway through the second chapter. It didn't help that Reba the Reading Puppet's Friday evening reading hour was in full swing in the kids' section at the back of the library, riling up a bunch of kindergartners.

"That's some heavy-hitting prose."

Indy glanced up, mortified. Sawyer, dressed in a sweaty navy tee and a pair of gray running pants, leaned over the counter, looking down at the book she was reading.

"I wouldn't have guessed you for the type." He grinned.

"What type?" she frowned.

The side of his mouth tugged upward. "Wackadoo."

"Seriously?" She pointed to the books under his arm. "You know, you could have showered before dropping those off. You stink." *Like clean sweat, and pressed linen, and lemonade on a sunny summer day. And ugh, Indy.*

"I ran here." He shrugged. "And I'm only joking, India."

Indy stared at him, trying to tame her lame mouth *and* her hormones. "Why?"

"Why was I joking, or why did I run?" The neon *Duh* emblazoned across Sawyer's forehead made Indy squirm. "I'm training for a meet next week. You *do* know I'm on the track team, right?" Except, the way he asked her, it was more like, *what kind of idiot wouldn't?*

"Yes. I'm not *totally* clueless. I just meant—I don't know . . . you're sweaty."

"And you're reading about dead people."

She met his eyes. "Touché."

"How are you?" He smiled, and his eyes lit up. "I mean, after last Saturday. After White Rock?"

"How come you're talking to me?" she answered without thinking. "You never talk to me."

He snorted. "Didn't we just have like a whole conversation last weekend, India?"

"Stop calling me India."

"Why? That's your name."

"I like, Indy." Because damn her mom for naming her after some stupid punk song from the Eighties.

Indy looked down at the books under Sawyer's arm, hiding her blush. After an awkward moment, he held one up, waving it at her. "You going to take them?"

She grabbed the worn copy of *The Plague*, looking up sharply when she noticed the title. "I thought you hated *The Stranger*."

"I did," he said. "But, *The Plague's* your favorite book, and I'm a good listener."

Indy's heart thumped erratically. She'd only mentioned it was her favorite book once and then just in passing. And why did he have to be so stupidly cute about it? *Gack.* He made her want to curl up in his sweaty arms and debate the meaning of life.

Sawyer raised an eyebrow in sync with his upper lip. "I do pay attention."

Indy shook her head like it was stuck in tar, slowly and with less umph than she'd like. Because, well, the fact that he paid attention floored her. Cheeks burning, she took his other book, *Heart of Darkness,* flipping to the barcode inside its jacket. "Did you like it?"

He shrugged. "Not really."

"Me neither," she said, surprised once again that their reading tastes were so similar.

"But you were right about *The Plague.* That book killed me."

They stared at each other awkwardly, Indy's heart beating so loud she cringed. Finally, she sighed. It was possible she'd misjudged him. And after the way she'd acted in White Rock, it was equally possible it was also way too late to make up for being the biggest idiot ever.

Sawyer looked conflicted, like he was working hard to hide what might be some glimmer of insecurity and still entirely amused at the same time. He ran a palm through his limp pompadour, and Indy swore his eyes caught fire, momentarily blazing a brighter green around his mossy irises. "I've been thinking about that storm last weekend," he said, finally breaking their awkward standoff. "You ever listen to this show, True North?"

Choking on her swallow, Indy gritted her teeth, trying to force down the saliva lodged in her throat. "True, what?"

"True North. It's like . . . like this internet site that also has a late-night radio program."

"A podcast?" she asked, trying her best to look oblivious.

"No." He shook his head. "Like an actual radio show, except from the Internet. About UFOs. I listen to it sometimes. The whole team does. When I miss it, Manny tapes it. Then Augs and I listen to it in the gym."

And just like that, Indy's heart tried clawing its way up her throat. It bashed against her sternum, rattling loudly against her chest wall. She was so sure Sawyer heard it, she folded her arms over her t-shirt and hunched over.

"You believe in UFOs?" she croaked out.

He stared down at her book. "I'm not saying they're aliens or anything, but sure, why not? Anyway, I brought it up because last week, the host, Orion, predicted something might happen in the skies in White Rock. I caught the archived show last night and instantly thought of you. You know, because of what happened."

"That's wild." Indy pulled her hair off her neck and self-consciously twisted it into a bun, using a pencil to hold it in place. A wave of relief washed over her. She'd obviously made the right call *not* posting those drawings. "What do *you* think happened?"

"I mean," he ran a hand through the damp ends of his hair, "I'm not sure, but it didn't seem . . . normal, you know?"

"Are you saying you think it was more than a storm?"

"Don't you?"

"Maybe?" She shrugged.

"Well, check it out—the show. Tell me what you think when you do, and we can talk about White Rock more later. Until then, I gotta run. I still have a couple hours of training left before meeting the guys. Maybe I'll catch you at the bonfire tomorrow."

Sawyer hunched a little, uncharacteristically awkward. He turned and ambled out the front entrance instead of wandering back to the stacks to grab a new book like usual, leaving Indy standing there with her mouth unhinged. She checked herself. Beneath all that purple nail polish, her fingertips were tingling. And her chest felt tight. *And fishsticks.* It wasn't just physical. She definitely liked Sawyer.

Her mind on Sawyer and White Rock, Indy tuned out Reba the Reading Puppet for the rest of her shift best she could, which thankfully wasn't very long. After she clocked out at six, she headed across the lot to her Jeep, her head in the clouds as she rehashed her conversation with Sawyer earlier over and over and over. Indy felt like a broken record. Caught so deeply in a Sawyer groove, she almost didn't notice the black GMC idling across the dark parking lot.

The GMC's blacked-out windows glimmered under the halo of light from the streetlamp in the corner behind the library. A silvery glint caught Indy's eye, and she turned toward it, her hackles suddenly at attention. Normally, she wouldn't think twice about tinted windows. Everyone in New Mexico had them. But it was nighttime, and hers was the only other car in the lot.

Indy barely made out two shadowy figures through the truck's front windshield. Otherwise, she was alone. And it freaked her the hell out. Nervous, she pulled her phone from her jacket pocket.

"Call Lior," she said out loud, clumsily searching for her car keys as her phone dialed.

"Hey," Lior answered after two rings. "What's up?"

"Just being paranoid about this truck across the parking lot," Indy answered breathlessly, still rummaging through her backpack. "And I can't find my stupid keys. Stay on the line with me for a sec?"

"Of course." Lior paused. "You know you're not supposed to go out to a parking lot in the dark without them in your hand, Indy."

"When has knowing anything ever stopped me?" Indy snorted.

"Front plate?" Lior asked.

"Nope."

"Local, then."

"Maybe."

"What's it doing?"

"Just sitting in the corner of the lot, idling. I can't really see in through the front. But it's got this vibe, you know. I just want . . . shit, found them." Indy squashed her backpack under her arm, using her shoulder to hold the phone in place while she quickly unlocked the car door. "I'm in. Sorry, Lior. I got a new set of numbers earlier. Then Sawyer came in and brought up True North and White Rock, and now I'm just kind of freaking out."

"Indy . . ." Lior sighed heavily, and Indy immediately knew what came next. "You've got to tell Cora you're Orion. It's going to piss her off when she finds out you've kept it from her."

Pulling out of the lot, Indy watched the GMC in her rearview mirror. "Sawyer told me August and Manny both listen to True North."

Lior sniffed as if to say, "See, you better *tell Cora now if you know what's good for you.*

"I get it, Li. And I feel terrible about it. Obviously."

"You mean like how you made up a lie and ran out of Starbucks earlier? Where'd you go anyway? I thought you were on shift at three."

"Technically, I was supposed to be. I figured I'd head over early, but then the numbers came . . . in my Jeep in the parking lot. They kind of knocked me out. Like literally. I must have passed out or something because next thing I knew, it was three thirty." The line went quiet, and for a moment, Indy thought Lior had hung up. "You still there?"

"Indy," Lior breathed out, "Cora and I walked past your Jeep after you left. We literally peeked in the window, wondering where you went. You weren't in there."

"I was lying down on the front seat. You probably just couldn't see me."

"Uh-uh. Cora climbed up on the running board to look in."

The hairs on Indy's neck bristled. "You must have checked the wrong Jeep, then."

"Right, like I don't know my best friend's car . . ."

"Whoa!" Indy cut her off. "I think the GMC is behind me."

Indy tilted her rearview mirror, aligning it with the pickup's front end pulling up behind her. In the dark, she couldn't be sure if it was the same truck, but her gut said she'd be an idiot to assume it wasn't.

"Okay, I'm staying on the phone until you get home," Lior told her.

"Should I drive around a little?"

"Yeah. See if it follows."

Indy turned off Guadalupe onto a backstreet, waiting to see if the pickup followed. She drove slowly, holding her breath until a pair of headlights turned onto the road behind her. Cutting through the neighborhood's cramped streets, she watched the vehicle's lights turn left with her, then right, sweating bullets as she babbled into the phone at Lior.

"Should I call the cops?" Lior asked.

"What if it's not the GMC?"

"What if it is?"

"Why would anyone follow me?"

"True North?"

"Maybe they want an autograph," Indy tittered.

"Hilarious. Indy, maybe it's time to . . ."

Indy cut her off again, exhaling loudly when the vehicle made a right turn onto another street. "It's gone."

"Oh, thank God!"

"Guess I am just being paranoid." She exhaled. "I'm really sorry."

"Indy, your numbers, White Rock, I get why you're paranoid. *I'm* starting to worry. Things are starting to feel out of hand."

Turning back onto the main road, Indy headed down Agua Fria toward her house. It irked her that Lior suddenly seemed interested in White Rock. Since the incident, Lior had been less than enthusiastic about rehashing what'd happened. "A couple days ago, you said it was *just a storm.*"

"I didn't see what you did. Okay? But I believe you. And whatever it was, it clearly affected you. Your nose. The numbers are starting to make you sick, Indy."

Indy pulled into her driveway and shut the car off. "Maybe. But what am I supposed to do about it? I mean, I haven't even figured out why I get them, Li. I only know they're getting closer. These new numbers, they're in Cloudcroft." She sighed heavily. "I'm going live with them tonight."

"You really think that's a good idea?"

"I don't know." Indy sat in the cab woefully. "But it's better than doing nothing. Guess I'm about to find out."

QUEUE THE REVOLUTION

INDY FLIPPED HER laptop open, feeling slightly more nervous than normal now that she *knew* people from Corazon were listening. She hit return and grabbed her microphone. "Good evening," she crooned into it just as the alien GIF started dancing. "The only way to deal with an unfree world is to become so free that your very existence is an act of rebellion—so which are you tonight, warrior or follower?"

As soon as the words were out of her mouth, True North's burner buzzed.

"Warrior!" a male said when she answered it. "And it's Mayberry."

"Hey, Mayberry. What's up?"

"You know those White Rock coordinates you dropped? It happened. Wednesday night. Big disturbance out at a place called Overlook Park. People were freaking out. Like this thing just came out of nowhere. I took pictures. I'll upload them."

True North's chat room went crazy.

Indy held her breath to keep her voice from wavering. Even before that stupid truck, she'd spent plenty of time worrying about what might happen if her premonitions proved otherworldly. A lifetime fan of (especially bad) conspiracy theories, she'd read enough to believe the government had a knack for threatening people. And real or not, being cannon fodder wasn't one of her life's endeavors.

"Mayberry, def post the pic, but can you tell us what you thought it looked like? And whether you're local. Did you drive to it, or were you just there doing something else?"

"We drove there from Trinidad, Colorado. When we asked around, people in town told us they'd seen something weird at the park a few days before, so we set up camp there and waited. At first, we thought it might be a storm, but then it . . . it's hard to describe, but it was like a fake cloud. Like the cloud was just camouflage for whatever was hiding inside it."

As Mayberry spoke, a picture filled Indy's monitor. Shocked, she sat frozen at her desk. On the screen, a display of rainbow lights softened the otherwise crisp edge of what looked like an enormous tear in the sky. Parts of the rift were dull enough to blend with the night, but others were luminous where moonlight touched its edges. And that's where she saw it—something mechanical, like what she'd seen in the funnel cloud in White Rock Saturday.

"That's it?" she gasped.

"Yep."

"Unbelievable," she breathed into the mic.

"It really was," Mayberry said excitedly.

"I wish I could have been there."

"I wish you could have been there too. Maybe next time."

Indy sat back, almost disbelieving, even though she'd seen nearly the same thing just days ago. She shook her head at the egg-carton ceiling, wondering whether to share the new coordinates with her listeners after all. The closer they got to home, the more she worried someone might connect her to Orion.

"Speaking of," she finally breathed into the microphone, "I've got a new set of numbers. I'm sorry that I went ahead and figured out the location without y'all. But here they are."

Indy sent them to the chat room, reading them out loud simultaneously.

"Cloudcroft," Indy echoed into the microphone. "You got it."

The chat room filled with commentary, and the people meter on Indy's site counter jumped by forty. She stared at it incredulously.

"You still there, Mayberry?"

"Yeah, but I gotta go. Just wanted to share that with everyone."

Hopefully, Indy typed without thinking. ***It's close by.***

As soon as she hit return, she cursed herself. Close by? She may as well have just said, "Hey, yeah, and while you're there, I'm five-foot-five, boob-length black hair, gray eyes, purple-framed glasses, right-side Marilyn piercing, and married to my beat-up oxblood moto boots—because *that* wouldn't be nearly descriptive enough to give herself away, either.

"Right, well, I'm outta here for a few, but stay tuned for the next interview," she rushed out, "an oldie for sure. Be back in a sec."

Unsettled and unable to digest Mayberry's picture live on air, Indy booted up an old interview with Rob Mazar, an employee who claimed to work at Area 51 back in the seventies when they reverse-engineered alien technology (his words). Then she sat back, exhaling slowly. Her stomach felt pressurized. Like something so big was about to materialize, she might birth it herself. Mayberry's picture was unreal. And though the disturbance looked a little different than what *she'd* seen in White Rock, it still confirmed she'd seen *something* inside the clouds.

When the interview ended, Indy's burner flashed again. She crossed her fingers and answered quickly, hoping to speak to Visitor, forgoing her usual quote-happy *hello*.

"True North," she nearly whispered.

"Your show's dangerous."

"Dangerous?" Indy chirped. "Why?"

"Life sucks. It's like we're all hoping for something bigger or better that never happens, and here you are, pretending it's out there. Spreading a big, disappointing lie."

"Asking people to trust in something they can't see, or that they can see but don't understand yet is the stuff of dreams and history books, Caller. Sorry, but I disagree. Dreaming big isn't dangerous. Besides, ever hear of a self-fulfilling prophecy?"

"Yeah, well, tell that to my mom. Or my boyfriend. Or my geometry teacher. I live in the real world, and bigness isn't always inclusive. Especially since what makes some people feel big often makes the rest of us feel small. And most of us, Orion, we're small enough already."

"*You* get to choose how big you are in this life. Not your boyfriend, or your mom, or your geometry teacher," Indy countered.

"Easy to say . . ." the caller trailed off.

Indy nodded. *Easy to say* was right. Orion talked big, bigger than Indy in real life. In fact, she often wished she could take her own advice. "Listen, look around. Then ask yourself—does anyone *really* have that much power over you? You're the only one who can permanently alter your future. Do something about it, Caller. Seriously, get your ass in gear, girl. Prove you're more than just an idea. I mean, you're not their stupid puppet unless you want to be."

"You really believe that?"

Indy frowned. Orion's bravado aside, she doubted herself immensely. Not that she'd ever share that fact with her listeners. Because what was that saying . . . *fake it till you make it*? "I'm trying to," she admitted. "Yeah."

"Get my ass in gear?" the caller echoed.

"Yes. We're all rooting for you for sure."

"All right. You're on."

"Awesome! Come back some time and tell us how it's going."

Ramping up a track from LCD Soundsystem, Indy grinned at her Dean Winchester bobblehead bobbing next to her computer screen. When it came to taking her own advice, no doubt, she was still a coward. But it felt freaking great living vicariously through other people.

As the song wound down, True North's IM box lit up.

VISITOR: You're going to Cloudcroft?

Indy spun in her chair, stopping herself mid-turn to type out:
And to whom do I have the pleasure of conversing with?

VISITOR: Visitor.

Orion: Oh, shit. Hold up.

"Hey," she chirped into the microphone, "taking a permanent break from the heavy tonight to share this stellar vid on-line. Worth the watch, I promise. Someday we'll all have a voice. I trust we'll all be stars in our own skies. But for now, let's just be okay with being all right." She hit *return*, initiating a UFOtv video she'd been engrossed with for the better part of the month.

Orion: Still there?

VISITOR: Paraphrasing a bunch of shitty song lyrics doesn't prove you're a sage.

Orion: If you don't like what I have to say, don't listen.

VISITOR: Just mulling the self-help/psychic thing you have going on. So, are you going?

Orion: Don't know. How do you know I'm close enough?

VISITOR: You went to White Rock.

Orion: Is that a question?

VISITOR: Not really.

Indy twisted her mouth into a frown, working the muscles around it as if sucking on a lemon. Visitor seemed pretty sure she went. Which probably meant he knew her. But he also seemed to want to remain anonymous as badly as she did. Crossing her fingers against her forehead, she leaned into them for good measure. If they did know each other, and Visitor really wanted her help (and she totally wanted to know more about him), Indy sure as heck planned to use that to her advantage. But before tipping that hand, she had to find out.

Orion: How did you know the last numbers weren't like a barcode or something?

VISITOR: The same way you just knew.

Orion: But I didn't at first.

VISITOR: And yet you went. They've all been coordinates,
Orion.

Orion: But how do you know?

VISITOR: Meet me in Cloudcroft, and I'll tell you.

Orion: What? No. I don't even know if I'm going.

VISITOR: You just said you were.

Orion: Yeah, about that . . . it's far. And I've got a lot to do.

VISITOR: It's not that far. It's in your home state. Besides,
I was right about White Rock. I know you saw something,
and I know you can help me.

Orion: What if it's a hoax?

VISITOR: It's not a hoax. If someone were trying to punk
you, they'd have to be goddamned geniuses. It'd be a
pretty elaborate prank, right?

Indy chewed on her bottom lip. Visitor *had* to know her; otherwise, how would he know she lived in New Mexico. If they didn't go to school together, maybe he was a library patron or one of Cora's co-workers at Starbucks.

*Orion: Okay, then tell me what *they* want. And how*
we're connected?

VISITOR: Not like this. Meet me in Cloudcroft, and I'll tell
you everything I know then.

Orion: Did I do something to piss them off? And if you're
right, and that's a big 'if,' why are they broadcasting
numbers to me?

Indy's particular talents included being able to recite the alphabet backward in ten seconds flat, a scary good photographic memory when it came to what people wore on any given day (that she often called on at parties to freak people out), and a killer soprano.

She played a mean game of poker and made even meaner scrambled eggs. And she spent a good deal of time contemplating meaning, including whether wondering about meaning meant she was uber deep or just too freaking clueless for words. But besides the numbers and being the only human she knew of who'd been resurrected, she was pretty middle-of-the-road normal.

VISITOR: I'm not doing this online, Orion.

Orion: And I'm not meeting you until I know more. Or at least until I know who you are.

Indy waited, but the message box just blinked. After a moment, a time stamp popped up, letting her know he'd signed out. She dropped her head on the desk, resting her cheek against its cool pressboard surface. She'd gone live again, and nothing had changed. Like most everything else about her life—drowning, Sawyer, the coordinates, the sightings—Visitor remained a mystery.

NEW MOON FEVER

IF LIOR EVER stopped talking, Indy might be able to convince her to drive down to Cloudcroft after school next Friday. But stars shimmered like diamonds across the crisp sky, and along with the unseasonably warm, late February weather, the night screamed romance. Lior had August in her crosshairs; nothing but death could divert her focus.

Indy probably shouldn't have bothered coming to the tailgate. Despite Lior repeatedly insisting they were only going to support Corazon's basketball team, Indy and Cora both knew they'd be playing wing women to Lior's not-so-subtle pilot. 'Accidentally' bumping into August maybe two seconds after getting out of the car proved it. Not that August seemed to take offense. He looked like he'd happily suck Lior's face off if she let him.

"He's so into her. Why doesn't she just tell him?" Cora whispered, knocking up against Indy's shoulder. "It's totally obvious."

"First, she'd have to admit it to herself."

Cora nodded and linked arms with Indy, drawing her closer. "Beer?"

"Hot dog," Indy countered. She jingled her keys in her jacket pocket. "Sober driver."

Indy and Cora walked toward a pack of kids thrusting sticks at a raging bonfire. When Indy spotted Jay Maisy from her AP lit class, she managed to finagle two hot dogs from his stockpile. Starving, she downed hers quickly, mingling with Cora and a bunch of kids as the crowd grew.

Shadows shaded the cars and trucks parked around the lot. As Indy watched other kids roasting food over the fire, she tried to ignore the aspens looming in her periphery. The secluded space was Corazon's favorite make-out spot (not that she'd know personally). Sitting high on the crest of a mountain above the city, Navajo Point came to an end at a steep drop-off overlooking Santa Fe. Except for the bare cliff face, trees surrounded the plot, and its seclusion made the place feel just the tiniest bit otherworldly.

Indy gazed out at the forest, trying to imagine Cora's reaction to an alien suddenly walking into the clearing. She looked up at the sky, trying to guess how the crowd would react to some something suddenly just materializing.

"Earth to Indy." Cora snapped her fingers below Indy's nose. "Where'd you go?"

Indy hugged her shoulders and met Cora's eyes, nodding up at the firmament. "Do you think there's something else out there?"

"You mean like aliens or parallel universes?"

Indy nodded.

"I hope so."

"Do you think they're like us?" Indy looked around at her classmates, feeling guilty for hoping aliens were nothing like humans—unless they were evil. She'd happily take cliques and clichés over extraterrestrial conquistadors.

"Eh. If there's something out there, my bet is on evil lizard creatures."

Mountain air filled Indy's lungs. She held it in for a moment, thinking back to Holy Ghost River. Whatever she'd seen that night, she was sure it wasn't evil lizard people. "I have to pee," she told Cora, tugging at her sweater. "Come with me?"

Cora handed her beer and hot dog stick to the guy standing next to her. "Lead the way." She took Indy's hand and let Indy drag her around the bonfire across the clearing and into the woods.

A barely-there moon made the woods hard to maneuver. Shadows loomed from every dark nook, and the silent forest made everything seem doubly eerie. Tittering nervously, they stumbled between tightknit trees. Indy tripped over a root, then pulled out her phone, squawking as she turned the flashlight on. She held it over a swath of bushes, searching for a good place to pee.

As she settled on a chaparral, something to their right rustled, then grunted. Indy shielded the flashlight, motioning for Cora to be quiet.

Cora held a hand over her mouth, trying not to giggle.

After a moment, Indy's eyes adjusted, and a whitish flicker flashed between the trees. On the heels of Cora's whole evil lizard quip, it made Indy nervous. She glanced up, scanning the sky, then back at Cora. Cora shrugged just as something to their right grunted again. Her eyes popped, and she pointed between the trees.

Maybe thirty feet away, two bodies stood twisted together against a skeletal aspen. Naked from the waist down, their bare parts glowed under the sparse moonlight. Within seconds, Indy realized she was staring at Sawyer and Corazon's head cheerleader, Mina Starkey. And she was pretty sure Sawyer wasn't performing CPR or anything.

"Shit," Cora whispered.

Stepping back, Indy tripped on a root. Sawyer glanced over his shoulder; his eyes shadowed but somehow still glowing. Cora started giggling. She tugged Indy's hand, and after an infinity where it felt like all of Indy's limbs turned to stone, they took off running.

Indy held her phone up, shining the shaky light forward as they tumbled into the clearing.

"Oh. My. God!" Cora pronounced when they stopped. "Mina-freaking-I'm-so-perfect-Starkey! Didn't she just spread a rumor about him? I swear that boy must own a master panty-dropping key."

Sawyer *did* have a slick reputation; almost all of Corazon's female population could attest. But Indy had always sort of hoped that, like all the other high school gossip, it was more of a rumor. She nodded, trying to ignore her smarting cheeks. "My eyes are burning!"

"Good luck trying to unsee that!" Cora grinned. "Though Sawyer's got a pretty fine ass, Indy. Not one-hundred percent sure I want to."

Sawyer definitely had a fine ass. But seeing him like that just confirmed Indy's fears; he was also a player to the Nth degree. One canceled the other out as quickly as control+alt+delete. Indy could care less about Sawyer banging Mina against a tree—at least that's what she told herself. She chalked the tug in her stomach up to a bad hot dog or nerves over her next set of coordinates; it had nothing to do with seeing him half naked up in another girl's business.

Besides, she told herself, when Sawyer finally ambled out of the clearing, *you have other, more pressing things to obsess about. Like telling Cora about Orion. And Cloudcroft. And Visitor.*

LAY IT BARE

BY MONDAY MORNING, Indy managed to convince herself Sawyer was just a boy she helped at the library. Still, when she had to veer out of his way to avoid being run down in the hall before first period, she suddenly wanted to beat the smug-ass expression off his face. Slamming her locker door shut as she watched him head toward August and his bunch, she inadvertently rolled her eyes at him.

Across the corridor, Sawyer cocked his head at her. He ambled over, gazing down at her balled fists. "What's up?"

"You, apparently," she grumbled.

Sawyer burst out laughing. He glanced at her hands again, which she'd managed to unclench and shove into her pockets. "You're priceless."

Roiling with snark, Indy opened her mouth to tell him exactly where to shove it, but a commotion broke out down the hall. They both turned in time to catch Corazon's math teacher, Mr. Bines, jumping up to rip down a sprawling, hand-painted poster hanging above his classroom door. It read: BEWARE OF MR. BINES. HE'S AN ASS-GRABBING OLD PERV!

Students hooted, and as the crowd grew outside Mr. Bines's classroom, he totally lost it. "Who did this?" he yelled just as the first-period bell rang. "Go! Go to class. Get inside." He point-stabbed at the classroom door. "Now! Get your butts out of the hall!"

Beverly Mendes, whom Indy and Lior had both grown up with, stepped out of the crowd, glaring at him. "Keep your grabby hands off me from now on, and I'll take it down, perv."

"How dare you!" he fumed.

Beverly placed her hands on her hips defiantly. "Me? How dare *you!*"

"Way to get your ass in gear, Bev!" someone shouted from the crowd.

"Yeah, way to get your ass in gear," a few more people echoed.

Indy froze, nearly choking on her chewing gum. She took one look at Sawyer, who seemed riveted by Beverly's demonstration, and hightailed it toward first-period English. *Get your ass in gear?* She never meant True North to be more than a quiet, down-low show. But somehow, there it was, on full display smack in the middle of Corazon.

Corazon reeked of lemmings and conformists, so it was a massive deal for Beverly to single herself out in front of everyone. All morning kids gossiped about her 'Big Moment.' But they also talked about the radio show Beverly swore set her in motion, whispering about True North like it was the holy freaking grail.

"It's the one I told you guys about!" Cora proclaimed around a mouthful of pizza during lunch. "Beverly called Orion Friday night and got all riled up after talking to him. UFOs and anarchy," she smacked her hand on the tabletop, "we've so got to listen!"

Indy glanced at Lior, whose eyes were so wide they nearly swallowed the lunch table. Eager to derail Cora, she quickly changed the subject. "So, how'd it go with August Saturday night, Li? You were Velcroed to his side when I left. And *someone* neglected to mention him on the phone last night."

Lior wanted to keep glowering at Indy, no doubt. But Lior was also like a dog on a squirrel. Indy said August's name, and Lior's eyes bloomed for an entirely different reason. "Weeeeell," she drew out, "he wants to hang after the game this Wednesday night. But like as a group. Like you, Cora, Manny, and Sawyer."

"Manny Cassavetes?" Cora asked. "For real?" She licked her bottom lip. "He's kind of savage."

"I think so too," Lior agreed.

This time Indy gave Lior a death stare. "Forget it."

"Indy, I already said you would. Pleeeaaassseee," Lior pleaded.

"So much for not liking August," Indy pouted.

Lior scrunched her nose at her sandwich, smiling big as she spoke through her teeth. "I don't," she said, more like a question than an answer. "But *you* know how it is."

Indy glared at her; Lior may be on to her crush on Sawyer, but damned if Indy was willing to admit it. "Ugh, Li, I don't want to go on a triple date. Especially not with you-know-who."

"Oh my God, he has the whitest ass on the planet!" Cora burst out laughing.

Lior looked puzzled, and Cora promptly filled her in.

"Manwhore!" Lior tittered. "Okay, well, I promise to make sure he keeps his butt covered Wednesday night."

"*Lior!*" Indy yelped.

Lior smiled sweetly. "Just try to say 'no' to me again, India."

Indy sighed. Her chances of getting out of Lior's triple date were dismal. Arguing with Lior was like digging a hole with a silicone cup. And good luck with that. Still, after seeing Mina squashed between Sawyer and that aspen Saturday night, Indy really didn't want to be alone with him, maybe *because* she wanted to be alone with him. Besides, what was she supposed to say about it? I thought your butt was the moon until I realized it was in orbit around Mina Starkey?

Indy one-hundred percent didn't want to go on Lior's triple date, but by the end of the day, she realized it was the leverage she needed to persuade Lior to drive down to Cloudcroft with her—not that it took much convincing. Standing on the front quad as they said their goodbyes after school, Indy got maybe two sentences into her proposal when Lior cut her off, entirely down with the idea, if not too freaking excited for words.

It seemed like a fair deal. But by dinner Tuesday night, Indy seriously started thinking about doing something utterly ridiculous, like outing Sawyer on True North—maybe telling people he was an alien from a far-off galaxy or something like that to raise his Corazon stock and keep him busy. Sawyer already had enough fembots chasing him around school. Indy could only imagine what a rumor like that would do for his reputation. Though, she assumed it'd include keeping him far too engaged to do something as lame as triple dating.

Grumpy about it, Indy took her dinner out to the back porch and ate in solitude. Afterward, she went upstairs and opened her laptop, heading straight to True North. When the alien GIF on True North's home screen started dancing, she sat back in her chair and popped a can of Dr. Pepper open, throwing half of it back before leaning into the mic.

"It only takes a single spark to ignite a fire." Indy grimaced at the computer screen, thinking about Sawyer and that stupid bonfire

Saturday night. "But someone's got to be the wood. Any volunteers tonight?"

After booting up one of her favorite punk songs, Indy played air drums furiously in front of the computer before beating the crap out of the desk, making everything, including her precious Dean Winchester bobblehead, rattle across its surface. As the song ended, her burner flashed. She answered it, cuing the theme to *The X-Files* simultaneously.

"Howdy, Caller, wood or spark?"

"Depends on the day . . . today, though, maybe spark. Because of you, O. I mean, you're off the charts! Like you should have seen my school this morning! You know that girl you told to get her ass in gear? She nailed it. And it was a thing of beauty."

Slapping a hand over her mouth, Indy tried muffling a hiccup as Dr. Pepper shot up her nose. *No freaking way!* The caller had to be Cora.

"Thanks. I appreciate the support. Sometimes I wonder if anyone's actually listening."

"Really?"

"You have no idea. It's hard talking about something that feels so crazy. And sometimes, it feels like I'm talking to myself. Or like I'm imagining you all and *I'm* crazy."

"We're here, O. Totally. And everything you say . . . I mean, it matters. Obviously, because that chick at my school just totally kicked ass. I guess you could say that means we're the wood, and *you're* the spark."

Indy blushed. She wanted to kiss the caller, even if it wasn't Cora. "Thanks. I couldn't do it without y'all."

True North's chatroom buzzed with commentary. Most of it positive. Though a few complaints made Indy laugh—messages from people who just really wanted her to know she was a liar (likely to be struck down by God), or a poser (who never got laid—true, unfortunately), or just outright dumb (not true at all). She'd grown used to the dissing, and the encouraging comments more than made up for the freaking trolls who took their stupid grievances out on her show.

"Well, thanks for being you," maybe-Cora gushed. "I mean, *awesome.*"

Red-faced, Indy said goodbye. She propped the burner against the mic base and shared a few UFO videos, crossing her fingers that Visitor called. As she waited, Lior messaged her.

LiLi: OMG. Wuz it, Cora, earlier? So dope—she murdered it.

Indy smiled at Lior's message. **Cora. Yeah, probs. Li, I don't think she murdered it.**

LiLi: Seriously, I liked what she said. Totes authentic.

***Hugs* You meant she killed it?**

LiLi: Whatever. Yeah. She killed it!

Agreed.

LiLi: So, are u looking forward to tomorrow night?

Indy rubbed her palms over her head, dragging them down her face, accidentally catching her Marilyn piercing. If wishes were fishes, she'd be far away tomorrow night, like on a beach in Jakarta.

Not really.

*LiLi: Well, whatevs. You'll survive. And, so you know, you were atomic tonight! *Explodes* C U tomorrow morn, quad. LOVE YOU. Pop's here. Got to go.*

If it was possible to feel any worse than she already did about going on a triple date tomorrow, Indy didn't know how. Sighing heavily, she located an exposé about the Phoenix lights from YouTube and booted it up. While it played, she opened True North's inbox and rifled through emails. Most were the same, "Oh my God, I'm your loyalist listener, tell me all your secrets," or "Please take me away to Nirubu with you" types. But one was tagged *Visitor*. She opened it, scanning the note.

Orion, I don't know if you'll be at Cloudcroft, but I need to meet you. I know you value your anonymity. But I could really use your help. If you are going, we can arrange a covert way to meet that will keep both our secrets—secret. When we meet, I'll tell you everything. You'll understand, I promise. Visitor.

Indy stared at the screen, her fingers hovering over her keyboard. She could write back and say she was going. She could agree to meet Visitor and get to the bottom of her numbers and Visitor's big mystery. But it could also be a lie. What if Visitor was pulling a prank, or worse, trying to dig up her identity for less-than-honorable reasons?

"Sweets!" Indy's father bellowed up the stairs, startling her. "You there? Need your help like yesterday! I'm coming up."

Indy's doorjamb rattled, and she slammed her laptop shut, nearly catching her now-forest green nails between the screen and keyboard. "I'm here." She jumped up, running to the rail near the stairs leading to her bedroom door. "Hey, Dad."

Clunking up the steps, her dad stopped at the top, grinning. His floppy curly hair fell over his face like always, tinged with speckles of acrylic paint that matched the splotches on his jeans and navy t-shirt. How he managed to get so dirty when he painted was an even bigger mystery to Indy than her numbers.

"What'd you do, roll around on your canvas?" She faux-frowned.

"Took a nap on it," he grinned.

Indy shook her head, biting back her smile. Her dad, goof extraordinaire. She loved him to death despite all the ways he and her mom tended to discount her ideas or drive her crazy.

"Can you help me re-balance Old Glory?" he asked, referring to the massive pile of recycled junk he'd meticulously stacked and arranged in the garage to look like a dynamic American flag. "It's pretty precarious right now. If I touch it without help," he smacked his hands together quickly for emphasis, "BAM!"

Indy jumped. "Jeez, Dad! Scare the crap out of me while you're at it, why don't you?"

"Oh, you're a sensitive soul, aren't you?" His eyes twinkled, but Indy knew he was only partly joking. She and her dad had what her mother called an 'artist's sensibility.' They'd always shared a sort of us against the noisy, smelly, too-loud-world bond.

"It's like eleven thirty? Why are you even still working?"

Her dad grinned, and because she knew him, she knew what he was thinking even without him saying it—*I'll sleep when I'm dead, Indy.*

"You know you could have just texted. I would've come down."

"Could I have now?" He crossed his arms over his chest. "Check your phone."

Indy ran to her desk and grabbed her phone. She frowned at it, rolling her eyes at him. "Sorry." She shrugged.

But he'd already turned around and headed down the stairs. "Not sorry enough," he joked over his shoulder. "Now get your butt moving down to the garage."

Indy followed her dad downstairs, through the dark kitchen, and out to the standalone garage that her parents renovated years ago and used as a workspace. One corner, messy and full of canvas and paints, belonged to her dad; the other, a neat, quiet writing space, belonged to her mom.

Half the garage had been jury-rigged with construction lamps. As Indy rummaged around her dad's toolbox for a clamp under the strange light, she stopped to stare at the eerie shadows looming in the corners, flashing back to the night she drowned. Suddenly, she remembered a string of unfamiliar mechanical parts that seemed to hum through the clouds, almost as if they were trying to communicate with her just before she fell into the river. Similar to what she'd seen in the clouds at White Rock.

"Indy?" Her dad held his hand out.

Stunned by the memory, Indy startled, handing him the clamp.

"There," he said, motioning for her to grab hold of a tin-can-constructed corner of Old Glory. He tinkered with something on the flag's side, tightening the fasteners between several old pipes and wind vanes he'd bolted together. "Did your mom tell you about the article she's working on for the *Santa Fe Voice* about some internet radio show that's apparently causing a brouhaha?" His head dipped at an angle so Indy couldn't see him, and his voice came out muffled as he spoke. "It's called True North."

Indy inhaled and mentally tried to say her ABCs backward, still shaken by the new memory. "Brouhaha, Dad?" she tried to laugh. "Seriously? What're you like eighty or something?"

Her father's arm snaked out around one side of Old Glory, his hand morphing into a fist capped by a single, upright middle finger.

"Dad!" she barked. "I'm telling Mom. You know you're a bad influence, right?" Except she'd always really loved him for being this *live and let live* Bohemian kind of guy. Plus, her mom was just as bad. Indy could walk around the house yelling *fuck* at the top of her lungs, and her parents would probably just say something like *stop fucking yelling.*

Both her parents clung to their anarchistic attitudes when it came to navigating mainstream society. Because of it, they often related to Indy's teenage angst like they were still there in the thick of it with her—even if not so intentionally. Cool. But also sometimes awkward.

Indy's dad straightened up and set his wrench down on the workbench beside him. "Perfect." He appraised his handiwork, clapping his hands together as though dusting them off. "Now, what'd you say, kiddo? You're narcing me out to Mom? Good luck with that."

She rolled her eyes at him.

"So, did she tell you?" he asked, squeezing cerulean blue acrylic onto his stained paint palate. He picked up a sable-haired paintbrush and pointed it at her. "Apparently, it's a *thing*. Mom says it's a clever hoax."

"Why does Mom think it's a hoax?" Indy asked casually.

Indy's dad used the sharp end of his paintbrush to scratch his head. He shrugged. "Ask Mom. Something about the DJ promoting mischief through fake visions, or something like that. Haven't heard it yet. But it revolves around this whole UFO-type mythos, so you, my dear, should adore it."

For a moment, Indy wondered what he'd think if she just admitted right then and there to hosting True North. That it was all true and that she'd seen two UFOs for herself now. Then she remembered her parents' freak-out session after she drowned. How when she told them she'd seen figures near the river and a spaceship, they'd stared at her like a psycho-kitten.

They'd humored her, sure, but Indy never forgot the worry weighing their expressions down for months afterward. She knew they'd spent too much time pondering what they thought was her fragile grip on reality. If making her go to therapy for years 'just because it was good for the soul' wasn't proof of that, she didn't know what was.

Indy bit her lip. Her mom especially would love Indy's ingenuity, but they'd also probably program the state hospital into their speed dials. "I'll have to listen, then," she said casually. "You know, 'cause aliens, right?" She stood on her toes and kissed her dad's cheek, faux yawning. "Sounds chill. Now I gotta go to bed. Test tomorrow."

"Cool," he said absently, already engrossed in his painting. "Sleep well and don't get abducted, K?" He looked down at her and winked. "By aliens, I mean, all right?"

"Sure thing." She smiled.

At least not tonight.

STAND UP AND FIGHT

INDY WALKED DOWN the crowded Corazon hallway beside Lior toward physics. They found seats near the back of the classroom and only nominally listened to Mr. Blake drone on about some conference on mater he attended, texting viral videos to each other under their desks instead. Indy already had an A in physics. She felt bad, kind of, for blowing the lecture off. But it was hard to stomach Mr. Blake's speech about how someday scientists might invent anti-matter reactors that could power spaceflight when she already believed it was possible.

U c Sawyer? Lior texted. *I think he's staring at you.*

Indy kept her head straight. Only her eyes moved peripherally. Far as she could tell, Sawyer was staring down at his desk, his eyes fixed on something that definitely wasn't her. Seriously, if Sawyer *had been* staring, it was probably only because he was waiting for her to start levitating or speaking in gibberish.

Indy texted back, *No, I think he's actually paying attention to the lecture.*

"Ms. Lewin-Kaminetzsky? Please, enlighten us."

Indy looked up. The classroom snickered. "Dancing bears?" she told Mr. Blake, shrugging.

"Hentai," someone fake-coughed behind her.

"Enough!" Mr. Blake shared his best evil eye, then held his hand out impatiently. Indy handed him her phone, grimacing as he glanced at the screen. He raised an eyebrow at her, shaking his head. "UFO videos, India? Good to see you're finally taking a serious interest in physics."

The whole room broke out in titters. "Sorry," she muttered.

He handed it back. "On your own time, understand?"

Smarting, Indy sank in her seat, fixating on her boots. The only good thing about having a mother who was still married to the *good ol' days* was that she'd kept all this super old clothing she let Indy steal. Like her oxblood leather moto boots, marked by ten still-semi-burnished steel buckles. Indy stared at the shiniest one, willing it to turn into a spaceship and fly her to somewhere more hospitable.

When the bell rang, Indy was first out the door. She followed Lior to the cafeteria and stood beside her in the lunch line, obsessing about Sawyer, and Cloudcroft, and Visitor, while Lior went on about their triple date later that night. Because she *wasn't at all* excited to get with August.

"Hey, girls." Cora ran up behind them. "Got a surprise for you in a few." She wriggled her eyebrows. "Just wait."

Indy grinned, excited by Cora's enthusiasm. Cora was the coolest of them. Plus, Indy was especially enamored after that True North phone call. Plus, *plus* she could really use the distraction. "That's fa-sheezy." She smiled wickedly.

"Huh?" Lior said.

"Nothing," Indy giggled. Sometimes she just really liked confusing Lior.

Cora nodded knowingly, making a face at Lior that likely translated to, *despite being a dork, we still love you.* Lior glared at them, filling her tray with three sides of pudding off the lunch line. "Moving on," she sniffed. "So, I think we should meet at Shakeup tonight."

Lior rounded the lunch counter, and Indy reached out, stopping Lior's pudding from careening off her lunch tray. She started to say something sarcastic, but Lior looked so sincere it sucked the snark right out of her. Instead, Indy just sighed. "All right."

Grinning, Lior butted Indy's shoulder. "You're so easy." She grabbed a piece of cheesecake off the very end of the lunch counter, adding it to her arsenal, and shooed Indy toward the register. After they paid—all sugar for Lior, lettuce for Cora, and pizza for Indy—Lior thrust her tray toward the quad. "Let's go outside. It's gorgeous today."

As they stepped onto the patio, fresh air caressed Indy's face. She stopped walking in the middle of a sea of students and closed her eyes. The sun made her feel like a solar battery. Temperatures were nearing a record-breaking sixty, and though the snowcapped mountains still said winter, the crisp, high desert air and brilliant sunshiny day whispered spring. Indy felt newly charged. For a moment, she was perfectly willing to believe that everything—the numbers, Cloudcroft, their triple date—would turn out okay.

"Come on, Zoney." Lior grabbed her arm and shooed them to an empty lunch table, one of the last in the courtyard. When they were situated and Indy finished arranging her pizza, carrot sticks, and chocolate milk into a lousy facsimile of an even less recognizable UFO on the table, Cora cleared her throat. She jerked her head toward Sawyer and his jock bunch, sitting a few tables over. "Watch this."

Cora climbed onto the bench Indy sat on before stepping onto the tabletop, her high-heeled calfskin boots clunking loudly as she caught her balance. She stuck her chin out, her body confident and erect, smiling radiantly while she waited for people to notice she was standing there. "Hey, Corazon, can you hear me?"

Everyone who hadn't already noticed Cora turned and stared. In the sun, her forest green jeans and matching emerald-dyed hair tips stood out like the pines surrounding the withered grass blanketing the yard. Cora clasped her waist, calling attention to its sleek circumference. "This stupid school is broke and failing, and failing us, and falling apart," Cora shouted, stomping on the ancient, already cracked tabletop for good measure. "Y'all know someone who's dropped out, right? They've cut band and half our arts programs. But we walk around like all we care about is whether our hair looks okay, or if we'll win the football game, or if you're that bunch over there, get laid." She pointed at Sawyer's table.

Kids on the quad started laughing. Some pitched their trash Sawyer's way, which started a mini trash fight. Indy looked for Corazon's outdoor lunch monitor, fearing she'd have to lay her life on the line in Cora's defense should Ms. Muñoz suddenly decide to charge. But Ms. Muñoz just stood on the side of the quad, looking bored, shaking her head reprehensibly.

"My point," Cora yelled over the din, "is that they treat us like we don't matter, and *we* respond by acting like they're right. And then Monday, Beverly shows up and does something awesome. And even though we think it's the coolest thing in the universe for like four hours, we go right back to being idiots. People, this school is here for *us*!"

Someone on the quad yelled, "Fuck yeah!" which set off a series of quad-wide hoots and hollers.

"Get your freaking asses in gear!" Cora demanded, fist-pumping the air.

"Get your asses in gear!" a few people yelled back.

As chaos in the form of chanting students, sailing trash, and chucked food filled the quad, Indy reached out and grabbed Cora's calf, desperately trying to pull her off the table. She ducked to miss a flying hamburger bun but kept tugging with all her might.

Cora trip-stumbled off the table, landing beside Indy on the bench with a humongous grin. "Well?" she asked, her eyes shining.

Indy swallowed, aiming for at least a few notches below hysterical. "Are you freaking crazy?"

"What? You didn't think that was cool?" Cora looked genuinely dumbfounded.

Indy paused. If Cora's 'get your ass in gear' spiel hadn't come from Indy's very own lips just days before, she'd think it was the coolest damn thing in the universe. "So cool," she made herself spit out. "I just don't want to get booted off the quad."

"Screw that. That's my point. They never let us do anything around here. It's always what *they* think. You know Beverly got in trouble for putting up that sign? Even though she had pictures that proved Mr. Bines is a letch. Because the poster was 'unsuitable' for a high school environment. I mean, when did free speech stop being a First Amendment right?"

Lior reached out and squeezed Cora's arm, shooting Indy side-eye. "Ignore her. You're a god!"

"I get it, Cor. And you're a badass for saying something. I'll worship you from now until we graduate," Indy promised. "I just . . . don't want you to get in trouble."

Cora shrugged. "Some things are worth making waves over."

Normally, Indy would be bursting with pride for Cora. But the fact that True North, even if inadvertently, inspired Cora to action overshadowed it. The last thing Indy wanted was to call Corazon's attention to her UFO adventures. And the fact she knew kids locally were listening to her show messed with her head.

Cora's performance provoked a kazillion high-fives and congratulations. More people crowded their table in ten minutes than Indy probably talked to in a lifetime. Which is probably why, when the end-of-lunch bell rang, Indy waited until Cora and Lior were distracted and tried to sneak off. Because. Too. Much. Talking.

"Not so fast!" Lior yelled after her, chasing her down the hall. Looking around to see who was watching, she caught up and whispered, "So, now are you going to tell her?"

Indy shrugged woefully. She *really* wanted to. But. After Cora's big scene, Indy couldn't imagine Cora taking it well when she found out Indy was her new secret hero. "It's going to piss her off, Li. I mean, like the fact I never said anything and then let her get up in public and everything? What if she feels humiliated? She'll hate me."

"Cora's tougher than that. She'll probably be annoyed for a few days, but no way is she going to feel humiliated. Besides, it seems like she kind of worships Orion. And you *are* Orion. So, get over it. Cora loves you now just the way you are. Imagine how much more she'll adore you when she knows the truth."

"I'll think about it," Indy sighed. "You're probably right."

Lior shoulder-bumped her. "We just decided; meet us tonight at six thirty?"

Already overwhelmed, Indy muttered, "Do I have a choice?"

Lior pulled at Indy's ponytail and ran off toward Student Council, waving down the hall as a sea of students swallowed her. On Indy's way to class, she passed a group of freshmen huddled together talking about Cora and her stunt. And the way they went on about it, you'd have thought Cora was Superwoman. Indy slowed down to eavesdrop, picking out the words *extraterrestrial, revolution,* and *Orion* as she passed. She had no idea if they actually listened to True North, but it was clearer than the day through her glasses that they blamed the show for Cora's rallying cry at lunch.

DATING FOR DUMMIES

INDY GRABBED A bagel, smeared it with peanut butter and honey, and took it upstairs to her laptop. She threw an extra-loud record on her old turntable and went straight to True North, checking the boards for updates. Reading through post threads, she skimmed through everyone's plans for Cloudcroft, then froze. Though Cora's 'Corazon sucks' speech happened only hours ago, people were already sharing shots of her standing on the lunch table, labeling them with chat threads like 'Cool Chick Kicks Ass,' and 'Fuck the Establishment.' Someone even uploaded a video.

Panicky, Indy snapped her computer shut, breathing in the dry attic air. Her bedroom smelled like old cardboard boxes and cedar wood, and the combo often, especially in winter, made her nostrils burn. Not that she'd change it for the world. The textured walls and ceiling comforted her. Better yet, she valued her privacy. Lior's parents were always up in Lior's business, which drove Lior crazy. And maybe if Indy's parents were less hippy-dippy and more type-A, Indy wouldn't have wandered off and drowned in the fifth grade.

But then she wouldn't be sitting there playing the *Dead Kennedys* at top volume, either. Lior could, like, play John Legend on her headphones, and her dad would still bust a gasket.

Exhaling, Indy checked the time, then unenthusiastically pushed away from her desk. Five thirty. One hour until date night. She spun in circles, slowly breathing out all the crap she'd stored up before making herself get up and search for an outfit. Staring her closet down like she was looking into Hell's maw, Indy sniffed. Why did she care what she wore? And why did she care what Sawyer thought? After running into him in the forest last weekend, she was sure this was a date in name only.

Opting for comfortable, Indy changed into a black ripped tee, tight black pants, and a pair of canary yellow high-top Docs. Then she added the spiked bracelet her mom gave her last Hanukkah for good measure—Sawyer and his glowing butt could bite it. When she got to Shakeup's parking lot, she hunkered down in her Jeep, staring through the windshield at her friends inside. Scrunched into a booth together, they sat shoulder to shoulder like sardines, Sawyer and Manny capping both ends. Which . . . *great*. Where was she supposed to sit? Beside Sawyer?

Indy pressed a finger against her right nostril, inhaled through the other, then switched sides before letting her breath out slowly to master her calm (props to her dad for teaching her how to yoga breathe). Then she pulled the keys out of the ignition. She hopped out, stood up straight, and strode toward the restaurant like a self-assured person, completely faking confidence.

"Kicking Docs," Lior said, grinning at Indy when Indy approached the table.

Sawyer threw his arm over the backrest, managing to both melt into the shiny red booth *and* lean toward Indy. He was almost incorporeal, able to morph like a chameleon into his surroundings and still stand out.

Inwardly, Indy sighed.

"You're late. I ordered for you," he said, motioning for Indy to sit next to him. "Anyway, you've got balls," he turned back to Cora, obviously already in the middle of a conversation. "Supersized. I'm impressed. The sky could be falling, and there's still no way I'd stand up like that in the middle of the quad." He grinned this *look-you-and-I-both-know-I'm-sexy* grin but sounded genuinely impressed by Cora's gumption. "Corazon's a dump. It's about time someone called it."

Unlike Sawyer, Manny was all about the seatback. As Indy nervously sat down, Manny slinked backward, arms stretched over it, cocking his head before winking at Cora slyly. "You're def the shit, Cor."

Cora giggled and flipped some side bangs, twirling the green tips of her layered haircut around two fingers. "You think?"

Cora had her game face on, and Manny was eating her up.

"You guys seen the True North boards yet?" August asked. "Cora, someone put pictures of you up on the site."

"That was you who called in the other night, right?" Manny grinned.

Cora nodded, basking in the attention. "Totally. Orion's pretty legit." She shook her head. "I just had to call. I wanted to see what he'd be like."

"*He?*" Indy frowned, gulping back her surprise.

"You think Orion's a dude?" August asked.

Indy flared her nostrils. Orion forecasted UFOs, yet there they were, spazzing over whether Orion was male or female. *Hello*, bigger issues at stake, people.

"He's a dude," Manny said around the straw sticking out of his mouth. "Anyway, we should go up to Cloudcroft this weekend. A bunch of kids from Corazon are caravanning up there after school Friday." Manny slapped August on the back. "My man and I were talking about joining."

Indy's mouth dropped open, as vacuous as her mind while she searched for some excuse to dissuade them. Something like Cloudcroft was under quarantine all next week because of some top-secret, crop-spraying experiment out of Sandia Labs. But Cora cut her off.

"Oh my God! We should!" Cora half-yelped. "I don't work this weekend. Li, Indy?"

Lior lobbed a Morse code eye roll at Indy, silently nagging her to spill it already.

"That'd be cool," Sawyer interjected. "Camping weekend. The six of us."

Sawyer and Manny nodded at each other. August nodded at Lior, who sat like a deer caught in some poor dude's headlights. Lior wanted to go; the wanting blazed across her face. But she also knew the stakes. August or not, Lior knew Cloudcroft meant so much more to Indy than just bonfires and an excuse to drink beer and make out.

"Indy?" Lior asked tentatively.

She and Lior had already agreed to head to Cloudcroft Friday after school, so it was hard to lie and say she wasn't free to go. Because what if they went up there and ran into Cora and the rest of them? Uncomfortable would be an understatement. "Erm," she scratched the bridge of her nose, displacing her glasses, "why Cloudcroft? I mean, it's a school thing?"

"You don't know?" Manny shook his head. "Orion's numbers. Cloudcroft's supposedly the next UFO hotspot."

"Indy's married to her books," Lior tittered, blowing Indy a kiss for good measure. "She barely pays attention to us as it is. So uncivilized."

"Just because I don't know one podcast from another doesn't mean I'm uncivilized," Indy mumbled, playing along.

"It's not a podcast," Cora rolled her eyes. "Jeez, Indy. Get with the program."

Manny gave Indy a look. "Aren't you that UFO girl anyway?"

Indy choked on her iced tea. She swallowed it down, backhanding her mouth. "Thanks, Manny," she said sarcastically. And people wondered why she didn't like jocks.

He held his hands up in surrender. "Whoa, I didn't mean it like that. I think it's cool. I mean, I've always believed you. I just figured you, of all people, would be listening to True North."

Hitching sideways, Sawyer met Indy's eyes. And ohmigod, she wanted to die. He must have heard all the rumors, but he wasn't in school with all of them when she drowned. Which meant he had no idea how bad it was or how awful their taunts were afterward.

"Maybe she doesn't listen *because* of what happened at Holy Ghost," he volunteered.

Their server stopped at the table, offloading a massive tray of goodies. She placed a double green chile cheeseburger, an order of red chili fries, and a chocolate shake in front of Indy. Grateful for the interruption, Indy almost laughed out loud. Awesome for Sawyer for not ordering her a salad. But also, if she ate even half that much food, she'd die.

Indy met his eyes. Sawyer's smile made her heart flutter, and for a fleeting moment, she thought she might jump in his lap and stick her tongue down his throat. "Thanks," she blushed, nodding down at the table. "And I . . . I guess, yeah. You're probably right about the drowning thing." Under the tabletop, she played her knees like a piano, drawing her nervous energy away from her mouth. "So, what, you want to go up there to see a UFO?"

"I mean, hopefully." Cora nodded enthusiastically at her hamburger. "But there's also the whole camping with friends part."

"And partying." Manny grinned mischievously.

"It'll be fun," Sawyer assured Indy. "The UFO part's just the icing."

Indy gripped her knees. "Uh, okay—I guess." She shrugged, avoiding Lior's eyes. "As long as I can get Saturday off."

Cora burst, squealing like a toddler. "We can leave straight from school Friday. Three hours down there, right? I've got two tents. Indy, you've got tons of camping gear; you bring what you have."

"Sure." Indy faked enthusiasm. "How long do you want to stay for?"

Cora surveyed the table. "All weekend?"

"Cool, as long as I'm back by midnight Sunday." August nodded.

"What are we supposed to do there?" Indy asked innocently, picking at her chile fries.

How she was supposed to play dumb for forty-eight hours was almost as perplexing of a mystery as her numbers. What if something happened again? Something *big*? Or worse, nothing happened? Or worse, *worse*, they somehow found out she was Orion? Chewing, she looked down at the table. Thank God she hadn't agreed to meet Visitor. Because bringing five friends along would put him at ease for sure.

Manny plopped his huge hands on the table and brought his thumbs and pointer fingers together, making a circle. He closed his eyes and hummed. "Meditate?" he said between an *Om* and clenched teeth. "Yoga?"

Lior smacked him playfully.

"What? My mom teaches it," he grinned.

"The whole thing's woo-woo enough," Lior giggled.

Sawyer caught Indy's eyes. "You look sick." He laughed.

Indy looked down at her hamburger. "Too much food?"

"Or maybe you don't *really* want to spend the weekend with us?" he teased.

"No. That's not it," she answered quickly. "I mean, I do. It sounds fun. I just . . . I'm not a good camper."

"Amen!" Lior concurred, clamping her hand over her mouth after the word slipped out. "I mean, you know, you hate bugs and all," she added, mumbling between her fingers.

Indy loved being outdoors, but ever since that night at Holy Ghost, sleeping in a tent in the middle of nowhere made her itchy, and Lior knew it. Indy still went camping to humor her parents, but she slept with one eye open and one hand on her cell phone, which meant she never slept at all.

"You're seriously afraid of bugs?" Sawyer asked.

"So afraid," Indy lied.

"More than aliens?" He hiked an eyebrow at her.

Indy held her breath. Sawyer was probably just teasing her, but something about his tone made her waver. She smiled, ready to fake-laugh it off, but August saved her. Hamming it up, he launched into a conversation about whether it'd be cool to be abducted. Indy absolutely stayed out of that one. It might be cool. It might be horrible. It was also entirely possible that some otherworldly creatures had plans to probe her as they spoke. Whatever the case, she was conflicted about finding out.

When the conversation fizzled, Manny threw a wad of bills on the table. "Let's get out of here. Dad said there's a demonstration squadron flying into Santa Fe Airport tonight. A bunch of old military planes. We can watch them land."

Nodding effusively, Lior slid out of the booth, hugging herself over her flimsy spring coat. August followed and quickly slipped out of his letterman jacket. He threw it over Lior's shoulders, grinning like a crazy person when Lior looked up at him bashfully.

She *so* had him.

Cora followed Lior out of the booth, and Indy followed her lead, wondering how to make a suave exit—maybe head home and eat the last of her parents' Girl Scout cookie haul while she streamed something dumb on Netflix. But Cora grabbed her arm.

"Uh-uh. You are not ditching us," she whispered.

Indy met Cora's twinkling eyes. Nope. No suave exit for her tonight. Leave it to Cora to read her mind. "I wouldn't dream of it," she muttered.

"Mind if I ride with August?" Lior asked everyone.

August grinned. "They don't mind. Sawyer, Manny, go with Indy." He wrapped an arm around Lior's shoulders and maneuvered her outside into the crisp night air toward his GTO.

Sawyer harumphed, grumbling about cramming himself into the backseat of Indy's Jeep before yelling, "Dibs on the front." Manny followed and hopped in the back seat when Indy let them all in, scooting closer to Cora.

Indy drove behind August, heading toward the airport on the outskirts of Santa Fe, sneaking glances at Sawyer when she thought he wasn't looking. Sawyer's profile was the stuff of legends. Roman, though probably broken, nose. Army green eyes. Wide cheeks. Top lip like a meandering river. Not to mention golden-brown skin offset by black hair that he usually slicked into a pompadour. Indy loved it when Sawyer styled his hair like that. But she also loved it when he ran, and got all sweaty, and let it fall over his forehead.

And oh my God, yuck.

Weirded out by her serious crush on him, Indy forced herself to keep her eyes on the road until August stopped outside the airport. He pulled off the street and parked in a turnout beside a cracked, retired runway that bordered the main one, about three hundred feet from where most of the planes touched down. Two massive, old cargo planes idled on the strip, waiting for a hangar.

Indy parked beside August's car. She pulled the hand brake and sat awkwardly for a second, unsure what they were all supposed to talk about. Praying for some cue, she peeked through the window over at Lior, who shot her a peace symbol and scooted across the bucket seat toward August.

"How many vehicles do you think that thing holds?" she asked out loud, motioning at one of the cargo planes. "It looks like it could carry a T-Rex."

Manny leaned through the space between Indy and Sawyer, arms spread-eagle across their seat-backs. "That's a Lockheed Galaxy. My pop used to load them. They hold a butt ton of armored vehicles." He looked back at Cora. "Want to see it up close?"

"Totally!" Cora kicked the back of Indy's seat. "You coming?"

"Nah. We'll stay," Sawyer answered for her.

Cora caught Indy's eye in the rearview mirror, grinning when Indy's eyes popped. She winked, wiggled her eyebrows, and gave Sawyer a slight behind-the-head nod, switching into freak mode. "So, you can let me out now," she said in Indy's ear, purring seductively.

Faux-glowering, Indy popped her seat forward, throwing the door open simultaneously. She scrunched against the steering wheel while Cora climbed out.

Cora winked over a salacious grin and ran off behind Manny toward the fence. Indy watched them search a length of chain-link before stopping. Manny crouched down. He pulled a spoke up off the ground, bending the chain-link at its corner where it met the post. Cora crouched beside him, smirking at Manny before scurrying through the makeshift hole.

"Cora's into dudes?" Sawyer asked, breaking the awkward silence.

"Cora's into everyone," Indy corrected him.

Cora's last long-term relationship (as in, more than a month) was with Corazon's dance squad leader, Trish Mealy, so Indy wasn't surprised Sawyer asked. Before tenth grade, though, she'd been hella boy crazy, and anyone who knew Cora well enough knew she still had much love for certain male anatomical parts. She'd come out as pansexual last year. But she was still fond of saying that if chicks had dicks, she'd be at least ninety-five percent lesbian.

Snorting, Indy scooted sideways toward the door, turning to face Sawyer. He made her super nervous, and that nervousness oozed from her pores. Confused by her feelings, she inhaled and started to count backward.

"Why do you do that?" Sawyer cocked his head.

Indy's face went scarlet, but thankfully the red and blue runway lights shining through the windshield masked her embarrassment (fingers crossed). "Breathe?" she asked. "Isn't that what humans do?"

"I mean. . ." He sucked in air and held it, mimicking her.

Indy grimaced. "I didn't think it was that obvious."

Above them, an old bomber flew in, lining up to land. It swooped over Indy's Jeep, close enough to make Indy's heart skip.

"I may have given up on trying to *get* your attention, India, but I still see you."

"You make me so nervous," she blurted out. "I figured if I count to five and still can't breathe, I probably really am asphyxiating, not just freaking out."

"So, can you? Breathe?" He bit back a smile.

Indy licked her lips. "Yep. Not suffocating." She nodded at the plane that now taxied down the airstrip. "It's definitely you, Sawyer."

He leaned closer. "I'm glad you came out tonight."

Indy's ears rang. She pulled at a lobe, pretending to itch it while she sorted that one out.

"What?" He laughed.

"I just, I thought you hated me."

"Hated you?" He tilted back. "Why?"

"Because you give me that eye roll. The things you say. Because you avoid me. I don't know." She shrugged.

Sawyer jacked his mouth to the side before bursting out laughing. "I'm sorry, India. I don't mean to laugh. That's just . . . stupid. I don't avoid you. I told you last week that I *gave up* trying to get your attention. And when in the history of us not talking, did I ever say I don't like you?"

"That's it. In the history of us *not talking*. Plus, you make these faces. I mean, like these, *you trip me out* faces."

Sawyer threw his hands up, holding them palms out near his shoulders. "I make faces at you because I catch myself looking at you and think, 'Oh shit, stop staring at her, Sawyer.' Because if anyone hates anyone, it's obviously the reverse."

"But I don't hate you."

"Well, we're both idiots, then."

Indy's mouth dropped open. "So, you like me?"

"I did." He shrugged. "Honestly, India, I don't know what to think anymore."

"So, you don't *not* like me?"

Sawyer winked at her. "I don't *dislike* you."

Indy had no idea how to react to flirty Sawyer. And because of it, she found herself speechless.

"No comeback?" he joked. "I'm disappointed."

Above Sawyer's glorious but subdued smile, his green eyes glowed, almost as if powered by a generator. Astounded, Indy leaned in to get a better look. Just as Sawyer leaned in to kiss her.

"Sawyer!" she yelped, backing away. "What are you doing?"

"Trying to kiss you."

"That's not what . . ." She stopped and just stared at him.

Indy *wanted* to kiss Sawyer. She wanted to kiss him so badly she felt the want grow through her limbs like roots, breaching her skin, making their way toward Sawyer across the console. Every inch of her felt possessed, and every inch of her wanted Sawyer to possess her. The problem was, she liked him. *A lot.* And she didn't want to be just another one of his conquests.

Sawyer's dark eyebrows met in a ball above his nose. "You don't trust me?"

"I don't want to be just a hook-up."

"You think that's what I'm doing here?"

"I mean, that's . . . that's kind of your thing," she stuttered. "Right?"

Sawyer's front teeth landed dead center on his bottom lip. He worried it a little as he narrowed his eyes at her. "Right. Got it."

"Sawyer, I didn't mean . . ."

"It's fine, India," he cut her off. "You don't have to explain."

Indy felt shitty. She hadn't meant to hurt his feelings. "I feel like I do."

"Let's just take a walk."

Sighing, she pulled the keys out of the ignition and hopped down, inhaling the sharp smell of engine fuel mingling with mountain air. "I kind of love that smell," she said softly when Sawyer walked around to her. "Reminds me of traveling."

Sawyer fell in step beside her, heading toward a fence that spanned the runway. "You travel a lot?"

"Not really. I mean, we go west a lot—lots of road trips. My mom's brother lives in Santa Cruz. And a couple years ago, my dad took me to Japan for an art exhibit he was part of. That was awesome. But otherwise, not much. You?"

"We used to. Before we moved back here. My parents still travel, but now that Riley and I are older, they leave us at home when they go anywhere."

"Moved back?" Indy focused on the tiny plumes of breath that branched out in front of her, afraid to look at him.

"I started elementary school in Los Alamos. Dad worked at Los Alamos SciTech, but we moved to Louisiana and then Alabama for a few years before moving to Santa Fe."

"Oh." For some reason, Sawyer didn't strike her as a dyed-in-the-wool New Mexican. He just seemed—different. Different from what, though, she wasn't sure. "How was Louisiana?"

"Lame. Humid." Sawyer stopped walking and looked down at her. "We lived on a joint reserve base. Barely ever left. It wasn't that exciting." His top lip curled, pulling his mouth into a rakish smile that made Indy blush again. "So you think I'm a manwhore, India?"

"What?" she squawked. "I don't."

"Then why are you so sure I'm only interested in a hook-up?"

Sawyer's one-eighty threw Indy for a loop just as she was starting to settle into a kind of chatty rhythm. She'd already lined up three more questions. Enough to keep him talking for at least fifteen minutes. "That was a weird segue."

"It's not a trick question."

A brisk wind blew dead leaves into eddies that skittered over the tarmac. Indy looked down at the cracked blacktop. She pulled an errant hair off her cheek and made herself meet his eyes. "I don't think you're a manwhore, Sawyer." He stared, and she looked away bashfully. "This is embarrassing."

"Imagine being in my shoes." He grimaced.

"It's just . . . I guess because of Mina? I know it's not fair," she raised her voice over the bomber touching down, "but you have a reputation."

"Reputations are bullshit. You of all people should know that."

"Except yours isn't, is it? I mean, I've seen you, Sawyer."

"Honestly, India?" He ran a hand over the top of his stiff pompadour. "I'm lame around girls. I never know what to say, so I usually just skip past that part."

Indy frowned. Sawyer seemed plenty good with girls when they ran into him in the forest last weekend.

"I'm not saying I'm lacking in the attention department, alright?" Sawyer looked off toward the bomber taxiing down the runway. "But I promise you; it's a ruse. Inside, I'm more like you, insecure when it counts. I don't know jack about love, for instance."

Indy's face flushed. Insecure? Probably. But who was he to call her on it? She swallowed hard, spitting out, "Who said anything about love? *God*."

"I'm just saying it's easy to mess around. Not so easy to connect."

"If you want love," she scrunched her nose up at him, "maybe try dating someone who isn't all about your looks and status." Indy briefly pictured Lydia Rose, the captain of Corazon's color guard. "And maybe aim higher. Like for someone who has an IQ over twenty."

Sawyer's laugh exploded from his chest. "Why do you think I've been trying to get your attention?" His eyes glimmered, and she nearly melted. "India, *you* are smart, funny, *and* beautiful. You know that."

Indy wanted to believe Sawyer with every fiber of her being, almost as much as she wanted to kiss him. But she had no idea how to navigate his sometimes flirty, sometimes aloof personality. So she reverted to sarcasm—her go-to—instead. "You know you can't just do that charming bad boy thing with me and expect me to melt because you're gorgeous, right?"

Sawyer's eyes positively glowed, making Indy secretly eat her own words. Because, yeah, in theory at least, substance beat gorgeous. But holy hell, could Sawyer hold his own in the looks department.

"Don't scowl at me, India." He laughed.

"Don't laugh at me."

"Look, if you don't want to date me, just tell me. I can deal with that. But don't pretend you don't want to if you don't mean it. I have a heart, too, you know."

"You're so weird."

He winked at her. "And gorgeous, right?"

Embarrassed, Indy turned sharply, walking away from him with a wave of her hand as if to say, *done with you, buddy*, but Sawyer just kept laughing.

Back at the Jeep, Indy tried to ignore Lior and August, making out in the front seat of his GTO. She plunked down on her Jeep's front bumper, stretching her legs out to plant her feet against the chain-link fence. A moment later, Sawyer plopped beside her, stretching the chain-link even farther away from the Jeep's grill with his long legs and beat-up burgundy Chucks.

The Jeep heaved a little, jostling her. Indy lost her footing for a second, nearly falling off the bumper before dropping her foot on the dirt ground with a thud. Sawyer reached out to grab her shoulder, but she recoiled, her head suddenly mimicking a watermelon hitting the ground after being dropped from a skyscraper. She tried speaking, but the words came out garbled. Instead, she shook her head, squeezing it between her palms as her brain throbbed.

Reaching out to hold her in place, Sawyer dipped his head to see her eyes better. "Hey, what's going on?"

Indy took her glasses off, pinching the bridge of her nose between two fingers. Where the hell were the stupid numbers?

"India," Sawyer said softly, pointing at her upper lip, "your nose."

Indy pitched forward, leaning over her knees as she stared at the ground. If this wasn't the most mortifying thing that'd happened to her in years, she didn't know what was. When she moaned, Sawyer's hand appeared below her face, gripping the wadded-up edge of his jacket sleeve. Gently, he nudged it against her nose.

"Your jacket," she garbled into the denim.

"Will survive." Sawyer held on tight to Indy's right shoulder. "This happen a lot?"

"Lately," she told his sleeve. "I get migraines."

"Can I take you home?"

"Indy!" Lior yelled out the window, startling her before she could answer. "You okay?"

Indy waved Lior off. "I'm fine," she mumbled. From Lior's vantage, it probably just looked like she was hugging Sawyer. "But I think Sawyer and I are going to take off."

"Cora?"

"She's with Manny," Sawyer answered for her. "You okay to give them a ride?"

"Sure. It's okay. Right, Augs?" Lior asked.

Indy registered August's "Peace out" followed by Lior's "See you tomorrow." She looked up at Sawyer. "Take me home now?" she whispered into his arm.

Sawyer helped Indy up into the Jeep's passenger seat. He tossed Cora's purse to Lior through the GTO's window, then started up the engine and drove off. Indy rolled the window down, letting the cold night caress her face. Her head was on fire, and the air felt freaking wonderful. Leaning back, she pulled a wad of tissue from the glove compartment, flipped her visor down, and opened the vanity mirror. Thankfully, it pretty much just looked like she'd smeared lipstick over her top lip. She looked down at Sawyer's denim jacket—his jacket sleeve, on the other hand, wasn't so lucky.

Indy tried on a smile. Doing it made her feel a little better. "Thanks for driving. I appreciate it," she said as nicely as possible.

He glanced at her. "How are you?"

"Embarrassed."

Sawyer met her eyes just as blinding light swallowed the road ahead of them. He hit the brake, skidding into the glowing circle before coming to a dead stop. Indy braced for impact, ready to meet an oncoming car head-on. But the light came from above them, not in front of them, and as soon as Indy realized they weren't crashing, an odd calmness gripped her body. Searing brightness enveloped the Jeep, bringing with it a muted silence. Time slowed, and Sawyer's mouth moved as if speaking, but it was like someone had shoved cotton in her ears. His words came out garbled, like a recording of his voice playing at quarter speed.

Indy shook her head, staring at him wild-eyed. Everything about Sawyer's demeanor went against the grain; he was too calm and seemed unaware of the blinding light invading the cab.

Sawyer cocked his head and reached out to touch her arm. When his fingers made contact, her ears popped. Sound flooded her ear canals. It came in a rush, overwhelming her with staticky waves of airplane engine, and street noise, and Sawyer's worried voice.

"Hey," he gripped her forearm. "Can you hear me?"

Indy nodded.

"What happened? Is it your head? Where'd you go?"

"Go?" she chirped. "What the hell was that?"

Sawyer wavered. "You mean the plane?"

"What? No. The light."

"An airplane, India. Right over us. Came in way too low."

"But . . ." she looked at him, trailing off. Why would a plane make her feel like someone ripped her brain out and put it back inside out? "I couldn't hear you. And the light. There was something inside it. Like at White Rock."

Sawyer flipped the Jeep's hazards and pulled onto the side of the road. "You saw that too? At White Rock?"

"Isn't that why you told me about True North?"

"I told you about True North because Orion predicted something would happen there, and it did. But I wasn't sure if you saw more than a hella weird cloud."

Indy nodded vigorously. "There was something shiny in it. Like tonight."

"India," he pursed his mouth a little, "a plane just almost landed on your Jeep. That's all it was."

"And White Rock?"

He dropped his chin, tracing the corded edges of her worn leather seat with a single finger. "I mean, it could have been a plane, I guess."

Sawyer seemed open to something unusual hiding in the clouds at White Rock. And she wasn't one-hundred percent certain he was wrong about tonight. They *were* right next to the airport. Plus, what was she supposed to say? That she *knew* there was more than just airplanes and weirdo clouds hogging their skies? She shook her head, resigned. "I don't know about just now. I mean, I guess what you said makes sense. But White Rock *wasn't* an airplane, Sawyer."

Sawyer's fingers crossed the seat to Indy's knee, finding her hand in her lap. He hooked them around her pinky and tugged. "I think that True North show's getting to everyone. And you just basically popped a vessel." He met her eyes almost bashfully. "I'm not saying you're imagining things, all right. But I think your head's playing tricks with you right now. And it makes sense you'd be sensitive to the light. So tonight, I'm running with airplane. White Rock . . ." he paused and shrugged, "I don't know. Even more reason to head down to Cloudcroft this weekend, I guess."

Indy exhaled, wilting into the seat as all the air left her body. "Why did you ask me where I went?"

Sawyer stared out the window beside her for a moment. His pupils wavered so slightly it could be a trick of the light. Still, he smiled when he answered, shooting her that infernal smirk, a Sawyer expression if there ever was one. "You checked out for a moment, you know. Like, umm," he scratched his forehead, "like you went somewhere."

Indy flashed him an odd grin. She meant it to be a reassuring smile. But something about Sawyer's answer felt like a lie—the way his eye twitched maybe. Whatever he meant, he was side-skirting the truth, and it unnerved her that she knew it so concretely.

BOOKS VS. BOYS

"YOU ARE A serious wanker," Cora frowned, leaning over the circulation desk. "Don't think I didn't catch you slinking around pretending you didn't see us."

Arguing with Cora was pointless. Indy *was* a total wanker. Especially after coming up with one excuse after another to avoid Lior and Cora, and particularly Sawyer, at school all day. "I wasn't slinking, all right? I just have a boatload of crap to get done before we leave for Cloudcroft tomorrow."

"Really? Like what? Avoiding Sawyer?"

"Maybe. But I wasn't avoiding you guys. You just happened to be near him every time I turned around. Anyway, I did all my homework over lunch. Now I don't have to worry about it this weekend."

"I don't get it. What happened last night?"

"Nothing. Sawyer is just Sawyer."

Cora's face shifted from a frown to a smile. It touched her almond-shaped eyes, giving them wings of sorts. "Oh. My. God. Indy! You do like him!"

"Okay, wait now." Indy held her palm up. "I think he's hot. There's a difference."

Cora ogled Indy curiously. "Fine. You think he's hot. So do most of the girls at Corazon, Moi included. And you don't see *me* hiding from him."

"Yeah, well. . ." Indy tried for something snappy. But Cora was right. Indy liked Sawyer even more after last night, and she was avoiding him because of it. Between White Rock, Visitor, and what happened at the airport, her head was already so full of Cloudcroft and anxiety over what might go down, she couldn't deal.

Cora planted her hands on her hips. "India, you're a smart girl. So, I'm just going to assume you already know he's not that bad. And that he's really kind of nice. But I'm not going to overlook the fact that you're a total slouch when it comes to any boy and the possibility of dating. When it comes to the male species, you are the biggest excuse generator I know. Don't you get sick of yourself?"

Indy threw a paperback at her. It bounced off Cora's chest and landed on the counter with a thud.

"Ouch," Cora said dryly.

"I can make a shiv out of a book in five seconds flat," Indy cautioned.

"I have a shift in ten. I'm leaving your pouty ass. But I'm warning you. Sawyer or no Sawyer, you're going to have fun this weekend, or I'll personally stalk you for the rest of your life. You hear me?"

Indy snickered. "Yep. Me and the whole library."

Cora pointed two fingers at Indy's eyes, moving her hand back and forth in the air between them. She walked backwards to the entrance, squinting threateningly while she mouthed *you like him.*

Indy flipped her the bird. "Yeah, Cor. Whatever."

"I'll be seeing you tomorrow, India," Cora answered menacingly.

Indy smiled, watching Cora strut out of the library. When the door shut behind her, Indy wearily gathered the mound of books piled on the counter, threw them on a cart, and wheeled them over to the stacks. Crouching to shelve one of her favorites, *Contact*, she accidentally dropped it, cracking its well-used spine as it landed open on the floor.

Indy picked it up. Gingerly, she smoothed the book's pages, pausing to grab the library slip that landed upside down beside it on the carpet. Someone had written on it, and she stopped to read what it said.

It's bigger than us. But I've come a long way to find you. What would Sagan say? Space is bearable through love.

Indy let herself fall back on her heels, landing on her butt. Up against a bookshelf, she pulled her knees toward her chest and picked at the ratty neon purple laces holding her old white Chucks together. The canvas was full of holes, and little patches of her old but beloved hedgehog socks shone through their tops. From one rip, a pair of tiny hedgehog eyes stared up at her accusingly.

Space and love. An incredible heaviness settled over her. Well, didn't that just sum up her predicament perfectly?

Lingering in the stacks, Indy thought about what it would be like to own up to being Orion, wondering whether her confession would piss Cora off. She wondered whether Sawyer wanted more from her than just another conquest (and God, what did she do then?), and if aliens *were* about to invade, whether what Sawyer wanted even mattered.

Indy's uncertainty overwhelmed her. What did they want? Why were they contacting her? And what if they made themselves known to the world over Cloudcroft in front of all her friends? If another UFO appeared from the ether smack in front of them, and something terrible happened, her life really would change forever. If that happened, in the grand scheme of things, she wasn't even sure anything outside that moment would count.

Indy dropped her head back against a row of books. After a moment, she hopped up, smoothing the creases in her black skinny jeans with her palms. She pulled her hair off her shoulders and from around her face, twisting it into a bun high on her head. Then she walked back to Circulation and grabbed a pencil, weaving it through the dark hump on her crown. Soon enough, her neck cooled, and the lack of weight on her shoulders made her feel lighter.

Still too hot in her baggy blue and purple argyle sweater, Indy pulled it off, revealing her favorite pro-Marx tee. After she bought it, she'd poked holes through the fabric on both sleeves and the collar, liking how the controlled mess made her feel unburdened. She fancied it her very own shirt sieve; like all her crazy had escape routes whenever thinking about the numbers overheated her circuits.

Calmer and more relaxed, Indy settled on a stool behind Circulation and grabbed a book from her stash under the shelf, a treatise on everything from time travel to string theory she'd been struggling through. She skimmed it half-heartedly, occasionally pausing to answer patrons' questions and check people out. Then she remembered the note on the back of *Two for the Road*'s library slip and that Sawyer once checked out *Contact* as well. She tried recalling Sawyer's last return, snapping her fingers excitedly when she came up with *The Plague* and *Heart of Darkness*.

Dropping her book on the counter, Indy jogged to the 'C' stack near the back of the building and pulled the library's only two copies of *The Plague* off the shelf, shaking as she flipped them open. She tugged out their library slips. Except for its barcode, the first one was empty. But the second one was golden. Its backside read, *I'm an impartial observer, but I still have a disease. Only you can cure me. See through me. To the heart of what makes me tick. Save me soon, please.*

She took the book with her to the 'H' stack and found *Heart of Darkness*. On the slip inside the library's only copy, someone wrote,

Humans share the same strange savagery no matter their status, united in their egocentricity. But you are light. And because that's so, my own blank spaces will never be spaces of darkness.

Indy gripped the slip, staring at it curiously. She squinted at the blocky yet fluid handwriting. The notes could have been there for years. Just some poor dude's brief ode to Camus and Conrad that never saw the light. But her gut told her Sawyer wrote them.

She chewed on a thumbnail, grinning. She loved what they said and how he'd related it to both stories. She loved how finding them was like unearthing a secret society of library slip poets. But mostly, she just loved thinking that Sawyer wrote them. It meant that he paid attention.

Excited by the idea that Sawyer was probably her secret library book vandal, Indy peeled the barcodes off each slip, then tucked them into her pocket before bringing both books to the counter to issue them new identifiers. If she could manage to work up the nerve to ask him about the notes this weekend, she would.

If Sawyer still seemed interested.

If the numbers didn't kill her before they got to Cloudcroft.

If the sky didn't open up and swallow them all before she got the chance (which maybe wouldn't be such a bad thing considering how she'd left Sawyer after the airport last night).

Shadows crept across the library's dingy white foyer as the sun set in the west behind the Jemez Mountains. Indy watched them mute the already somber space. The dark fit her mood. Uncertainty never did anyone any favors, but in her case, uncertainty was the antagonist in her unfolding story.

Near six o'clock, when the automatic lights finally flipped on outside, Indy heaved a sigh of relief. She packed it up, punched out, and drove home. Her parents were at some art shindig for the evening—again—and the empty house was a blessing. Balancing a

Mountain Dew, a bag of chips, and a cup of instant macaroni and cheese between her hands and chest, she headed up to her room, arranging the smorgasbord across her desk. Then she pulled the library slips out of her pocket and propped them against her computer.

The note on the slip from *Heart of Darkness*—*my own blank spaces will never be spaces of darkness*—made her feel especially pensive. Indy owned a lot of blank spaces, particularly when it came to what happened at Holy Ghost River. She'd also done a bang-up job of glossing over them these last few years. More light in her life would be a welcomed shift, and she hoped, at the very least, Cloudcroft would shed some.

Sipping her Mountain Dew, Indy scanned True North's boards, allowing herself time to unwind. A slew of new threads filled the screen; all centered on two things, excitement about this coming weekend and support for the growing number of mutineers who considered themselves part of a True North rebellion. Reading the commentary, Indy whistled through her teeth, inhaling to counteract the tightness in her lungs. True North had sprouted wings. Like ten-million pairs of them.

Without really thinking, Indy hastily grabbed the burner off the desk. In a panic, she flipped the microphone on and hit the prompt button to let people know she was going live.

"Ladies and gents, truth, as you know, is often stranger than fiction." She exhaled quietly into her hand, steadying her voice. "I try to tell you all the truth here. But reality isn't always objective, and when it comes to my life, nothing so far has been fixed. I don't know what's out there, but I believe something wondrous is happening. And because of that, I'm willing to leap. But I also worry—a lot. Honestly, I started True North to connect with other people who feel lost, like I do. You helped me figure out what to do with the numbers. And I love you for that. But I have no clue where the numbers are taking me now, and I have no idea where they'll take you. And I'd be lying if I promised you anything more than *this, right now*. Honestly, at this point, you know as much as I do. We're all in this together."

Cranking a dial on the monitor, Indy blasted *The X-Files* theme, followed by a classic anti-establishment song courtesy of The Psychedelic Furs while she scanned the comments. As she read, her body unspooled. Going live on a lark was out of character, much less spilling her guts. But listeners seemed sympathetic. She half-grinned. Maybe she should step out of character more often—like with Sawyer (wishful thinking).

The song ended, and Indy's burner rang. She reached for it quickly, steadying her shaky hand. "Hiya, Caller, and welcome. It's normal to peddle parts of yourself in order to control your destiny. So, which are you tonight, seller or buyer?"

"Thanks for taking my call, O. And I'm a buyer. Just wanted to say there's a difference between belief and truth. Belief doesn't require proof for something to be factual. Just faith—however you define it. Even if you're wrong about shit, I'm behind you. Anyway, no one re-ally knows anything for sure, so maybe we should all just be real and stop fronting. I mean, that's what you're really saying, right?"

Was it? "Maybe? That's what it feels like sometimes."

"Well, keep nailing it then."

The line went dead for about half a second before ringing again. Indy had just enough time to take a swig of Mountain Dew and clear her throat.

"Good evening," she crooned. "Faith is taking that first step even when you can't see the top of the stairwell."

"You do know you're not a philosopher?" a deep, decidedly male voice barked.

"Thanks for enlightening me. Props to Martin Luther King, Jr."

"What?"

"That's who I just paraphrased."

"Same thing. Same point. You talk big, but you're obviously an insecure, nut-job, idea-stealing loser. You're pushing anarchy, sweetheart. Look, my guess is, you're sitting there with a tinfoil hat on and eight cats. Leave us sane people alone and get some help, why don't you."

Indy laugh-snorted. For some reason, jerky callers bothered her less than the things people wrote on True North's boards. Writing, especially on the Internet, had this tendency to be indelible—verbal dumbassery was not.

"Actually, two cats," she replied. "And the fact that you called in just to share your special brand of obnoxious speaks magnitudes. I'm guessing *you're* the insecure nut-job."

The caller fake laughed. "All I hear is *blah blah blah*. How about you just shut up now? I'm sick of your ridiculous bullshit. Get a life, sweetheart. Quit your lying and whining and buck it up. There is *nothing* bigger out there than God and *nothing* so special about you or any of you other nut-job True Northers that justifies being disruptive."

Indy's board blew up.

Bragalicious: HANG THE F UP!

69694EVA: I knew it! Orion's a girl.

STARBUCK: I seriously love the trolls that call in. Makes me feel better about my $100,000 student loan debt. That's what happens when you don't go to college, kiddos.

TREKKESTER2: Seriously, though. Orion, U R a Grrrrl, right?

Skimming the commentary, Indy prodded the caller. "Why are you so threatened? You may as well get used to it, 'cause I'm going to keep on talking here, and you can't do a damned thing to stop me." She hung up with flair, simultaneously setting off a twelve-bit fireworks show on her home page and an audio clip from Carmen Burana. Then she typed out:

> *Orion: Small minds. Funny how people can blindly believe in God but not themselves or other bigger possibilities. Faith is an equal opportunity concept. Not a vacuum or shield. You either have an open mind, or you don't. Cherry pickers are the real disappointments.*

Indy believed it all the way, even though she didn't always live by her own credo. Selective faith was a terrible thing; she'd suffered the effects of it all her life, especially when it came to trusting people. But she'd also worked hard to put her money where her mouth was, to take chances on what she felt in her heart as well as the things she had a hard time comprehending.

> *SaffronRD: Everyone's entitled to an opinion, right?*
> *AreciboOne: God is dead. Faith is illogical. But that doesn't mean I don't believe.*
> *Orion: Good point. Let's all agree that it's all right to disagree. Define faith and belief however you want. It's all good by me, friends.*
> *SLIM: Ditto.*
> *Matty70: So . . . girl?*
> *Orion: OMG, stop.*

After battling that stupid on-air troll, girl power was foremost on Indy's mind. She wanted to own it. She wanted to write, *hell to the yes, I'm female.* But especially after that last call, she was cautious. There were already a thousand good reasons to keep her identity hidden—no need to add to the already-boiling cauldron.

"Hey, everyone," Indy said into the microphone. "Whew, that one blew, right? But as Saffron just pointed out on the boards, we're all entitled to our opinions. No casting stones on True North, peeps, all right? Unless you're a troll, in which case you can suck it. Also, for all you know, I'm gender-fluid, or a unicorn, or a computer program. What I am matters a lot less than what's happening in our skies. Besides, it doesn't matter. And I'm never going to tell you. Now, I'll take one last call. Then I'm leaving you with a vid from Hawaii. Strange lights and copious Air Force denials, hurrah!"

Indy sat back and gave Dean Winchester a hard flick, scrolling the boards while she waited. "Last call of the night," she breathed into the mic when the burner rang. "I'm just going to assume you're a warrior. Thoughts on Bigfoot or the Chupacabra? Or maybe Foo Fighters?"

A voice on the other end sniffed, "Not really."

"Then what's your pleasure?"

"Cloudcroft."

"Visitor?" Indy asked hesitantly.

"Are you going?"

"Not sure. But I see that bunches of people on the board are. You?"

"Yeah."

"Post pictures of it? A video, maybe?"

"Orion, I really need your help."

"How's that?"

Despite her paranoia, Indy wanted to help Visitor. She wanted *him* to help *her*. But she also sensed he wasn't budging unless she agreed to meet him in Cloudcroft. And now that Lior's grand triple date had turned into a camping weekend, no way was that happening. Indy wasn't even sure how she was going to fake not being Orion for the whole weekend as it was.

"You haven't returned my messages. We need to talk."

Suddenly, Indy's door rattled.

"Sweetheart?" Her father's voice, muffled by the door and staircase, made her jump. "Your door's locked."

"Shit." Indy cursed out loud, then covered her mouth. "Gotta sign off. Visitor. Peeps. Apologies. Remember, kindness can never come too soon because you never know how soon will be too late." She slammed her computer shut and rushed downstairs to unlock her door. "Sorry, Dad," she said breathlessly. "What's up?"

"Were you talking to someone?"

"Yeah, Facetiming with Lior about Cloudcroft this weekend. And listening to that show you told me about."

Her dad pulled his eyebrows into a furry black ball over his nose, his smile more skeptically amused than happy. "Your mom just caught some of it. 'Research,' she calls it. Apparently, she's not the only one."

Indy's heart skipped. *Please, God, don't let Mom have heard Dad call me sweetheart on air. Or anyone, for that matter.*

"Um, yeah. Well, you turned me onto it."

"You're going to Cloudcroft?" He shook his head. "She'll love that you're going. I thought you were going to Taos for some reason. She'll probably ask you to take pictures. Hey, you all right? You're kind of red, sweetheart."

"Did you have a reason for banging on my door at eleven at night?"

"Right. Yeah. Mom wanted to make sure you had enough money for this weekend. I'm going to bed, and neither of us will be home in the morning. She's driving to Albuquerque with me early to help set up my exhibit. Man, she's going to bust a gut when I tell her you're going to Cloudcroft, not Taos."

Indy's dad had a major art show at a major art gallery in downtown Albuquerque coming up. She was proud of him as all get out, but she also wanted him to stop talking about True North and Cloudcroft—because, among many things, *awkward*. "I'm exhausted, Dad." She fake-yawned. "I have enough money. But thanks. Can you tell Mom I love her and that I went to bed?"

"Why don't you come down and say goodnight. She's probably still listening."

"Tell her for me? Gotta sleep, Dad," she said, nearly pushing him out of the doorframe. "I love you. Have a good time in Albuquerque. Drive safe. Good luck." She just about slammed the door shut on his face, adding, "Don't do anything I wouldn't do," before closing it completely.

"What fun would that be?" he teased through the door. When she didn't answer, he said, "All right. Call us tomorrow night when you get there. Goodnight, sweetheart."

Indy dropped her head against the door and exhaled, her heart in gangbuster mode from being interrupted. Fingers crossed, only her, her beloved Dean bobblehead, and her cats Kepler and Hubble, who didn't give a poo about anything but Fritos and hogging the comforter, heard her dad interrupt True North.

Exhausted, Indy ran back up the stairs, grabbed the library slips off her desk, threw some PJs on, and settled into bed. Tucking both notes under her pillow (because that's not at *all* sentimental), she shut off the bedside light and thought about the males in her life. Her dad was a hardcore weirdo. Visitor was an enigma. And Sawyer, well, Sawyer was Sawyer, and that was confusing enough.

Add obnoxious caller number two to the mix, and she was good and done.

Indy buried her head under a pillow and closed her eyes. Uncertainty defined her, and yet she still felt as undefined as ever. Thanks to her dad, Visitor's call proved fruitless. Though honestly, at this point, she didn't even know how they could help each other. And Cloudcroft—she had less than a clue what to do with that.

A giant oak outside banged against Indy's bedroom window, tapping erratically as gusts of wind threw the night into chaos. Late winter in Santa Fe was a windy affair, and maybe the one thing she didn't love about living in the high desert. Shivering, she pulled herself into a cocoon under the covers, sinking into a dark swath of warmth, only half-aware as the wind died down and her muscles started twitching. After a while, her mind drifted.

Frigid air stung Indy's cheeks. In the dark, her eyes blurred. She rubbed them, squinting ahead at the glow her flashlight cast through the trees. Shuffling past shadows from the looming aspens toward the sound that woke her, her bare feet barely registered the rocks and twigs blanketing the ground. The blustery wind sent her long hair fluttering over her eyes. She hugged herself with an arm and tiptoed around an outcrop of smooth boulders, determined to track down the sound that coaxed her from her warm sleeping bag into the cold, late autumn night. The dry air smelled brittle and sharp, like pinion mixed with ice. Little plumes of her breath shot out in squat stacks, rising to hover above her head, and she watched them glow like miniature ghosts in the moonlight.

Ghosts.

The thought made her whimper.

Closer to Holy Ghost River, Indy stopped cold. Two luminous orbs hovered above the tributary's surface. One of them broke into bubbles like the fizz in her favorite soda, coalescing into a naked figure above the river, almost like a boy, feet floating inches over its surface. It saw Indy standing frozen near the shore and cocked its head.

Swim, it said, though its mouth never opened.

Indy took a few steps closer, mesmerized by its glowing eyes. "What are you?"

The creature floated nearer, its body flexing as its contours unraveled at the edges, morphing from skin to wisps of bubbles. She heard a sound in her head, followed by the word *you* as it lifted its arm to point at her.

Indy shivered, her body registering the cold night air. "Girl," she said out loud.

She stepped closer to the river's bank, but when the creature jerked forward, she startled and tripped, falling head-first down the embankment. Clawing at tree roots protruding from the dirt slope, Indy flailed, half catching herself before dropping into the water. Slush engulfed her body; it felt like an electric shock. She opened her mouth to suck in air and inhaled ice.

Numbness made it hard to move her arms or break the surface. Her lungs buckled, and she strained to see until brilliant green spheres lit the space around her, introducing her to tiny bubbles that teemed around her body underwater. She floated, only half aware of the barrage of rainbow lights that moved above the river's surface like an image dissolving into pixels. Then she heard the creature in her head again, whispering.

Sucking in dry air, Indy's lungs exploded. She sprung up toward the foot of her bed, wringing her sheets into cotton eddies she crushed with iron fists. Bent forward at the waist, she dropped her head to her kneecaps and tried to steady her hitched breathing. The taste of mossy ice water still coated her tongue, and her frozen limbs tingled. But she recognized her bedroom and the blankets covering her legs.

Focused on the small pool of red staining the sheets near her pillow, Indy touched her nose. She pulled her fingers away, smearing sticky spots of blood between them. It'd been a dream. But her head tingled like the numbers just paid her a visit. Except there were none.

32.9573° N, 105.7425° W

INDY DROVE BEHIND August, following his polished GTO down a worn stretch of highway past the ancient lava flows that blanketed the Carrizozo plains. Saturated with late afternoon sun, the wide-open sky promised a dry trip. At least until they climbed into the mountains around Cloudcroft. Adjusting the rearview mirror, Indy watched Cora, content to sit in the backseat with Manny, recap last night's True North broadcast in detail. Because apparently, it was *soooo awesome.*

"Orion totally bared her soul. Then she put this dumbass troll in his place," Cora gushed.

"Dude, Orion's a *she?*" Manny sniffed.

Cora waved him off. "Guys don't have that kind of empathy or gumption; they're all about bucking it up and shit."

Indy caught Cora's eye and winked. Though personally mortifying to listen to, one of the best things about Cora's in-depth analysis was that her recap made it clear no one heard Indy's dad interrupt the broadcast. Which meant, for now, at least, Orion's anonymity was still golden.

"Nah." Manny patted Cora's back good-naturedly. "Orion's a dude. Girls don't have iron balls."

Sawyer twisted in his seat, craning to give Manny a look behind his headrest. Cora choked on her soda. "Why would we want them?" she muttered.

"What do you think, India?" Sawyer turned to her.

"Iron balls?" Indy shrugged. "Sounds painful."

"No, he wants to know if you think Orion's a lady," Cora corrected her.

"I haven't heard the show yet."

"What?" Cora screeched. "You *still* haven't listened? You may be like the only living person at Corazon who hasn't."

"That's not true."

"It's totally true. And it's right up your alley, Indy. I mean, UFOs and shit. *Please.*"

Cora and Manny laughed, but Sawyer gave her one of his strange, half-assed eye-rolls, sniffing to convey his skepticism.

"What?" Indy frowned at him.

"You are way too curious, India. There's no way you'd agree to go to Cloudcroft and not check the show out first, especially . . . you know." Sawyer cocked his head, maybe hinting at the thing in the clouds at White Rock or what happened at the airport.

"It's not like I haven't tried to listen." Sawyer's spot-on opinion threw Indy for a loop. He must *really* pay attention. Plus, how was she supposed to play this out? "It's just never on when I do. I must have bad luck or something."

Manny leaned forward between their backrests, filling the tiny space with his football player's bulk. "Just pull up True North's home page after nine and leave the screen open. It almost never comes on before that, and this dancing alien alerts you when Orion's going live."

"Good idea." Indy nodded, ignoring Sawyer's curious stare.

Sawyer shook his head. His thin-lipped skeptical expression made her uneasy. On the other hand, when Sawyer wasn't strutting around sporting his should-be-patented, shit-eating grin, he pretty much looked skeptical 24/7—like she wouldn't be surprised to find out he walked around wondering if he existed. Sawyer was just kind of weird that way. But it was a weird that worked for him. Case in point being Corazon's female population. They ate that crap up.

The fact that Sawyer listened to True North made Indy anxious. It's not like she went around quoting philosophers and poets daily, but she'd recently discussed books with him; he probably knew all her favorites already. And he was keen enough to put two and two together.

"What do *you* think of True North?" she asked him.

Sawyer ran a hand through his hair, messing his only partially styled pompadour. "I like Orion. He's a blast."

"Blast?" Sawyer's word choice made her groan. Of course, she kept the groaning to herself, but still. He had this way sometimes of talking like her grandpa.

"Yeah. It's primetime, India. A low-key listen. You feel me?"

Cora burst out laughing. "You're priceless!" She patted Sawyer's shoulder.

Indy shook her head. "You're also an ass sometimes, too, you know that?"

He sat back in his seat, clearly satisfied with himself. "Yep."

Cora leaned forward, nudging Manny out of the way. "Oh my God, will you die if something happens this weekend? I don't know, I mean, if there really is something out there," she sucked in her breath, "I mean, I'd have to rethink everything I know."

Snorting his agreement, Manny bumped up beside her. "My ma's all up in arms about an impending alien invasion. So I almost hope it's a hoax. 'Cause if it's not, I mean, what do they want?"

Indy gave Cora a sideways glance over the headrest. She tried to look as utterly dumbfounded as Cora. Because, yeah, if Holy Ghost River, or just the fleeting moment she caught that glimpse of something in White Rock, were any indication, it *would* be life-changing. But she was a lot more worried about surviving it. "Nothing's going to happen, Cor. But if it does, do you think they'd be popping up all over the Southwest and giving away their locations if they wanted to conquer Earth?"

"Why would they bother coming here if they didn't?" Manny scoffed.

Sawyer dropped his head back and threw his feet up on Indy's dash, scrunching his long legs closer to his chest. "I agree with India. Why is it so hard to believe they might be peaceful?"

Indy stared at his oxblood Docs, kind of loving that in the shoe department, at least, their tastes aligned. "Is that a rhetorical question?" she asked him.

"Kind of. I mean, if something does happen, I'd like to think it's for noble reasons."

"Noble?" Manny snorted.

Cora dropped back in her seat. "What about you, Manny? You believe, right?"

"In God, yeah. The rest?" He shrugged. "I'm a good Catholic boy."

"Even the Vatican believes in ETs, Manny," Sawyer told him.

"Seriously, man?"

"He's right," Indy agreed. "They supposedly have all this secret documentation in their archives about it."

Sawyer's face twisted into an unreadable, glorious smirk. The kicker for Indy was, instead of teasing her, he took off running, launching into a discussion about the supposed secret pact Eisenhower made with an alien race back in the Fifties. And, for a moment, Indy fell in love with him.

As Indy turned up a narrow road off the highway into the Lincoln National Forest, climbing high above the golden plains into a pine-dappled pass, she cracked her window, listening intently to the easy way Cora, Manny, and Sawyer joked about aliens and UFO conspiracies. They sure seemed to enjoy the idea, the *something more* of it. And that's when it dawned on her.

Humans were drawn to possibility. Possibility was like a rechargeable battery; as long as some mystery remained to investigate, humans would keep coming back, regardless of how many times that mystery petered out. Whether something happened in Cloudcroft this weekend mattered less to them than the idea. Possibility *was* the something that kept them engaged, and didn't that alone *already* make those coordinates meaningful? One thing her life had proven so far, despite everything (or maybe because of it), was that anything is possible, no matter how many times it turns out it's not.

Glancing in her rearview mirror back at Cora and Manny, Indy smiled. Craning her neck to read the snow-covered sign they just passed, she asked, "So where did Lior say to turn off?" August and Lior had fallen behind them, and though Indy knew exactly where to go, they didn't know she knew—it was best just to play dumb altogether.

"Turn left up ahead on 244. Head for Lower Fir Campground," Sawyer told her.

"There's a lot of freaking snow up here." Indy shivered. She turned the heater up along with the defroster, marveling at how quickly little sprigs of rime took over her windshield.

"It is still winter," Cora reminded her.

Off to her left, Indy caught a dark smudge shadowing the otherwise glistening snow between the pines. For a moment, last night's dream returned to her full throttle. She suddenly *felt* the icy Holy Ghost River and remembered how scared she'd been until she saw the creature underwater.

"India?" Sawyer waved a hand near her face. "Hey, you all right?"

"What?" She blinked.

"What just happened?"

She shrugged, trying to shake the dream off. "Nothing."

"You just passed the exit."

"Oh. Right." Indy slowed and flipped a U-turn, trying to ignore Sawyer's questioning stare as she backtracked the half block to the campground entrance.

August and Lior, who were smart enough not to follow Indy past the campground, had already parked at their reserved campsite. It was a good thing, given how crowded the park was already.

Indy glanced around uneasily at the tents surrounding them. Swarms of people converged around bonfires and coolers. Kids tossed footballs across lots and over campsites, downing beer while they messed around. The whole thing reminded her of a snowy tailgate party.

Whooping his approval, Manny motioned toward the GTO. He and August went to work unloading supplies, periodically throwing coolers and camping gear to Lior or Cora. But when Indy moved to help them, Sawyer tugged her toward a bush.

"What's up with you?" he asked softly.

"Nothing," she lied.

"That's what you said in the car too. Also, obviously not true."

"Obviously?" She rolled her eyes.

"Queue the *Psycho* music," he added, smiling. "Yeah, *obviously*."

"I hate crowds." Factually, she was telling the truth. She did hate them, though she'd long since learned how to deal. Chalk it up to years of navigating packed school hallways and their sorry lack of privacy bubbles.

"Well, that sucks. Funny how it wasn't crowded in the car ten minutes ago, though. You know, when you first went white as a sheet?"

Indy sighed, deflating a little. Shivering, she waved toward Lior as if needing to help set up the site, then wrapped her arms around her torso, pretending to be too cold to answer. Barely missing a beat, Sawyer pulled his canvas jacket off (an olive color that matched his eyes perfectly, dammit) and wrapped it around her shoulders. Indy let him, but more because he did it before she could protest.

"Thanks." Indy stared down at the glittery snow-packed ground. "And so you know, I had a *moment* in the car. Old memories kind of thing. It wasn't a big deal, Sawyer."

"You want to take a walk and talk about it later?"

Sawyer seemed genuinely interested. Biting her lip, she mustered up half an iota of courage. "Not really. I mean, the walk thing, yes. But I'd rather talk about the notes I found in *The Plague* and *Heart of Darkness.*"

Sawyer's face unfurled; his eyes lit up, and the corners of his mouth raced for his cheekbones, imitating his beautiful arched brows. Even his straight, shiny teeth made an appearance. "You found them all?"

"All?"

Dialing back his expression a little, he asked, "Just *The Plague* and *Heart of Darkness*?"

"And *Contact* and *Two for the Road.* Are there more?"

Sawyer's eyes danced. "Yes."

"You wrote them?"

He nodded, beaming.

"Seriously?" She looked up at him, beaming back. No doubt she loved a good treasure hunt, especially one involving books, boys, and poetry. "That's awesome. I kind of love imagining that you're part of this secret society of library slip defacers."

"You're such a dork." Indy's face fell, and Sawyer added, "I mean that in the best possible way, India. So yeah, there are more, and yes, you should look."

Indy stood there grinning at Sawyer like a goon until something hit her head. Startled, she turned around in time to meet the soft edge of another pillow. It bounced off her shoulder and introduced her to two parka-clad jerks, hands planted on hips, laughing in delight. Howling, Indy scooped the pillow up off the trampled snow and ran toward them, wielding it over her head. Sawyer caught up and grabbed her around the waist, lifting her as he maneuvered her like a battering ram toward Lior and Cora. They chased them through the campground while August and Manny set up tents, Indy laughing hysterically as Sawyer rotated her in circles while she smacked everyone in their path with the pillow. For a few amazing minutes, all her serious melted away, and she forgot why she ever questioned Sawyer in the first place.

When Indy was laughing so hard that tears ran down her cheeks, freezing near her mouth, Sawyer put her down. "Teamwork," he said haughtily.

Indy high-fived him.

"Dick!" Cora yelled, jumping on Sawyer's back.

Cora wrestled Sawyer playfully, yelling *giddy up* as Manny cracked a Dr. Pepper and settled into a folding chair. August and Lior pulled up chairs beside him, throwing kindling into the nearby fire ring as dusk settled over the mountain. Before joining them, Indy went to her tent to change into something warmer, then returned and dropped down onto a rutted log near Lior. She planted her chin in her hands. Remembering the dream earlier freaked her out, but Sawyer was her knight in down-filled armor. He had this rebel/nerdy side but still managed to make himself socially relevant, debunking her long-standing theory that weirdos, and especially rebels, can't be popular. The more Indy got to know Sawyer, the more she saw all the ways she might be wrong about people. But she didn't mind being wrong. It was good knowing that at least some of her more cynical ideas about humans were total bullshit.

Done wrestling, Cora and Sawyer pulled up folding chairs nearer to Indy. Indy dug through one of the coolers, taking out Doritos, packaged hot dogs, and marshmallows. She threw everything on another unopened cooler nearer to the middle of their group, along with the long metal rods Manny brought from his dad's shop to cook their cache in the fire.

"So," Cora said after they'd eaten their way through two packs of hot dogs, "now that it's dark, want to tell ghost stories?"

Sawyer caught Indy's eye. "How about we take that walk?"

"Oh, Lord!" Cora exclaimed. "Don't do it. Remember the last time we caught him in the woods?" She cut up laughing.

"Cora!" Indy cringed. "Jeez."

"I'm reformed now, Cor," Sawyer said straight-faced. "Besides, I know better than to throw myself at a girl who doesn't want me."

What?

Noooooo.

Indy squirmed in her seat. The truth was, she really, really did want Sawyer. Maybe not *that* way (yet), but still. Anything involving arms and lips would work.

Sawyer waved a skewered marshmallow over the fire. He glanced over at her, holding his left hand up. "On my honor, milady, no funny stuff."

Indy sank into the wood beneath her, trying to will herself into the grain. She dropped her head, pretending to adjust her glasses. "Yeah, because you know I'll kick your ass if you do," she mumbled.

"All five feet what, maybe five inches of you?" Sawyer snorted.

She watched Sawyer devour his marshmallow, then stood up, dusting hot dog bun crumbs off her jeans. "Whatever. You want to walk or not?"

August threw an arm around Lior's shoulder. "Mind if we come?"

Indy started to nod *yes, come*, but Sawyer shook his head. "Yep. I mind. There's a lot of empty private space around here for everyone, Augs. Why don't you guys go that way." He pointed to a patch of trees east of their tents.

Sawyer stood, took Indy's hand, and led her past a couple of people he knew at different campsites, waving as they passed. They headed for the north edge of the mountain, past a dense line of snow-capped pines to a trailhead. "On the map, it looks like there's a clearing up ahead. I brought binoculars." He pulled them out of his jacket pocket and waved them at her. "Thought we could check out the stars."

"Sure," she said, watching her breath disperse into the radiant night. The little puffs reminded her of Holy Ghost, and she wondered which made her more nervous—being alone with Sawyer or something otherworldly happening. "I'm all decked out in my warmest winter gear." She held a hand up, showing off the triple-ply mitten her mom knit before shoving it back inside her down parka. "I'm set for at least two minutes." Truth be told, she was a weather wimp, and it was probably no warmer than thirty degrees out. Since drowning, anytime it dropped below forty, she froze.

Indy walked beside Sawyer quietly, following a glittering path of packed snow lit by moonlight. Trees lined the trail sides, and the shadowed spaces in between them lent the evening this extra air of mystery Indy kind of loved.

"You good?" Sawyer asked when they stopped in a clearing.

"Totally. Just need a sec." Indy inhaled high-altitude air, letting her breath out slowly. "Can I see those binoculars?"

Sawyer handed them over, moving behind her when she took her glasses off and tipped her head back, settling on a pack of stars in the Gemini cluster. "These are amazing," she gasped out loud, impressed with the clarity of the constellation.

He shifted closer, leaning over to speak near her neck. "Optics make a difference. You looking at the twins?"

Sawyer's voice resonated in Indy's ear as he pressed against her, tucking around her shoulder. She let her head drop back against his chest, too aware of all the muscled ridges beneath his jacket. "Right. How'd you know?"

"Your orientation."

Indy glanced sideways, meeting eyes that burned down at her like the stars. Still holding the binoculars, she slipped her glasses back on and let her hand drop to her side. Sawyer's irises were mesmerizing. They looked almost luminescent in the moonlight.

Breathing deeply, she asked, "What's up, Sawyer?"

"Up?" he echoed.

"Yeah." She swallowed. "With us."

"Us," he repeated, rolling the word off his tongue like it pleased him. "I don't know. But I'm not questioning it." His fine mouth pulled left, and he reached out to tuck a stray hair behind her ear, letting his fingers linger at her neck. "I'm running on instinct right now."

"I like you," she admitted. "Do you like me?"

Sawyer turned her to face him and grabbed her jacket lapels, pulling her so close their noses nearly touched. "You already know I do."

Time stopped, and everything around Indy narrowed to a halo. Shaking, she closed her eyes, tipsy over Sawyer's warm breath, and waited for his mouth. But Sawyer released her jacket. He stepped back, holding her gaze, staring at her with the goofiest half-grin half-frown. "Sorry," he said softly. "Guess the other night threw me off."

"Because I pulled away?"

He nodded. "I'm not as sure now."

"About me?" She swallowed.

"About me," he answered quietly.

Indy stared at the snowpack near her boots, trying to steady her erratic heartbeat. Repositioning the binoculars, she turned away and pretended to focus on the stars again. "I mean it that I like you," she told the sky.

"I believe you," he said. "But you put me in a box, you know? You said as much the other night. I think I'm afraid I'll disappoint you."

"You don't disappoint me," Indy whispered. "I disappoint myself."

She crossed her arms and tucked her mittens beneath her armpits, suddenly feeling a million miles off. Given everything else in her crazy life, it seemed lame now not to risk getting to know him better. But she'd basically called him a manwhore the other night and didn't blame him a bit for questioning her interest.

"How about this," Sawyer said over her shoulder, "tell me the truth about what *really* had you in a panic earlier, and I'll answer any questions about me you have. You can ask them all. As many as you need to until you trust me."

Indy mulled it over. There was so much she wanted to know about him. "I had a terrible dream last night, and something made me remember it earlier. Good enough?"

"What was the dream about?"

"I don't want to go there, Sawyer." She handed him the binoculars. "Not tonight. But not because I don't want to know you better."

Sawyer took the binoculars back hesitantly. Slowly, he pivoted away from her, carving out a half-circle in the snow with his Docs as he went. "Back to Orion then," he muttered.

Indy swallowed hard, staring bullets at his back. Was Sawyer doing that, *I mean so much more than what I just said* thing he was so good at? Or did he honestly just want to look at everyone's favorite constellation?

"Look." He waved her forward over his shoulder. "Nebula M42 in Orion's sword is pretty clear right now."

"You know your astronomy," she murmured.

He looked back at her, his eyes guarded. "I know lots of things."

Sawyer's expression raised the baby hairs on Indy's neck. She was pretty sure he wasn't hinting he knew about True North, but she felt just as sure his wheels were turning. And that whatever had him in a stew had to do with her. Sighing, she held her hand out like an olive branch for the binoculars again. "That doesn't surprise me."

"India, look," he said suddenly, pointing up at the northern sky.

Indy followed Sawyer's arm, staring up at a wavering swarm of moss and indigo-hued striations bleeding across the firmament. Hypnotized, she held her breath. "What . . . what is it?"

"Maybe the northern lights?"

Indy shook her head vehemently. It couldn't be the northern lights. Cloudcroft was too far south. And she knew Sawyer knew that.

Filled with anxiety, Indy's heart leaped in her chest, trying to bang its way outside. She wrapped an arm around Sawyer's waist, feeling like a rowboat facing a tidal wave. The lights flickered and flexed with the wind, shimmering in the sky above the hill for almost a minute, then as quickly as they appeared, they faded.

"That wasn't the northern lights, Sawyer," she whispered. Every molecule in her body felt electrically charged—like her body itself was humming some unknown song. Even if she wanted to write it off, she knew in her heart the way she knew how to count or recite her ABCs that it wasn't all just casually related.

"Rocket launches sometimes cause that. The White Sands proving grounds is what, thirty miles to the south?" Sawyer looked down at her. "Hey, you okay?"

Indy gazed up at him, her head still full of swirling colors. "I don't know."

"I don't think that was Orion's prediction," he told her.

She searched Sawyer's eyes, trying to unknot the uncertainty she saw lurking beneath his cool-guy mask. Did he truly believe they'd just witnessed the aftermath of some military operation? She didn't think so.

Placing one hand on each of his sturdy arms, she distanced herself from him a little. "Sawyer, maybe we should go back . . ." she trailed off.

He frowned at her. "Why?"

Indy shook her head.

"You're not going to tell me."

"I want to." Damn, could that boy read her mind. "But . . ." she sucked in cold air, wanting with all her fiber to trust him. Lying took way too much energy. "This is all just too strange." She pointed up. "That. The other night. You."

"Me?" His hands reached out for her, circling her waist to pull her close as he looked down into her eyes.

"Yeah," she whispered. "I mean, the *you* part's a good strange—I think. But the rest of it scares me."

'Scare' was an understatement. She could barely explain the paralyzing, incomprehensible feeling that something bigger than all of them was on the cusp of uprooting their lives. She wished it could *all* be about Sawyer and her fears about trusting him, maybe loving him, and nothing more. That it could be so freaking easy.

Indy pulled away from him.

"I wish you'd just talk to me," he sighed.

"If wishes were fishes," she tried to smile. She swept her hand out at the moonlit trail, quietly inviting him to walk with her back to camp.

"They'd still be worth nothing, India." Sawyer snorted. "You'd just act like they didn't exist."

Indy wasn't sure how she'd expected Sawyer to respond, but his anger surprised her. Even more miserable than seconds ago, she lumbered behind him, mentally kicking her own ass. On air, Orion always managed to find her voice. In person, Indy's foot lived in her cowardly mouth day and night.

As they walked, a palpable buzz hung over the mountain. Indy felt it thrumming in her chest even before the trail opened to the hemmed-in campground. After a short, uncomfortable jaunt across the vale, where Sawyer stopped to talk to, or high-five, a bazillion people, Indy breathed a sigh of relief when they met Cora and Manny back at the fire pit.

"You guys catch the light show?" Manny asked as they both pulled up lawn chairs. "Cora thought it was a spaceship."

"Looked more like a storm cell or rocket vapors." Sawyer frowned.

Indy settled into the empty chair on the other side of Cora, co-opting a portion of Cora's blanket. She pulled it around her shoulders, trying to work through what just happened.

"Wild, right?" Cora tilted her head back to look up at the stars.

"Sure. Yeah," Indy muttered.

Cora grinned. "You're such a bad liar."

"You're not even looking at me, Cora."

"Like that matters. I've known you long enough."

"Where's Lior?" Indy deflected, frowning.

"She snuck off with August just after you guys left. Also, what's up?"

"What do you mean?"

"Sawyer's over there, across the fire," she nodded toward him. "And you don't seem even remotely excited about Orion's prediction."

"I just . . ." Indy shrugged. "I didn't have any expectations."

Cora pursed her lips at the stars. "Are we talking about Sawyer or the lights?"

Indy sniffed. "Maybe both."

"Man, Indy, you're super freaking hard to pull things out of. I could torture you, and you'd just grin and lie." She snorted. "Why are you even here with us this weekend?"

"Because you guys wanted to come." She shrugged.

Cora leaned to her left, closer to Indy's ear. "Really? You sure it wasn't to see where things go with Sawyer? Or because you really do wonder about what's out there sometimes?"

"I mean, yeah, those things too."

"Dude, you spend a lot of time deferring. *We* wanted you to come. *We* wanted to see the lights. You're just tagging along *because*. Like nothing is ever your idea. Like you have no ownership over anything. Even though I know, that's not remotely true. It's like you're afraid to just say, 'yeah, this is me, this is what I want and think,' and then own it."

Indy held back her grimace. "I guess I see why you think that, but I swear it's not true."

"It is, though. You label and compartmentalize everything and then stay in this small orbit because of it."

Indy's heart hurt. Was that really how Cora saw her—as this narrow-minded, inflexible person? Was that how Sawyer saw her too? "But I'm here now, right?"

"Are you, though?" Cora dropped her voice, nearly whispering. "You've been so distracted this year. You don't even notice Sawyer stalking you at school or seem interested in anything but books lately. I mean, you barely paid attention when I climbed up on the table, and that rocked! Don't you dream about something bigger than just this, Indy?"

Indy swallowed, trying not to do something dumb, like cry. Lately, she thought about *bigger* every single second of every minute of her life. *Bigger* was all she could think about. And yet, Cora was right. Indy was so scared of making waves or taking chances that she stayed in this tiny orbit, running from things that might cast her out into the light. "Look, Cor, I promise you I'm not uninterested or just muddling through my life." She leaned forward, as close as possible. "I need to tell you something huge. Just not here, all right?"

Cora grabbed Indy's arm. "Ohmigod. You're pregnant!"

"God, no! Also, *Cora*!"

Sawyer and Manny both stopped talking. Cora tipped back in her folding chair, waving her hands at them. "Nothing to see, boys. I kid. She's still a virgin." She shot Indy a cock-eyed smirk. "Right, I?"

Indy buried her face in her palms. A Freudian trifecta, Cora played id to Indy's superego, and Lior balanced them out. Where the heck was Lior now when she needed backup?

Cora patted Indy's shoulder. Indy peeked up from her hand-cave, squinting ferociously. "You're so paying for that."

"Uh-huh. Sure I am." Cora grinned, leaning in closer to whisper in Indy's ear. "I planted the seed, Indy. You can thank me later."

Indy faux-glowered, peeking through her fingers past Cora for a second to see if Sawyer was still staring at them. Finally, she stood up. Saluting the campfire, she announced, "I'm going that way. To the bathroom."

Indy took off before Cora could stop her or volunteer to come along. She walked morosely through the campsite, catching snippets of conversations along the way. Most of the talk seemed to be about the lights, and more than a few of the people talking were drunk. She caught the words 'Orion,' 'alien invasion,' and 'probing' more than a few times before reaching the bathroom.

Stopping in front of the tree-shrouded building, Indy nervously chewed on a thumbnail. Except for shadowed moonlight, a flickering lightbulb, and her iPhone, it was super dark out, and she wasn't thrilled about entering the women's restroom alone. Talk about the worst possible place to get abducted. As she ruminated, debating whether to go in or just pee in the bushes, something rustled off to her side. Startled, she squeaked out loud just as Sawyer stepped out from the men's part of the building into a circle of canned light.

"Sawyer, thank God," she whispered. He may be perturbed, but she could totally deal if he'd just wait for her to pee and walk her back to their campsite.

Indy called out to him as he walked off in the opposite direction. "Hey!" she shouted, jogging nearer when he kept going. "Don't be like that."

Sawyer stopped. He turned, cocking his head at her inquisitively.

Indy froze, instantaneously struck by his dull eyes. She shivered, wondering how they could look so muted and empty. Confused, she dropped her gaze, staring at his black jacket. "How'd you get down here before . . ." she started to ask, but something hit her back.

"Boo!"

Indy grabbed her chest, flipping around to find Lior and August grinning at her. "Jesus, Li! You scared the freaking crap out of me!"

"What are you doing out here alone in the dark?" Lior asked.

"Using the bathroom. I mean, I was about to. I was trying to get Sawyer's attention so he'd wait for me and walk me back to the campground." She turned to point at him, but he'd already headed back.

Lior pushed Indy toward the bathroom door. "Go, then. We'll wait."

Glancing over her shoulder at Sawyer's behind, Indy walked into the bathroom. Apparently, he *was* mad at her. And she guessed she didn't blame him. But maybe if she spilled her guts when they got back, he'd give her a second chance. She was willing to try if it meant never seeing that awful expression again.

Indy squatted over the cold toilet seat, her teeth chattering. When she finished turbo-peeing (because *hello*, freezing), she walked with August and Lior back to camp. She wasn't sure how or why she pissed Sawyer off, but the look he shot her wasn't subtle. Whatever the case, she stood by the fire and swallowed down a heaping lump of panic as she warmed up, determined to find out.

"Where did Sawyer go?" she asked Cora as she scoped out their campsite.

"Sawyer?" Cora shrugged, rustling the blanket around her shoulders. "He called it a night. Headed for his tent as soon as you went off to the bathroom. Honestly, Indy, that boy deserves an award for the world's poutiest jock."

GIRL FIGHT

"STOP, INDY!" CORA screamed.

Manny swooshed in from the left, scooping Cora up in his arms, spinning her around so Indy could chuck a big-ass snowball. Indy threw the mass at Cora's head, doubling over with laughter as it exploded in Cora's hair.

Before Indy could chuck another, August grabbed her from behind, pinning her arms at her sides. "Run, Cora!" he shouted.

Suddenly, Indy's body jerked forward, ejected from August's arms. Using her elbows to block an epic faceplant, she rolled on her side in time to see Sawyer wrestle August to the ground. She scrambled to catch her footing and motioned at Lior, and as soon as Sawyer had August in a headlock, they rushed him.

"King of the mountain!" Lior yelled, taking him down into a snowbank.

Laughing, Indy rolled off the human ball beneath her, staring up at the brilliant, cloudless sky. Lior rolled beside her, stifling her giggles with a mitten. Covered in snow, Cora plopped down beside

Lior. "What are we doing?" she chirped. "Snow angels?" She spread her arms and legs out and swooshed them against the ground.

"Plotting," Manny said, dropping down beside Cora. "Isn't that what girls do? Conspire to take over the world?"

"Because we easily could," Indy told him.

"No freaking doubt," Manny concurred.

"It's because we don't have to work as hard as you guys." Cora smirked.

Sawyer stepped up, standing over Manny. "Don't you?"

"No." Indy grinned. "We get it right the first time."

Cora and Indy high-fived over the space between their prone bodies.

"Oh, crack!" Lior giggled.

"Snap!" everyone said simultaneously.

"Yeah, that too." She smiled.

August grabbed Lior's hand and pulled her up. "You're so freaking cute, Li." He planted a kiss on her forehead, then tugged her closer, oblivious to the look Sawyer gave Manny.

August and Lior headed back to the campsite, and the rest followed, occasionally stopping on the trail to chuck snow at each other. At her tent, Indy excused herself to search for drier jeans, goading Lior and Cora into joining her. She wanted the deets on Lior and August—as if their lovey-dovey display wasn't enough of a signpost.

"So, you slept in his tent last night," she said casually, wriggling out of her wet jeans.

"You're very observant," Lior snickered. "I thought we established that this morning."

"She's asking if you boned," Cora clarified.

Lior turned her head between Cora and Indy. "No."

"No?" Cora raised an eyebrow.

Lior shot Cora her infamous *give-me-a-freaking-break* look. "What about you, Cor?" she countered. "You and Manny look pretty chummy. You came out of his tent this morning. Something *you* want to tell us?"

Cora smirked. "Well, if I did kiss and tell, I'd say we have a *thing*. But since I don't, you will just have to guess. But I will say it's a lot more than whatever Indy and Sawyer have going. *That's* kind of pathetic."

"August says it's Sawyer's fault. That he's lame when he's really crushing on a girl. Which is, like, almost never." Lior fist-bumped Indy. "Don't sweat it, I. August said he'll get over it when he figures out how to talk to you right."

"You and August talked about us?" Indy felt an odd sense of protectiveness. Like maybe she needed to defend Sawyer's honor or something.

"Well, yeah. You guys went off into the woods last night without us, and then when we got back, he was in his tent all alone brooding."

Cora raised an eyebrow, directing her pointed stare at Indy. "You should have seen this one when they got back. She was just as bad—all pouty and flustered. What did he do, Indy? Or better yet, what didn't he do?"

Indy bit her lip. Truth or lie? Then she reminded herself it was Cora inquiring, not her parents or something mortifying like that. "I asked him if he liked me. You know? Because I can't read him. Then he pretty much said yes. And then I botched it." Cora opened her mouth, but Indy stopped her. "Yeah, I know what you're going to say, Cor. So please, just don't. I heard you loud and clear last night."

"What did you guys talk about last night?" Lior asked.

"You know," Cora nodded, "the things *we've* been talking about. How Indy's always so preoccupied and secretive lately. Taking ownership, etcetera, etcetera."

"You guys have been talking about me behind my back too?" Indy threw her hands up. "Great. Maybe you should start a 'gossip about India' club."

"Meeeooowww," Cora countered.

Lior shook her head at the ground. "Just tell her already, Indy."

Indy suddenly felt trapped. Like seriously tied, bound, stuck in a coffin, and buried deep underground, trapped. She swallowed and started to yoga breathe, but Cora interrupted her before Indy even exhaled.

"Lior already knows?" Her eyes smoldered. "Is it that big thing you promised we'd talk about last night? God, India, just tell me already."

Indy started shaking. She loved Cora. Why was it so hard to share things with her? "I'm Orion," she finally blurted out.

"Say what again?"

"I'm Orion, Cor."

Cora's face broke, caught between a smile and a scowl. "Yeah, you're priceless."

"I'm serious."

"Orion, True North Orion?" She stared between Indy and Lior, her eyes shifting from squinty to enormous.

Indy wanted to hug Cora, but instead, she gave her space, knowing all too well that Cora hated being coddled. "Yeah. That one."

Cora squinted at the nylon tent flap. "Asshole."

"I wanted to tell you, Cor. Like really wanted to. I've been planning to forever, but I keep chickening out."

"How long have *you* known?" Cora shot Lior a look so fierce it hurt Indy almost as much as if Cora stabbed her with an actual dagger. Cora looked like she might cry, but she also had this tough-girl thing going on, and it kind of broke Indy's heart.

"Since the beginning," Lior answered quietly. "Indy made me promise not to tell anyone. She promised she'd tell you herself. But I'm sure she has a good reason for waiting. Right, I?"

"Fuck," Cora said matter-of-factly. She dusted her palms over her damp jeans as though sloughing Indy off, then quickly crawl-squatted out of the tent.

Indy watched the tent flap close. "Cora's pissed," she breathed out.

"Yeeepp."

"This sucks."

Lior sighed, letting her shoulders droop dramatically. "You should have told her months ago, and you know it." She sat back on her heels, sighed again, and crawled out of the tent after Cora.

Indy stared down at her rumpled sleeping bag. Lior might be mad at her for all of three seconds, but Cora had a temper, especially when someone hurt her. She even used to joke that her middle name was Grudge. For half a second, Indy fantasized about pretending she had a giant migraine and staying in her tent all night. But she knew better. Cora might be mad for longer than a hot minute, but Indy was pretty sure she'd come around. Indy just needed to apologize again (and again and again) and a lot more profusely until Cora felt like talking.

Morose, Indy threw on another sweater, grabbed her jacket, and crawled out of the tent. She plastered on a goofy smile and joined her friends around a crackling fire, blending as much as possible with the noisy, burgeoning night. When Cora handed Indy a Coke and an already-charred hot dog, Indy took it. She chewed and listened to their raucous, subversive conversations and just told herself to nod, laugh out loud, and wait patiently for her opening. Cora would let her know when she wanted to talk, and until then, Indy needed to seem as un-pathetic as humanly possible.

Sawyer shared a story about Corazon's last track meet, and Indy watched him closely, looking for a glimpse of the boy she'd run into near the bathroom. All day long, his animated face haunted her; she found it hard to reconcile who he was right now with how he'd looked at her when she stopped him last night. After they ate, she observed him while they sat around the fire gossiping about Corazon's star quarterback, Niles Ryan (rumor had it he'd run off with a waitress from the Shakeup who was old enough to be his mother). No one admitted out loud that they were still waiting for something magical to happen. But it was apparent they were because occasionally, August stopped talking and glanced up at the sky, or Cora met Indy's stare with a cock-eyed *what's next* look.

When the conversation started to lag, and Sawyer passed his binoculars around, they took turns coining lewd names for the constellations. They drank beer pilfered from Manny's dad's stash and roasted marshmallows, which Cora, unfortunately, decided to chuck at Indy, culminating in an epic but sticky fight.

Somewhere around midnight, Cora and Manny snuck off. And by then, Indy could probably measure her exhaustion with a Geiger counter. Waves of anxiety rolled off her, and she had to work to keep her eyes open. Because seriously, best-friend fights, boys, and worrying about alien invasions took a lot out of a person.

Earlier, Indy had held out hope that Sawyer might ask her to take a walk again and maybe explain why he was mad. But by the time Lior and August said goodnight and headed for August's tent, Indy was so exhausted and frustrated she finally just asked Sawyer outright.

"I'm clearly great at pissing people off," she mumbled, covering a yawn. "So, I know how I offended Cora. But what about you, Sawyer? You still mad at me from last night?"

"Cora's mad at you?"

She raised a wary eyebrow, squinting at him over the crackling fire. "You can't tell?"

"Nope." He frowned. "Why is she mad?"

"Girl stuff." She looked at the ground. "Why are you mad?"

"Boy stuff."

Indy's neck tingled, sending tiny, uncomfortable prickles down her arms. "You *are* mad at me, then."

"Your words."

"Yours, too, evidently."

Sawyer glanced off at the fluffy tree line, then dropped his soda between his jean-clad legs, dangling it between his glorious runner's thighs. After a second, he met her eyes, the fire casting a rusty glow that ignited his olive irises.

"I keep waiting, India. I'm tired of waiting."

"Waiting for what?" she choked out.

"For you to stop being so clueless."

Sawyer's cool stare made Indy feel like part of a freeze-frame; his stillness unnerved her. But he also looked combustible, and she wondered how the two things could exist so synchronously inside one body. She inhaled, suddenly aware that the air around the fire felt suffocating. As if the fire itself just burned through all the oxygen on the mountain. Gasping, she jumped straight up and promptly tripped over a rock, her head swirling with numbers.

A shrill howl rattled Indy's eardrums. She pawed at her ears, hitting the ground hard before rolling on her side. In her periphery, a brilliant purple light cut a line like a zipper over their campsite. Speechless, she rolled onto her back, mostly oblivious to Sawyer, who'd dropped to his knees beside her. He hovered over her like the lights, calling her name, but it sounded muffled beneath all the cacophony.

Indy watched a swath of rainbow octagons spill from a jagged tear in the sky, shimmering like a hologram, exposing bits that looked both digital and mechanical. They constantly rearranged as though unsure what they wanted to become.

Sawyer looked up. His grip on Indy's shoulder went slack as he stared at the sight, mesmerized by a light show that couldn't be celestial. Indy squeezed her eyes shut, trying to keep track of the numbers, desperate to get them out of her head before her brain exploded. She felt for her phone, ripping it out of her jacket pocket. Her hands shook, but she opened her Notes app and started to type: 1, 6, 11, 4, 35, 57, 17, 10, 5, 75, 50, 34.

Sawyer gaped down at her. "What are you doing?"

"Trying . . . trying to take . . . a picture." Indy pressed at her left eye and quickly shut her phone down. She struggled to sit, half leaning against Sawyer's chest as she balanced on one hand, sucking in oxygen before projectile vomiting over his shoulder. Tremors racked her body, but she kept an eye on the sky, frozen until the glowing parade of lights flickered out.

The campsite seemed to roar. The lights disappeared, and people clapped and shouted while others stood frozen, still staring open-mouthed at the sky—including Lior and August, who must have come out of August's tent. They stood like statues near the opening until Lior suddenly realized Indy was on the ground.

"Indy!" Lior rushed over, squatting beside them. "Are you okay?"

Nodding pathetically, Indy tried to sit up straighter, falling back against Sawyer when he hooked a hand under her armpit and tugged her closer. Flush against his chest, she flung her arms around him and dropped her forehead against his collarbone, not even caring about the dribbles of throw-up still stuck to her mouth.

"You're shaking." He wiped damp hair from her temple. "And sweaty."

"I'm sorry." She spoke into his jacket, her words muffled by the fabric. "So sorry."

"For what?" he asked, his voice as full of awe as it was quiet.

Indy looked up at him wide-eyed.

"Indy!" Cora crashed into the campsite, followed by Manny. "What was that? You saw it, right?" She stopped, suddenly registering that Indy being in Sawyer's arms wasn't normal. Frantic, she squatted and grasped Indy's shoulder. "Wait, are you all right?"

"She had . . . like . . . a seizure," Sawyer struggled to get out.

"Shit. Indy! Your nose!"

Indy already knew. She felt it gush over her lip as soon as she lifted her head to look up at Cora.

Cora pulled her scarf off and shoved it at Indy's face. "Jesus, it looks like you're hemorrhaging."

Pushing Sawyer back to create some much-needed space, Indy held Cora's scarf to her nose, speaking through the itchy fabric. "I'm fine. I just . . . I need a moment."

"Man, that shit was real!" Manny exclaimed. He stood over them, still gazing up at the sky. "Ain't no damned rocket launch either. Never seen anything like that."

Indy struggled to stand up, staggering until Sawyer and Cora helped steady her. Lior handed her a water bottle, and Sawyer held onto her tightly as she downed it, saving only the tiniest bit to swish around her mouth and spit out.

They walked Indy to her tent, and after Cora and Lior hesitantly said goodnight, Sawyer crawled inside behind her. Keeping a hand on her lower back, he gently laid her down on her sleeping bag, zipping her into a downy burrito.

"Do you mind if I stay? If not, I'll get Cora or Lior. Someone should watch you tonight."

Indy grabbed his wrist. "Please don't go."

Stretching out long on a mat beside her, Sawyer turned on his side to see her better. Compared to the noise outside, the tent was mercifully quiet. Head still thrumming, she watched Sawyer examine the planes of her face, wondering what he was thinking. His eyes wandered slowly, taking in every freckle and pore, and on top of everything else, it made her uncomfortable.

"You're staring at me," she whispered, wiping at her nose again.

Sawyer's brows came together. "I know." He grabbed Cora's scarf and dabbed at her nostrils. "I think it's done bleeding."

"I guess I should be embarrassed."

"Why?"

"My nose . . . or because I threw up." Indy shrugged against the sleeping bag, feeling it catch her long hair. "That's why you're staring, right?"

He shook his head. "Not really. I guess I'm just trying to figure you out."

Indy adjusted her legs, pulling her knee against her chest, so it stretched out the bag. "You're trying to figure *me* out? Didn't we just see a spaceship or something? I'm the least interesting thing on this mountain right now."

"I don't agree."

Indy licked her lips, wrinkling her nose at the metallic taste that lingered. "What did you see this time, Sawyer?"

"Same thing as you, I suspect. Though it didn't make me puke my guts up."

She touched her temple. "It's my head. The lights . . . I think they set off my migraines."

Sawyer donned a skeptical face, cocking his head sideways doubtfully. "How long have you been getting headaches?"

"All my life."

"You got a nosebleed in White Rock too. And the other night."
Sawyer smeared a thumb over her upper lip, rubbing gently. "Think
there might be some connection?"

"What? No. Why would there be?" The tent's walls glowed,
and Indy threw an arm across her eyes as if shielding them from the
muted moonlight. Did he know? Had he unraveled her connection
to Orion?

He scrunched his nose. "Third time's a charm, I guess."

Indy frowned. Suddenly, throwing up again seemed like an excellent idea. "You said the lights Thursday night were from an airplane."

"Yeah, well, now I think I might have been wrong." He gently
swept a stray piece of hair off her cheek. "Look, I have no idea how
to feel about what just happened, but I do know how I felt when
you dropped. It scared the crap out of me. I just want to know
you're all right."

"I'm all right," she lied.

Sawyer tucked his chin, angling it to scan her face better. "India, my guess is something strange is happening . . ." he paused
again and poked a finger against her forehead, "something different
is going on inside that head. And I know it *sounds* crazy, but your
headaches, your nosebleeds, I'm thinking maybe they're connected
to whatever's happening up there." He tipped his chin up, motioning at the sky.

Indy balled a fist under the sleeping bag, trying not to cry.
"That is crazy."

"You haven't at least thought about it?"

Curiosity and concern colored Sawyer's voice, but his face
lacked any trace of judgment. Indy breathed out. She was pretty
sure he hadn't just divined she had an alter-ego, and for the moment, that was something. Focusing on the tent's apex where the

girders met, she let her vision blur and answered him quietly. "Okay, I guess I have thought about it."

"Do you want to talk?"

"Not really. Not now."

"Hey." He palmed her cheek. "You're white as a ghost."

"I'm just . . . baffled by what we saw tonight. I mean, it's life-changing like Cora said, right?"

"And that's bad?" he asked earnestly.

Indy hesitated, unsure how to answer. Because she did want her life to change, but in an ordinary way, like she wanted to get through junior and senior years, go to college, and spend the rest of her life doing mundane, everyday things that made her happy. And communing with strange beings wasn't one of them. "It's not, I guess. It's just, not *normal*, you know?"

He squinted at her. "I don't really. I figured you of all people understood extraordinary."

"What does that even mean, Sawyer?"

"It means you don't do *normal*, India. You haven't since the day I met you. It's one of the reasons I like you so much."

Indy's face burned. She wanted to be extraordinary. But if being extraordinary meant having to trade ordinary for an eternal rollercoaster ride, she'd take ordinary every time. She'd experienced enough excitement already to last an eternity. "That's part of the problem. I don't think I am normal. I never exactly feel like I fit in like everyone else. Also, what if we're being invaded? Or like, what if we're not, and this is all happening just because? That would be even worse, I guess. It's just super confusing, Sawyer."

"You think about it a lot."

Indy worked hard to keep the bile in her stomach down. It wasn't so much a question as an observation, and he had no idea how spot-on it was. "I do. I guess drowning messed me up. More than I let on."

Sawyer's lips parted below his glimmering eyes, but he waited for what felt like an eternity before finally answering her. "Whatever's happening, your life is going to change one way or another, whether you want it to or not. Them's the rules. You may as well enjoy the ride."

"You really believe that?"

"I live by it." He stared up at the tent top. "We're all just cogs in a much bigger wheel, India, and there's nothing we can do to stop it from turning. But you do have autonomy over yourself. Why not make the best of it?"

Tucking her chin against her chest, Indy pulled into a ball. Sawyer almost seemed resigned. "When those lights appeared, I felt it," she whispered. "At White Rock, and the airport too. But it wasn't bad. I mean, it was—the headache part. But there was also this overwhelming sense of . . . amity . . . or maybe connection, you know?"

"I think I do," he answered quietly.

Indy's head throbbed. Quickly devolving into a ball of ravenous, terrified, and delirious, she just wanted to stop thinking, eat an entire cow (assuming she could keep it down), and pass out. "I'm too tired to figure it out right now, Sawyer. Will you curl up with me?"

Sawyer unfolded, stretching to his full six feet as he scooted closer. Indy rolled on her side, waiting for him to tuck in against her back. When he wrapped a strong arm around her shoulders, pulling her tight against his stomach, she sighed long and hard.

"Better?" he whispered in her ear.

"So much better." Indy shivered. Sawyer's breath ruffled the baby hairs on her neck, warming her skin as she closed her eyes. "If I admit I'm holding things back but promise to tell you later, like when I'm ready, can you be okay with that?"

"Is that what you're doing?"

"Yes. I guess it is."

"Which means there'll be a later?"

"Do you want there to be?"

"I thought that was obvious."

"Then, yes," she said shyly.

"Are we done pretending?"

"You mean the part where you pretend you don't adore me?"

"I mean the part where you pretend you could care less whether I like you or not and hate the sight of me." He snorted.

"I love the sight of you," she admitted.

"So, we have a deal?"

She thought about it for a moment. "For a price."

"And what would that be?"

"Pizza. I think I threw up dinner. And I'm suddenly *so* hungry."

"Can't help you there."

"Then, I don't know," she faux-grumbled, wanting to see him again maybe even more than she wanted pizza.

"What about pizza every night for a week? I'll even drive."

"You drive? I've only ever seen you run."

"I drive, India. I don't run when I'm on a date," he answered huskily.

Indy turned in his arms and stared at him, not trusting her voice to do what she wanted. Instead, she peered into Sawyer's intense eyes. Of course, he wouldn't run, but that's how she always pictured him. In motion even when he wasn't. Because except for his face sometimes, nothing about Sawyer, physically, at least, was ever static.

Raising an eyebrow, he asked, "Do we have a deal?"

Inside, Indy melted. He said *date*, as in they would go on a date, or seven of them. "Okay?"

"Was that a question?"

"I just saw a UFO and barfed my guts out. I'm exhausted."

"But you'll get pizza with me?"

"Yes. I'll get pizza with you."

Sawyer stroked her cheek, and her whole face tingled. Every sense in her body was out of whack. Sounds were too loud, and even the dim tent was too bright, and her skin felt like an electrical outlet. The entire night was crazy; all she wanted (other than to snuggle with Sawyer and dream about pizza) was to go to sleep.

Indy gazed at him deliriously, memorizing his features as she drifted. For the first time in forever, she felt almost weightless, as though telling him even the little she did, reset her normal. Transfixed, she stared at his luminous irises. He probably didn't even know how much they affected her. How connected she felt when she looked at him. As if he was this dormant limb or lung that finally started working again. And then she just knew—whatever happened in the skies above, the real key to *her* something extraordinary lay right beside her.

FROM THIS INFINITE UNIVERSE CAME YOU

"DID YOU FIND them?" Sawyer handed Indy *Through the Looking Glass.* "The notes we talked about?"

Indy shook her head and placed his library book on the counter. "I haven't looked yet."

"You should, then." He ran a hand through his messy, product-free hair, and she nearly swooned. "We still on for pizza?"

"Sure." A pulse of excitement rushed through Indy's limbs, spreading out in a warm, diffused rush. She felt weirder around him than usual. It didn't help that after Cloudcroft, he looked more beautiful than ever. *Stupid Sawyer.*

"What?" he asked.

Indy covered her mouth. Did she say that out loud? "What, what?"

"So, when?"

Her stomach knotted, flipping forcefully enough that she looked down at her shirt. When she looked up again, Sawyer stared at her questioningly.

"When do you want to go for pizza, I mean?" He raised an eyebrow.

Indy shrugged.

"You all right there?"

She slouched a little as she leaned over the counter, too aware of the voltage bouncing between them. "I think so."

"So, pizza?" He suppressed a smile.

Indy's shift ended in just under two hours, and until Sawyer walked in, she'd planned on sneaking out early and grabbing a burger. A braver girl might say *tonight, let's get pizza tonight*. But she wasn't brave because Sawyer turned her to putty from the inside out.

Sawyer waved his hand in front of her face. "You still in there?"

She grabbed it without thinking and interlaced their fingers. "I'm here," she smiled.

His cheeks flushed, and Indy realized she was holding his hand hostage on the counter. Flustered, she let go quickly.

"How about tonight?" he asked.

"I . . . have a ton of homework," she stuttered, unsure why she couldn't just say *yes* and go through with it as she promised.

"Tomorrow night?"

"I promised Lior I'd study with her."

"Thursday?"

"I work until eight." She shrugged.

"Saturday?"

"Sure." Seriously, she'd completely run out of excuses.

"Awesome." He tapped his knuckles against the counter. "Guess I'm off to train for my meet next week, then. I'll call you later about that pizza."

Possibly frustrated with her evasive lameness, Sawyer turned and headed toward the door. He didn't even wait for her to say goodbye. Indy watched him walk out, mentally kicking herself, exhaling with enough force to scatter her homework across the counter. *Smooth, Ms. Lewin-Kaminetzsky.* Shaking her head at her reflection on the computer monitor, she opened the worn copy of *Through the Looking Glass* and scanned its barcode. Flipping through it, she touched the book's yellowed pages lovingly. Sometimes, she liked imagining her secret superpower was the ability to absorb the heft of a book's words through her skin.

Thinking about Sawyer's notes, Indy pulled the book's library slip out, curious to see if he'd defaced it like the others. She smiled. On the backside, he'd scrawled, *If I had one wish, I'd wish that you meant what you said. Come through the looking glass! I'm here on the other side. I may be mad for you. But I swear I'm not a mad hatter.*

Indy blinked, her heart thumping. Hastily pushing her homework aside, she keyed into the library's database, looking up Sawyer Reyes. She pulled up his borrower's record and hit print, chewing on a pastel yellow thumbnail as she waited for it to queue up.

The old printer beneath the counter sputtered. Eager, Indy grabbed the printout and scanned the top. The first book Sawyer ever borrowed was *The Time Traveler's Wife.* Thinking back, Indy remembered secretly loving that someone like Sawyer read cheesy love stories. Honestly, that book might have been when she first started paying attention to him.

Indy took the printout and walked to the stacks, locating *The Time Traveler's Wife* on the top shelf of a bookcase near the western end of the library. She pulled both copies down and opened them. The first housed a blank slip, but the second included a message. She turned it over, reading, *I traveled here to meet you. You don't recognize me, I can tell. But you will, eventually.*

Intrigued, Indy wandered to a stack across the hall and grabbed the next book on the list after *Contact,* pulling the library's only copy of *Anthem* off the shelf. Steadying her hands, she took out its slip. On the back, he'd scribbled, *Chaos necessitates change. Change forces us to make choices. You are an excellent option.*

A heavy burst of air left Indy's lips. She scanned the printout, nearly running to stack twelve to pull two copies of *Vanity Fair* off the shelf. On the back of the first slip, she hit pay dirt. He'd written, *Unlike Becky, my motives are pure. Will you ever find this? Do I deserve you?* Indy dragged a finger over each word, trying to picture Sawyer's hand moving across the stiff manila paper. Anxious to read more and maybe a little freaked out, she put the book aside and scanned down the printout. Sawyer's next choices surprised her. He'd checked out four books, all of them girly, young adult novels she'd refused to read on principle (at least that's what she told people). She ran to collect them, feeling sure she'd been off duty when he checked them out because, in theory, at least, she would have given Sawyer holy hell for choosing them, *and* she would have remembered it.

Excitedly pulling copies of *Twilight, If I Stay, Match,* and *Delirium* off the shelves, Indy flipped through their covers, disappointed to find them all empty. She re-shelved them and imagined confronting him at school, in front of everyone. Sawyer-the-jock reading angsty teen love stories seemed like excellent leverage. Though, she also kind of loved him for being such a dork.

On Sawyer's sixth visit, which she'd also been absent for, he'd checked out *Outlander* and *Wuthering Heights,* more books that seemed totally off his radar. Her heart sank as she searched through all four copies. Save for a barcode each slip was still an empty, pristine sheet.

Indy took a bathroom break, helped a few patrons, then went back to sleuthing. On Sawyer's seventh visit, he'd checked out *A People's History of the United States,* and *Eat Pray Love,* a combo she absolutely remembered (because weird). Housed at opposite ends of the library, Indy headed for *Eat Pray Love* first. Momentarily disappointed to find both copies empty, she crossed from the stacks near the stairs to the stacks near the front desk and struck gold. The slip in the library's only copy of *A People's History* read *Anarchy and socialism are fuel. You're fire. And I keep getting burned.*

Someone called Indy's name, and she jumped, hiding *A People's History* behind her back like she'd stumbled upon porn in the stacks. Her face flushed, and she giggled over feeling so embarrassed in the first place. Damn Sawyer and his stupid effect on her. Shoving the book back on the shelf, Indy skipped over to her supervisor at the front desk. As he explained an upcoming library event that he wanted her to work, she focused on looking engaged because inside, she was secretly *soooooooo* distracted.

When her boss finally headed for his office upstairs, Indy breathed an impatient sigh of relief. She pulled her hair into a messy bun high on her head and took off her glasses. Tossing them on the counter, she rubbed her eyes, careful not to smear her purple mascara. Twenty minutes in, and she'd barely dented Sawyer's borrower's list, but she also sensed a pattern. She hadn't personally scanned Sawyer's choices in or out on his seventh or eighth visits either—the last two of the *Twilight* series and the first *Harry Potter*—and when she went to inspect them, they were all disappointingly empty.

Indy penciled through the list carefully, crossing off all of Sawyer's visits she hadn't been there for, laughing out loud at times at his choices. Judging by the pattern she eked out, Sawyer went for fluff and romance when she wasn't around and literature and non-fiction when she was. Almost like he wanted to impress her.

Her.

She nearly choked.

Just how long had he been paying attention to her, really?

Indy stared down at the remaining titles. Sawyer acquired his sixteenth book during one of Indy's shifts. For good measure, though, she ran to find fifteen first. But as she suspected, *The Notebook* was empty. Number sixteen, though, *Flowers for Algernon*, rewarded her. She pulled out its slip, marveling at the now-familiar writing. *Humans are cruel. They judge like you judge. Sometimes I'm a mouse running in a maze, and sometimes I'm a genius, impatiently eager for you to catch up. I'm tired of waiting. Is oblivion better?*

Indy's heart skipped. *I'm tired of waiting.* He'd said those exact words in Cloudcroft.

Panicky, she nearly flew across the library to book seventeen, *Jane Eyre*. She pulled out its library slip and eagerly read each eye-searing word. *I'm a ghost. Yet physical. Fleeting and material. Still waiting for you to make me human.* Since she'd also been there for Sawyer's eighteenth and nineteenth picks, Indy suspected *The Alchemist* and *Ishmael* would also reward her. And she was right. Both copies read, *Wake up already.*

Book twenty, *1984*, held a message too. Its slip read, *If you roll your eyes any harder, you might catch a glimpse of me in your periphery. Watching you.* Book twenty-one, though, *The Stranger*, nearly fractured her heart. She stared at the blank slip, sure she'd been there to check it out for him.

Indy pinched the bridge of her nose, displacing her glasses. She leaned her forehead against the cool metal bookshelf and told herself just to breathe. Deciphering Sawyer's cryptographic way of expressing himself was a hundred times more confusing than trying to crack the new coordinates she'd channeled in Cloudcroft. And given how many times she tried doing it already, that said something.

Searching the end of the print-out kind of desperately, she quickly found *On the Road*, *The Plague*, *The Fountainhead*, and *Heart of Darkness*, whose note she'd already pilfered. Lungs in her throat, she walked to the counter to help a customer, then headed for *A Modern Study of The Old Testament* and *Bhagavad Gita*, the last two books on the list before Sawyer checked out *Through the Looking Glass.*

Upstairs, near the back of the north wing, Indy pulled *Bhagavad Gita* off the shelf. She tucked it under her arm and then searched for the library's worn, abridged copy of *A Modern Study of The Old Testament.* Holding her breath, she flipped *Bhagavad Gita* open first, looking down at Sawyer's scrawling handwriting. He'd written, *I've never been selfless or heroic. But you changed my absolute reality. Now I'm at war with my heart. Liberation, please?* Quickly, Indy placed it on a shelf and opened *A Modern Study of The Old Testament,* reading, *Willing patience from bone is impossible, like blood from a rock or wine from water. How did Moses do it? I'm the rock, not Moses. You're a burning bush. I keep waiting, repenting, trying to be better. Feel like I've been kicked out of Eden. Wandering the desert. Mixing metaphors until you finally call me (505-717-0106, btw. You've reduced me to begging).*

Stunned, Indy took a deep breath and pulled her phone out of her pocket. She snapped a picture of the slip, then quickly ran downstairs. At Circulation, she stared at the phone number, gawking at the screen. Outside, the setting sun cast warm shadows through the slats in the wooden shutters covering the windows in the main foyer. Twilight bustled, and scores of people strolled the Plaza's main streets. Inside, though, the library neared flat-line status. The entry, at least, was so quiet she was almost afraid to use her phone and break the silence.

Indy crossed her fingers and dialed, pressing her phone to her ear.

"Hey," Sawyer answered on the third ring.

"Sawyer," she nearly choked. "It's Indy."

"What's up? You still at the library?" He cleared his throat, and Indy could almost see him stand up taller, shielding himself behind this armor he donned before every competition. Secretly, she'd always loved watching him do it, the way he physically morphed from fidgety to unflappable.

"I . . ."

"You re-evaluating that pizza?"

"I . . . I read them . . . all," she stuttered.

Sawyer breathed out. "I'm hanging up. I'll be down there in a few."

"No. Wait. Sawyer!"

Sawyer didn't answer. The line disconnected, and she held the phone away from her ear, staring uncomfortably at his number. *Crap.* She checked the time on her phone. Twenty more minutes before her shift ended. Enough time left for the anticipation to kill her. Seriously, what was she supposed to say when he showed up? *Hey, read your dope notes; I'm chill?* Because she wasn't. Not at all. Truth be told, she might be wholly, irrevocably in love with him. And *that* was even scarier than her coordinates.

Indy waited fifteen long minutes before clocking out and stepping outside. Twilight was all crimson laced with indigo, full of huge fluffy clouds backlit by the last remaining rays of sunlight. She inhaled, filling her lungs with the sharp scent of burning mesquite, and stared up at the sky unfurling over Santa Fe, comforted that even amid the chaos, pretty things abounded.

A soft breeze sent cool air fluttering across Indy's face, masking the burn pinking her cheeks. She turned on the sidewalk, contemplating just walking to her car before Sawyer arrived. Then she spotted him jogging toward her down the aspen-lined street.

Standing still as a statue, Indy pushed her fist against her sternum to quell the thunder in her chest. He'd seen her for sure, so running away probably wasn't the best idea. Instead, she waited for him to catch up, digging deep to find her voice when he approached her.

"You . . . *ran* here?" she blurted out.

"Too nervous to drive," he huffed. Sawyer bent at the waist, then put his hands on his thighs, dropping his head for the briefest second. When he looked up again, he grinned, blowing a lock of hair off his forehead. "And I wanted to burn off a little steam before facing you."

She grimaced. "You make me sound like a death squad."

"Well?" he said almost shyly.

She shrugged. "I don't know what to say."

Sawyer stood up and wiped the sweat from his brow. "When have you ever not known what to say?"

"I just went through your library picks for the last year!" she chirped. "I'm kind of speechless. And I didn't ask you to hang up on me and run down here."

Sawyer reached out and hooked her chin, tugging her face up. "Do you know how long I've been waiting for you to find them?"

"You could have just said something," she whispered. Sawyer's hand on her face burned a crater in her skin. It was all she could do to stop herself from shaking.

"I tried. You never paid attention." His thumb caressed her jaw, sliding over her bottom lip, where it lingered.

"Sawyer," she breathed out.

"India," he echoed.

Tilting his head down, Sawyer aligned her face perfectly. Then he kissed her.

Indy melted. Sawyer's lips were magnificent and pliant, but the kiss was explosive. She kissed him back eagerly, winding her fingers through his hair almost territorially, oblivious to the people passing them on the street. Totally immersed in Sawyer's taste, and smell, and feel. Everything not Sawyer dropped away. Indy was vaguely aware that the world still moved outside her body, but her body itself stayed fixed to him, frozen, especially compared to the fireworks inside her heart.

Breathless, she finally broke away. "Wow," she murmured.

Sawyer exhaled. "Understatement."

She nodded slowly. "I . . . jeez."

"Still speechless?" He grinned.

"Your fault."

"Are we finally on the same page?"

"Uh . . ." she blew out, "yes."

He looked monumentally relieved. "Thank freaking God, India."

"I can't believe you wrote them. To me."

Sawyer smiled mischievously. "When I started writing, I thought you'd find them and figure it out. Then you didn't. Then I thought maybe you'd read them and just weren't interested. Then I realized you might actually be *that* oblivious. I got so used to doing it; I guess I figured I'd find out either way, eventually."

Indy stared at the sidewalk, following a crack to the street. *Unreal.* She swallowed, forcing herself to move her still stinging tongue and put words together. "The things you wrote, I mean . . . your actual words," she shook her head, "what does it all mean?"

He crossed his perfect arms over his perfect chest, stretching his Kelly-green t-shirt across perfect, muscled shoulders. "I guess you inspire me," he answered softly.

Indy looked off toward the snow-capped mountains hovering in the distance over the city. It didn't make sense to her; how life could deviate so thoroughly from one day to the next; how it could suddenly feel so right and set without any kind of forewarning, even when everything else seemed to be falling apart. "Will it be weird if I tell you I think I might be in love with you?"

"Totally weird."

"Weird enough, you'll stop liking me?"

"Never." Sawyer over-pronounced the word *never*, letting his tongue touch his top teeth before capping it off with a small, emphatic sniff. "Especially because I *know* I'm in love with you." His eyes danced, full of mischief. "I even remember the very first time I saw you at school."

"Me too," she admitted. "On the steps near the gym. You were wearing this shirt with a squirrel holding a switchblade. And your hair was all messy."

"For me, it was the morning my mom brought me in to register. You were standing at your locker with Cora. Wearing a black dress. Hair in a bun. I thought you'd caught me gawking." Sawyer's smile touched his eyes. "I wanted to drop through a hole in the ground."

Worried she'd morph into a messy puddle at his feet, Indy grabbed her arm, squeezing roughly to remind herself to breathe. "So, what next?" she asked shyly.

"Pizza," he said. "If you're done avoiding me."

Indy started to say she'd only avoided him at school all day earlier because she had a headache (a lie, but still). But Sawyer held a hand up, stopping her. "How about you *don't* make something up, and we just agree that whatever your reasons, we're done skulking around each other. Deal?"

Indy bit a thumbnail. She could think of a million good reasons to say *no, no deal*. If Cloudcroft proved anything, it was that life wasn't getting any less complicated anytime soon. But Sawyer wanted her to trust him. And he'd put his trust in her. Sawyer, with his arresting face, and athletic body, and stupid perfect brain, and quirky sense of humor, and thousands of other amazing things, she'd need a million terabytes of memory to log. She probably couldn't even walk away under duress even.

"Deal. No skulking." She snorted.

He held his hand out, laughing softly. "Pizza, then?"

"Now?"

"Please. I sprinted all the way here. I'm starving."

Indy took his outstretched hand, squeezing his long fingers between hers. She nodded enthusiastically. "Pizza sounds really freaking good."

I HEART TRUE NORTH

DELICIOUSLY FULL AFTER splitting a large pepperoni and green chile deep-dish pizza, Indy tossed her car keys on the hallway table next to a note with her name on it, holding her stomach as she locked the door behind her. She picked up the folded message, squinting to decipher her mother's messy handwriting.

Dad forgot he had a thing at Artemis Gallery tonight. Said he texted you, but you know Dad—just wanted to be sure. Sorry, we missed you again. Still can't wait to hear about Cloudcroft. We'll be home by midnight. XO Mom

And hallelujah for small miracles. Indy adored her parents, but she hated talking to them about personal things, like that she'd just gone out with Sawyer. Plus, she hadn't seen either of them for more than a minute since last Thursday night, and she knew they'd be all up in her business when they finally cornered her. Indy cringed at the thought. No way was she telling them the truth about what happened in Cloudcroft. Every time she relived those three long minutes when the sky filled with rainbow honeycombs, and she thought she might die, she came undone.

Indy hadn't even checked True North yet. It'd only been twenty-four hours since they returned from Cloudcroft, and she wasn't dying to go live and take a stab at what happened Saturday night—as Indy or Orion. Still, if being with Sawyer this evening taught her anything, it was that grabbing the bull by its horns paid off. Seriously, she'd lost a whole year of making out with Sawyer because she'd been too afraid to talk to him.

Nervous but resolved, Indy ran upstairs and threw her backpack on the bed. Ignoring the butterflies in her stomach, she stood in front of her computer, waffling.

"What do you think?" she asked her Dean bobblehead, flicking at it anxiously.

Dean bobbed his head *yes* at her, and she plunked down in her chair, apprehensively opening her laptop. No more procrastinating. She turned it on, leaning in before rolling back to distance herself from the overwhelming number of posts that popped up. True North's boards had exploded. The visitor counter at the bottom of the page for Monday alone tipped one thousand.

Based on the number of people still awake and outside their tents Saturday night, Indy's rough guess was that at least fifty people witnessed the lights over Cloudcroft. But fifty was enough. People posted pictures or described what they saw in the sky, and the opinions in the comments section bordered on hysterical. Scanning the page, Indy counted seventy-six separate threads and hundreds of comments in response to those posts already. Cloudcroft was a bona fide *ohmigod* event, even though speculation about *what* they all saw varied wildly. Theories ranged from a UFO encounter to a mass ripping of Earth's dimensional fabric to a glitch in the Matrix. One person even claimed they'd all been victims of government-administered LSD sprayed directly over the campsite.

Indy linked her hands behind her head and tipped back. Though elated to know she wasn't insane, part of her was terrified. Because *hello*? There it was. More than just speculation—enough to stir a big roiling pot. She'd seen enough movies to know; even using a proxy server and a VPN through Tor, if someone or something wanted her badly enough now, she was a goner.

Debating whether to go live now that concrete proof was out there, Indy scrolled through the pictures posted to the site, trying to deconstruct the ones that were grainier and out of focus—not surprising given the lack of light and shake-inducing shock factor. Despite being mostly inky and undefined, every single one of them proved something inexplicable appeared in the sky. Cameras didn't get high and trip balls. And they certainly didn't record honeycomb shapes breaking through a haze of color just to mess with people.

Overwhelmed, Indy moved on to the live feed. Tentatively, she typed:

Orion: Well, that happened.

The feed immediately went bonkers—message after message scrolled beneath her own.

CloudCROFTER: You went? We're dying to know.

Tobias456: Alien Invasion? WTF?

69694EVA: Shit went down, O. You're bona fide.

STARBUCK: More numbers?

SLIM: Pics b trippin.' Want to know what u think. Been debating all night.

Indy glanced around her room like she was being watched. She tried yoga breathing, then chewed off the edge of a thumbnail, then quickly typed:

Orion: So sorry. Couldn't go 'cause I was sick as hell in bed all weekend. Dumbass timing. But the boards and pictures, oh my God. No more numbers, but the last set

was a doozy, right? Yeah. A ship. Or something. Hard to
tell except for in a few frames. Looks mechanical?!?

Indy chewed her bottom lip as she wrote, unsure whether to share her new numbers. She'd already run a search on them a bazillion times and come up with zilch.

STARBUCK: Those pics, though. Looks like it's hiding.
Styxit2YA: Camouflage.
SLIM: Subterfuge :-)
69694Eva: Alien intervention. Maybe they've always been watching.
RodgerDodger8: Or you're a pawn. Mind control.
STARBUCK: Go live, O.
SLIM: Totally. Peeps wanna hear what U got 2 say.

Indy clenched her jaw hard enough to hurt. Prying it loose, she rubbed her chin and fidgeted with an old protractor, scraping it in circles on her beat-up desk. Part of her wondered if she should just quit True North, both the website and the show. Especially now that Sawyer was in her life. If the site went down pronto, it would only ever be an urban legend. And if all the sightings ever amounted to was a reason to hope or dream, that was plenty.

Frustrated by her choices, by not having answers, by everything, Indy got up and paced, stopping to pet Hubble and Kepler, lounging obliviously on her backpack. She chewed on a pen and spat the little blue plastic flecks from the cap across the floor. The other thing was that True North was the only way she knew of to talk to Visitor, who incidentally hadn't tried contacting her since last Thursday. Plus, it kept her grounded. It reminded her that whatever was going on, she wasn't alone in her panic *or* wonder.

Staring at the computer screen from her bed, Indy watched posts pop up. After a few minutes of anxiety-filled indecision, she finally grabbed her burner and turned it on. But before going live, it rang, startling the bejeezus out of her. Indy jumped, dropping it on the floor. Staring at the square plastic casing like a venomous snake, she grabbed it, holding it between her fingers away from her body. Suspicious, she answered on the sixth ring, propping the phone against her keyboard after switching on her voice modifier.

"I'm not live," she told the caller. "But I've got you. What's up?"

"What happened up there?"

Indy instantly recognized the voice. "Visitor?"

"In Cloudcroft. It stopped. In the middle of everything. It just stopped."

"You were there?" Her voice came out hollow, and not for the first time, she was grateful for the device masking her identity.

"Yes."

"You think it stopped? Like maybe it was interrupted?" she asked him.

"I know it was."

Indy watched the board fill with pleas for her to go live, peppered with proclamations that after Cloudcroft, she'd chickened out or succumbed to brainwashing.

"Orion, I'm running out of time. I want to go home, and I need your help."

"Have you tried Googling it?" she asked tersely.

Visitor sighed, audibly exasperated. "You and I both know I can't Google this address. There's no app for it. There's just you and me and your new coordinates."

"How do you know I have new coordinates?"

"You haven't gone more than a week between coordinates since December. Plus, I'm pretty sure you were there too."

Knowing that Visitor could have been any of the faces she saw at the campground made her nervous. She thought back, trying to remember if anyone stood out. But she also knew it was a dumb endeavor. The most extraordinary people often just looked normal. "All right, maybe I do have new coordinates."

"Tell me?"

Still unsure whether to believe him, she said, "Tell me who *they* are first."

"I will if you agree to help me."

"I might agree to help if you promise to tell me," Indy countered.

"That's not how it works."

"It is if you want those coordinates," she grumbled.

"I offered to meet you," Visitor reminded her. "In Cloudcroft. You turned me down."

"Right, because you could be like a serial killer or government assassin."

He was quiet for a moment. "I get that. But I'm not."

"Are we talking honest-to-God aliens, Visitor?"

"Call me Henry."

"Henry?" The name was so . . . so normal, she nearly laughed. "Seriously?"

"As serious as Orion."

"Okay, *Henry.* You're right; I was there. And I do have new numbers, but I don't think they're coordinates. Your turn."

He sighed. "*They* aren't human. But they are my people."

A dog barking in the background nearly sent Indy flying out of her chair. "Right," she whispered, rubbing out the goosebumps climbing her arms.

"You don't believe me."

"I don't know what to believe," she answered honestly. "But if you're right, why are *your* people communicating with *me*? Who are they? What do they want? Where are they from?"

"I've been thinking about that a lot. But I'm not going to tell you over the phone. We need to meet in person."

True North's feed quieted down. People still called for Orion to go live, but many also seemed to think she'd already bailed for the night. "I have to think about that, Henry. Honestly, I'm a little afraid of you. I mean, you could be lying."

"I'm not. I promise. I'll help you figure it out."

"Can I bring someone?"

"I'd rather you didn't."

"Where are you now?"

"In New Mexico."

Indy pulled her glasses off and kneaded her eyes and forehead. *That's* how he knew she went to Cloudcroft. Like she suspected, he probably knew who she was already. "Give me a few days to think about it?"

"Will you wait to share the new coordinates until you talk to me?"

"Yes."

"Thank you."

"But I'm not promising anything after that."

Henry exhaled so hard she almost felt it. Closing her eyes, she tried to see him, tried to picture this stranger she knew she was about to entrust with all her secrets. Indy hated that he probably already knew who she was. But it also made her wonder. If he did know her, why hadn't he approached her in person already?

"Imagine spending your entire life wondering who you are," he said quietly. "Then imagine waking up one day knowing there's an answer, but that finding it depends on the help of a single stranger. You'd feel powerless and maybe even desperate, right?"

"Yes," she admitted.

"Well, that's me. And I *am* desperate, Orion."

For the longest time, in grade school especially, Indy felt estranged and isolated. But at least she knew who she was. She hated knowing Henry, or anyone for that matter, could be that lonely. "I'm sorry, Henry. I'll help you if I can. But you understand why I'm cautious. Right?"

"Orion, I've listened to your show from the beginning. I know you want people to know they matter. That we're more than just skin and bones walking around independent from each other in an otherwise empty universe. I think you already know this, but you're putting yourself on a ledge going live with those coordinates. I respect that. And I trust you because of it."

She swallowed, then stuttered, feeling like a poser. "Th . . . thank you."

"I'll call again Sunday night. Ten o'clock. Is that enough time to figure it out?"

"Yes."

Indy started to say more, but Henry hung up.

Henry.

Visitor was less of a stranger now, but her strange constellation had grown. *They* were out there, like another layer superimposed over the world she'd always known. And people other than her were in on the secret.

Sighing hard enough to make her bobbleheads bounce, Indy leaned over her keyboard and typed out:

Orion: Still here. Sorry. Not feeling so chatty. Staying on the boards until I get my voice back.

Lior, who'd joined the feed, responded immediately.

LiLi: U okay, O?

Orion: Good as gold, LiLi. Just not up to live chat tonight.

MrDark: People are saying Cloudcroft was just the beginning.

Orion: The beginning of what?

MrDark: The end.

Indy smiled. She'd never known Cora to troll the internet, but Cora also wasn't subtle. Plus, Indy knew Cora was now regularly monitoring the boards—she'd said as much. Coralicious *had* to be her handle.

Indy sat back, fingers hovering over the keyboard. Let them debate humanity's merits. For now, it was so much better than having a heated conversation about what they'd all seen in Cloudcroft.

TINFOIL HATS AND FERAL CATS

CORA GRABBED INDY'S hand and pulled her past a row of lockers plastered with blocky stickers proclaiming, *Get Your Ass in Gear!* Indy reached out and brushed one with her fingertips, affirming they were real. She couldn't quite wrap her mind around the fact that her show had become this phenomenon.

"You see that, Cora?" she asked, trailing behind Cora out to the school's side quad.

"There's a poster in the main entrance, too. Bet Principal Garcia tears it down by day's end. Asshole."

"He probably should." Indy dropped her voice to a whisper. "Imagine how people are going to react if they find out . . . you know."

Cora stopped for a moment, turning to face Indy.

"I mean . . . it's just me. I bet they all think Orion's some mystic guru or something."

Cora tugged at Indy's arm, continuing her trek to the quad. "You kind of are. I mean, think about it. But for real, maybe you should worry more about what the people who *do* take you seriously think. As in, watch your back kind of shit."

Indy nodded dejectedly. It's not like she hadn't been worrying about that basket of crazy on and off since that truck followed her home from the library. Especially after seeing the same truck drive past her house just before bed last night.

Lior waved at them from a picnic table near the stucco wall adjacent to the media center. As soon as Cora dropped down on the bench beside her, Cora pulled out a nail file and placed it and a bottle of yellow nail polish next to Lior's lunch. As far as Cora was concerned, there wasn't anything a good manicure couldn't sort out.

"Gross," Lior snipped. "Can't you wait until later?"

"No," Cora answered. "I've got a shift after school, and we're pushing our new Sunshine Spring mix. I want to be matchies."

"Oh, my Gawd." Lior rolled her eyes at the sky, then winked at Indy, totally messing with Cora. She picked up Cora's nail file and poked her with it. "You're such a conformist." She shook her head and motioned at Indy. "So, what's next?"

Indy frowned. "Figure out what the next set of numbers means?"

"You have them?" Cora's now purple and blue hair tips shimmered. She shook her head, bumping off a ripple of glossy highlights. "First off, can I just say I'm still so freaking in awe that you're Orion. Bitch, you are cooler than me. It's totally not right."

"Thanks," Indy answered bashfully. The truth was, she'd never be cooler than Cora; she didn't want to be. Cora was a queen, and Indy was perfectly thrilled to be her subject.

"Are you posting them?" Lior asked.

Wavering, Indy shook her head. Lior and Cora still didn't know about Henry, and until she figured out whether to trust him, she didn't intend to share any time soon. She knew what they'd say—don't meet him. "They're not all one coordinate. I haven't figured out what they are yet."

Cora waggled her eyebrows. "What does Sawyer think?"

"About what?"

"The numbers. About being Orion?"

"You mean like when he finds out in never years?"

Cora arched a manicured eyebrow. "Look how well not telling me worked out."

"But it did work out."

"Only because I'm awesome. And also not making out with you, or spilling my deepest, darkest feelings when we're together, or pledging my undying faith and love. Well, I am, I have, but you know what I mean. Dudes you date and best friends are totally different."

Indy pulled a carrot from her lunch bag and waved it in the air. "How do you know we're dating?"

"Oh," Cora grinned, "you mean other than how obvious it was Sunday that you like each other? Sawyer and I talked this morning." She fake-coughed into her fist, mumbling, "At least admit I was right."

Lior nodded. "If you're serious, you should tell him."

"Define serious." Indy grimaced.

"Indy!" Lior yelped.

"I know, all right. Just, what if he thinks I'm crazy? Or he tells everyone."

"He won't. Come on, I—you two wouldn't have hooked up if you didn't trust him."

Lior and Cora knew Indy well. She would never seriously date someone she didn't feel she could confide in. "We didn't *hook up*. Also, what if he hates that I'm Orion?" she whispered, scanning the quad cautiously.

"Then he's not the guy for you. *And* he's an ass," Cora reassured her.

"Indy, Orion's always telling people to take chances. Try taking your own advice for once."

"That's the thing. Orion said it." Indy frowned. "*I* didn't."

"You *are* Orion," Lior reminded her, rolling her eyes.

Cora grabbed her hand. "Sawyer's good beans," she said, squeezing reassuringly. "Manny says he's super into you. Anyway, frankly, the boy's just weird enough that I think he'll like you even better once he knows."

Cora's insistence inspired Indy. And after digesting the idea, she couldn't think about anything *but* telling Sawyer. He'd understood when she explained her nose bleeds and headaches. He'd even come to her defense when Manny called her 'the UFO girl' last week. Plus—and she shivered at the thought—he claimed to love her. The solution seemed obvious, and later, when Sawyer pulled up in front of her house for their pizza date, she peeked out the window, took a deep breath, and decided to spill it. She wanted to trust Sawyer completely and telling him the truth about being Orion felt like an excellent first step.

"Gary Indiana, there's a boy at the door for you," Indy's mom yelled up the stairs.

Indy cursed her under her breath. *Gary Indiana, Mom, really?* Rolling her eyes at Kepler, she grabbed her purse and jacket, torpedoing down the stairs before her mom inflicted more damage. In the hallway, she stopped and smoothed her skirt, running her hand over a leather pleat. She'd gone all out; red, high-heeled booties with hella shiny buckles, black leather mini skirt, black fitted t-shirt, and a fire engine red biker jacket, all courtesy of her mother's 'vintage' (i.e., old) high school wardrobe.

"Hiya." Indy walked around the hallway wall; a grin plastered on her face. At the same time, Sawyer and her mom gave her the once-over. But Sawyer, his expression was everything; he did a dou-bletake as his mouth dropped open.

"Sweetheart!" Indy's mom proclaimed. "Well, damn. Kickin' outfit."

"Don't say 'kickin,'" Indy begged. "There's like, a law about things you're not allowed to say out loud after thirty."

Her mom's eyes glittered. "Is there now? Must have missed that memo. Good thing I've got such a good daughter. Always willing to fill me in."

Indy grabbed Sawyer's arm. "We're going now."

"I don't think so." Her mom gripped her shoulder, stopping her. "Not until you tell me where you're going. Are you on a *date*, India?"

Indy buried her face in her palms.

"Oh my. You're wearing contacts! You must be . . ."

Holding up a single hand, Indy waved a palm near her moth-er's face. "Don't even."

As usual, it took about a decade for her mom to catch up. Also, as usual, she seemed to have forgotten this one little word called *tact,* along with the credo *thou shall not embarrass thy daughter in front of a potential suitor.*

Sawyer kept his cool, obviously squelching a laugh. "I'm Saw-yer Reyes." He stuck his hand out toward her mom. "And it is a date," he said amiably. "Thank God. You have no idea how long I waited for Gary Indiana to finally notice me."

"Jenny Lewin." Indy watched her mom go all melty before shaking his hand, moving on to drape her fingers over his nice-ly dressed shoulder like they were fast friends. "And that's lovely. I didn't know." She stepped back, but not before giving his shoulder a squeeze (and for real, with shoulders like that, it probably happened every freaking day).

"So, what's up with Gary Indiana?" Sawyer asked, grinning. "The name, I mean?"

Indy shot her mom the iciest stare. Gleefully ignoring her, her mom said, "India used to be obsessed with *The Music Man*. She's seen the movie at least fifty times. And she adored that song. Gary, Indiana. Not Louisiana, Paris, France, New York, or Rome. Sang it everywhere. We just thought it was so cute."

"Completely adorable." Sawyer's eyes twinkled.

Indy wanted to kill them both.

"Would you like to come in? Meet Indy's dad and have a soda?"

Eyes abloom, Indy stared darts at Sawyer. Behind her mother's back, she shook her head. *No. Please, God, no.*

"That's nice of you, Ms. Lewin. But we have reservations at six."

"I understand," she beamed. "Just don't forget, Indy. It's still a weeknight. Be home by eleven thirty."

Indy squeaked something unintelligible, grabbed Sawyer by the arm, and yanked him outside onto the front porch. On the steps, she breathed out, "I'm soooooo sorry."

"It's fine." He shrugged through a smile. "She's nice. Plus, I wanted to meet your dad. You, though . . . seriously, you and that death stare, it's scary effective, India."

"Trust me; you do not want to meet my dad tonight. He's stressing out about a show he's about to do. He would have talked your freaking ear off about it." She hopped up and down on the steps, anxious to escape the front porch before her dad came out and tried talking to them. "So, did you really make reservations? What happened to pizza?"

"No. I just wanted to impress your mom. I would never deprive you of your pizza." Sawyer's eyes wandered from her head down to her pointy boots. He let out a long, slow whistle before biting his bottom lip and meeting her eyes again. "Also, would it be too jockish of me to admit I think you look so hot right now I want to go for pizza just to show you off?"

"Yeah, kind of." She blushed. "But I'm still flattered."

"You know I dig your glasses, though, right?"

"I thought you liked my eyes."

"Your eyes are beautiful, but your glasses are also super sexy."

"Eh, they're not punk enough." She sniffed.

"So, you're punk tonight?"

"I don't know. Maybe. Or rock and roll. I for sure have a major case of the screw-its right now. Whatever I am, it's all anarchy, baby." She laughed.

Sawyer's grin exploded. He grabbed her lapels and pulled her closer, kissing her hard enough to make her head spin. Indy happily kissed him back, coming up for air only after she noticed that truck again, cruising up the street in her periphery. It slowed near her house, idling for a moment.

"Sawyer." Indy grabbed his arm. "Turn around."

The truck drove off as he pivoted, speeding up around the corner.

"What am I looking at?"

"There was just . . . there was a truck there." She pointed at the street in front of her house. "Sorry. Guess I thought they were gang-bangers or something."

"Pizza." He shook his keys in the air. "You need pizza, stat. And let's grab dessert at the Plaza Café afterward. I love their tres leches."

Trying to ignore her gut, which was all kinds of roiling, she nodded. "Yes, please."

Sawyer walked her to his car, a big old Escalade Sawyer's daddy bought him on his sixteenth birthday. Though it hardly mattered anymore, in some ways, Sawyer was *that* boy. Without even really meaning to, Indy quickly ticked through an internal checklist.

Wealthy family—totally. Smart—yes. Athletic—bonanza. Handsome—hella. Popular—yes, yes, yes. Honestly, she still wasn't exactly sure why Sawyer liked her. Or, well, that wasn't right. She understood why he liked her. She just didn't get why he didn't seem to care that she wasn't like any other girls she knew he'd dated.

"Glaring isn't going to make my ride go away," he said, opening the passenger door for her.

"What? I'm not."

He made this face, sort of a *don't mess with me, you amuse me* frown-smile. "So judgy."

"What's that supposed to mean?" She climbed into the Escalade and buckled up.

"Why do you even care about the car?" he asked, settling beside her.

"You don't drive it to school." When he didn't answer, she added, "Obviously, you care what people think too."

"I don't drive it to school because I knew you'd have issues with it," he admitted. "I stopped driving it to school right after I figured you out."

"What?" She turned sideways on her seat, staring at him.

"India, you're more hung up on things like status, or maybe I should say anti-status, than anyone I know. And you're not the Escalade type."

"And you are?"

"I'm just happy to have a freaking ride. There's this little word called *gratitude* I take kind of seriously."

Indy felt like a jerk. A wounded jerk. But still. "Why would you stop driving it because of me?"

He shrugged, looking at her with a cocked eyebrow as if to say, *Duh.* "I wanted you to notice me. But I didn't think you'd look past the car."

"Are you serious?" She almost laughed.

"I'm pretty sure it would have cut my chances in half."

Indy thought about it for all of a second before flushing with embarrassment. He was so on point. A hundred times over. She was just as bad as some jocks and popular kids she harped on. "I'm sorry I made you feel like that. But I still would have liked you." She grimaced. "You really think I'm that judgmental?"

Sawyer paused for a second before starting the car, scanning her face. "I've seen you form opinions about things pretty quickly. But I guess I'd say you're more like stubborn. Because I've also seen you give people you've already decided suck second chances. And you're forgiving when it comes to things most people actually do judge others about."

Indy swallowed down a lump. She'd adopted the bad habit of pigeonholing people as a defense years ago and had clung to it ever since. But she was trying hard to change her ways. Sawyer himself proved that most of what she thought she knew about humans was off the mark. He was nothing like she'd thought, and she'd never been so happy to be wrong.

"I'm trying to be more open-minded. I mean, I'm here with you, right?" she ribbed.

"Uh-huh." He squinted a single eye at her. "And you're already better for it."

Pulling away from the curb, Sawyer maneuvered his shiny white behemoth down the narrow street. The setting sun dipped below the Jemez Mountains to their left, and its ginger-orange rays brushed the side of his face, painting it golden. He looked sure of himself but not angry, and when he glanced sideways at her, his smile transformed his already perfect mouth.

"I'm joking, India."

She looked down at the floorboard. "I know you are."

Indy's stomach growled. She grabbed Sawyer's hand, trying to ignore all her jumbled thoughts and emotions. As they drove toward downtown, she made a deal with herself. She'd tell Sawyer about True North and the numbers later. Just not before food—she wasn't about to let her paranoia ruin her dinner. Also, once she started talking True North, she was pretty sure the topic would rule the night.

Sawyer parked in the lot at Indy's favorite pizza joint. For more than an hour, they talked about school and growing up, almost like Cloudcroft never happened. Like neither of them witnessed the mass of colors and mechanical parts over the mountain Saturday night. Afterward, they strolled past historic adobe buildings housing modern boutiques and funky galleries, hands linked as they headed toward the Plaza Café and the heart of downtown. At the café, they settled into a window table looking out at the Plaza and ordered two slices of tres leches. Riveted by Sawyer's stories about living on different military bases, Indy listened intently, trying to gather up the nerve to tell him about True North.

Sawyer spoke passionately about the things that mattered to him, and Indy happily listened. But as he sat across from her, highlighting his words with mad gesticulations, something out on the Plaza caught her eye. In the park across the street, a figure in a plain black suit loitered near a tree, staring through the restaurant's window at them. Wearing sunglasses. At night.

"Hey, there." Sawyer forked Indy's cake playfully. "Am I boring you to death?"

"Sorry." Squinting, Indy pretended to focus on Sawyer's perfect hair, swept up in a low pompadour. "It's just . . . your hair looks super dope tonight."

Sawyer shifted, twisting in his chair to look out the window before Indy realized what he was doing. "Sawyer!" She grabbed his forearm. "Stop."

He glanced at her over his shoulder. "You're not staring at my hair, India."

"Please," she whispered.

Sawyer turned back to face her. Indy held her breath, quickly sorting through options. The man on the Plaza could be the opening she needed. But between the truck she saw earlier and the guy outside, she was starting to wonder if she *should* tell him. Just being Orion, host of True North, was one thing. Admitting she was Orion, potential danger magnet, or would-be murder victim was another. It was starting to look like someone really was following her. And if it was like, *Men in Black,* or even Henry, she could be putting Sawyer in danger.

"We should leave," she said abruptly.

Sawyer stared down at his frosted slice of half-eaten tres leches woefully. "How about you tell me what's bugging you, instead."

Digging her nails into her palms under the table, she briefly closed her eyes. *Courage, India.* "There's a man outside on the Plaza. In a suit. Wearing sunglasses. He's watching us."

One of Sawyer's eyes twitched. He rubbed his chin, hiding what looked like a grimace. "Well, I said it earlier; you're off-the-chart hot tonight."

"That's not why he's staring."

Sawyer rested his palms flat on the wood table. He leaned forward a little, squaring off with her. "Okay, then why *is* he watching us?"

"You know what?" Indy made herself meet his stare. "I'm sorry. I'm just being weird tonight." As she said it, the man slithered behind a tree before reappearing on the other side. He took his glasses off, and his eyes reflected the Plaza's yellow lamplight, glowing a silvery amber. Indy gasped, then clamped a hand over her mouth. Her nerves got the best of her. She shot up, almost knocking her high-backed chair over.

"Let's just go," she pleaded.

Sawyer stood up, pulled out his wallet, and threw a bunch of bills on the table. But he didn't say anything.

"Don't be mad," she said as he ushered her out of the restaurant.

"I'm not mad, I just wish . . . look, if you don't want to be here with me, India, just say so."

"Sawyer, I swear on my life, that's not it!"

Outside on the sidewalk, Sawyer stopped and licked his lips, looking up at the star-saturated sky before finding her eyes. "Sometimes, I think I know you *so* well. And other times, you're a stranger."

Indy's teeth clenched so hard that her jaw felt like granite. Quietly, she spoke between them, pretending to glance down the street toward the Governor's Palace casually. "Listen, please. He's across the street toward the center of the Plaza against a tree. Kiss me or something but try to peek out at the Plaza when you do."

Sawyer stared at her for a moment before pulling her in for a kiss. Grasping her hands, he balled them against his chest and looked down at her, closing the space between their foreheads. "Okay, that is weird. He's been out there for a while?"

"Yeah, and I'm *sure* he's watching us, Sawyer. It's really creepy."

Sawyer wrapped an arm around Indy's waist and maneuvered her without another word toward the parking lot. He walked fast, periodically glancing over his shoulder.

When they climbed inside his Escalade, Indy said, "Now *you're* being weird."

"Being watched is weird."

Sawyer sat hunched over the steering wheel, abandoning his usually confident posture. She searched his face, afraid to tell him the truth. But explaining she was Orion was the right thing to do. At least then, he'd probably understand why someone might be stalking them. "Can we just go? Please," she pleaded. "Drive to the airport, watch the planes and talk?"

Sawyer started the Escalade, double-checking all his mirrors before heading toward the highway. When they entered the Relief Route, he turned the radio on and tapped his fingers against the steering wheel in time to some rap song, but she could tell he was still uneasy. He glanced in his rearview mirror a lot, and she didn't blame him. She spent most of the drive with her own eyes glued to her side mirror.

At the airport, Sawyer stopped in the same dirt lot they'd parked in last week. He shut the engine off and turned toward her, draping an arm over the white leather steering wheel.

"So," she started tentatively, "that happened."

"Yeah," he said quietly. "It did."

Her heart skipped. "You all right?"

"I don't know. Life has been like a strange dream lately, India. Haven't you noticed? True North. Cloudcroft. The guy on the Plaza. I've been thinking about it since the airport last Thursday."

Indy's stomach turned in somersaults. "Do you know?" she blurted out.

"Know? Know what?"

Sawyer's baffled expression reassured her. Best she could tell, he hadn't suddenly concluded she was Orion. "How much I adore you?"

"I think I do," he said thoughtfully. "But you can still tell me."

Desperate to distract him, Indy crawled over the center console, planting herself in his lap. She placed her hands on his chest and fiddled with the buttons on his shirt, unbuttoning two before leaning forward and whispering in his ear, "This much."

Sawyer locked his hands around her lower back, tipping his head away against his headrest. He stared at her, fluttering butterfly lashes before running his fingers through his coiffed hair, sculpting it into a perfect mess. "What are you doing?"

"Trying to show you," she answered shyly.

"I want you, India. But I also want this to be real, and I want it to last."

Indy loved that being with her mattered to him, that *she* mattered to him. But his hesitation took her aback. Because according to legend, Sawyer never turned down a girl in his lap. "It is real, isn't it?"

"Then why do I feel like you're keeping me at an arm's distance?"

"Honestly, I'm just being lame right now because that's not what I thought you'd say." She kissed his nose. "You keep surprising me and doing or saying the opposite of what I expect."

"You expected me to jump you."

She shrugged. "I'm in your lap. I might have been hoping you'd notice. Plus, you know . . ."

"That's what I do," he said gruffly.

Indy leaned back against the steering wheel. She'd wanted to distract him, not hurt his feelings. "Sawyer, I couldn't care less what you did with anyone before me, honestly. I just care that you know how I feel. Because I'm new at this. I have no idea what I'm doing."

Moonlight highlighted his faint smile, igniting his face. She reached out to touch it just as he opened his mouth. "It's good to know that. And a great reason to go slowly. But I wasn't talking about right now. I meant you keep me at arm's distance always."

Indy swallowed the lump growing in her throat. She was way too emotional now to think rationally. "You're right; life's all out of whack lately. And I don't know what that . . . that whole thing on the Plaza was. But you're here. And I'm here. And I'd just like to pretend things are fine for a while and make out."

"Hard to argue with that." Sawyer tapped a finger to his pursed lips, beckoning her closer. "But we need to talk, India. Promise we will, later?"

Indy leaned forward, nodding *yes* as she went, full of something that, until recently, she'd only ever read about in her favorite romance novels. She kissed him gently, tracing Sawyer's tongue as he explored her mouth. For a few moments, she was the queen of freaking everything, and despite being the conduit for some possibly hostile alien Morse code, she had no trouble letting everything go but Sawyer. The only thing she *could* control right now was this. This moment. The first moment in a long time that she wanted to last forever.

REASON IS OVERRATED

WATCHING TARA BOLES tell off Corazon's principal, Mr. Garcia, Wednesday morning was pure entertainment. Red-faced and like he might bust a vein in his temple, Mr. Garcia stood in the hall near Administration bellowing like an elephant, demanding Tara take down the poster she'd just shellacked across the wall.

Talk about tenacity—the girl had balls. Tara had used maybe two whole rolls of clear industrial packing tape to secure her totally legit statement to the brick hallway. A hurricane, at best, had a minimal chance of tearing it off.

"It's called free speech!" Tara yelled around her chewing gum. "You want it down? Call my lawyer!"

"It's called vandalizing public property, Ms. Boles. And hate speech isn't protected speech. Neither is defamation." Mr. Garcia put his hands on his hips like someone's old grandma, striking a pose that made everyone in the hallway snicker.

Someone in the crowd yelled out, "Did he just say defecation?"

"Hate speech?" Tara sneered, yelling over the gaggle of students who started chanting *defecation*. "It says," she pointed to a defaced picture of Corazon's meanest lunch lady, pointing at each word as she read, "Stand up to faculty lunch-shaming."

Arlo Walker, Corazon's junior class president, stepped into the circle other students had formed around Tara in the hall. "It's not defamation, Mr. Garcia. Because it's true. Every time someone goes over balance or uses a voucher, the staff calls us out in public and refuses to serve us. It's like Corazon has a beef with poor students."

"That's ridiculous!" Mr. Garcia shouted. "Corazon values and respects economic diversity. I'm disappointed in you, Mr. Walker. Both of you—in my office NOW!" He held the Administration door open, shooing them inside. "The rest of you, vamanos! Go to class!"

"'Economic diversity' my ass," Cora hissed. "I should write him a list of the things I haven't been able to do since freshman year. He'd be up all night. Not that I'd want to," she added under her breath. "I hate this place."

"Everyone!" Tara yelled defiantly. "You're all my witnesses. He's busting me for getting my ass in gear and defending our student body. He *says* Corazon cares, but actions speak louder than words." She stomped a pastel pink heel on the floor and tossed her head back, jangling her enormous earrings. "If y'all don't see me tomorrow, call Orion!"

Indy froze, hugging her notebook to her chest. Beside her, a girl whispered to her friend, "Seriously, my dad's law firm is looking into that show. Like because it's so disruptive. God, adults are so uninspired."

Cora poked Indy's side. "All you," she said under her breath. "See what you started?"

"It's out of hand, Cor," Indy whispered. "I mean, people are getting in trouble. And her dad's law firm? That can't be good."

"You're not doing anything illegal."

"Yeah, but I am pissing people off. Plus, I think I'm being followed."

"What?" Cora hissed.

Quickly, Indy described the truck she kept seeing and the man she saw last night with Sawyer.

Cora blanched, tugging her forward. "I don't like it, Indy."

As the crowd dissipated, Indy spotted Sawyer across the hall. Their eyes met, and he waved her over. "Look, can we talk about it later? Sawyer's staring." She nodded toward Sawyer, standing near his locker tossing a football around in a group with Manny and August.

"Yeah. I'll see you after fourth."

Indy wove her way through a throng of bodies over to Sawyer.

"Hey." He kissed her cheek. "What was that all about?"

"You mean Tara?" she asked.

"I mean you. You looked like you might faint for a second after Mr. Garcia yelled at her."

"I guess I felt bad."

Maddy Goldberg, one of Corazon's cheerleaders extraordinaire, walked past, giving Sawyer some serious eye. She stopped at her locker, whispered something to her hideous cheerleader girlfriends, then blew him a kiss.

When Sawyer grinned, Indy socked him. "You're a heathen."

"At least someone appreciates me," he gloated.

"Yeah, like half the school, Sawyer."

He let go of her waist and crossed his arms over his chest, leaning back against the row of lockers behind him. "That includes you, right?"

"Are you serious?"

Sawyer bit back a smile. "At least half-serious." He let his face break, easing into a grin that could mesmerize most of the cheerleading squad into doing his bidding.

"Stop being charming. It doesn't work on me."

"Really?" He cocked an eyebrow. "It did last night."

"Mostly because I mixed sugar and anxiety. You just happened to be there to reap the benefits." She smiled despite wanting to snort bullets at him. Stupid Sawyer. He was so hard to be angry with.

Sawyer pulled her into another hug.

She chewed on her bottom lip, scrunching her nose in the process.

"You still upset about the Plaza thing?" he asked.

"Little bit," she said into his chest. "You?"

"Yeah." The bell rang, and he hugged her. "Talk about it later?"

"After my library shift?"

"Better yet, come over for dinner this weekend. My parents are going out of town Sunday for a week. I'll cook. Then we can *really* talk. About everything."

Indy tugged away a little to see his face better. Sunday was her phone date with Henry. Also, *everything*? "Monday, maybe?"

"Sounds good. But I am free after school today too," he said enticingly.

"I work until eight. After that?"

He shook his head woefully. "I promised Manny and August I'd hang out. But I'm also totally free tomorrow night. And I still owe you pizza."

"Okay. Tomorrow night. We'll eat pizza and make out."

He smiled. "Then Monday night, promise we'll talk?"

"Yep. About stalkers, and your library notes, and Cloudcroft." By Monday night, she hoped, she'd know more about her numbers and have the courage to tell him about Orion.

"My library notes?"

"Yeah. I've been thinking a lot about what you wrote. What you meant."

His eyes gleamed, sparking this crazy squeezing feeling in Indy's heart. "Ten-four. Tomorrow night, pizza. Monday, we talk.'"

She shook her head, making herself smile. She deserved a guy who could make her smile even when she didn't want to. At least that's what she'd read in last week's Cosmo Girl. "Can't wait."

Indy said goodbye and moved through the following few periods in a semi-daze, distracted by conflicting thoughts about Cloudcroft and Henry and what exactly she'd tell Sawyer next Monday night. Because Tara's outburst had her all mixed up. *Get your ass in gear?* WTF?

By the time school let out, gossip at Corazon was rampant. Between the lights at Cloudcroft Saturday night and Tara's big moment, the school's rumor mill was in overdrive. People were staking odds on an alien invasion, and the whole Lizard-People-from-Mars eating them for dinner thing started grating on Indy's nerves—probably because she half-worried it might be true herself. It didn't help that the truck she kept seeing pulled up across the street from the library when she got off shift later that evening. Or that she saw it again Thursday morning in front of her house. Or again the following night, when she walked Sawyer to his car after he joined her family for dinner. And it especially didn't help that Cora seemed to be point-stabbing at it out the Starbucks window now.

"Whoa. It's right next to your Jeep," Lior gasped, motioning out at the Starbucks parking lot. "That's the one you described, right?"

Sawyer lurched forward, nearly tipping his metal chair over. "How many times is that now?"

"You should call the police, India," Cora frowned.

Indy gulped. "And say what?"

"That someone's following you."

She shot Cora a look. Because, for real, unless she absolutely had to, she had no desire to explain to the police why someone might be stalking her. "I'm just saying. What would I tell them?"

"That you've seen the truck like five times now," Lior spoke up.

Indy gave Lior a look. It's not that the Santa Fe Police sucked; it just took murder to get anyone in the city to pay attention to anything. Santa Fe was like that. *Carpe Mañana* was legit its motto. The only way they'd even listen to her was if she admitted she helmed True North.

"It's a small city, Li. We see the same cars every day all the time. And it's probably not even the same one," she said as convincingly as possible. "Besides, I don't even know if it's following *me*. I mean, I've been with Sawyer almost every time," she tried to joke.

"Are you serious?" Cora squawked. "The same black truck with tinted windows just happens to drive down your street, and past your work, and cruise up next to your Jeep? And you think it's about him?" She pointed at Sawyer, totally oblivious to Indy's attempt at humor. "Indy, notice its back plates? They're some kind of special issue."

Sometimes, in haste, Cora had a habit of speaking without thinking. Mentally reminding Cora to keep her mouth shut, Indy flared her nostrils, making them as big and round as possible; *seriously*, she tried to bore into Cora's head, *I cannot just call and claim someone's following me for no reason. And also,* she nodded toward Sawyer, *keep your mouth shut.*

After a few minutes of idling next to Indy's Jeep, the truck finally backed out and drove away. Indy started breathing normally again, unaware she'd been holding her breath until she realized her lungs burned. "We're just being paranoid, right?" she asked weakly. "Everyone's been on edge since Cloudcroft."

"Or maybe we're not," Cora sniffed, "and it's reasonable to assume that if a strange black truck keeps popping up every time you go out, something's going down. If a bear shits in the woods and no one's around to see it, the bear still shit in the woods, Indy."

Sawyer nearly spat his iced coffee out.

"Cora!" Indy frowned at her. "That's nasty."

"I'm just saying, don't be the girl who figures out there's a problem *after* it knocks on her door. You, of all people, know better."

Sawyer furrowed his brow, staring at Indy curiously. "You have problems with bears shitting in the woods?"

Indy caught her face with her hands. "Oh my God, people." She peeked through her fingers at Cora, who looked seriously worried. Which Indy supposed was understandable. The truck worried her too. She just didn't know what to do about it without confessing everything. "Let's see if we keep noticing it around, alright?"

Sawyer ran a hand through his messy pompadour, resting his palm on the back of his neck for a moment. "The minute you see it again, if we're not together, you call me."

"*If* I see it again."

"*India.*"

"Yes, sir." Indy snorted.

Cora's ferocious expression made Indy quiver. She knew she'd get an earful later. Just like she also knew Cora wanted her to hurry up and tell Sawyer about True North. He should know because, *hello,* a mean-looking truck might be stalking her. But what if the truck *was* the police? Or, like, the FBI? Or worse, something much, much more sinister?

CALL ME MAYBE

INDY CHECKED HER phone. 9:57 pm. She'd been out with Sawyer way longer than planned and barely made it back under the nose. Anxious, she stared at the burner and sat back in her chair, waiting for it to ring. Crossing her fingers, she counted out loud and concentrated on breathing while scanning True North's chat room. She hadn't been live since just before Cloudcroft, and people had started to take notice.

> *69694Eva: Where'd you go, Orion?*
>
> *Annie: No show for a week? What gives?*
>
> *TREKKESTER2: Coincidence O disappears shortly after Cloudcroft?*
>
> *SLIM: O where u at, DUDE?*
>
> *Matty70: Maybe O got his message across and went back to be with his people.*
>
> *STARBUCK: People, like alien people?*
>
> *SLIM: Straight as shit. I knew it!*

Indy ran a hand over her face, pushing her glasses away to rub her eyes. No matter how weird things got, for everyone not her, True North was still entertainment. She wondered how they'd feel if someone suddenly tossed them into a never-ending *Twilight Zone* episode along with her.

Weeby: Maybe he needs a break. Or biding his time?

69694EVA: Or maybe she's in trouble.

TREKKESTER2: What if there was more to Cloudcroft than O let on?

The burner rang, and Indy jumped, nearly knocking it off her desk. She grabbed at it as it skittered across the surface. "Hey," she gasped, turning away from her computer. "Henry?"

"Hi," he said. "Sorry I'm late."

"Someone's following me," she blurted out. "You have anything to do with that?"

Henry was silent for a moment. "You *are* female," he said quietly.

"Oh, shit!" Indy gripped her throat. *Dammit!* So much for remembering to turn on her voice modifier. She'd never slipped up before. Not once. How could she be so careless now?

"I basically already knew. But even if I didn't, I would've figured it out when we met," he reassured her.

"I'm pretty sure someone's watching me, Henry. And if it's not you, do you really want to risk it?"

"It's not me. I wouldn't send someone to follow you if I knew how to find you. I'd come to you myself. And yes, I'll risk it. I'm running out of time."

"You're positive we haven't met before? Because I've been thinking maybe you already know who I am."

Henry was quiet for a moment, and as far as Indy was concerned, his silence said more than he ever could. "It's . . . complicated."

"But you know where I live."

"I only know you live in Santa Fe."

"Alright, you said you're also in New Mexico, right? Where do you want to meet?"

"I can come to you."

"There's a place on the outskirts of town, Southside. Leo's. It's a dive coffee house."

"Done," Henry said. "When?"

Indy swallowed. The sooner, the better, or she'd lose her nerve. Plus, she needed to figure out the numbers thing pronto. After Cloudcroft, she worried they might kill her if she channeled another set. "Tomorrow too soon? Around four o'clock?"

"No. I can do that."

Henry almost sounded excited. Indy checked herself. What if he was just some fanboy after all? "How will I know you? I mean, you don't like, have tentacles or horns or some super alieny appendage, right?"

"No." He laughed. "Not normally. I blend in like everyone else."

"Not normally?" She gulped.

"I'll be wearing a green shirt. Brown hair. Green eyes. About six feet tall. You?"

"I'll find *you*. Your description is good enough."

Before Henry could say anything else, Indy hung up. She held the phone against her chest, gripping it tightly. *Good God, girl. What are you thinking?* Maybe it was the worst idea of all time, but by five o'clock tomorrow—fingers crossed—she'd finally have answers.

THE OTHER SHOE

MONDAY MORNING, INDY was an epic mess. It didn't help that she was worse than Godzilla tiptoeing through Tokyo when it came to hiding her emotions. And unfortunately for her, by lunchtime, both Cora and Lior noticed.

"What?! No!" Lior screeched when Indy finally fessed up. "You're not going!"

"It's fine. I'm fine. And I have to, Li. I have to know."

"How come you never told us about this Henry dude?" Cora squinted at her. "Why are you so freaking secretive?" She stared darts at her peanut butter and banana sandwich. "That's it; I'm calling in sick for my shift. We're coming with."

"Cora, I can't ask you to do that. Besides, Henry wants me to come alone."

"Oh, that seals it," she said obstinately. "And you didn't ask. I'm telling you."

Lior twisted the ends of her ponytail around a metallic gold fingernail, nodding her agreement. "I'll just tell my dad I'm study-ing at your house after school."

Out of nowhere, Sawyer, August, and Manny darted up be-hind Indy. Sawyer leaned over her shoulder and pecked her cheek. "Going where?" he asked, hugging her tightly.

"To the mall after school," Cora told him.

Sawyer moved Indy's Wonder Woman lunch box off the bench and sat beside her. Manny followed Sawyer's lead, scooching in be-tween Sawyer and Cora. He threw an arm around Cora's shoulder. "The mall? Count me in. I need a new mitt."

August sidled in beside Lior. "You promised me a do-over at All-Star after school, Manny. No way you're getting out of that."

"Manny kicked August's ass at the batting cages yesterday," Sawyer clarified. "It was epic."

Cora laughed. She kissed Manny's cheek. "Yeah, baby, go kick his ass some more."

August threw a fry at her. Lior followed up with a grape.

Indy just felt grateful the stars had aligned. Truthfully, she wanted Lior and Cora with her when she met Henry. She just hadn't wanted to ask. She couldn't ask; she really was *that* bad at seeking out support sometimes.

Sawyer took a bite of Indy's salami sandwich. Chewing, he turned sideways to look at her. "Sorry, babe. I can't go, either. But we're still on for dinner?"

Indy wrinkled her nose.

"It's not a zombie revolution."

She squinted at him, studying his face. Despite bad manners and a mouth full of food, he was still drop-dead gorgeous.

"I just mean, don't look so horrified." He winked at her. "It'll be a great night."

Though anxious about it, Indy *was* looking forward to their dinner later. But she'd been a basket case overall since hanging up with Henry. "I'm just nervous," she admitted.

"Me too," he said sweetly.

She scrunched her nose again, shooting him a playful look. "*You're* nervous?"

Sawyer grabbed her hand and pressed her palm tightly against his chest. Leaning in, he whispered, "There's more here than you think. And I worry you won't like it. We're similar that way."

Indy's breath caught. "That's not the answer I expected."

Sawyer grinned, though he still looked thoughtful. "Guess I like surprising you."

More curious about him than ever, she nodded. If everything went well, by dinnertime, she'd have a surprise for him too. One she hoped she'd finally understand well enough to explain without struggling to fill in the blanks.

Lunch ended, and Indy said her goodbyes, making herself sludge through the last two periods of the day, which passed about as quickly as a slug stuck in molasses. At three, it started raining, but by four, the torrential storm that had everyone clamoring for their cars when school let out passed, leaving Santa Fe's narrow streets swamped with water. Indy steered her Jeep through floodwaters to Leo's. She drove carefully, trying to avoid a smattering of potholes before slowing to a crawl as she got closer to Leo's parking lot.

"What if Henry's just a serious fanboy?" she asked Lior and Cora.

"Or what if he's MIB?" Lior countered, leaning forward between the Jeep's front seats.

"We run?" Fanboy-stalker Indy could probably handle. Anything else, not so much.

Indy pulled into the lot and briefly searched it for the truck she thought might be following her. Inside, Leo's looked empty, but the flooded parking lot was even emptier. No menacing black pickup, thank God. She parked and braced both hands against the steering wheel, locking her elbows. "You guys wait here, okay?"

"Uh-uh. No way," Cora insisted.

"It's safer for all of us this way. He won't know you're watching. Plus, I don't want to blow it."

"You go in first, then," Cora said. "We'll wait a few and go in after. Pretend we don't know you."

Indy pinched the space between her eyes, pulling at the skin on the bridge of her nose behind her glasses. She'd worn her boring brown frames today; being less conspicuous felt safer. "Fine. Just be chill, all right? And wait until I've sat down with him. If he sees you getting out of the same car as me, we're busted."

"Done," Cora agreed.

Stepping down from the Jeep, Indy straightened her denim skirt, pulling her black leggings tighter above her vintage harness boots. She flipped her hair back over her left shoulder and took a bunch of deep breaths, standing up straight as an arrow. Muttering, *get your ass in gear,* Indy tiptoed over a string of puddles into Leo's.

At the main counter near the front of the coffee house, she ordered an Americano, searching the room through the muddy mirror over the row of coffee machines on a neighboring countertop. Toward the back of the coffee shop, she spotted someone wearing a green t-shirt. He stared away from her out a window, absently flipping a pencil, but he was the only person in the room wearing the right color.

Indy paid and grabbed her drink, weaving around mostly empty tables toward Henry. Absorbed by something outside, he didn't even glance her way. He seemed oblivious, and Indy liked that she had a minute to observe him before he saw her.

When she was halfway to the table, Henry shifted, looking anxiously toward the front door. He wore a 'Kiss Me I'm Irish' shirt. But he also sported something more recognizable—Sawyer's face.

Indy nearly choked on her coffee. Her heart exploded, and she pivoted quickly, moving back toward the front door. Walking slowly, she tried to look inconspicuous, attempting to breathe as she made her way outside. Externally, she appeared calm, but inside she was panic-stricken.

Near the Jeep, Indy started to hyperventilate. She put her coffee cup on the hood and attempted to unlock her driver's side door, mostly oblivious that Cora had come around and was now shaking her arm.

Just need to sit. Just need to breathe. Just need to open this freaking door.

Indy's hand quivered, sending her car keys skittering over the metal door panel. Her ears rang, and her head throbbed. But worst of all was her lungs. They felt almost empty.

"India!" Cora chirped, yanking the keys out of Indy's hand. "It's open."

Indy doubled over, grasping her knees.

"Hey!" Cora pulled the door open and dragged herself and Indy behind it, out of view, using the door panel for shelter. She put a hand on Indy's back. "What the hell just happened?"

"Sa . . . Sawyer," Indy stuttered. "Look."

Cora seemed confused. She volleyed her head back and forth between Indy and Leo's. Then, it registered. "You mean . . ." she trailed off. "Jesus. I'm going to go in there and give that asshole a piece of my —"

Panicked, Indy grabbed Cora's arm, stopping her before she could march into Leo's. "Cora, don't go in there, please! I don't think he saw me. Just tell me it *is* Sawyer. That I'm not hallucinating."

Cora squinted toward Leo's. She craned her neck, standing on her tiptoes to see better over Indy's still open car door.

Inside the Jeep, Lior dropped her head over the parking brake, nearly resting her chin on Indy's seat. "Dudes, what's up?"

"Indy says Sawyer's in there." Cora's voice came out hushed.

"What?" Lior squealed.

"There." Cora pointed, pressing a finger against the door's window. "I see him. Looks like Sawyer, Indy. From here, at least."

"Shit," Lior mumbled.

"Get in." Cora gave Indy a push, nearly boosting her into the Jeep. As Indy climbed up and gripped the steering wheel, Cora quickly ran around to the other side, scrambling into the front seat. "Maybe it's a coincidence," she huffed, slamming her door shut.

Staring out the windshield like a madwoman, Indy fought to control her voice. "Coincidence? You don't believe that for a second, Cora."

"You're right," Cora said. "But I mean, Sawyer? Sawyer's Henry? Really?"

"It doesn't make sense," Lior concurred.

"It must be a joke." Indy almost choked on her words. "Either that or he *is* one seriously deranged fanboy."

Lior pursed her lips for a moment, mulling it over. "Or maybe he knows you're Orion, Indy, and is done waiting for you to tell him. Maybe he wants to confront you."

"Henry started calling me *before* I started dating Sawyer."

"Okay, well, maybe that's why Sawyer finally ponied up and asked you out. Because Orion listened."

"Or maybe he's psycho," Indy countered. "Or screwing with me after all."

Cora took Indy's keys off Indy's lap and shoved them into the ignition. "Drive," she demanded. "Before he sees us because I seriously don't think he's screwing with you. I don't even think he knows you're Orion. He may be an asshole jock sometimes, but he's not *that* much of a douchebag. I don't think he'd purposely try to hurt you. He's totally in love with you."

"He made me think he might be an . . ." she almost choked, "an alien!" Indy was so perplexed she wanted to smash her fist through the windshield. Instead, she bashed the heel of her palm into the steering wheel. "Ouch! Shit. I feel so freaking humiliated."

Indy tore out of the lot, her shaky breathing exaggerated in the suffocating quiet that suddenly engulfed them. Uncomfortable silence accompanied them down Cerrillos toward her house. No one knew what to say because the truth was horrible. She'd really fallen for Henry-slash-Sawyer's sob story. She'd really fallen for *him*. How could Sawyer be Henry?

"What do I do?" Indy finally whispered.

"Meet him like you planned tonight," Cora said. "Find out what he's up to."

"I don't know . . ." Lior trailed off.

Indy caught Lior's eyes in the rearview mirror. Even if Lior didn't want to say it, Momma Bear Lior had her doubts. Her face was like a bright neon sign flashing *stay the hell away from him*.

"What don't you know?" Cora twisted in her seat, looking back at Lior.

"I mean, he lied to Indy at lunch about where he was going after school today. And he's never mentioned calling into the show, has he? I think he's up to something."

Indy almost wished for an actual hole in the ground to drive her Jeep into. Talk about a heart-crushing turn of events. Except for Sawyer's sheer weirdness sometimes, nothing about him set off her warning bells. "I'm so stupid," she mumbled.

Indy pulled into her driveway and parked. Sitting back, she tugged her glasses off, throwing them onto the dashboard. Scattered raindrops hit the Jeep's hood, leaving crooked trails that matched her mood. Blurry, isolated, and aimless.

"If Sawyer is Henry," Cora said, making no move to get out, "I'm betting he either doesn't know you're Orion, in which case he's probably doing some kind of undercover investigation for the school or something like that and doesn't want to tell you, or he's a nut job and is obsessed with Orion and True North."

"You think he might be doing something for school? Like an article for the paper or something?" Indy asked, grasping at straws.

"Or shit, maybe he's a narc, or the feds got to him, or something." Cora let loose a long, breathy sigh. "Maybe the government approached him and made him do their bidding. Maybe that's why he suddenly got so friendly."

"Cora!" Lior chastised her.

"And all those library notes?" Indy whispered. "He started writing them when he first moved here. Before I started True North."

Lior scratched her head. "Huh, stumper. It does kind of support that he doesn't know you're Orion. Or at least that he didn't know until recently."

"And that he's into you for real," Cora said.

"But maybe also psycho," Lior added.

"Maybe give him the benefit and find out?" Cora suggested.

Indy opened her car door and hung a leg out. "I'm supposed to meet him at seven. Assuming he didn't see me, what do I say? How do I play this out?"

"Just be cool, super cool," Cora told her. "Lay the groundwork and let him trip himself up."

"Easier said than done," Indy grumbled.

Cora and Lior trailed Indy to the front door. A rumbling hum filled the air, mixing with the steady drumbeat of falling rain. "Your dad in the studio?" Cora asked.

Judging by the sound of his buzzsaw coming from their garage, Indy guessed so. "Yeah."

"Mmmm, I'd like to see him handle that thing," Cora snickered.

"Cora, gross!" Indy swatted her.

"What?" Cora waved a hand in the air. "Clearly, you have good genes, India. Just appreciating."

Inside the house, Lior and Cora plunked down on the living room couch. Cora pulled out her nail file. "You know, if you're worried about later, Lior and I could come with. Wait in the car or whatever if it makes you feel better. We've got your back, Indy."

Indy sat down beside them, and Lior draped an arm around her neck, pulling her close. "Totally. One-hundred percent."

Indy rested her head on Lior's shoulder. Now that she had a moment to think, it seemed more likely Sawyer was messing with Orion on a dare. He'd never call True North if he knew it was *her* show. Sometimes, especially lately, she forgot that Sawyer was a jock. And it wasn't some big secret that the jocks at Corazon did stupid things. Just like it wasn't a secret she judged those things—Sawyer knew she did. It was conceivable that he didn't want her to know he was being an idiot.

"I'm fine," she reassured them. "I'll go and see what he says. If he's a jerk about it, guess I'll know he's a jerk, period. But if he doesn't bring it up and doesn't seem to know I'm Orion, do you think I should tell him? I mean, I should know if he meant what he said about wanting to go home, right? Like if he's crazy?"

"See what he says first," Lior advised. "If he doesn't bring it up, maybe find a way to dig deeper. Give him a chance to explain what he was doing at Leo's. If you like what he says, and you trust him, then yeah, tell him. If not, wait and see."

"Just don't kick him to the curb unless he's flat out screwing with you," Cora added.

"Why?"

"Don't you want to see how things play out?"

Too many unknowns crowded Indy's plate already. Sawyer was supposed to be her reprieve, not another problem. But furious or not, Indy couldn't just walk away. She was in love with him for one. Plus, Cora was right. She absolutely wanted to know what he was up to.

BOY WHO FELL TO EARTH

RAIN BEAT SIDEWAYS against Rojo's foggy windows. Indy ran for the restaurant's entrance, grateful she'd exchanged her vintage boots and merino sweater for a pair of red slickers and a hoodie before leaving the house. The evening seemed to be coming down in sheets. At this rate, she'd need an ark just to make it back home safely.

"Hey, babe!" Sawyer, wearing the same black V-neck sweater he had on at school earlier, stood up when she walked in, holding his arms out for a hug. "I just downed a red chile Oreo shake. It was awesome. Want one?"

Indy stomped water off, peeking to see if he had a green t-shirt on beneath his sweater. Instead of hugging him, she sat down across the table, dropping her soggy purse on an empty chair.

Sawyer sat down slowly. "Everything okay?"

"You tell me," she said sharply.

A server brought Indy water, giving Sawyer a moment to look her over before answering. He stared at her across the table, one eyebrow cocked, left ear at an angle to his shoulder. Fluttering criminally long lashes, he narrowed an eye, mimicking a pirate. "Is there a right answer?"

Indy shrugged. She looked around the empty room at the warmly painted walls covered in adobe pinks and oranges. Torrential downpour aside, Monday night almost guaranteed her Rojo would be empty. It's why she chose it.

"I guess I'll go with *yes, something's wrong.*" He tried to smile. "That's why you wanted to meet here instead of at my house, right?"

She shrugged again.

"Are we playing games now?" he asked.

Indy just wanted to know about him being at Leo's earlier. It wasn't her intention to act so prickly. But she couldn't help herself. Whether he meant to or not, he'd hurt her. And her nerves were too frayed to outright ask. Plus, not knowing what she was dealing with made her feel irrational.

"Okay," he said, reclining against the wood-backed chair. "Game, it is."

"I'm not playing with you, Sawyer."

"Then why do I feel like this is you looking for a way to get out of talking tonight?"

Indy couldn't tell if Sawyer was mad or just perplexed. He seemed a little put out, and since she'd only ever seen him mildly annoyed before, it threw her. Forcing a small smile, she did her best to look apologetic. He might be Henry, but on the drive over, she promised herself she'd give him the benefit of the doubt. "I'm not. I'm just . . ." she paused, startled by the massive crack of lightning that suddenly lit up the night sky through Rojo's front window. "Confused, I guess."

Sawyer reached across the table and grabbed her hand. "What's up, India?"

"I'm not sure I even know how or where to start."

"Is this about Cloudcroft? I was there, too, remember? And I want to help you understand what's happening. But I can't if you keep everything bottled up."

Yeah, you were there—you and Henry.

She squinted at him. "Who are you really, Sawyer?"

Shadows slunk across Sawyer's face; he suddenly looked guarded. But in more of an, *I'm worried about you*, than an, *I'm lying and trying to play it cool* way. "We should talk about that," he said, dropping his voice.

"Okay, talk."

Sawyer ran a hand through his hair, letting it linger at his crown, and she knew he was sitting on a problem. "I know why we're being followed."

"You do?" she chirped, waiting for the other shoe to drop.

"Yeah."

Indy bit her bottom lip hard enough to leave a dent. *Here we go.*

"Do you know who *I* am?" she asked softly.

Sawyer let go of her hand, crossing his arms over his chest as he sat back. His eyes caught fire, full of emotion Indy barely knew how to decipher. He was too quiet and too still— until the server came and set two burgers down, and Indy shrugged at him inquisitively.

"Yeah," he finally said. "I do."

Indy calmly picked up the hamburger he ordered her, silently willing her heart to stop bruising her chest. She'd listen to what Sawyer had to say before deciding what and how much to tell him before asking him why he'd pretended to be Henry and broke her heart. "Okay, then, you start."

His nostrils flared. "Promise me something first."

Indy held her burger mid-air. "What's that?"

"That you'll at least try to keep an open mind."

"Okay." Indy's stomach lurched. "I promise."

Sawyer palmed his face, running a hand back and forth over the rounded apple of his left cheek. "I wanted to tell you before, India, so many times, but I thought . . ." he shook his head. "I wasn't sure how you'd react. I guess I was afraid you'd push me away. Because it's weird. So weird, right?"

Indy's eyes carved out pits in her skull. They were so large that even she was aware she was gawking. "Clarify, please?"

"What happened. I mean, it was so long ago. Honestly, I wasn't even sure you remembered."

"Remembered?" she asked, still confused. "Remembered what?"

"Me. From before."

"Before?" she rasped. Indy dropped her burger on her plate and wiped her hands, working to keep her voice steady. She tried to recall the first time she spoke to Henry. "When before?"

"Holy Ghost River."

A lump caught in Indy's throat. She coughed and grabbed her glass, dribbling water over a hand when she couldn't make it go down. Her heart slammed against her ribs so hard she half worried they'd crack. "I don't understand," she sputtered.

"Holy Ghost. I was there. I thought . . . isn't that what you meant?"

"There?" She felt like an echo.

"In the river."

Indy froze, one hand halfway above her plate, the other struggling to hold onto her water glass. She flexed her jaw, overwhelmed by the prickly rush of heat racing up her neck. "Explain," she managed to garble out.

"You tripped and tumbled down the bank. I went in after you." He rubbed his face again. "I knew it was you the first time I saw you at school. I *know* you, India. That's what the library notes are about. That night. All the time that's passed since. That we found each other again."

In sync with her heartbeat, the room seemed to dim and then swell with light, surging brightly around her. Everything suddenly felt big, too big, and she worried she might keel off her chair. Trembling, she nearly dropped her glass when she set it down, spilling water across the table.

"India." Sawyer quickly grabbed her shaking hand.

Water seeped over the tablecloth, spreading into an uneven blotch. She watched it and tried to swallow, then swallow again.

"Say something."

Indy pulled her limp hand away. "How? How were you there? I mean . . ." She trailed off, finally looking directly at him.

His eyes. They were so green.

Too green.

Oh, God.

"You understand?" he asked quietly.

Indy pulled her glasses down and jabbed at her eyes as if trying to stamp out her bewilderment. Narrowing her pupils, she sculpted Sawyer into a fuzzy pinpoint of doubt. "You're the thing in the river?"

"Yes."

"The night I died?"

"Yes. No," he coughed. "You didn't die. I stayed with you until the helicopter came."

"What?" she croaked. "How were you . . . with me?"

"I merged with you, India." He dropped his head, looking up at her through dark lashes sheepishly. "I kept you alive. We shared a body and life force."

As though backlit, Sawyer's intense eyes glowed—just like the moment before he dispersed into bubbles underwater. "But . . ." she stumbled over her words, "I don't understand. How is it possible?"

He tugged on an earlobe, leaning over the table to whisper, "I'm not constant." When Indy's face fell, he added, "I mean, I *am* me. This body belongs to me. But *it's* not constant."

Indy stared at him so hard her eye sockets ached. "Explain *not constant,* Sawyer. Explain how your body is *not constant.* Do you know how insane that sounds?"

Sawyer sniffed, leaning even closer. "It's a lot to process. I get that." He scanned her face, waiting for her to say something. When she didn't, he said, "Everything in the universe, it's all matter. We're all made of the same atoms, and energy, and particles."

"You . . . you scattered," she whispered. "Underwater." Sawyer's pupils constricted, and the worst sensation gripped her; she felt like a stranger. Like she was suddenly viewing him through some far-off window.

"Right. That's right. Energy is transferable. I just, I rearranged myself."

"Inside me?" she chirped.

He nodded.

"All this time—everyone said I hallucinated." Indy gulped, breathing in before letting out a gusty whistle. "I don't understand how you did it, Sawyer."

"I don't know how to explain it better. Your cells were my cells; your breaths were my breaths, etcetera. I learned so much about you in those twenty minutes. I *was* you, kind of."

She pinched the bridge of her nose. "I . . . how is that even remotely possible?"

Sawyer's jaw sharpened around his mouth. "You're asking me to describe something that's an inherent part of my makeup. I don't know how to do that."

Indy shook her head, staring wide-eyed around the dining area as she struggled to find room in her brain to store what he'd just told her. The information felt heavy. As if each facet of what she learned took up physical space that weighed down all her other thoughts. Quietly, she said, "I feel like I'm having an aneurysm."

"I get that. But it's like asking you to explain why humans only breathe air, not water."

"But I *can* explain that."

"Because someone taught you how to understand the difference."

"You don't know why you're different?" she asked, dumbfounded.

He sat back, exasperated. "Big picture-wise, I know why I'm different. Physiologically, not so much."

A surprising, tsunami-like wave of relief washed over her. She wasn't insane; something inexplicable really had happened that night. "Sawyer, I don't ..." She chewed fiercely on a thumbnail. "I don't know what I'm supposed to say. Or think."

The very idea that Sawyer could do something so extraordinary was crazy. But it also didn't matter to her how he probably thought it did. It was a kind of crazy she didn't have to carry around or own like the rest of her secret burdens. His revelation freed her; at that moment, nothing mattered beyond that after all these years, she finally knew with one-hundred percent certainty she hadn't imagined the boy with the glowing irises turning to bubbles underwater.

Indy scanned the room. She leaned forward, whispering, "What are you? Like a mutant?"

He snorted. "I'm not a comic book character."

"Then, what?" Her eyes felt like marbles inside her skull, making her feel all kinds of dispossessed.

"I'm adopted. And other than what you saw for yourself at Holy Ghost, I don't know that much more about where I came from than you do."

Indy's head spun. How could Sawyer be the creature that saved her six years ago? How could he be a real, living, breathing person?

Much as she wanted to, for Sawyer's sake especially, she couldn't just get over the fact that he'd possessed her and somehow sustained her and, because of it, saved her life. Because unless she'd missed some super important memo, humans *were* constant. They drowned when submerged for too long. And they wasted away when they weren't, imprisoned in the body they were born with as they aged. They did not, could not just up and become something else.

"Wait," she nearly squeaked. "You're worried *you're* the reason I'm being followed! Because you're . . . different."

"Is that a question?"

"Am I right?"

His eyes flared. "Is there another better reason?"

"Better than being . . . inhuman?"

Sawyer looked hurt. "Inhuman, India?"

"I mean . . . shit, I don't know what I mean. Otherworldly? Different?"

Sawyer's face relaxed. "You believe me?"

"That you were there that night? That you saved my life? Yes. I never forgot your eyes. And, God, now that I know, I see it. I remember you. I can't believe I haven't known it all along."

He hesitated. "When you asked if I know who you are—I thought you did remember. I thought that's what you meant."

She shook her head, suddenly flooded with memories. "Underwater, the things I saw, they were so incredible. The doctors said I was delirious because I went without oxygen for so long. But, I mean, was that you, then? Was I in your head? Because of how you saved me?"

Sawyer looked down at the table, masking an emotion that burned through him as he nodded.

Indy covered her mouth. She closed her eyes for a moment, conscious of the tears that pooled at her lashes. "Your thoughts and memories?"

"Yeah."

"Sawyer, the things I saw, they were so . . . fantastic. So . . ." she trailed off, unable to say the word *alien*.

"Until that night, I'd only ever watched people from afar. When we merged, I was mesmerized." Sawyer cocked his head, staring at her longingly. "The pictures in your head, your memories, they fascinated me as well."

Indy sank into the chair, struggling to process. She lacked words to describe the things she'd seen when he saved her. Adding it up, it seemed clear. Sawyer *had* to be Henry. Henry, who implied he wasn't human.

"You're *not* human," she whispered. "Are you?"

Sawyer shook his head deliberately, holding Indy's gaze.

"Then . . ." She shrugged, silently finishing the question.

He met her stare, lifting a finger slightly off the table, pointing up.

Sawyer's finger stopped time. Indy registered how his expression changed as he tilted his chin upward. She watched the set of his mouth and how his muscles tensed across his chest, pulling his shoulders tighter. But everything happened outside of her, slowly and far away, like she'd been wrapped in a thousand sheets of filmy vellum. And because of it, her mind wouldn't turn over.

"You get why I waited to tell you, don't you? I didn't want to scare you. And I wasn't sure if you remembered. Not until just now when you asked . . ." He trailed off. "India, I understand if you need time. I know it's a lot to process."

A million questions rushed Indy, like whether Sawyer knew what was going on with her numbers and whether he knew what *they* wanted. But she also had to resist the urge to stick her fingers in her ears and sprint away as fast as possible. And she was angry (or maybe hurt) that he'd waited so long to tell her the truth. Though, she also understood. Sawyer's secrets were big and dangerous. Bigger and more dangerous than hers. He risked a lot by finally exposing himself.

"I'm just . . . in shock, I guess."

"You hate me now?"

"No!" she said, barely thinking before blurting out, "I still really, really like you."

Sawyer schooled his expression, but his voice softened. "You do?"

She nodded *yes*.

He stood up and held out his hand. "Let's go."

"Where?"

"Somewhere not here. Somewhere where we can talk openly."

Indy pushed her chair back and stood up. She took his hand, tugging him around the table to her body. When he pulled her closer, she wrapped her arms around his neck and buried her face in his chest, suctioning herself to his wiry contours. There was so much to hash out; she had so many questions. But she needed to be reminded that he was still made of flesh and blood. Standing pressed against him, Indy felt muscles stretched tight over tendon and bone. She smelled his scent, a mix of clean sweat marked by cedar, dryer lint, and rosemary. She kissed him. And at that moment, it didn't matter that he wasn't the same as her, as long as he existed.

RESURRECTION 2.0

INDY TURNED INTO a gated roadway behind Sawyer's Escalade. As her Jeep climbed a hill, she eyed the tawny desert xeriscape and manicured lavender bushes lining his driveway. Even pummeled by rain, they looked perfect; a sure sign Sawyer's parents kept gardeners on staff. Indy snorted. Already, in every way she could think of, Sawyer was a walking contradiction—rich kid, rebel, hot boy, brainiac, sci-fi nerd, jock. Adding alien to that list was just crazy.

"You sure it's okay to be here," she asked at his front door.

"Yes, it's *still* okay." He stressed the word *still* without making her feel like an idiot. "My parents are visiting colleges with Riley. They won't be home until Wednesday. Besides, I'm allowed to have human girls over."

"Hysterical," she mumbled.

The inside of Sawyer's house felt like a museum. Indy followed him through a long, terracotta-tiled hallway decorated with curio-filled cutaway shelves, then upstairs over a winding maple staircase to a room big enough to house a trapeze. Mimicking him, she plopped down on his huge, four-poster bed, staring up at an ornately carved, wood-beamed ceiling.

"You are spoiled," she breathed out.

"Sort of," he agreed.

"Must be nice."

"I never got the impression you lacked for anything." Sawyer turned his head sideways to stare at her.

Indy grimaced. He was right. She didn't lack for anything, really. Just her fallback was stereotyping people. Probably because it was easier than admitting she disconnected when she worried someone might reject her, preemptively alienating herself. Jeez, was she really so bad it took an actual otherworld encounter to wake her up?

"Not judging. Just saying," he reassured her.

"How old were you when your parents adopted you?" she asked.

He shrugged. "The papers say ten."

Why were you adopted? What happened to your birth parents? And if you're so happy here, why do you want to go home?

Home . . .

Indy gazed down her nose, suddenly overwhelmed by emotion. "You want to go back?" she asked shyly.

"Back?" Sawyer glanced sideways at her quizzically.

"I mean." She pointed up.

"No," he said, stressing the word by squeezing her hand. "This is my home."

"Really?" Henry seemed intent on going somewhere else. He'd said as much. But maybe she'd misread what he meant. "What about . . . where you came from?"

"I'm guessing it's like emigrating when you're young. Home is where you end up. Besides," he said softly, "you're here. Now that I've found you, I'm not going anywhere."

She snorted before she could stop herself. "For a while, you seemed interested in being *everywhere* else."

Sawyer shifted on the bed, looking up at the ceiling as his jaw popped. "If it makes you feel better, call it a defense. A way to fit in. Whatever."

"I'm sorry. That was really low." She rolled on her side and ran a palm down his arm, nudging his fingers apart when she reached his hand. "I meant it when I said I don't care about your past. I'm just a mess right now. But people love you, Sawyer. You fit in everywhere."

"It's nice you believe that." He rolled on his side to face her. "I know you think you know what it's like to feel different, but you're not *that* different. Not like me. Sometimes I just really want to *feel* human. Not like some . . . some weird fucking space alien reject."

"Sawyer!" Indy's heart sank, but she also wanted to laugh. Sawyer couldn't be further from a reject; his bazillion friends at school proved that. Still, being a quirky human was hard enough. She imagined being inhuman among humans would be unfathomable. "That's not true."

"I still remember my real parents. I remember what it was like . . . up there. Adjusting to all this," he sighed. "For the longest time, I was just going through the motions. I had to *learn* to be human. And it doesn't help that they left me here to swim on my own. What else would you call me?"

"I can't answer those questions, but I promise there's nothing remotely rejection-worthy about you. You're the most awesome person I know."

He shot her a look.

"The most awesome non-human person then." Indy grinned.

"I'm the only non-human person you know."

"Fine, you're the most awesome living being in the universe."

Sawyer's strained smile lit his face. He reached out, wriggling an arm underneath her neck to pull her closer. "Come here."

When Indy was flush against his body, she asked, "The night at the river, what were you doing there?"

Sawyer closed his eyes for a moment. "My parents were stationed here, part of a group of scientists and surveyors monitoring Earth. I snuck out. Down. Whatever." He shifted on the mattress, obviously bothered. "I remember watching you. I wanted to meet you. To touch the earth and meet a human."

Indy shot up, looking down at him through a veil of wild, loose hair. "Wait," she yelped. "You're here because of *me*?"

"I don't know why they never came for me afterward. That's on them." He sighed. "But we weren't allowed to leave, so I figured out a way to sneak down. And I stayed longer than I planned to make sure you were safe after you fell in the river. But I couldn't find my way back once the helicopters left."

Indy was both angry for Sawyer and mesmerized by the idea that aliens were studying humans, that *he'd* been studying *her* from somewhere above the campsite. "You don't think they just left you, do you?"

"Not on purpose. Especially not now, with everything going on."

"You think they've come back for you?" Suddenly, her connection to the numbers seemed crystal clear. They were looking for him. They probably wanted him back as much as he wanted her help to find 'his people.'

"All I know for sure is that I was in the river with you until the paramedics showed up. When they left, I lost my way. And it took a couple days for hikers to find me." Sawyer grasped her arm, trying to pull her back to him. "We were supposed to study Earth, not get involved. When the helicopter came, I think it scared them off. At least that's what I tell myself."

"But you were just a little boy."

Sawyer succeeded in tugging her back to his chest. He wrapped an arm around her back, securing her tightly to his body. "I don't resent them if that's what you're thinking. Sometimes I just feel lost."

"I would too," she whispered. "I'm so sorry."

"I'm not. Not anymore." He nuzzled her neck, gently grazing the skin beneath her ear. "I love you, India."

Overwhelmed, Indy balanced on an elbow and stared down at his beautiful unguarded face. She smoothed a swath of hair off his forehead and threw a leg over his waist, climbing on top of him. "I love you, too."

"Yeah?" Sawyer caught her hand at his stomach and wrapped it into a ball in his palm. He reached up and brushed her cheek, then wrapped a hand around the nape of her neck, prompting her to meet him face to face.

"What about your parents now?" she whispered.

"What about them?"

"I mean," she nodded at the ceiling, "you said you still remember *them*."

"Gina and Mike, my mom and dad now, they saved me. They raised me as their own and never judged me for being who I am. They were there for me. As far as I'm concerned, they are my *real* parents, India."

Indy felt Sawyer's answer in her bones. But she also wondered why if it was true, he seemed so desperate to find his birth parents. "You're lucky you ended up with them."

Sawyer's mouth met hers, brushing her lips with feathery kisses before speaking. "You have no idea. The forestry service took me to CPS in Santa Fe. I didn't speak any English, but mom and dad, they'd been on a list to adopt another child forever. Someone from the service knew my mom. I guess they called her. They didn't care that I was older. And they were there for me from the get-go, even though I was this weird-ass, terrified, mute kid."

Indy stared down at him. Through him, really, trying to picture ten-year-old Sawyer lost and wandering the Pecos wilderness on his own. Her heart skipped; he must have been petrified. "Do they know what you are?"

"They've been secretive about my health since the day they brought me home. I never get sick, but all my doctor's appointments are with one of their colleagues up at Los Alamos—my uncle, Perry." Sawyer let go of her to make air quotes around the word 'uncle,' "So, yeah, maybe."

"You haven't talked to them about it?"

"Nope. I mean, if I'm wrong, and they don't know, they'll flip, right?" He stroked her cheek. "One day, when I'm ready, when I understand myself better," he paused. "I might."

She kissed him again, lingering on his plush (and for real inhuman) lips. "What am I supposed to do with such a big secret?"

He smiled at her expectantly. "Keep it safe."

Indy wanted Sawyer to tell her he was Henry. But after everything he shared, she also knew he had no idea she was Orion. And she was even less sure than ever he'd accept the truth. Orion must have been Sawyer's go-to. Someone he thought he could trust with secrets he hadn't shared with her yet. Admitting who she was now felt like a betrayal. The worst thing, though, was how much she feared that once she did tell him, he'd admit he wanted to go home after all.

"And tomorrow we're supposed to just, like Netflix and chill over pizza?"

"I'm hoping." He grinned.

"What about the truck that's been following me? And the guy in the park?" Indy still believed *she* was the target. It seemed even more likely given everything he just told her—other than Sawyer's parents and maybe his uncle, no one knew the truth. Sawyer's secret was safe. Hers, on the other hand, wasn't so ironclad.

"I guess I'm worried someone else figured it out. Maybe someone from my parents' lab." He ran a hand over his face. "I still think you should file a report. But if things get really weird, I admit it'll be hard to explain why you think someone's following you. No matter what, though, swear you'll let it go if something happens to me. You can't tell anyone. You can't make a deal out of it. I don't want you getting hurt, India."

"What, no!" She shot up arrow-straight, perched over him. "First, I'm not letting anything happen to you. Second, forget that. If something does happen, I'll kick every ass in New Mexico until I find you or kill the bastards who found you. Either way, Sawyer, if anything happens to you, someone's going down!"

Sawyer burst out laughing. "You watch way too much television."

She leaned over him, nose to nose. "I'm serious. Promise me we're in this together."

Sawyer's face cracked. He looked both elated and miserable and reached a hand up to swipe a thumb down her bare forearm, raising goosebumps. "After Cloudcroft, I think you're right." He sighed. "And I think it's probably time we talk about why."

DISINFORMATION

"TALK ABOUT WHY!" Cora squealed. "Jesus, Indy, explain that."

Indy chewed on a nail, still a little bewildered by Sawyer's confession. "He thinks that when he saved me, he left a physical imprint, or maybe a part of himself inside me. My nosebleeds and headaches—he thinks that whatever's going on up there, it's operating on some frequency affecting me now because of our connection. And after everything he told me last night, I think he could be right. Seriously, Cora, it also kind of explains why I've always been *so* into him. But I mean, he doesn't even know how he did what he did that night. So, it could also be anything."

"So then why can't *he* channel your numbers?"

"Assuming they're about him?" Indy grimaced. "Maybe because that's the part he left behind."

Cora folded her Starbucks apron and threw it on Indy's kitchen table. She kicked her heels up beside it and pulled a nail file from her purse. "I can't believe he's actually," she stared at Indy, her peacock-blue eyes wide, "you know."

"You can't tell anyone, Cor! Swear. You have to promise me."

"Swear on my life! I pinky promise!" Cora dropped her nail file on the table and hooked Indy's pinky to seal the deal. "So, then you told him you're Orion?"

"No."

"*Indy*," Cora croaked. "If he thinks the numbers have anything to do with him, he'll put it together eventually."

Indy rummaged through the refrigerator for leftovers and sat down at the table. She unwrapped a chicken leg and started chomping on it, chewing while she ruminated. "He doesn't seem to know that I know he's Henry. So I don't think he's made the connection yet. And after everything we talked about last night, I'm afraid he'll hate me when I tell him." Indy let her shoulders droop. "Worse, I'm afraid he'll admit he wants to go home once he knows."

"What if he does?"

"I . . ." Indy fumbled over her words. "I guess I'll try and help him."

"But?"

"But nothing. I mean, it'll suck. I'm in love with him, Cor. But he deserves to know who he is. If that's what he really wants, and I'm somehow able to help, I have to. I just don't want to lose him, you know?"

Cora frowned. "Yeah, I get it."

"Want to come upstairs with me?" Indy tossed a plateful of chicken bones away and stood up. "Mom and Dad are at an opening. I'm thinking I should go live. I haven't since before Cloudcroft."

"Seriously?" Cora jumped up.

"I think it's time."

Cora started up the hallway stairs before Indy could process her response. "Hells yes," she called back. "Let's do it."

Comfortable as always in Indy's room, Cora sprawled out on Indy's bed, butt-bumping Hubble off the comforter. Turning her nose up at the intrusion, Hubble *meowed,* then jumped up on Cora and plopped down on her stomach as if to say, *eat me, bitch,* lazily kneading her claws against Cora's sweater.

"That cat hates you so much," Indy snorted.

"Totally," Cora grinned. She spread out over the bedspread, kicking her long legs to each corner as she tucked her hands beneath her head. "So, what's TN's standing? I need the haps before you go live. Between your stalker and the shit that went down last week, I kind of figured you might be done with it for good."

Indy plopped down in a chair near the desk. She turned in circles, flicking at Dean Winchester with each pass. "I'm more than a little bent about going live again. Maybe if I just don't share these new numbers . . ." she shrugged. "I promised Henry, err, Sawyer, I wouldn't, but I don't know." Wrapping her mind around the fact that Sawyer wasn't human was hard enough. She hadn't even tackled the whole maybe he *was* the reason for the numbers part yet. "What if I'm supposed to help Sawyer? What if that's what this is all about? Now that I know what he is, I guess I don't need True North any-more. Not if I tell him I'm Orion."

"But True North's bigger than that now, Indy."

"You mean all that *get your ass in gear* stuff?" Indy sniffed.

"Yeah."

"You could carry that mantle."

Cora sat up. "Really? You think? Or maybe we could do it together."

"New show?"

"Sure. Something like."

Indy nodded. She loved the idea.

"So then, what now?" Cora asked.

Indy opened her computer. "I haven't talked to Henry since I made plans to meet him. It's got to be driving Sawyer crazy. Maybe the best way to let Sawyer know who I am is just to let him figure it out."

Booting up True North, Indy shushed Cora silently with a finger as she readied to go live. When Cora nodded, Indy winked, simultaneously activating her mic and voice modulator. She cleared her throat. "Love seeketh not itself to please, nor for itself hath any care, but for another gives its ease, and builds a Heaven in Hell's despair. Hey, friends. It's been a while, and I'm sorry. But I've been busy building bridges beyond Cloudcroft." She paused and sucked in, holding her breath until her lungs felt tight. "You probably have a lot to say, and I want to hear it, but I'm also waiting on a particular caller tonight. Visitor, if you're out there, I'm listening."

A sound clip from *Close Encounters of the Third Kind* played as the chatroom lit up. At the same time, Indy's non-burner phone vibrated, signaling an incoming text from Sawyer.

Sawyer: It's on NOW. True North.

Indy: Kk :-)

Sawyer: I was thinking I should call in and ask O about Cloudcroft.

Indy: Maybe that's a good idea.

Sawyer: Maybe he can help us.

Indy: Or maybe help you.

Sawyer: Turn it on and listen?

Indy: Sure. Was going to anyway.

Sawyer: Ok. Love you.

Gearing up a YouTube clip before texting Sawyer that she loved him back, Indy glanced at the chat threads. As she suspected, the board was on fire. She grabbed her phone again, typing out a string of heart emojis to send to Sawyer, but True North's burner flashed.

Exhilarated, she dropped her private phone on the desktop, scrambling to answer.

"Hello, love is the space and time measured by the heart. Got a good love story tonight?"

"No," a girl said. "Love sucks. I've got a question, or maybe a complaint."

"Listening," Indy prompted her. "All straight-talk encouraged."

"Where've you been? I'm mad at you, Orion, because Cloudcroft blew my mind, and then you just left us all hanging. Something big AF is out there, and a lot of us are just waiting for what comes next. We need you, O; you're our flippin' guide."

"I get it. But I'm still figuring out the big AF part. I swear I didn't abandon you. The thing is, Cloudcroft stirred the pot. I'd be lying if I said strange things weren't afoot. Problem is, I don't know which foot they're about. I've just been laying low, hoping it'll blow over soon."

"Cloudcroft got their attention?"

"Which *their*?" Indy snorted.

"Like the feds or whoever. The people in charge who don't want us knowing what's out there."

Indy shrugged at Cora, who mouthed '*crush it*' over Hubble's furry head. Disturbed by the caller's probable assessment, she turned back to the microphone. "Yeah, them."

"So, you're in trouble?"

Indy thought hard for a second before answering. Was she? And which was more dangerous? Whatever was in the skies, or the people following her? "Here's the thing, you and I *know* something's going down now. Even if we don't know what it is, something bigger is out there. If I never go live again, even if *they* find me, they can't take that truth away from us."

"No, but they can cover it up. You disappear, and suddenly True North's some Snopes-debunked rumor Bob the troll turns into an internet meme. Stay safe, O, and keep True North alive. Truth is objective when you've got facts on your side and people in your corner to back them up. If something happens to you, anything at all, you come back here and start making noise. They can't silence all of us."

Indy nodded at the burner. "All right. Makes sense. Just remember, if something does happen before I get back here, or if I never go live again, you guys can still make a difference. You're a wave with momentum. A tide to be reckoned with. You really don't need True North." Breathing deeply, Indy gave her words a moment to sink in. "Promise me, all of you, that no matter what happens to me, or this show, you'll keep fighting for what you believe in. And always remember you're part of something bigger. You've seen that now for yourselves."

"We got you, O," the girl said, her breathy voice ending on a high note. "We've got your back!"

A surge of emotion overtook Indy. Even Cora's eyes looked a little damp. "Thanks, Caller," she said, nearly choking up. "For the straight-talk."

Indy hung up, punctuating her goodbye with a quick clip from *Futurama*. Seconds later, the burner flashed again. She had just enough time to exhale and gesture at Cora before answering. "Hello. Neil deGrasse Tyson says the universe is under no obligation to make sense to you. And that may be true. But it still pisses me off. So, believer or skeptic? And what can I do for you tonight?"

"Believer! Dude, I love your show." A male voice, heavy with weed-induced euphoria, funneled through the receiver. "Just knowing something's out there is enough. In case they grab your ass, I want you to know I'm going to spend the rest of my fucking life watching the skies. Because it's full of fucking wonder."

Indy glanced at Cora, smiling. Cora shook her head exuberantly. "No truer words, Caller. I couldn't say it better myself."

"Like the lady said before, we've got your ass."

The line went dead again, and Indy sighed, blowing out slowly. Still waiting for Sawyer, she read from a dated *New Yorker* article about the psychology of mass hysteria. Fielding phone calls in between, she offered her own two cents about UFO sightings, about how after Cloudcroft especially, she didn't believe they were all just a product of the power of suggestion. Almost an hour in, as Indy rambled about the Phoenix lights, publicly erring on the side of *totally alien* and *government cover-up*, the burner rang again. Finally, this time, she recognized the voice.

"You never showed up," the caller accused her when she answered.

Indy's skin tingled, puckering from her scalp to her toes. Though muffled and maybe even intentionally disguised, how she missed the similarities between Sawyer and Henry's inflections baffled her. Damn, they sounded alike.

"I did show up. I saw you there."

"But . . ."

"But I left."

"Why?"

Indy chewed on her lip, tripping over her tongue before shooting mental laser beams at Cora. Even just a nod Indy's way would make Indy feel a whole hell of a lot better about spilling it publicly.

"You still there?" Henry asked.

"I'm here." Indy sighed. "Just thinking about how to answer."

Cora smiled kind of lamely. She motioned at the mic and mouthed something unintelligible. Indy sat back, and as she gathered up the courage to explain, True North's chatroom went ballistic.

Indy ran a hand through her hair compulsively, fighting a tangle. Her temple throbbed, and she wanted to rip the damn thing out.

"I waited for an hour, Orion," Henry told her.

"Let's take this off-air," she finally answered.

"Why? Afraid your callers will figure out you're a liar?"

"I'm not a liar. I didn't go over and talk to you because I recognized you, and I panicked."

"Wait, what?"

"I *was* there," she said calmly—much more calmly than she felt. She took a deep breath, looking to Cora again for strength. "It was raining out, and you were wearing exactly what you promised you would be. You were sitting at the rear of the shop near a window. There was a book on your table. And when I walked in and saw you and realized I knew you, I chickened out."

"How is that possible?"

"We know each other well, actually. We've spent a lot of time together. In fact, I saw you again later, at another restaurant. You wore a black sweater and seemed pretty blissed out over a red chile-Oreo milkshake. I get it now. I really do. And I promise, if I can,

I'll help."

Henry was quiet for so long, Indy worried he'd hung up. She cleared her throat and started to ask if he was still there when he sighed.

"All right, Orion," he said flatly. "Take me private."

ALL OF THIS AND NOTHING

"WE'RE OFF AIR," Indy breathed into the phone.

"You know who I am? Why didn't you say something earlier?"

Henry's biting tone threw her off. "I'm sorry! I should have. I should have said something in Cloudcroft or last night. I just, I chickened out." She looked to Cora for encouragement, swelling a little when Cora winked her support.

"Last night," he echoed before pausing. "We saw each other last night?"

"Look, I get why you didn't tell me you've been calling True North," Indy continued, afraid if she slowed to listen, she'd lose her nerve. "I'm not mad at you. I didn't tell you I'm Orion for some of the same reasons you didn't tell me the truth about where you came from. But now that I know your big secret, and you know mine, we can be straight with each other."

"What big secret is that?"

"Are you messing with me?" Indy nearly screeched.

"No. I'm not."

"That I *am* Orion."

"Yeah, I got that part."

"Then what's your deal?"

"You sure we know each other?"

"Yes!" She nearly shouted. "Look, I understand if you want to back off, but I swear to God, I was only trying to protect you. Especially after what you told me. I have a lot on my plate, you know? And then I went to Leo's to meet Henry and saw you. You can imagine what that probably felt like. And then later, I mean, I thought you were going to tell me that you are Henry, or that you know I'm Orion, and instead you tell me . . . well, that you're visiting. I didn't know what to think. All I knew then was that you'd already been talking to Orion and wanted to go home. And I suddenly really didn't want you to do that."

Sawyer's long pause plunged Indy's comfort level to zero. "Where'd we meet?" he finally asked, rippling the deafening silence.

"Which time?"

"The first time."

Maybe Sawyer was testing her. Maybe he worried she wasn't really Indy. She wouldn't blame him for being overly cautious. But something felt off. Like, what if she was making the biggest mistake of her life kind of off. It was a horrible feeling.

"Holy Ghost River," she said quietly.

"That was six years ago." Sawyer's voice sounded hollow.

"Right, then we ran into each other again at Corazon sophomore year. You recognized me from the river. I didn't recognize you until you told me last night."

"Corazon High?"

Indy started to say *yes*, but the line went dead.

"Hello," she said into the receiver.

Across the room, Cora's eyes bloomed. "Indy?" she asked.

"Hello?" Indy said again, slowly moving the phone away from her ear as if it'd contracted the plague. She stared at Cora. "He hung up on me."

Indy focused on a bedroom wall, reeling. Was he really that mad? Because he'd lied, too. For a lot of the same reasons. And she'd forgiven him. She picked up her phone, taking a deep breath before texting.

> *Indy: Why'd u hang up, Sawyer? I know ur mad, but plz give me a chance to explain.*
> *Indy: Sawyer, I'm really sorry.*
> *Sawyer: . . .*
> *Indy: Sawyer, plz call me back.*
> *Sawyer: . . .*
> *Indy: Let me at least explain be4 u shut me out.*
> *Sawyer: . . .*
> *Indy: Shit, Sawyer, what if I'd given you the same cold shoulder after you told me about, you know.*
> *Indy: I can't believe you hung up on me just because I'm Orion.*
> *Indy: But I mean, I understand. And I love you. Call me.*
> *Sawyer: . . .*

Indy stared at the ellipses on her phone, flickering like ghosts as they came and went beneath her texts. Sawyer, it seemed, was reading her messages; he just wasn't responding.

Frustrated, Indy held her breath until she felt dizzy, then she dialed Sawyer's number, ready to leave a lengthy phone message if he didn't answer. After reaching his voicemail, she sighed into the phone and shored up her tears. "Sawyer," she warbled, "I should have told you I'm Orion before tonight. We should have told each other everything weeks ago. You have every right to be mad. But I love you, and I want to help. I only care about working this out. I'll do whatever you need, all right? Just please give me a chance. Like I gave you. You told me your secret, and I didn't run away screaming, right?"

Then she texted:

Indy: Me being Orion doesn't really change that much.

Sawyer: . . .

Indy: Hello?

Sawyer: WTF, India?

Indy breathed a sigh of relief. At least he responded.

Indy: Does it?

Sawyer: . . .

Indy: Sawyer?

Sawyer: . . .

Indy: Sawyer?

Sawyer: It changes everything.

Indy: Like u and me, everything?

Sawyer: . . .

Indy: Sawyer?

Sawyer: Especially you and me, India.

Indy didn't wait to read more. She dropped her phone, or more like flung it. The purple outer casing hit the edge of her bed, startling Hubble, then rebounded, careening toward her toes. She kicked it, swiping it under her mattress.

"That can't be good," Cora said.

"Um, no. He's really pissed. I don't think I want to read anything else he writes until he's had time to think about it. 'Cause I think he just tried to break up with me."

Cora motioned Indy over to the bed. Indy obliged, dropping down beside Cora on the purple patchwork bedspread. Wiggling toward her friend, Indy butted her forehead against Cora's bony shoulder.

"It's okay, sweetie." Cora stroked her hair. "Remember, you're O-freaking-rion. He'll get over it. He's too smart not to understand why you kept it a secret. Just give him time to process. Anyway, he's a dude, you know? He probably feels stupid. They all have little baby egos." She dropped her voice, imitating what Indy presumed was one weird freaking baby.

Indy giggled. Even thinking about alienating Sawyer made her feel like falling into a black hole, but somehow, like always, Cora found some ridiculous way to turn it around. Indy was on tumble-dry and might very well be unraveling, but no matter what, no matter how inside-out things got, Cora was a constant. At that moment, Indy felt like puking her guts out, but knowing Cora had her back made it easier to deal with accepting that she might lose Sawyer.

CONSPIRACY THEORY

IN THE MORNING, after the worst night of sleep, Indy pulled her phone out from under the bed and checked her messages. Nothing. Even the ellipsis would be better than the blank white space that stared back at her; at least then, she'd know Sawyer hadn't written her off.

Like a zombie, she lumbered through breakfast, barely listening to her dad talk about his friend's art opening the night before while obsessing about whether Sawyer would forgive her.

"And then his head exploded!" Indy's mom stared at her wryly.

"Huh?" Indy mumbled.

"That's what I thought."

"Rough night?" her dad asked.

"I guess," Indy mumbled into her palms.

"We haven't talked much since before you went to Cloudcroft." Her mom closed her laptop with a thwack and tapped a short but manicured nail on its shiny surface, beating out a disjointed melody that made Indy's head throb.

"Stop. Please," Indy begged.

Her mom stopped tapping. She leaned forward in her chair and crossed her arms over her chest, giving Indy her fiercest mom look. "What's going on, Gary Indiana?"

"Ugh."

"*Ugh* isn't an answer," her dad said.

"Then don't call me that."

"Fine. *India.*"

"Fine, *Mom.*" Indy rolled her eyes at her mother dramatically. "Boys. Boys are the problem. Mine specifically."

"Lover's quarrel?" her dad asked.

"Sweetheart!" Indy's mom admonished her dad. "Is he right?" She stared at Indy.

"Sawyer's mad at me."

"Should he be?" she asked.

"Probably. But he doesn't have to be a jerk about it. I tried apologizing, and he won't return my calls or texts."

Indy's mom stared at Indy intently. She moved her head from side to side like a bird, studying her daughter far more seriously than she previously let on. Indy watched her do it with a sense of dread. Her mom was making that (should be patented) *gotcha* face, and it only meant one thing; Indy was about to get one serious lecture.

"Was that after you went off air last night?"

Cereal caught in Indy's throat. She coughed so hard as the lump went down, she shot milk out her nose. Scrambling for a napkin, she knocked her water over, spilling it across the table, soaking her dad's open paper.

"Shit!" her dad yelped.

"I take it that's a *yes,*" her mom said.

Indy held a napkin to her nose, blinking. A thousand responses trucked through her head, but she kept her mouth shut. Because what could she say, really? The truth was, she felt almost relieved they knew about True North.

"We need to have a serious discussion, Indy. Since you'll be late for school, now is not the time but consider yourself on notice."

"Am I grounded?" Indy managed.

Her dad's dark eyebrows bunched together at the bridge of his nose. Indy almost giggled; she wanted to tell him he looked like a male Frida Kahlo but figured it wasn't the right moment. "You're not grounded, kiddo. Frankly, we think it's kind of a cool hoax. But you're walking a line. I gather you know you've sparked a revolution o' sorts. It may be a joke to you, but a lot of people clearly take True North seriously. Including your principal. He put all of us parents on notice about student conduct over the show lately. He finds out you're Orion, and he may very well expel you. Look, kiddo, I know it's hard to believe, but Mom and I were teenagers once, and we both agree that it's normal to act out. But we don't want you ruining your future over an internet show."

"Also," her mom chimed in, "I'm not okay with you running off to meet strangers you've only ever talked to on the radio. Especially not ones who think you're some kind of messiah."

Indy stared at her parents, dumbfounded. They weren't mad. But they also didn't believe the sightings were genuine. "I think one of my callers might be Sawyer," she said softly. "I took him offline to confront him. So yeah, that's when he hung up. Also, the sightings aren't a hoax. The numbers *are* coordinates. Something super weird is going on."

Indy's mom straightened, her suddenly tense spine pulling tight. She looked to her right at Indy's dad, concern etching outlines around her eyes and mouth. "Sweetheart . . ." she started.

"No." Indy held up a single hand. "Don't. I know how it sounds, and I also know I'm not crazy. I saw something unreal in the sky over White Rock *and* Cloudcroft, Mom, and I'm not the only one. The numbers in my head, they *always* correlate with some crazy event. It's bona fide. And I'm pretty sure it has to do with what happened in fifth grade at Holy Ghost River."

Her parents exchanged worried looks. "India," her dad started.

Indy held up both hands, palms facing out, adamantly shaking her head. "Before you decide to lock me up, hear me out. I promise to explain after school." Dropping her hands, she looked down at her wristwatch. "Because if I don't go now, I'm going to be late, and I know how much you hate that."

Indy's mom looked at her dad briefly before breathing out, "M-kay, India. Go. But you come straight home after school, understand? No dicking around until we talk."

Nodding, Indy jumped up and grabbed her backpack from the floor near her chair. She pocketed her keys and rechecked her phone before dashing for the door, yelling, "I promise," on her way out.

In her Jeep, she let out the longest sigh. She'd been half-holding her breath for the last five minutes and felt light-headed. No doubt her day would be all full of explaining. Though, the only person she really cared about getting through to was Sawyer.

At school, Indy parked at the very far end of the lot, near a swatch of gnarled trees leading to a wooded area that doubled as Corazon's deadbeat smoking area. It was a dregs spot, but at least she'd found a place. Arriving like she had, minutes before the bell rang, almost guaranteed she'd have to park down the street and walk.

In Building C's main hallway, Indy nearly ran straight into Sawyer. As she rushed toward first period through the dwindling crowd of other late students, he stepped out of the boys' restroom right into her path.

"Whoa," Indy held her hands out to stop the restroom door from hitting her shoulder. She stood, startled for a moment when she realized it was him, and started nervous babbling. "Oh. The door . . . I . . . you're late."

Sawyer gave her the once-over. But he didn't respond. Instead, he pursed his perfect lips and shook his perfect head, then proceeded to stomp-walk off toward building B. Indy watched him go, staring at his flawless back dejectedly. Yep, he was pissed. But at least he hadn't yelled at her or outed her in the hall.

Sawyer ignored Indy all morning, winding past her in the halls without a glance. At lunch, he disappeared altogether, and Indy dragged Lior and Cora out to the sliver of dead grass between the auditorium and gym that doubled as the social reject quad. Even if Sawyer wasn't outside eating lunch, hiding was better than facing his posse.

"I'm one part devastated, and one part pissed at him," Indy admitted. "I mean, he held back for weeks before telling me the biggest secret ever, and I spent the hour after he told me assuring him I still adore him. You think he might be just a tad more supportive or sympathetic."

Cora and Lior exchanged looks. "He might not be mad for the reason you think," Lior mumbled.

"Just tell her," Cora prodded.

"Tell me what?" Indy dropped her sandwich on the wood table. She made a menacing face at Lior.

"Weeeeeeell," Lior dragged out, "he kinda cornered me before class this morning. I don't think he got that you're, you know, until . . ." she stopped.

"Until what?" Indy nearly screeched.

"Err," Lior scratched her head with a pointy, black-lacquered nail, "Until you texted him after the show."

"What?" Indy looked off toward the still snow-capped mountains. It didn't make sense. They'd talked for at least five minutes before he hung up on her.

"He said you texted him that you're . . ." Lior nodded conspiratorially. "And it freaked him the fuck out because of the whole Henry thing. He said he understood why you'd keep the O thing a secret, but not the Henry part, not from him."

"So, he's what . . . jealous of himself?"

Unbelievable.

"Maybe just that you were so secretive about Henry when he was so open with you? I think he's still just processing. I mean, he did stop me to ask me if I knew anything about it, so I doubt he's decided it's over. Besides, he needs you, right?"

"What if you didn't know I was O yet, Lior? I mean, did he even seem like he cared about blowing my cover?"

Lior shrugged. "He started out talking in code. Like, hey, you ever listen to True North? You know about Orion? He squinted when he said it. I knew after listening last night and talking to Cora where he was going with it. But he didn't admit to being Henry. He still has no idea *I* know about *him*. I only guessed he was mad about your talking to Henry because he asked, *she ever tell you about Visitor? What's up with that?* Like he wanted to know what you'd said about him behind his back but wasn't about to admit it was *his* back unless I outright asked. Which, so you know, I didn't. I mostly played dumb."

Indy rolled her eyes but more to hold back tears than anything. Why was being in love so overwhelming? "Maybe what he's really mad about is that I figured him out."

"Or maybe he feels bad he didn't tell you about Henry to begin with. It can't be easy for him, Indy. Maybe he does want to know where he came from *and* loves you but doesn't know how to address or reconcile both."

"Boys are masters of denial," Cora harrumphed.

Indy almost felt bad thinking Lior might be right. She believed Sawyer loved her; maybe he felt guilty for omitting that he really did want to know the family that left him behind. Maybe he lied to protect her feelings. Maybe he lied because he didn't want to admit those things to himself.

Twisting the end of her ponytail into a tight coil around her finger, Indy sat like a skittish mouse, obsessively peeking to her right, then left, every few seconds hoping to spot Sawyer. She listened half-heartedly to her friends' well-intentioned advice, wondering if they truly understood how insane it was to masquerade as someone else, especially knowing what she did about the universe and its secrets.

Indy pulled at her ponytail until Cora set her hot dog down and placed a hand on Indy's head mid-motion. "You're going to rip that thing off your scalp," Cora warned her. "Just chill; it'll work out. I may not be you. I may not understand those numbers in your head or why Henry-slash-you-know-who is drawn to them, but I do know he didn't tell you something that weighty just to go and disappear from your life. He trusts you, Indy. And he needs you. Trust *me*. He'll be back soon enough."

Maybe, but Indy wasn't about to bank on it just yet. Feeling pessimistic, she looked down at her sandwich. Suddenly, her egg salad on rye looked more like flea-infested yellowing maggots. Evidently, the whole eating lunch thing wasn't on her stomach's list of priorities. And she didn't blame it. "The numbers from Cloudcroft are different this time." She wiped her mouth and pushed her food away. "I still haven't figured them out. But I know it's not a single coordinate. Best I can tell so far, they're maybe coordinates *and* a few something elses. Sawyer knows that I have them."

"So maybe that's where you start. Talk to him about them and play it off like you don't give a crap about anything but figuring the new string out. For sure, you still have *that* in common. I mean, that's why he started calling the show in the first place, right?"

"You mean like when Sawyer stops ignoring me?"

Cora gave her a playful push. "Buck it up, lady. Since when have you ever needed a male to get your shit in order?"

"Umm, never," Indy mumbled.

The end-of-lunch bell rang, signaling the demise of Indy's reprieve from Sawyer's bitter cold shoulder. Indy sighed dramatically. Still mopey, she gathered her trash, resigned to keeping the promise she'd just made to herself. She would not apologize to him for the millionth time, but she would try to understand why he might be so mad. Cora was right. Sawyer needed Indy. Beyond that, she *desired* him. And patience, she decided, was the best way to get what she wanted.

DOUBLE JEOPARDY

INDY BLINKED, THEN blinked again. After smiling at Sawyer in the hall following fifth period, only to watch him turn the other way and stomp down the wrong wing to avoid speaking to her, there he was—leaning casually against her Jeep, as if annoyed she'd taken so long to pack up and walk out to the parking lot.

Hopeful, Indy walked closer, jangling her car keys in the air as she waved hesitantly. Sawyer uncrossed his ankles and stood up straighter, but he didn't wave back. Instead, he cocked his head, sizing her up with a distant flat look that made Indy all kinds of uncomfortable.

"So now you want to talk to me?" she asked when they were face to face.

"India?"

"In the flesh." She pursed her lips and raised an eyebrow.

He nodded toward the wooded area behind the lot. "Can we take a walk?"

"Back there?" she asked, suspicious.

"You have a better idea?"

"Yeah," she jangled her keys, "hop in. We'll go get a shake or something."

Nodding, Sawyer stepped back to let Indy unlock the passenger door. When it was ajar, he hopped in, and Indy sighed long and hard. *Thank freaking God.* Climbing in beside him, she buckled her seatbelt and gazed at his profile, hating how perfect it looked—especially now. Like she needed the distraction. Were all aliens this stupid-beautiful?

"What?" Sawyer asked.

"What *what?*" she answered.

"You're staring."

"What else is new?"

Sawyer's eyes narrowed, focusing on her as if learning something unexpected. "You're an interesting person, India."

"So interesting you're not mad at me anymore?" She pulled out of the parking space, backing up before straightening out behind the row of cars streaming from the lot.

"I was never mad."

"That's why you hung up on me?"

"I hung up because something you said made me realize it wasn't safe to talk on the phone anymore. I knew we had to talk in person."

Indy gave him a look. Sawyer was acting weird and not his normal weird, which said a lot. Straining to see over her shoulder as she made another left through the maze of Corazon's parking lot, she cranked her steering wheel to avoid hitting August's car as he and Lior jetted out of a nearby spot. Lior caught Indy's eye through the windshield, winking as she mouthed *sorry.* Then she pointed to Sawyer beside Indy and gave Indy the thumbs up.

Indy straightened her Jeep, returned Lior's wink, and gave August the bird as he sped off. "Your friends. Jeez, Sawyer," she said, heading for the main gates behind August.

Hoping to break the ice a little, she turned to rib him.

Then, she froze.

Stunned, Indy hit her brakes hard. She stopped the Jeep in the middle of the exit lane, holding up traffic as she stared out her windshield, ignoring the honking behind her. Standing on the sidewalk, gaping at her as if she just sprouted a head of mutant dandelion fuzz, stood . . . Sawyer.

Indy's record-breaking doubletake between her passenger and the boy on the street made her head spin. She felt lightheaded and short of breath and was seconds from swinging her car door open and jumping out of the Jeep when the Sawyer in her car put a hand on her knee. "Please, India. Let's just go," he said. "We have a lot to talk about."

"But . . ." she pointed out the windshield.

Sawyer number one sat forward, gripping the dashboard. "Oh," he said quietly.

"*Oh*, is right," she repeated as her heart crawled up her throat.

The Sawyer standing outside, gaping at Indy, dashed for her Jeep. As he approached, the crowd of kids milling near the front quad parted, forming a semi-circle around her car. Within seconds, a rush of finger-pointing, camera-phone-waving students surrounded them.

"Open up!" Sawyer banged on Indy's Jeep hood, startling Indy into motion. She threw the door open and quickly jumped down, staring wildly at the boy sitting in her passenger seat. He wore a black hoodie, blue jeans, and checkered Vans. Not Sawyer's usual attire or what he'd been wearing while shunning her in the halls earlier. She'd been so discombobulated all day and so happy to see him in the parking lot she'd completely missed it.

And duh, Indy.

"Henry?" she gasped, looking up at him.

The boy nodded.

She swung around to face Sawyer.

"You're Visitor?" Sawyer asked him, glaring over Indy's shoulder.

"You're not?" she swallowed.

Sawyer grabbed Indy's waist and scooted her out of the way. He leaned into the Jeep, seemingly unfazed by his doppelgänger. "Irreal?"

Henry nodded.

"How . . . what are you doing here?"

He pointed at Indy. "Orion promised she'd help me go home."

Indy grasped Sawyer's arm. She shot him a look, silently begging him to shut Henry up. But it was too late—all around her, people started videotaping their standoff.

Henry leaned across the center console and popped Indy's seat back, motioning hastily at them. "Get in."

Sawyer waffled, gawking at Henry as the whispers around Indy's car grew louder.

"Come on," Henry implored. "I need to talk to Orion now!"

Someone yelled, "Orion?" and like an idiot, Indy turned around, searching for the loudmouth offender. The ripple was immediate; a collective gasp moved through the crowd.

"Just get in the Jeep!" she yelled at Sawyer, pushing him forward. "Go!"

Sawyer sprang into the backseat. Indy followed close behind, pulling her door shut with a rattling thud. She honked as the crowd swallowed the Jeep, threatening to run everyone over.

"Orion!" someone shouted, banging on her grill.

Someone else yelled, "We love True North!"

As the group parted to let Indy's Jeep out, a small cluster of people started chanting, "India, India, India."

"Shit!" Indy spit out. "Thanks a lot, Henry!" She glared at Henry's twin over her shoulder. "You, too, Sawyer!"

"Me?" Sawyer gasped. "Jesus Christ, India, just drive."

Indy continued to honk her way through the crowd, peeling out of the parking lot as soon as she hit the driveway. She drove fast, white knuckling the steering wheel, worried someone from school might follow. As she sped down Cerrillos, Indy stole incredulous glances in the rearview mirror, alternating between watching the street behind her and peeking at Henry and Sawyer. Damned if they weren't identical. Even the scowls on their faces were alike.

Indy headed straight home. High on adrenaline, it was the only thing she could think to do. She needed to be somewhere she could figure out this new reality without looking over her shoulder in fear every second.

A tense five minutes later, she pulled into the carport behind her house. She put the Jeep in park, then finally turned to face Sawyer. "I'm sorry I didn't tell you about Orion. And I'm sorry I didn't tell you about Visitor. After what happened last week at Leo's, I thought *you* were Henry."

Sawyer examined Henry before meeting Indy's eyes. "I get that now."

Indy turned the car off. "You know each other?"

Sawyer ran a palm over his head, stopping to grip his neck. "Yeah. We know each other."

"Twins?" she whispered.

"Something like that," Henry snorted, looking between her and Sawyer. "You're a couple?"

Indy stared back at Sawyer. Henry's question sounded more like an accusation than a question. Still, she stopped herself from nodding defensively and sat up straighter. It was up to Sawyer to decide; he already knew what *she* wanted.

Sawyer nodded at her affirmatively.

"Yes?" she half-asked.

"Yes," he said out loud.

"Does she know?" Henry asked him.

"Know?" Indy frowned.

"About you." Henry stared Sawyer down.

Sawyer tipped forward on the bench seat. He grabbed Indy's shaking hand and met her gaze, holding her hostage with a soulful expression. "She knows I was in the river that night. She knows I love her."

Indy's heart burst. She felt a ping and then the warm rush of blood that traveled through her body, making her feel dizzy with emotion.

"*She's* the reason I'm stuck here," Henry said.

"*I'm* the reason you're stuck here."

"*She* fell," Henry sniffed.

"Wait, what?" Astonished, Indy gaped at Henry, overwhelmed by his anger.

"I'm sorry," Sawyer said, deflating. "I thought you went back with them."

Henry tilted his chin, looking down his nose. "I stayed. You should have known I'd stay. I never went anywhere without you."

"I swear, I would never have left the river if I'd known that. I hid after the helicopters came. I thought you went back with them." Sawyer's voice came out hitched, and Indy realized he was working hard to keep it together.

"I thought *you* went back. I've been on my own since then. All this time, it would have been good to know I wasn't alone here." Henry's tone sounded curt but strained; he seemed to be working even harder than Sawyer to stay collected. "I guess they left us both."

Indy felt like crying. So much more had happened that night at Holy Ghost River than she ever guessed. *She'd* drowned, and somehow, two other people lost everything. Her actions had altered three whole lives. She grabbed Henry's hand, trying to imagine what they must both be going through. More than ever, she just knew she had to help.

Stumbling, she managed out, "I'm . . . so sorry, Henry. If I'd known all this earlier, I never would have waffled. I promise I'll do anything I can to get you home now."

"I'm sorry too," Sawyer said softly. "I know I was supposed to stay with you. But she would have died."

Henry's gaze fell on Indy. "You still think you can help?"

Indy lowered her eyes. Henry's voice simmered with emotion, and she knew without looking at him that he was still wrestling with his anger. "If we can figure out the new set of numbers."

Henry cocked his head questioningly, but a rustling on the back porch distracted her. Looking up, she met her father's stare. He stood barefoot on the back steps wearing his finest paint-strewn overalls, waving an indigo-splattered paintbrush at her. With a hand cupped around his mouth, he shouted, "The school called, India. Get your rebel arse inside. You, my love, are in boatloads of trouble."

VISITOR

HOVERING NEXT TO each other in Indy's small sunny kitchen, Indy's parents volleyed their heads between Henry and Sawyer as if watching an out-of-control tennis match. Sawyer stood near the enameled oven, as far away from Henry as he could. Henry just stood in the corner near the back door like a stalk, sloughing off pent-up resentment.

Watching them all awkwardly watch each other, Indy wanted to laugh. She felt too full of the absurd, or like she was stuck in an awful ninety's sitcom. "Soooo . . ." She tapped a combat boot against the tiled floor nervously. "Can we go upstairs now?"

"Which one of you is Sawyer again?" her dad asked, still staring between the two boys.

Sawyer raised his hand.

"And you're twins?"

Henry nodded.

"And this is what kind of messed-up game?"

"It's not a game, sir," Henry replied. "Everything India told you is true. Sawyer saved her when she fell into the river. When the medics came, we were separated. And our parents took off. They left us both behind."

Indy closed her eyes. When Henry told them his story, including how he wandered the Pecos Wilderness for days before a hiker found him and took him to social services in Albuquerque, where they stuck him in an orphanage, she cried. Sawyer grew up loved. Henry hopped from foster homes to orphanages until he turned fifteen when he finally ran away. Since then, he'd lived on society's periphery, working odd jobs around New Mexico.

With a raised eyebrow, her dad said, "Son, I believe parts of your story. I'm sure it's shocking to suddenly, after six years, find your long-lost twin. And I'm damned sorry your parents abandoned you two. Seems Indy can claim more than just teenage rebellion came from this whole True North experiment. As for the rest, despite my youthful looks, I wasn't born yesterday."

"He's telling the truth," Indy insisted.

"*India*," her dad sighed.

"Why can't you just believe me for once!" Her parents always humored her, but they never actually listened to the things she said. She loved them, but they were sure as hell part of the reason she had such a hard time trusting people.

"Indy," her mom said firmly, "I don't think these boys are being straight with you. Think about it. They both came into your life *after* you started True North. Didn't *you* say you weren't sure if the numbers even meant anything until Henry started calling?"

Afraid she might actually burst into burning embers of rage Indy glared darts at her mom. Not one atom of her doubted Sawyer or Henry. And she knew she hadn't imagined the disturbances. "Something happened at Cloudcroft," she persisted. "We all saw it."

"Honey, mass hysteria is a common phenomenon."

Indy clasped her hips, digging her fingers into her sides. "Why don't you just commit me, then? If you're sure I'm so fragile, I can't tell fiction from reality!"

"That's not what we think," her mom insisted.

"Really? Because it sounds like it!" Indy shouted. "And it's how you've always treated me!"

"Do you have any idea how much trouble you're in at school?" her mom asked. "We are behind you, India! But we're also trying hard to understand what's going on here. We can't know how to make things better until we straighten this out."

"I get it, Mom. You're my parents. You want to protect me. But you can't fix everything or explain it away. I am telling you the truth. I've always told you the truth. And the best way to help right now is to trust me."

"We do trust you." Her mom looked crestfallen. "But, honey, come on."

"God!" Indy inhaled slowly to draw her rapid heartbeat out. She was *sooooooo* pissed at them right now. "You don't! And you know what, because of that, for the longest time, I didn't trust myself, either." She pointed between Henry and Sawyer. "These two right here? Other than Lior and Cora, they're the only people who've ever had complete faith in what I tell them. They believe in me. And they've helped me see that I'm not some delusional kid, or head-in-the-clouds dreamer, or nut job. They were both *there* at the river. Their stories match mine. And because of what happened that night, they're here now. If they're lying, then they're the best-damned liars on this planet, and psychic, and probably super geniuses too. I mean, how else do you explain pulling off such a convincing con job?"

Looking between Sawyer and Henry, her dad said, "Can either of you prove it?"

"Dad!" Indy blurted out.

Abruptly, the air in the kitchen grew heavy. A wave of static swept through the room, and in a heartbeat, Sawyer disappeared. He dissolved, turning to colorful tiny wisps that swirled into filmy tendrils before dispersing into nothing.

Sawyer's body disintegrated, then quickly reconfigured next to Henry. Jumping back, Henry clumsily knocked into the wall. Indy's parents both gasped. Her mom balled a fist at her chest, looking genuinely stricken by heart palpitations. At the same time, Indy's dad threw his arms out; his chest puffed, presumably protecting her mom behind some make-believe man-shield.

Indy stared wildly, gulping as if to digest the show. It was exactly how Sawyer came apart underwater at Holy Ghost River. Except instead of bubbles this time, he morphed into air. And instead of terror, she felt awe. "Sawyer!" she gasped. "How . . . I didn't know you could still . . ." she fumbled for the right words.

"I don't make it a habit. Because," he pointed at her first, sweeping his finger slowly over all of them in a row, "that."

Indy's dad ran a hand through his hair. He dropped his arms and pulled out a chair, plopping down at the kitchen table as if burdened by the sudden, mind-blowing knowledge that he was not, as he worried, alone in the universe.

"Indy," he said softly. "Baby, I'm so sorry."

"How?" Henry asked Sawyer.

"It's just something I've always known how to do, I guess. The first time was at Holy Ghost. I went in after her without thinking, and it just . . . happened." Sawyer cocked his head, looking Henry over curiously. "It's been a part of me since then. I don't understand why or how it works. All I know is, I think it, and poof." He snapped his fingers. "You can't?"

Henry shook his head slowly. "But . . ." He held a finger up and pointed across the kitchen.

The faucet over the sink sputtered on, spitting water out like an abrupt, deep cough. Henry grimaced, then glared at it. As he stared, a glass floated up from the counter, hovering under the faucet shakily until it filled. Then it dropped into the sink and shattered, startling the crap out of everyone.

Henry sighed deeply. "It's a work in progress."

"Jesus," Indy's dad muttered.

Sawyer linked his hands behind his head, squeezing as if holding his brain in. "Yeah, can't do that."

After a moment that seemed like an eternity, Indy's mom stood up straighter. On the surface, at least, she transformed before Indy's eyes, morphing back into parent mode. "Maybe you should go upstairs now and show Henry those numbers. We can talk about school later, Indy." She glanced at Indy's dad, silently exchanging concerned parent looks.

"Yep." Indy's dad stood up, running his hands down his overalls as if straightening out his wobbly legs. "Good idea."

Indy rushed her mom, throwing her arms around her neck. "Thank you," she whispered.

"I'm sorry I didn't believe you, India," her mom whispered back. "You understand why, right?" She shook her head, still visibly stunned. "Now go upstairs and help them. Dad and I will figure out how to hold the school off for now. But please, for God's sake, don't go live with True North again until we've talked. This is some serious, out-of-the-ordinary shit. And Lord knows what alarm bells you've rung already."

Indy hugged her mom again and headed for the stairs, trailed by Sawyer and Henry. In her room, Sawyer and Henry hovered on opposite ends of her purple shag carpet, divided by a palpable wedge of tension as they sized each other up, jerking their heads in and out and back and forth like pigeons. Indy watched them from her periphery while she worked on her numbers, grimacing as they duked it out. After unsuccessfully configuring and reconfiguring the string on the pad in front of her, she finally said something.

"Stop," she pleaded. "You're acting like rodeo ponies."

Sawyer shot her a look. "Rodeo ponies?"

"All your preening. I mean, I get it. This situation sucks. But it's no one's fault. You at least liked each other once, right? Just talk it out already."

Unfolding his arms, Sawyer dropped his hands to his sides before tucking them into his pockets. He hunched, propped against Indy's dresser as he leaned toward her. "Neigh," he snorted.

"I somehow had this idea that aliens would be way more advanced," Indy muttered. She rolled her eyes and tapped the notes in front of her, caught up on the first four numbers in the string: one, six, eleven, and four. "I know this is crazy, but my birthday is January sixth. And Sawyer, aren't you in November?"

Sawyer took the paper from her hands. "These are the new ones? From Cloudcroft?"

Indy nodded.

"You're not crazy." He held the paper out, looking down at her. "If you break them into chunks, say into your birthday and mine, that leaves a whole block left for coordinates. The only thing is, I don't know when my real birthday is. My parents made November fourth up. The day they officially adopted me. You?" He turned to Henry.

"November fourth," Henry said. "The day I officially entered the system. Same as yours."

"You picked the same date?" Sawyer looked stupefied.

Henry shrugged, but Indy caught a slight twitch near the right side of his (also perfect) mouth before he spoke, almost as if the idea made him happy. "Not on purpose. But yeah, guess I did."

"Eleven-four then?" Sawyer raised an eyebrow and looked directly at Henry. When Henry nodded, Sawyer handed him the paper.

Henry quickly scanned the sheet, then excitedly scuttled over to Indy, nearly launching himself off the bed. "Pull up Google Earth," he told her, crouching beside her desk. "Then type in the string minus our birthdays."

Indy typed in 355717105755034. When nothing came up, she shrugged and looked at Henry. "We still have too many numbers."

"Drop the three at the beginning," he told her.

She tried again. "Nothing."

"Drop the four at the end."

"Still nothing."

Henry rubbed his jaw just the way Sawyer did when Sawyer puzzled out a problem, except Henry used his right hand instead of his left, and he pressed his pointer finger into the depression at the tip of his chin instead of tapping it. It was weird to see, like watching an alternate, slightly less attuned Sawyer.

"Try dropping the three and five at the beginning," he suggested.

Indy tried, then shook her head.

"Try dropping the three and four at the end."

Indy typed in the string of numbers, minus the three and four, and waited. Within seconds, a satellite image for Pigeon Ranch, the Civil War battlefield near Pecos in the Glorieta Pass, popped up.

"Coincidence?" Henry asked her.

"It's not far from Holy Ghost River," Indy whispered.

"That's it." Sawyer leaned over Indy's shoulder. "Call it a gut feeling." They stared at each other wide-eyed for a moment, mentally high-fiving their small victory. "But the three and four?"

"An address, maybe?" Henry volunteered.

Indy shook her head. "Doubtful. Why give me exact coordinates *and* an address?"

A sudden, insistent knocking made Indy jump. She shot up and raced down the attic stairs. "What?" she barked through her bedroom door.

"Dude, open up," Cora answered. "Your mom let us in."

"Us?" Indy's forehead hit the cool wood panel.

"Just open up."

Cora, Indy could deal with. But if *us* included more than Lior, Indy worried she'd freak. Trying to explain two Sawyers to anyone but her best friends was one chore she wasn't sure she could handle just now.

Indy unlatched the door and swung it open. As soon as she did, Cora and Lior *and* Manny and August barged past her, August high-fiving her on the way through. Cora led them all up the stairs, stopping at the top to shoo everyone into the heart of Indy's bedroom.

Indy closed the door behind them, then tromped up the stairs. She stopped at the top next to Cora and took in the scene. They all stood there gawking at each other.

"Dude!" August stared at Sawyer and Henry. "Dale called Milo, who called Manny. You two," he pointed between them, "it's all over school. And you," he turned and faced Indy, "what the hell?"

Lior struck a pose, leaning into August intimidatingly. She looked fierce enough in her blue high-top Docs and black grommeted t-shirt dress, but the stance made her seem mighty. "We already talked about this in the car, Augs. Like two minutes ago. To reiterate: you better be nice, or I swear you'll live to regret your poor decision-making skills."

"WTF, Li? I am being nice. Sawyer's my best friend. And I'm staring at his doppelgänger. I'm freaking entitled."

"Yeah, well, Indy's my best friend. You want to beat Sawyer up, go ahead. But hands off the guru."

Guru. Indy couldn't help it. She giggled.

"You're really Orion?" Manny asked her.

"Yeah. I really am," Indy said. There wasn't any point in being modest. That ship had sailed. Obviously, her friends had blown her cover.

Manny grinned. "Cool."

"We were so worried, I." Cora sat down on a patch of fluffy purple carpet, leaving the bed open for August and Lior. "I was with Manny when Milo called. People are capital F freaking the fuck out. But like, mostly in a good way. Have you checked True North's boards yet? Or at all since yesterday?"

August turned to Cora. "Wait, you knew she was Orion before today?"

"I mean, yeah. *We* did." Cora beamed and winked at Lior. "Best friends," she said. "Duh."

"I haven't been online yet," Indy told them. "The school called. My parents were freaking out when I got home. And that was before they saw these two. I promised them I'd stay off True North for now."

"About that." Sawyer swooped a hand across the room. "Irreal . . ." he paused when Henry bristled. "I mean, Henry, meet everyone. Everyone, meet Henry, my brother."

"Your brother?" Lior squawked.

"No shit?" August did a doubletake.

"No shit," Sawyer echoed.

"You didn't know?" Manny asked.

Sawyer shook his head. "It's a long, complicated story."

"But Henry knew about Indy? I mean, Orion. *He's* Visitor?" Manny sized Henry up, still obviously on the fence about whether to greet him.

Indy wondered how Manny figured out that Henry was 'Visitor.' Based on her best friends' expressions, Indy guessed Cora and Lior were just now putting everything together. But Cora spoke up before Indy could ask him. "Everyone heard you bickering about it in the parking lot at school earlier. It's all over True North, too. That's why I asked if you'd gone online yet. It's crazy right now. Your site. Like Boom!" She flittered her hands in the air, wriggling her fingers to imitate an explosion. "Everyone wants to hear from you. From Orion. There's like a thousand messages begging for you to go live and explain your doppelgängers, and how you managed to pull it off, and . . ." Cora stopped. She looked nervous.

Lior exhaled dramatically, picking up where Cora left off. "And a couple of people mentioned driving over here. They're worried you're gonna get arrested or something." She giggled, then covered her mouth. "Sorry, Indy, I know this is serious. Just some of them sound like militia. Like they're gonna stand out in front of your house with bats and guns and protect you in case the feds come."

"Shit," Indy and Sawyer said in unison.

"Are they sharing my address?" Indy asked nervously.

Cora nodded.

Reeling, Indy hurried over to her computer and keyed in True North. At least, she tried. The router seemed to work, but her computer repeatedly claimed that she wasn't online.

And what the hell?

"It's not working," she said out loud. She jiggled the router, then checked her computer's system. "It's telling me there's no service." Indy shot up and ran down her bedroom stairs, throwing her door open. "Mom!" she yelled down the hall. "What's up with the internet?"

"What do you mean?" her mom yelled back.

Indy heard her mom walk up the steps to the second floor. Indy ran to meet her. Rounding the hallway corner, they nearly bumped right into each other.

"Whoa!" Her mom threw her hands out to stop them from colliding. "I thought I told you to stay off True North until we figure something out."

"I'm not on True North. I was trying to check my email," Indy lied.

"So, what's the problem?"

"It doesn't work."

"The internet's fine."

"It's not fine."

Indy's mom looked surprised. "I don't know why it wouldn't be."

"Hon!" Indy's dad yelled up the stairs. "What's wrong with the internet?"

Indy and her mom looked at each other. Indy's mom shrugged and rolled her eyes. "I'll go call the cable company."

Indy nodded. "Thanks, Mom."

"Everything . . . all right?"

Her mom looked wary, and Indy guessed she knew that 'all right' was both the most inappropriate and yet spot-on two words to use given the situation. Indy was *just* 'all right.' She had to be. But 'all right' was also the very best anyone could hope for until they figured out what to do with Henry.

"Indy! Get up here," Cora yelled from Indy's bedroom.

Indy's Mom grimaced and nodded down the hall toward the stairs. "Go," she said. "I'll let you know when I've talked to someone."

Indy quickly hugged her mom and ran back to her room. "For some reason, we don't have service right now. Mom's calling the cable company. Wait, what are you doing, Lior?"

Lior stood on her tiptoes on Indy's bed, peeking down at the front yard through the stained-glass window above Indy's headboard. "Like three cars just parked out front," she said breathlessly.

"One after the other." She turned and stared at Indy, wide-eyed. "Shit, there's also a truck. Black with blacked-out windows. Government style. Like the one that followed you."

Sawyer hustled to the window. He turned to face Indy. "She's right."

Suddenly it dawned on him. Indy watched Sawyer's expression change as he put it all together. They hadn't imagined the man in the park or the truck tailing them. But their shadow likely had more to do with her, because of True North, than Sawyer. Either way, if the truck was out there now, it meant at least one of them was in more than just school trouble.

"We have to go. Now!" he said, nearly shouting at her.

"Yeah, get out of here and get your asses somewhere where you can go live with True North," Cora insisted. "People will help, Indy. I know they will. Just do it ASAP, before the feds come and snatch you."

"Cora!" Lior scolded her.

"We have to get to Pigeon Ranch," Henry said quietly, speaking up for the first time since Sawyer introduced him.

"Why?" Indy asked.

"I just figured out the last numbers."

"And?" Sawyer asked impatiently.

"It's a date. Today. March fourth."

ON THE DOWN LOW

A STREAM OF cars cruised down Indy's block. Some even parked, dumping groups of spectators out in Indy's front yard. Except for whoever was still sitting inside the four ominous-looking vehicles idling at the curb, most of the people looked like they went to Indy's high school. A few carried homemade signs. Some chanted. Indy heard them clear as a bell even in her room, yelling, "We know the truth," and "We've got your back, Orion."

Being the focus of all the commotion made Indy's heart race. Seeing her mom and dad down on the lawn trying to shoo people away made her want to drop through a hole in the ground. Indy winced. Despite what her parents said earlier, she knew that when it was all over, she was so completely grounded.

Whipping away from the window, Indy stared at Sawyer frantically. She ran to the window over the carport where she'd parked her Jeep, relieved to find the driveway empty. "We can sneak out back," she said quickly. "My parents are busy holding fort. They won't notice at first. Hopefully, no one follows us. But just in case, I'll drive like a demon."

Manny plucked Indy's car keys off her desk and jangled them in the air. He grabbed Indy's sweater off the floor and the sunglasses that sat near Indy's keys and tossed them both to Cora. "August parked down the block 'cause he was all about keeping his car in the shade. It's under the big cottonwood a couple houses down. You guys go out back and follow the arroyo around the block, then double back to it. Augs, you take them in your car. Cora and I will take Indy's Jeep. Cora can drive. If she puts Indy's sweater and glasses on and takes off fast, they might think we're Indy and Sawyer and follow."

Cora nodded enthusiastically. "I'm so in."

"What if you guys get caught?" Indy balked. This was her problem—hers, Sawyer's, and Henry's. She didn't want her friends getting in trouble.

"Manny's right," Lior agreed. "You've got to get out of here and to the ranch. You can't do that without a good head start. Let us help. We'll call Cora in a little bit and tell her where to meet us."

Everyone nodded their agreement. But Indy still faltered. She had no idea what would happen when they got to Pigeon Ranch. And she was scared. Genuinely scared—for so many suddenly serious reasons.

Indy hugged her shoulders to hold herself together. Being Orion in the safety of her room was easy. But life just got real, fast. Something terrible could happen. She could lose Sawyer. Or Henry. And she hadn't even really met him yet. Her friends could get hurt. They could get arrested for helping. She could be arrested and thrown in jail. And she'd read enough to know she and juvie would never be besties.

Reluctantly, Indy looked up from the carpet stain she'd focused on, meeting Sawyer's eyes. Sawyer nodded to the stairwell, motioning for her to meet him at the bottom. Halfway down the steps, Indy let him wrap her in his arms.

"I'm so sorry I dragged you into this mess." She buried her face into his chest.

"It feels more like *I* dragged you into this mess," he said against her crown. "But at least I got to meet you again. Kind of proves life really is full of wonder, India."

"Yeah, like you wonder how you'll survive it," she muttered.

Sawyer chuckled. "I love you, you know. I think I have since that night at the river."

Indy hugged him harder. "I'm sorry I lied about Orion."

"I get it. I don't blame you for keeping secrets. I mean, it hurts a little, but the reason it hurts is stupid. And I'm just as bad. I told you about Holy Ghost. But I never told you I had a copy."

"Copy?" Indy stared up at him. She searched Sawyer's beautiful face. For just one minute, she wanted to shut everything out and focus on it, a reminder, maybe, that even when life seemed impossible, good things still thrived.

"It's . . . a thing. Like two different sides of the same coin. Or mirror twins." Sawyer rubbed his jaw, pressing his fingers against his jawline. "It hurt to think about losing him. And I never thought I'd see him again. I thought he went back with them, and I used to imagine him living this perfect, unapologetic life. One where he didn't have to pretend or hide who he was. It made me angry." His voice hitched. "Also, andyesiknowthisisdumb," he mumbled quickly, "when I found out about Orion last night, I might have been a little jealous of Visitor."

"Of Henry?" she squeaked.

"Yeah."

"That's like being jealous of yourself," she said into his chest, nuzzling her nose against the depression between his muscles.

"Except I didn't know that."

She tried to laugh through tears. "So stupid."

"Right?" He raised her chin, staring down at her. "I think I kind of knew about the Orion thing after Cloudcroft. At least, I was starting to wonder. What threw me off last night was hearing that you'd gone out alone to meet Henry somewhere. After everything we talked about the night before, not telling me everything at that point felt like a bigger, more serious betrayal than just you being Orion."

"But I didn't say anything the other night because I thought you *were* Henry."

"I know that now." He shook his head, bewildered.

"We have to help him, Sawyer."

"*I* have to help. I owe him that, at least." Sawyer leaned to kiss her, lingering tenderly before pulling away. "We have to go now, India. Do what Manny said. But once we're out of here, we're dropping you and Lior off somewhere safe."

"Uh-uh," she said firmly. "No way. I'm not letting you go out to Pigeon Ranch alone."

"Henry and I, if we get into trouble, together we can . . ." Sawyer looked at a loss for words, "do things. Things you can't."

"Yeah, but they didn't send *you* coordinates. And you won't know if another message comes through. Another place we might have to go. Without me, Sawyer, you're in the dark."

Henry's ominous cough interrupted them. "Another black car just parked in front," he muttered. "Damn, check out the driver."

Indy and Sawyer rushed up the stairs, over to the window. Outside, a lanky man dressed in black coveralls with cropped hair and too-obvious mirrored sunglasses stepped out of the car and walked up to Indy's mom. He pulled something out of his wallet and shoved it in her face. Indy's mom gestured at him, and the man gestured back, and Indy couldn't for the life of her make out what they were saying. But her mom looked pissed *and* scared, and that had to be a bad sign.

Manny gave Cora a gentle nudge. "Ready?"

Cora took Indy's keys and nodded.

Sawyer placed a hand on Indy's shoulder, turning her toward the stairs. "We're out of here. Grab your backpack and that burner. We can use it to keep in touch with Manny and Cora."

Indy's group tiptoed down the stairs, quietly making their way out the kitchen's back door. Outside, Manny clapped a hand on Sawyer's shoulder, stopping him near Indy's Jeep. "So, I may not be the world's smartest guy," he sized Sawyer up as though meeting him for the first time, "but if Henry is Visitor, and he's . . . visiting, and you're brothers . . ." he trailed off.

"Then Sawyer is still your best friend," Indy finished for him. "And we don't have time for this."

Manny threw his hands up defensively. "Dude, you're my best friend. I don't give a shit who you are or where you come from. I'm just setting it straight. Inquiring minds and all."

Sawyer nodded affirmatively. "You're right *and* smarter than you give yourself credit for. We square now, Manny?"

"Absofreakinglutely."

Sawyer and Manny did this macho boy handshake thing that ended in a hug. When Manny let go, Sawyer peeled off behind Indy, trailing August and Lior toward the arroyo. Manny and Cora hopped into Indy's Jeep and drove backward out of the driveway. Indy heard the car pick up speed, but once her group reached the arroyo, she had no idea if Cora and Manny made it down the street without a tail.

DANCING BEARS

AFTER DAYS OF rain, the muddy arroyo slowed them down. Indy huffed, grateful she wore her Docs. Running through the muck in heels would have sucked big time. Gripping Sawyer's hand, she rushed past bare, twisted cottonwoods and still fluffy pines, heading up a rocky embankment behind Lior.

Back on the street, they walked quickly toward August's GTO. Down the sidewalk, Indy watched people mulling in her yard. The crowd had grown, but everyone seemed focused on her house. From a distance, at least, no one looked like they had a clue she was on the lam.

Sawyer opened the GTO's passenger door and ushered Indy and Henry inside. Lior hopped in the front, and August followed Sawyer, starting the engine quietly. Slowly driving away from the curb as if he had less than a care in the world, August headed north, out of Indy's neighborhood toward Interstate 25.

Once they cleared Indy's neighborhood, Lior twisted in her seat. "I have my laptop. Here." She shoved her backpack toward

Indy. "We can stop at a coffee house on the way. You can check the boards."

"You think that's a good idea?" Henry asked. "What if it's being monitored?"

"Good point," Lior muttered.

Indy's cell phone chimed, signaling an incoming text. She pulled it out of her bag, reading Manny's message aloud.

2 cars followed us outta ur driveway. 1 more picked up our tail. C's insane. Thank G she's driving. Sent our location to posse. My boys headed 2 of them off up Cerrillos near St. Michael's. C's driving in circles now, trying to lose the last 1. You guys?

"Tell Manny to text when they're sure everything's free and clear. We'll meet them up at the historical mile marker just outside Pigeon Ranch. The one with all the boulders," Sawyer told her.

"Shit," August muttered, twisting in his seat. "I think *we've* got a tail."

Sandwiched between Sawyer and Henry, Indy craned her neck to look back out the rear window. Behind them, a white car with blacked-out windows and missing plates followed just a little too closely. Not inconspicuous at all.

"Hold on," August told them. He cranked his wheel to the right, cutting across the lane, off the road sharply onto a side street, throwing Indy against Henry's side.

Henry put his arm out to steady her. "You okay?"

Indy nodded. "Thanks." While August drove, she attempted to text Manny back, taking sharp turns that both Henry and Sawyer tried to steady her against. *We picked up a tail off 2nd Street. Out of nowhere, headed for the highway,* she wrote back.

Manny returned her text almost immediately. Indy read it out loud.

Tell August 2 head for Galisteo. Sending backup.

Nodding, August stepped on the gas. He drove dangerously fast, weaving through a neighborhood full of narrow streets. Seconds later, the white car, and the same black truck that followed her before, suddenly appeared out of nowhere behind August, continuing to trail them. Indy tried to see if she could make out any passengers through the rear window, but the sun's glare and the cars' blacked-out windows obscured her view. All she saw were blurry outlines.

As August entered Galisteo, running a red light when he made a swift right turn, a posse of lowriders appeared out of nowhere behind the GTO, cutting off August's tail. The white car came to a screeching halt just before ramming into a purple Oldsmobile bedecked in shiny chrome and orange flames. The pickup behind it nearly smashed into a tree, swerving up onto someone's front yard before stopping. Four lowriders blocked the street, barring the other cars' passage entirely.

"Yes!" August shouted. He drove like a bat out of hell, heading for the interstate.

Her heart still racing, Indy texted Manny: *Thanks! Close call.*

Within seconds, Manny responded. *Got my boys on lookout. They b keeping up with peeps at Corazon. Lots of 'em keeping an eye out for u. Peeps positioned all over SF, ready 2 help. C lost our last tail. Just running circles now to make sure. Meet u?*

Indy texted Manny Sawyer's instructions, then waited.

"Manny says they'll meet us at Pigeon Ranch. I'm supposed to text when we get there. I'm going to try signing into True North on my phone," she told everyone. "I've got the burner in my bag; I may as well go live now."

"Wait." Sawyer put a hand on her forearm. "Seriously? Why?"

"It's out there now, Sawyer, and people are paying attention to what's going down. They could be backup if whoever just followed us shows up again. I mean, seriously, some a-holes just chased us through a neighborhood. They could've killed a pedestrian. I think we're probably already screwed. And we need all the help we can get."

"You go live," Henry said, "and they'll know where we are."

"Not if we're roaming."

Indy took a second to pull up True North on her cellphone. Except for once in a blue moon under her covers late at night, she barely ever looked at her site on anything but her home computer. Like if she acknowledged True North's presence when she wasn't in Orion mode, she might somehow blow her cover.

Fiddling with the screen, she went straight to the boards. And Boom! Cora was right. They'd totally exploded. The current trending topic, which had some nine-hundred-and-eighty-six comments and two-thousand views, was "The Feds Are After Orion!" Second to that was, "OMG, Orion is India Lewin-Kaminetzsky!" followed by a whole lot of commentary about how publicly outing her was the dumbest thing ever (seriously).

Indy quickly scrolled some of the live feed as well.

69694Eva: O's on the run. Heard cops at her house. Total mayhem.

TREKKESTER2: MIB. Was at O/India's house. Saw them. She's out. Escaped.

STARBUCK: %$#! Yeah. Called it. Female.

SLIM: I'm in SF 2, O. U need my help, U got it.

Quickly, Indy typed out:

Thanx, everyone. Especially peeps not hating on me right now. I'm safe. Was chased but lost tail. Anyone wants 2 help, text my TN call-in number with ur name and #, and maybe a clue if ur regular so I know ur 4 real. Not taking anyone live but will call u back.

Almost immediately, Indy's burner buzzed. She pulled it out of her bag and read the text out loud:

Hey, lady. Slim. Aka, Milo Torres. Small world, right? Been following u since the beginning. Totally bonkers ur O. And the strange girl I grew up with. And Model UN buddy. Manny says you need help.

"No, shit? Milo?" August said, peeking back over his shoulder at Indy. "He's the best kicker we have."

Indy stared at her phone. How weird. How impossible. She texted: *Milo? K. Tell me what last year's assignment was in Model UN.*

Milo texted back: *They gave us Pakistan. On UNESCO team. We blew Santa Fe Academy outta the water. You said like 0 words until the meet but then killed it. Guess u were saving them up for True North.*

Indy smiled. Until last year's Model UN, she'd assumed Milo was this wannabe, but not really, intellectual. Like his parents made him join Model UN for the college resume cred. Then he gave his speech, and Indy realized she'd totally miss-pegged him. Now, knowing Milo was also SLIM doubly made her want to eat her pre-model UN thoughts. She really had to stop assuming the worst about people.

As Indy started to dial Milo's number, her phone buzzed again. Another text, this time from Marta#1, who had a cousin outside of Pecos in La Luna who worked in the sheriff's office. Indy wrote Marta#1 back and thanked her, promising to call if she needed help once they got to the pass. Then she called Milo.

"O!" he yelled into the phone. "India! No way! You're like, a goddess for pulling this off."

"Thanks, Milo," she said breathlessly. "So, we're headed for Pigeon Ranch. It's been sort of a madhouse. Think you might be willing to get some people together and meet us at the lot near the ranch marker off Highway 60—the one with all the boulders? Just in case, I'm hoping people will block the trail and make it harder to follow."

"Us?" he asked. "Who've you got with you? Sawyer?"

"And August and Lior. And Henry."

"August! My man!" Milo yelled loud enough for the entire car to hear. Then, he paused. "Henry, you mean V-man?"

"V-man?" Indy asked.

"Yeah, dude. Visitor."

"Right. Yes."

"No probs. I'll spread the word."

"Thanks," she said, staring at her phone incredulously. Just like that, she'd asked, and he hadn't even blinked or questioned her. "Milo's sending backup," she told everyone.

"Awesome," Sawyer said, sounding almost uncannily cheerful.

August looked back over his shoulder, nodding out his rear window. "Not so much." Sawyer twisted in his seat just as August swerved left, sending everyone flying. He stepped on the gas, weaving in and out of traffic up St. Michael's.

Indy counted the cars edging up behind them. One. Two. Three. Four. All suspicious-looking, pretentious monsters—seriously, you'd think the government or whoever would choose more inconspicuous vehicles.

"They came out of nowhere," August breathed. He threw an arm out to hold Lior against her seat. "Hold on." With a controlled twist of the wheel, August spun the GTO, stepping on the brakes at the last minute to orient the car opposite the direction they'd been going. The cars behind them (now facing them) also hit their brakes, momentarily unsure how to proceed.

August took off down St. Michael's again, hooked left, and then swerved from side-street to side-street, doubling back in a series of zees toward Interstate 25. Indy texted Manny their location. She waited for his response, gripping Sawyer's hand hard enough to rip his fingers off.

"Shit," August muttered. "These assholes can drive."

Behind them, in the distance, at least two of the cars were catching up. Indy checked her phone and caught a glimpse of Henry from her periphery. Henry's closed eyes made him look calm, but he seemed to be muttering under his breath. Cautiously, she elbowed him, dipping her head a little to look up at his face from a closer, more private angle.

Henry's lids fluttered open. *Can you stop them*, Indy asked without words, widening her stare for effect; God, she hoped he understood. Henry flared his nostrils and shook his head. He closed his eyes again, except this time, he sat up straighter and pursed his lips.

Behind them, Indy heard tires screech. She whipped around in time to see a trash can bounce off the windshield of the car leading the pack. Another flew from the street into the wheel well of the car behind it, throwing it off its trajectory. All down the street, trash-cans and recycling bins jumped from the curb, pummeling the cars that followed, halting their progress.

Henry shook. Sawyer hooted and shot Henry a high five over Indy's head. Surprisingly, Henry responded, grinning sheepishly as their palms connected.

"I don't know how you did that," Sawyer beamed. "But major awesome!"

"Me neither." Henry tapped the side of his head. "Hurts, though," he mumbled.

August sped away from the bins littering the street, whooping his excitement. As he headed back up St. Michael's, Manny texted them again. "Manny says to head for the intersection up where St.

Francis veers off," Indy told everyone. "He's got guys ready." She turned to Henry. His face looked worn and a little gray, like he'd flung all those containers himself, which she guessed he kind of had. "You're a rock star," she told him, reaching out to grab his hand. "You, okay?"

"Tired." His slight smile only reassured her so much. The object was to get Henry home intact, not maim or even kill him in the process.

"Well, don't force it. Seriously. Don't do anything else, Henry. Not if it's too much."

"I had no idea that would happen. I was just trying to get one to fall into the road and block them. I'm stronger each new time I try."

"Save it, then, for when we're desperate. You look awful."

Henry's face fell, but then he smiled. "You do have a way with words, India."

She laughed. *Don't I, though?* "I just mean . . . you couldn't look awful for real if you tried. I mean, you look tired. Worn out. I'm worried whatever it is you did hurt you."

Sawyer watched them talk, his solemn eyes flitting around the backseat. He looked pensive, maybe even sad, and like there was a lot on his mind, he wasn't saying. Indy felt his heavy gaze. When she shrugged questioningly, he nodded, motioning toward Henry as if to say *don't stress, India. Please make him your priority.*

Letting go of Henry, Indy grabbed Sawyer's hand off her knee and threaded their fingers. Leaning into his shoulder, she whispered, "You are identical. I can't help but notice how handsome he is." She spoke playfully, trying to alleviate any weirdness. "But he's no Sawyer."

The truth was that Indy cared most about protecting the boy she loved. She wanted to help Henry, no doubt, but Sawyer was her heart; and she needed that intact, whatever the cost. Plus, Sawyer wasn't gunning to go somewhere . . . else. Not to mention, he lived on Earth as a *human*. That little bit of info she'd rather die protecting than jeopardize.

Sawyer lowered his mouth to Indy's ear, his breath fluttering her hair. "But if it comes down to it, you'll help him first."

His statement wasn't a question. It came out like a command, rattling around her head. She met his eyes firmly and shook her head *no*.

"He's here because of me."

"And *you're* here because of *me*."

Sawyer kissed the side of her ear. "Please, India."

"If you make me choose, Sawyer, there won't be a contest. I promise to do my best by you both. But you're my priority."

"He should be," Henry said quietly.

Sawyer tipped forward, staring across Indy at Henry incredulously.

Henry flicked a hand in the air. "Don't bother whispering."

"You can hear us?" Sawyer asked.

Henry grimaced. "Sorry. I have to fine-tune my senses to make things move. Unintended side effect."

Sawyer grimaced, then smiled. He nodded vaguely at Indy before leaning across her again to address his brother. "I wish we had more time," he said woefully, "to get to know each other again."

Henry stared straight ahead, speaking to Lior's seatback. "Me too."

"I'm sorry, Henry," Indy added. "I didn't mean I won't do all I can to help you. I mean, I'm here, right? I just . . ."

"Don't want to lose Sawyer," he finished for her.

"Don't want to lose Sawyer," she agreed.

"I get it. I didn't either. I think that's why I didn't go back right away when he went in after you that night." He tipped forward, finally meeting Sawyer's eyes. "I'm sorry I didn't help you."

"We were little kids. I don't blame anyone, Henry," Sawyer assured him. He squeezed Indy's hand. "And you're not losing anyone, India."

As Indy clung to Sawyer, August sped through the intersection past St. Francis, picking up a new flock of lowriders. They streamed out behind his GTO, a few fanning into flanks on either side of the car. The lead lowrider, a glittery orange, mint-condition Buick Regal, pulled beside them on August's left. Its driver projected a peace symbol out the window before pointing forward. August waved his assent, letting the Buick take the lead. Together, they headed for the highway in tight formation.

"Text Manny he's a freaking God," Lior told Indy.

Everyone except August sat torqued in an unnatural position inside August's car, watching the road behind them. Just before the interstate, Indy spotted a group of black chrome cruisers appear out of nowhere, maybe fifty yards behind. "I think they're back," she announced anxiously.

August checked his rearview mirror and then signaled out his window. Within moments, a few of Manny's posse fell back, fancy driving into a gridlock around the growing motorcade. Seconds later, August's GTO broke clear, and August entered the highway tail-free, speeding toward the pass.

"How do they keep figuring us out?" Lior asked, looking back over her shoulder.

Sawyer nodded down at Indy's burner. "It's got to be your phone." Before Indy could answer, he grabbed it, cracked a window, and chucked it out.

"Sawyer!" Indy briefly watched it bounce off the road, splintering into pieces. She stared at Sawyer, mouth agape. But she knew he was right. "They have all of our phones on record then, probably."

Henry dug into his pocket. "Not mine." He handed her his phone. "Use it."

"We'll have to trust that Manny and Cora know where to go," Sawyer told her. "And they may have picked up on Milo's phone, as well, when he called into True North." He grabbed Henry's phone from her hands. "I wouldn't use it unless you absolutely have to."

Indy grabbed it back. If they were going down, they were going down in style. She owed her friends that much. "I have to."

Flicking through Henry's screens, she pulled up True North. In the chatroom, she wrote furiously about their plight, fingerpicking out a live update. She told everyone who might be reading where to meet and what to do should the chrome caravan catch up. If the feds were coming for them (or worse), she might as well call her own cavalry to the fight.

PEDAL TO THE METAL

A HIGHWAY MARKER off the side of the freeway announced the exit to Pigeon Ranch. August rechecked his rearview mirror, scanning the blacktop past the pack of low riders flanking his GTO.

"So far, nada. Looks good, peeps."

Indy exhaled. She'd been holding her breath for what felt like miles. Hopefully, the message she left on True North's board would rally the masses—or at least a few people. They'd been tail free for a couple of minutes now. But just in case, they could use all the help they could get.

August made a smooth exit off the interstate onto a narrow road sprinkled with old adobe buildings past a Mission-style church and a couple of ancient trailer homes. He sped past street signs announcing the towns of Glorieta and La Luna, heading down Highway 60, densely lined on both sides with pinion and junipers. Indy watched everything speed by, blurring into one giant wall of green-brown foliage.

"I'm not exactly sure where to go when we stop," she informed everyone, "other than toward the old battlefield. We'll have to use Henry's phone and pray his GPS works."

Lior turned in her seat, then stopped cold, eyes wide as she craned her neck to see better.

"Lior?" Indy asked anxiously.

Lior pointed behind them through the rear window.

Everyone pivoted in unison. Behind their own car procession, a line of government-looking vehicles appeared, spilling onto the highway from a side road.

Whistling through his teeth, August signaled out his window and popped the GTO into high gear. He stepped on it, pushing the engine to its limit. Lowriders fanned out on either side of him, blocking both sides of the road around his car. They flew down Highway 60, engines revving, boxed in by what looked like a blur of colorful distorted ribbons.

When a helicopter appeared on the horizon behind them, Indy was minutes from freaking out. But as August navigated the road that cut through the foothills of the Pecos Wilderness, nearing the outskirts of the ranch's boundary, she saw cars in the near distance lining the narrow highway. Crowds of kids stood next to them. Some held signs with bold letters that read "Get Your Ass in Gear" and "We Believe." People hollered and waved, and as August passed them by, cars began pulling off the dirt embankment onto the highway behind them, blocking its passage entirely.

Indy inhaled hard, staring up at the sky as a cloud of remote-controlled model airplanes and drones flew toward the approaching helicopter.

"That must have been some message you left on True North." Sawyer wrapped an arm around her shoulder. "You rallied an army."

"They believe in you," Henry told her.

"*We* believe in you," Lior corrected him.

As August's GTO approached the trailhead, cars swallowed them up, blocking the highway entirely from both directions. In the distance, the first helicopter met a second. They rose and then dropped to the north, attempting to maneuver around the drones Indy's supporters launched into the waning, late-afternoon sky.

Surrounded by an army of cars, August stopped in a small, near-completely full lot at the base of the trailhead. Other vehicles parked him in, close enough on either side that it'd be hard to pick the GTO out from a distance. Pleased with himself, he turned in his seat and stared wide-eyed at Indy, waving his hand in front of his face with a flourish. "Your Highness," he said, bowing his head.

Indy tried to smile. "Thank you, August. You're amazing."

Lior patted the GTO's dash. "You should take this monster out to the speedway."

"Yeah?" August beamed.

"Yeah, baby," she grinned.

"What next?" Henry asked, turning to Indy. "It'll be dark soon."

"I've still got all my camping gear in the trunk from Cloudcroft," August told everyone. "Thankfully, I ignored my mother's nagging."

"Freaking boys." Lior sighed.

"Are awesome," August added.

They scrambled out of August's car just as Manny and Cora ran up to them. Cora grabbed Indy and pulled her into a bear hug. "You made it!" she shouted. "I was so worried!"

Indy hugged Cora back, squeezing so hard that letting go again felt like lopping off a lifeline. Still gripping Cora's arm, she turned to Manny. "Thank you! I owe you everything."

Manny bowed, tipping a fake hat. "Cora got us here. This girl is a hella miracle."

Cora blushed.

Indy hugged her again. "He's right."

Sawyer and Henry grabbed every bit of gear left in the GTO's trunk. In the distance, helicopters whirred. People Indy didn't know surrounded them, and as she searched the crowd, anxious to get going, she spotted SLIM, aka Milo Torres. He held his palms up like a scale as he broke through a group of kids, levering them up and down.

"Well?" he asked. "How'd I do?"

Indy ran to hug him. "Thank you!"

"We have to get going." Sawyer's hand closed around Indy's bicep, tugging her away from Milo toward the trail. "Now!"

"Make it back safely!" Milo shouted over the din. "We need you, Indy."

"Keep it together?" Sawyer shouted back at him.

Milo gave them a thumbs up. He pointed at the tight-knit crowd of people holding colorful signs and the sea of rusted, old trucks and tricked-out low riders. Then he held up a microphone, speaking into its mouthpiece. "We've got Orion covered, right?"

The crowd cheered, and someone yelled, "Go! Get your ass in gear, Orion!"

Indy felt a rush of elation. She looked up the hill at the trail leading into the forest, wondering what lay beyond those trees. Wondering whether she'd finally get to meet *them*—Henry and Sawyer's people.

Grabbing Sawyer's hand, Indy scrambled up a rocky path, staring down at Henry's phone as she checked their coordinates. Helicopters still buzzed in the distance, but the thick canopy of spiky, coniferous tree limbs overhead muffled the sound. "This thing is sending us to the north end of the ranch's boundary. About five miles that way." She pointed up a slope.

Henry looked up through the treetops at the darkening sky. "The branches are almost too dense to see through. I think we're pretty well hidden."

"For now," Sawyer added.

Indy followed the GPS, and the group followed Indy, climbing up, then down rocky slopes and mesas, eventually moving off the designated trail. They hiked into increasing darkness, haunted by coyotes howling in the distance, maneuvering through tangled foliage. When the sun set and the forest turned so dark, they couldn't see, Sawyer and Lior walked beside Indy holding their phone flashlights out. In the pitch night, the cool light cast a blue glow that made the forest look spectral.

Indy rechecked their coordinates. "Two more miles."

Licks of Indy's breath billowed in tendrils around her face when she spoke, perceptibly measuring the temperature outside as it plummeted. In her jeans and light sweatshirt, she wasn't dressed for nighttime in the wilderness. None of them were, really.

"This blows," Cora said, her teeth chattering.

Manny adjusted the pack on his shoulder. He threw an arm around Cora's back and pulled her close, keeping pace beside her. "Stay close to me, babe."

"We're almost there, Cor," Lior added. "We'll break out a sleeping bag when we stop."

Nodding her agreement, Indy pulled her free hand out of her jeans pocket, loosened Sawyer's from his, and knitted their fingers together. But Sawyer tugged his hand away and briefly blew on his palm.

"Better?" he asked, joining their hands again.

Indy smiled, trying to project positivity. It was freaking cold out, and the cold had started sapping her already-diminishing energy the moment the sun dipped below the Jemez Mountains to the west. Still, she especially didn't want Sawyer worrying. Deflecting, she nodded back at Henry. "What do you think he's thinking?" she asked quietly.

Henry, who'd fallen to the group's rear, had been silent for what felt like forever. After years of searching for a way home, Indy imagined his anticipation must be overwhelming. She wasn't going anywhere (she hoped), and she still felt like she was hanging on tenterhooks.

"Who knows?" Sawyer shrugged. "Honestly, I'm not even sure what I'm thinking."

Dogs barked in the distance, echoing eerily through the forest. Indy swallowed, wondering how close they were and whether they'd bite or just bark when they caught up. She inhaled deeply and silently recited her ABCs, making it to 'P' before asking, "Are you scared, Sawyer?"

"Yes."

"Really?" her voice wavered.

He tried to laugh. "Surprised?"

"What are you scared of?"

"I have no idea what they want. I'm not even sure I *want* to know anymore."

"Do you want to go with him?"

Sawyer met her eyes. "You mean, back?

Indy nodded.

"No. But I'd be lying if I said I wasn't curious, India."

"I understand," she said quietly.

"Pissed too. Seriously, after all this time, why now? And why you? Are you really the only way they had to contact us? And were they even looking for me? Or just him?"

"I wish I knew." She shrugged.

Sawyer squeezed her hand. "I'll probably just be a big disappointment anyway. I mean, I'm *so* human. But not. Sometimes *I* don't even recognize myself."

"You're what's in here," she pointed to his heart, then touched his head, "not here. You're special because you're not human, yeah. But you'd be special even if you were. Because you're you. Because you *can't* be sorted."

He gave her a look.

"What?"

"Take your own advice?"

Indy started to protest, but Sawyer shushed her. "If you even try to say it's different for you because you're human, or anything even remotely stupid like that, you'll undo everything you just told me."

Even in the dark, Sawyer's eyes shined. Indy stopped briefly and pressed up against him. For a moment, the rest of the world melted away, and she knew as much as she knew anything that no matter what happened later, it would all be worth it.

"I was just going to say that I *am* trying to take my own advice. Strangers put their trust in me. In Orion. If they can do it, so can I. It's up to me to own it. To be bigger than some girl who hides behind a mic."

"I guess we're both special," he said softly.

"Yeah, I guess we are," she smiled.

Sawyer wound an arm around Indy's waist and started walking faster, keeping her close as they hiked up yet another steep incline. The forest thinned out, and the air grew thicker. The atmosphere felt electrically charged, and when Indy climbed over a craggy outcropping of granite up an embankment, little sparks of static erupted out of nowhere. They kindled fairy bursts of light that hung in the air like fireflies.

"What the . . ." Cora stopped, turning in circles.

Dogs barked in the distance, and the staccato sound of chopper propellers echoed through the forest. "We're close." Indy nodded up the hill. She squatted in a nook between two boulders, looking down at the glowing coordinates. "Less than a quarter mile." She glanced up at the crest of the incline.

What were they going to find up there?

Lior clapped her hands together, trying to trap a dancing spark between her palms. "What do you think they are?"

"Some sort of massive electrical disturbance," Henry said.

"He's right," Sawyer concurred, sniffing the air. "You can smell it."

Indy inhaled. The night smelled like wet bark and burnt saltwater.

Hidden between craggy boulders, Manny squatted beside Indy, pulled a can of Coke from his backpack, and passed it around. Indy drank some and took the beef jerky August offered her, realizing after she started chewing that her stomach was growling. Man, if she'd only eaten that egg salad sandwich earlier.

"Ready?" she asked after they rested for a moment.

"Almost there?" Cora asked hopefully.

"I think so."

Indy stood up again, marveling at the light show. The electrical disturbance glowed brightest in the dark, narrow crevices between each boulder, making each ink-black space look a little bit like a gateway to another world.

Single file, they followed a stream of crackling lights, moving through nooks in the rocks as they continued to climb uphill. After a few minutes, the trail leveled off, and they spilled out onto a rocky mesa. Trees surrounded the circular expanse except where the land at the other end of the plain dropped away, lurching precariously downhill. Indy ran across the plain to the other side, staring down into an open valley.

"What now?" Lior asked, catching up with her.

Indy gazed at Henry's phone. "We climb down?"

"We'll be sitting ducks down there," Cora said breathlessly.

Indy stared at the sky, dense with shimmering stars as if someone seeded diamonds across the firmament.

"I don't see anything," Henry murmured, scanning the heavens.

"I don't think we're supposed to. Not yet." Indy's gut told her she wasn't wrong. They were heading in the *exact* right direction. Straight downhill. Whatever was waiting for them would be there.

Henry stared at her. "You're sure we're in the right place?"

She motioned at the GPS on his phone. "Positive."

Sawyer searched the valley below. He pointed toward the base of the cliff at a pile of stacked, flat slabs—slices of sheared rock that must have broken off the side of the mesa and tumbled down the hill. "We can hide in there until something happens. From above, at least, they won't see us."

"*If* something happens," Henry breathed out.

Indy shook her head. *They* were there already. She felt it. "Not if, Henry. When."

Air as crisp as a fresh-picked apple filled Indy's lungs as she slowly made her way down the steep hill, clinging to uprooted tree limbs and branches. Usually, she loved the way nighttime in the wilderness smelled. But the heavy atmosphere weighed her down, and the effort it took to make it to the bottom of the slope in the dark made her lungs feel like they were drowning in liquid nitrogen.

At the bottom of the hill, Indy's knees nearly gave out. Finally on steady ground, she sat on a granite slab and swallowed gratefully, waiting for everyone else to follow.

"In there," Sawyer said when he caught up, pointing to the space beneath an awning of sheered rock. "Just a few more feet."

Indy nodded and turned to scurry under the canopy, but Sawyer grabbed her arm.

"You're right that they're here," he said, offering her his sleeve.

Indy touched her upper lip, already knowing what she'd find. Her head was pounding. Then, she shrugged. If Cloudcroft was any indication, a nosebleed was the least of her worries.

CASTLE IN THE SKY

SITTING CROSS-LEGGED ON the dusty ground under a granite ledge, Indy peeked over her shoulder to spy on Lior and August. Toward the back of their little cavern, the two sat huddled against each other, wrapped in an unfurled sleeping bag. Beside them, Manny and Cora lay on their stomachs in the dirt, their heads upright as they stared out at the night. They'd shimmied into the other sleeping bag together to stay warm and looked like a human enchilada.

Cora smiled at her. "You sure you don't want some of this?" she asked, holding up the edge of the bag. "We'll make room for you." She patted a space between her and Manny.

Indy tried to smile back. "Thanks. But no." She was too busy holding fort, both watching the sky and watching out for Sawyer and Henry. "Feeling warmer yet?"

That 'I'm actually alive' pinkish pallor had finally returned to Cora's lips, thank God. Hers? They felt like the frozen lima beans her mother always bought, almost always forgot to use, and then years later, after they'd hardened into one solid chunk, finally threw away.

285

For the first time in her life, she felt more than disgust for those lima beans. She felt an odd kinship laced with sympathy. *She* was the lima bean in this picture, though possibly even more disposable.

"Any signs of anything?" Lior called up to her.

Indy shook her head and looked dejectedly back at the sprawling glen, searching for Henry and Sawyer. They'd walked the valley's perimeter a handful of times now, ducking into thickets of trees bordering the open field whenever a helicopter swept the valley.

So far, not one of the now three choppers scanning the area had spotted them. Sawyer and Henry's Spidey senses seemed to work better than a fine-tuned clock. But each time they doubled back over the partially snowy field, Indy found herself chewing on an already-ragged thumbnail.

Every second Indy watched Sawyer and Henry interact, another chunk of her heart sheared away. She ached for Sawyer especially. In a way, he'd hidden from the world his whole life. Henry was probably the only person on Earth who completely understood him, and if all went well tonight, they'd never see him again.

Rounding a bend, Henry and Sawyer stopped in front of another thicket of trees. Indy watched Sawyer's hands gesture wildly, their discussion most definitely heated. She sighed, feeling sad for them. Trying to catch up on six years in one hour would be like struggling to stuff a mattress into a pillowcase.

As if reading Indy's mind, Sawyer pivoted. Indy waved at him, then froze, holding her hand suspended in the air when Sawyer cocked his head. Finally, he returned her wave, nodding to Henry before jogging back to their encampment. Glancing briefly toward the middle of the field before ducking under the ledge, he plunked down beside Indy as near as possible without sitting in her lap.

"Hey," he said quietly, wrapping an arm around her shoulder.

Sawyer radiated heat; the weather didn't seem to have the same effect on him. "You're not cold?" she chattered.

He shook his head slowly, deliberately avoiding her eyes. "Henry taught me a trick."

"What, like internal combustion?" she tried to joke.

"Something like that," he answered thoughtfully.

Indy tucked into his side, absorbing his body heat. Sawyer's answer was weird. But what could she say about it, really, other than thank the universe for small miracles (and alien biology)?

"How's it going with Henry?" she whispered.

"Bad. Strange. Good. Hard. We're like two halves of a whole, you know? Symbiotic. I guess I got used to being without him after a while. But I realize now how much of me has been missing. And I feel terrible, India. All this time, at least I had my parents and sister. He's always just been alone." Sawyer palmed his temples. "Part of me wishes I could go back to that night at Holy Ghost River and do things differently."

Indy's eyes watered. She understood, but she'd also lost check of her emotions the moment she'd set foot on the dale. "Like, if you'd left me instead?"

"What?" Sawyer pulled back. "No! I just . . . Henry's the smart one. The careful one. I was the idiot who always got in trouble. Case in point—I wanted to see you up close. To see the river in person. To touch running water. If I'd just stayed put . . ." he shook his head. "But I would never leave you in the river. That's not the part I would change. Even if I knew then that we'd end up here, in the exact same spot."

"You're not an idiot, Sawyer. I think you're smart, and curious, and brave."

"What if I'm not brave enough?"

"You mean if *they* want you back?"

Sawyer nodded.

Indy swallowed her tears. Sawyer had to decide for himself whether to stay. She never wanted to be his reason for second-guessing his feelings. "You'll do what's in your heart, what's right for *you*, Sawyer. Whatever that is, I've got your back."

"I know you do," he whispered. "And I'm grateful for it."

"So, what's he doing?" Indy asked quietly, nodding toward Henry skulking across the field between the trees.

"Concentrating. Trying to communicate with them."

"Can he?"

"He says sometimes he thinks he can. He picked up some of the numbers you channeled before posting them but never channeled the full strings like you did. And he knew it was them, somehow."

Sawyer shifted a little, tucking his chin into the sweatshirt-covered concave of Indy's collarbone. His breath condensed in front of their faces, and Indy imagined it forming a shield that protected them from the suits out hunting her and Henry.

"India," he nudged her, "whatever happens, I have no regrets. Because of you, I finally get to be myself around my friends. I've never let my guard down before. And pretending all the time . . . not having anyone to talk to about . . ." he paused, searching for the right words, "being so different, sometimes it wore me out."

"I hope you stay." Indy squeezed his hand. "But you should know that getting to love you for even just a little bit is better than never having met you. I'll understand if you want to go back. I know they're your people."

Sawyer hooked her chin and met her eyes. "You're my people."

Indy swallowed, too full of an emotion she couldn't articulate. It didn't matter where she was or what she was doing. When she was with him, she felt grounded. "I'm just saying," she whispered. "You need to do what's best for you, despite what I think. I don't want you to wake up one day feeling like maybe you were wrong about being here."

"What if you change your mind about loving me?"

"Not going to happen," she answered confidently.

He held her chin, gently caressing it with a thumb. "Well, then."

Sawyer leaned in and kissed her so lightly, he may as well have been a ghost. His feathered lips traced magic across her skin, and as he lingered, Indy's face flushed with heat that burned from her head to her toes, turning her brain into a molten lump that, at that moment, forgot its purpose entirely.

Then Cora happened.

"Room, much?" she snickered.

Slowly, Indy came to her senses. She blinked, still breathing Sawyer in.

Sawyer snorted. "Jealous, much?"

Cora started to answer, her expression full of mettle, but a sharp, piercing noise stopped her. Sawyer jumped up. He held out a hand, frantically pulling Indy to her feet. In a jumbled rush, everyone scrambled from under the ledge onto the field.

"Cloud?" Lior murmured, looking up at the suddenly turbulent sky.

"Hell, no," Sawyer answered reverently.

Manny crossed himself. "It's like someone dumped a bucket of glitter over the valley."

Indy stared up in awe. Above them, a massive cloud hung low in the atmosphere. It flickered in and out of backlit focus until it finally caught purchase, expanding outward at its scalloped edges like a pooling spring. All around them, the air shimmered, bumping off sparks of gold and indigo that traveled in waves over the basin.

Sawyer grasped Indy's hand. He met her eyes before following her lead, running toward the center of the field. Everyone moved quickly, looking up as they rushed toward Henry.

"I think they finally heard me," Henry said when they met, his voice full of wonder.

Indy shielded her eyes to block the brilliant glow igniting the sky. Whatever the object was, it filled the entire nightscape and then some, sitting over the forest like a massive sombrero. At first, it hovered silently. Then, it inflated, audibly popping as it swelled, generating a deafening rumble that echoed across the vale.

Indy covered her ears. For the briefest second, she wondered if noise alone could kill her.

"India!" Sawyer yelled as she doubled over.

Indy puked on her shoes. The noise had started like static, messy, and singular. But now, bursts of competing bass and vibrato grated like an out-of-sync symphony, causing chaos in her head. She saw numbers in it, outlines embedded in each screeching eruption, bubbles that burst behind her eyes, and bled color.

Palming her ears, she barely noticed that her nose started bleeding again. Too aware of the dogs pulling commando-clad soldiers onto the glen, she tried to block out the rotor noise above, already knowing those choppers would never make it past the valley's treelined perimeter. Gales of wind threw her hair into a torrent around her head, reducing her already blurry vision to smears of shapes and colors. The air surrounding them went mad, and somehow, Indy knew they needed to reach the heart of the growing miasma.

"Run toward the light," she shouted.

"Which light?" Sawyer shouted back.

Indy pulled hair off her face, holding it at bay as she pointed to an iridescent patch of glowing ground in the center of the field. Above it, the sky pixelated, briefly projecting honeycombs through the clouds that stood out like crisp cutouts against a Technicolor backdrop.

Sawyer tugged her forward, motioning for everyone to follow. Heavy-footed, Indy moved toward the light, watching each honeycomb burn distinct shapes in the clouds before flickering out as though branding symbols in a tidy line across the sky. More figures trickled onto the field near the forest's edges, people clad in military garb and those awful barking dogs—blurry forms that slowly filled the valley's borders.

Indy kept going. Nearer to the center of the glen, the air became parched and heavy. Dry heat seared her lungs, and she stopped again, tugging Sawyer to a halt. "Something's off!" she shouted over the din.

Shielding his eyes, Sawyer looked up. "We need to keep going, India," he pleaded, pointing to the soldiers dismounting from ATVs they'd managed to maneuver into the valley.

As people closed in on them, Lior tugged Indy's arm, looking stressed to the high heavens. "Get your asses in gear!" she shouted over her shoulder, dragging Indy toward the light. "All of you! Now!"

Staring up at the pixelated cloud, Indy waffled. Suddenly angry, she balled her fists, working up a lung full of oxygen-fueled courage. "I helped you find Henry! He's right here!" she yelled, pointing at Henry as she tried to hold back another round of vomit. "But you can't have Sawyer!"

The air crackled, lighting brilliant bursts of electricity that charged the surrounding snow and dead grass, compressing Indy's lungs. She gasped, clutching at her chest, and the miasma above them sputtered like an old film reel before abruptly snapping, leaving an enormous, gaping void in the cloud.

"What the hell?" Sawyer turned to Henry.

Forming a tight circle, Indy's group faced outward, bracing themselves for whatever came next as a slew of important-looking people rushed toward them. Sawyer muttered *shit*, then just as some suit approached, faltered. An eardrum-splitting hum pierced the night. The sound sent shockwaves through the valley, nearly knocking Indy to the ground. She grabbed Sawyer's arm to steady herself.

A bolt of lightning struck the heart of Indy's circle. It came from the sky and spread over the ground like a shockwave, immersing them in a rainbow of electric color. One of the government suits stepped forward, skirting the light's perimeter. The woman held her hand out toward its border, then stopped, hurriedly drawing her fingers away. Cradling her hand against her chest, she yelled something Indy couldn't hear, motioning for the rest of her cohorts to halt.

Indy sucked in dry air, wheezing with the effort, then doubled over again. Cora turned in circles, stunned by the light show. But Henry just stared up at the sky. Blinking, he said, "I'm sorry, India. I don't think they're the negotiating type."

IMPOSSIBLE POSSIBLE NIGHT

PEOPLE IN SUITS and military garb moved like snails around their circle, slowly staking out a perimeter around Indy and her friends as though trudging through quicksand. In the distance, Indy picked out people she recognized in the crowd gathering on the glen. Some kids on ATVs had made it past the tree line, breaking through a newly erected military barricade. Farther off, Indy spotted her mom. She stood with an official-looking group of would-be suits, dressed down in less-official jackets and jeans, wringing her hands. Behind her, Indy's dad loomed over an officer near a bunch of pop-up tents that seemed to appear from the ether, his arms flailing in slow motion. Probably, knowing him, threatening to commit bodily harm.

Indy inhaled and held her breath to slow her heartbeat, counting while she licked the blood off her lips. Suddenly frozen in place with the rest of her friends, she couldn't turn her head in either direction, though she managed to force it sideways enough to find Sawyer's eyes. She locked gazes with him, and a string of numbers exploded like fireworks in her head. Sawyer blinked in sync with each flare as though in a trance, fluttering his eyelids as if someone possessed him.

The numbers moved through Indy's head in ribbons, polluting her brain with continuous strings of code-like structure. Her temples throbbed, and she worried she might have a stroke and die. Then, abruptly, the slipstream stopped. Just as suddenly, Sawyer vanished, flaring like a candlewick for a second before disappearing.

A burst of floodlight lit the basin, highlighting the sparkles that hung in the air, illuminating every nook and cranny. Staring wildly at the scene outside their circle, Indy saw that every living thing on the glen had frozen. People stood in weird positions, mid-motion, hovering millimeters off the ground. As her mind registered it, her limbs relaxed, untethering her from her paralysis.

Frantic, she whipped around. Equally panicky, Cora rushed to her side, trailed by Lior, August, and Manny. "Indy!" Cora tugged on Indy's arm. "What happened?"

"Sawyer . . ." Indy barked hoarsely.

"Henry *and* Sawyer," Lior breathed out. "Oh, oh God. Oh, Indy, I'm so sorry."

"Thank God, they sent *you* back!" Cora shouted breathlessly.

"Me?" Indy screeched.

Manny wrapped an arm around Indy's shoulder, pulling her close. August stepped in after him, protectively closing their circle. Above them, the cloud began to hum. Forms shimmered inside it, growing as they pushed outward, breaking through a membrane before dropping mechanical appendages that hung awkwardly in the sky. A blinding red flash introduced a disharmony of oddly shaped machinery that glowed blue against an angry backdrop, flailing to find a foothold before tumbling into tidy formation. The objects came together with a snap, and a parade of glowing octagons formed another long, parallel line beneath the cloud. What looked like an enormous chunk of seamlessly welded skyscrapers materialized like an upside-down city in the sky. Below it, a wide ribbon of dancing color, like an elemental moat, winked down at them.

Indy leaned over and tossed her cookies again, grappling with a new rush of numbers. The baby hairs on her nape and arms stood on end as an unearthly screeching rang out deafeningly over the valley, followed by a blinding flash that smeared everything into a haloed blur. Cora screamed, and Manny's arm went rigid. Together they stood in a blinding-white cocoon, exhausted by the disharmony.

The air smelled like water and dirt and tasted like salt and blood. But as the sound morphed into a frenzied thrumming, the numbers in Indy's head slowed. An indescribable tickle skated through her, top to bottom, tugging out at her toes. And in an instant, she understood everything. Then she slumped to the ground.

A figure stirred on the fringes of their halo, tuning in and out of focus. In a daze, Indy still recognized the fluid way it moved. Detaching herself from the human ball surrounding her, she struggled to stand and dragged herself toward the phantom.

"Sawyer!" she screamed as she connected with his solid frame.

Sawyer's arms surrounded her. He smelled like pine trees, and snow, and burning plastic.

Tightening her grip on him, Indy tilted her chin to meet his eyes. Sawyer had soulful eyes. She could swim in them. Lose herself in them. Read them like a book for the rest of her life and never get bored. And yet she didn't need to look at him to know he was hers now, lock, stock, and barrel if that's what he wanted.

"Are you staying?" she asked anxiously.

Sawyer nodded.

"Henry?"

"Is home now."

She exhaled, expelling the terror she'd stored up. "Finally."

Sawyer stepped back. He pulled something out from under his arm and handed it to her, speaking hoarsely. "I think this belongs to you."

"Boo!" Indy took the ragged, dirty bear, staring at it wondrously.

Above them, the massive mechanical city bounced as though suspended by threads before slowly pulling into a ball. The light washing the glen dulled, and people descended on their circle, moving quickly as their malaise faded. Badge-wearing suits rushed Indy's group, and the object belched out a series of high-pitched timbres. Unfamiliar sounds permeated Indy's skin, and a feeling so foreign, yet so welcome, traveled up her spine. It lingered in her chest before spreading through her body. Her muscles relaxed, and her mind cleared, and as the sensation reached her scalp, dissolving at her crown, the object disappeared, vanishing completely with an audible pop that echoed through the valley.

Indy scanned the surrounding field. Both strangers and people she'd known all her life stood staring up at the sky, wearing the same expressions—a mix of amazement, confusion, and rapture. The air still felt buoyant and charged with expectation, but a sense of calm also suffused the suddenly still, cloudless night. Everyone, including suits and soldiers, smiled. But no one moved. As if people just knew life would never be the same again and, knowing it, wanted to savor the moment.

ROADS LESS TRAVELED

"ARE YOU TELLING me that *they* achieved or attained whatever *they* came for and left? That it's as innocuous as that?"

Fidgeting in her seat, Indy nodded at the woman questioning her, choosing to smile instead of telling her what was on her mind. That Special Agent Crane was incapable of grasping that just because she didn't understand something didn't make it malevolent.

"And your friend, Henry . . ."

"He wasn't my friend," Indy interrupted. She hated saying it but pretending was for the best. "I barely knew him."

"Nonetheless, you claim he's gone now?"

Indy nodded.

Agent Crane stroked her chin, playing the tough gal part. "You say he's not your friend, India. And yet you risked a lot for him. I find that curious."

"Is that a question?"

"If you have an answer."

"The whole thing was like a treasure hunt. I had no idea what the prize was until the end. Henry was the key, and once he contacted me, I knew helping him would be worth it just to find out."

"And was it?" Agent Crane raised an eyebrow.

"You were there. You felt what I did, didn't you?" Indy was sure Agent Crane felt the same thing they all did just before the object disappeared; she'd been at the edge of their circle, itching to reach them, reeling in the rapture of it all.

Agent Crane studied Indy, looking down her nose from a semi-perched position on the table. She wore a tight gray suit over a black blouse and tiny, black pearl earrings. With her severe ponytail and arched eyes, she reminded Indy of a cat. "Contrary to what you probably think, India, it's not my intention to harm you. Defensiveness isn't your friend here. There's no reason for it."

After 'the event'—Crane's term for it—hostile-looking soldiers gathered Indy and her friends, threw them in a blacked-out van, and took them to this stupid complex. Agent Crane was probably military or NSA or something. They'd separated Indy from her parents and, later, her friends and Sawyer; she didn't know where she was or whose hands she'd fallen into, though she was reasonably sure she wasn't going to be tortured or locked up (fingers crossed). But still. *No reason for it?* She'd watched them forcibly round up everyone in the valley before they dragged her to who-knows-where without so much as a *sorry.* How was she not supposed to be defensive?

"You didn't answer my question," Indy mumbled.

"Which question was that?"

"About how you felt right before it disappeared."

Agent Crane squinted down at her. "I felt . . ." she paused, "something we'd all like to understand better."

"You felt *possibility.*"

"What?" Agent Crane arched an eyebrow.

"It was possibility. The feeling that anything's possible. Because it is."

"I'm not sure that's how I'd characterize it."

"Okay. Well, that's what I felt." Indy squinted up at her.

"India, how long have you known about these people?"

"I don't even know that they are people."

"Do you have any reason to believe they're not?"

"Does it matter?" Indy exhaled, overwhelmed by what she'd learned on the glen. That Sawyer and Henry hailed from a galactic crew of historians, scientists, and observers. Intra-spatial travelers. Beings from other planets and galaxies, but also different dimensions. Part of a band that for millenniums moved between realms, monitoring and inscribing their findings in a sort of universal, multi-dimensional sourcebook before settling in a dimension above Earth's orbit. They'd been here longer than humans, just not always perceivable—like a radio signal relying on an unreliable transmitter.

Agent Crane inhaled and lifted her chin, affording her a better angle to look down at Indy. "You're a bright young woman, India. I don't think I need to explain why this is of the utmost importance. So yes, it does matter. Wouldn't it be wonderful to finally know for sure we're not alone? And wouldn't it be wonderful to know they're like us rather than worry we're being invaded or annexed by a wholly different . . . civilization?"

"We're not alone. Obviously. We've never been alone. And another world full of people just like us?" She pretended to gag herself. "God, no. That's scarier."

Agent Crane crossed her arms over her chest and tipped back. She sized Indy up thoughtfully. "Do you think they mean us harm?"

Indy eyed her, remembering what Sawyer said just before Agent Crane and her cronies grabbed them all.

They're cleaning house. Collecting surveyors and informants, retrieving associates they've lost. Returning humans they've studied. Getting ready for when our worlds collide. Because they will, India. Some day. The veil separating Earth and the Etherverse is fading.

"I don't think so," she gulped, crossing her fingers under the table. Sawyer swore his people had less than no desire to harm humankind. But that didn't mean they wouldn't if they decided eradication was for the greater good of their people.

"What *do* you think, India?"

"I think they want us to be better. I think tonight was a lesson. Or maybe a gift."

"What kind of gift?"

"Certainty," Indy answered resolutely. "I think they want us to know humans are both unique to Earth *and* a part of a much bigger collective. I think they're hoping it'll help us figure out we're all the same species. That knowing there's more than just humans out there will help us learn to get along."

"Are you implying they think we're dangerous or myopic?"

"We kind of are, aren't we?" She shook her head. "I think they're hoping we figure out that we can be unique and still similar simultaneously, that there's no reason our 'differences' can't co-exist harmoniously given the big picture." Indy threw up air quotes around the word 'differences,' understanding, finally, just how loaded the word was when used to pigeonhole people. "Because there's no way we'll be able to accept *them* or anything else that might be out there until we do."

"Interesting." Agent Crane tapped a short, neatly manicured nail against her chin. "And why do you think they care?"

Indy dropped her face in her hands, rubbing her tired eyes. "I don't know," she mumbled into them. "Maybe just because. Or maybe because they're better than us at being awesome."

"And Henry? Did he share this sentiment?"

"Henry just wanted to go home," Indy said softly.

"You started True North because you already knew about them? To spread their word?"

Indy wasn't sure whether Agent Crane just asked a question or stated something she already believed, but it made her curious. She looked up at the woman, intrigued. She wanted to know what Agent Crane knew, especially if it helped her figure out what *not* to say.

"I had less than a clue why they were even here until a couple hours ago." Indy tried to keep a straight face and sit very still. She'd never been a good liar. "Did you know? That they were here before True North?"

"We've had some indication over the years. But your show helped us better frame the information we'd already gathered." Agent Crane cleared her throat. "You should be proud of True North, India. Your show exposed them. And now that we know what we're up against, we can address the problem."

Problem. Indy covered her mouth, holding back a giggle. Exhaustion made every already-stupid thing Agent Crane said seem absurd. "They're visitors, Agent Crane, not colonists."

"That's what they told you?"

"It's what I know."

"What else do you know?"

"Not much," Indy sighed. Other than that, observers often viewed their subjects through the lens of their own biases. And that when it came to humans, boy, did Sawyer's people have a few. Not that Indy blamed them. It couldn't be easy knowing your entire existence might someday hinge on the behavior of an irrational species. "Are my friends and I in trouble?"

"Not if you continue to cooperate. What made you think of colonists?"

"I read a lot. Besides, isn't that what always happens in the movies?" Indy crossed her arms and leaned forward, sliding them across the top of the metal table. After a moment, she dropped her head, resting her chin on a forearm. "When can I go home?"

"Do you have any reason to think they'll come back?"

"I don't know," Indy lied.

"And all this 'let's all get along' kumbaya business, you know this how?"

Indy tapped a finger against her temple. "I heard it in the valley."

Agent Crane stood up and clasped her hands in front of her pelvis, exhibiting prim but shrewd confidence. "They spoke to you?"

"Not exactly. I think they were trying to communicate with Henry before they took him. There were these numbers, like code or something. I saw them before he disappeared, and I just . . . figured it out, I guess."

"Like the numbers you started seeing last June?"

"Something like that."

"Why do you think they chose you?"

Indy struggled to stay composed. They didn't *choose* her, exactly. She'd chosen them all those years ago when she fell in the river and dragged Sawyer into her life. Since then, she'd just been their means to an end—a simple human with basic-enough DNA to track down. A conduit, if not a beacon, a way to find their boys and finally bring them home. "I've thought about that a lot. And I still don't know. Believe me; I wish I did."

Agent Crane tidied her suit jacket before undoing its buttons. She pulled a chair out and sat down again across the table from Indy. "You drowned in grade school. Records indicate your heart stopped."

Sucking in her surprise, Indy sat up straighter.

"It's called 'clinical death,'" Agent Crane continued, training her intense gaze on Indy's face. Cocking her head slightly, she tipped her chin toward her chest as she pursed her lips, possibly trying to look sympathetic. "A handful of studies have found that certain resuscitated patients wake up with new abilities. Just know you're not alone, India."

"You think I have . . . abilities?" Thanks to Sawyer's lingering signature and the clever way his people put Boo through simple DNA electrophoresis to track her down, Indy already knew she'd forever be an alien cellphone. If she wanted to, *she* could communicate with *them*, too, but it would always be hard on her physically.

"Possibly." Agent Crane squinted at her. "But I'm willing to bet there's more to it than that."

"Well…" Indy snorted, breathing in quickly to slow her thumping heartbeat down. "I'll let you know if I ever figure it out."

"I'll hold you to that."

"Can I go home now?"

Agent Crane leaned forward, squaring off with the table. "None of you know what happened to Henry?"

"They took him." Indy shrugged. "You saw what I did."

"Nothing was clear through the halo that surrounded you, India."

Indy frowned at her. Why were adults so clueless? "Except he disappeared."

"Was Henry born on Earth?"

"No. I don't think so."

"And none of you knew where Henry meant when he said he wanted to go home?"

"Not at first. Not until I finally actually met him."

"Not even Sawyer?"

Unnerved by Agent Crane's line of questioning, Indy sat back, putting as much space between herself and the annoying agent as she could. "How would Sawyer know?"

"You tell me."

"If I knew I wouldn't be asking *you*, would I?"

Agent Crane sat back in her chair, looking down at the table as she casually traced a finger across its top. After making a long, straight line, she looked up and met Indy's eyes. "And no one else in your group tonight sought you out because of, or through, your show?"

"No. They're all my friends. I've known them all for years."

"Even Sawyer?"

"I mean, kind of? I've known him for a few years."

"And no one else in your group was involved with True North?"

Indy met Agent Crane's stare. No way was she letting the woman talk her in circles. After a moment, she answered, "No. True North was all me. My boyfriend didn't even know I was Orion until last week. At first, he was kind of pissed off."

Arms crossed; Agent Crane nodded toward the glass pane behind Indy's head. If it weren't for the scowl on her face, Indy would say she was pretty. As it was, she reminded Indy of a shrew. A cat-shrew in a lousy mood stuck with an anemic mouse. Indy would bet she'd have more fun interviewing Cora. At least then, she'd have a feisty contender.

"Sawyer is your boyfriend?"

"Right."

"Are you aware that other observers we interviewed tonight stated they thought Henry *was* Sawyer?"

"That's dumb." Indy faux-huffed. "Obviously, he's not."

"Do they look alike?"

"Not really."

"Did Sawyer know Henry before tonight?"

"No. Like I said, he didn't even know I was Orion."

Agent Crane raised an eyebrow, her eyes simmering with suspicion. "And yet he was with you earlier."

"Sawyer may have been pissed at me for lying to him, but he loves me. It's not like I had to brainwash him." Indy pronounced the word *brainwash* testily. "He always has my back."

"Apparently."

"What's that supposed to mean?"

"Your stories are nearly identical, India. Word for word. He must *really* love you."

The room's dim lighting hurt Indy's head. After everything that happened, and at what had to be the crack of dawn, she was through talking. "Seriously, I've told you everything I know. I'm exhausted, Agent Crane. And unless I'm in trouble, and you're holding me here for some reason you haven't told me about yet, I'd really like to go home now."

"You realize that no one outside your group recalls tonight's events quite the same way. You six share the *only* consistent story."

Indy shrugged. "And?"

"And it doesn't add up." Agent Crane leaned in closer, smirking at Indy for good measure. "Nonetheless, if there's something more to find, we'll find it." She nodded up at a camera in the corner of the room. "Let's bring your parents in."

Seconds later, a disengaging pressure lock whooshed, signaling that Indy was no longer a prisoner. To Indy's right, a metal panel popped open, and another suit walked in, swinging the behemoth door inward. Her parents followed just behind him.

"Indy!" Her mother rushed over to hug her. "Thank God."

The male suit tossed a file on the table. He rifled through it and pulled out a stapled group of papers, then started regurgitating information like an automaton. Indy couldn't leave the state of New Mexico for six months and, afterward, would have to register with DOAB—the Department of Alien Biology—when she did (and who knew *that* existed?). She wasn't allowed to talk about The Event with anyone outside her group. She wasn't allowed to communicate to outsiders what she saw on the glen, not even in fanciful stories or drawings. She was to continue airing True North and debunk all postings about the 'incident' at Pigeon Ranch. They expected her to feed people misinformation. And when she turned eighteen, she'd have to register with the NSA, and the DOAB for life or until DOAB decided otherwise. The list went on and on.

"Seriously?" Indy whistled through her teeth.

Indy's mom tried to interject. "India's not signing this without consulting a lawyer. She has rights."

Agent Crane stood up, looking almost sympathetic as she shook her head. "Not in this case." She nodded at her colleague.

The man cleared his throat and recited some gobbledy-gook-sounding government statute, denying Indy her right to representation in the face of national or international security threats involving non-terrestrial intelligent lifeforms.

Indy's mouth dropped open. *For real? They have a statute dealing with non-terrestrial intelligent lifeforms? How often did this kind of thing happen?*

Agent Crane smiled briefly, obviously reading Indy's mind. "Just assume you're in good company. And be grateful you still have any freedom at all."

"So, my daughter will be a prisoner all her life?" her dad barked.

"Maybe refocus that question. She'll be protected. To do that, we must keep an eye on her. She's free to do whatever she wants within the bounds of that waiver."

"And my friends?" Indy whispered.

"Didn't predict an alien visitation or channel alien visitors," Agent Crane answered. "Unless there's more you'd like to tell us."

Indy shook her head adamantly.

"Well, then, they've signed entirely different waivers."

The man pushed the stack closer, along with a pen.

Indy looked at her dad, who nodded slowly. "I don't see that we have a choice," he told her.

"India, this is about protecting you as much as it is about national security," Agent Crane assured her. "I don't think you've quite grasped what it would mean to garner attention like this on a worldwide scale. You're better off being thought of as an instigator or charlatan."

"Except people will think I'm a fake," she murmured.

"As they should. Yours and your friends' stories may be consistent, but they'll be easy enough to discredit. You are easy enough to discredit, my dear. Trust me when I say it's much better to be pegged as a phony than to be known as the girl who channels aliens and can usher in an apocalypse. Until we know more, plausible deniability is better for everyone. And people will still have their epiphanies. Let them wonder. Isn't that what True North is ultimately about?" Agent Crane paused and swept the room with her eyes, landing on each of their faces for a second. "No one is going to call you a fraud unless you try to convince them aliens made contact tonight. Every single person in that valley has or will sign a waiver under serious threat of perjury. Anything leaked will be discredited. And leakers will go to jail. You say what we tell you to, and listeners who weren't there will blame Orion's denials on the government. They'll form conspiracy theories. Your show and your coordinates will become an urban legend. However it plays out, True North will still be celebrated. *You* still end up the hero in this story, India. And real or not, *this* outcome leaves everyone asking exactly what you wanted them to in the first place, questions that provoke wonder and promote possibility."

"But it's a lie," Indy whispered.

"It's for the greater good. We all lie sometimes," Agent Crane said knowingly. "Even boyfriends. Though something tells me Sawyer, particularly, will understand."

POSSIBILITY

TWO CAMO-CLAD SOLDIERS shuffled Indy and her parents down a brightly lit concrete hall. Moving like wind-up dolls, they maneuvered through a maze of walkways lined with discreetly closed doors, out through a warehouse, into a fenced-in courtyard bordered by muddy-looking cement blocks and barbed wire. Tall, looming mountains surrounded the tight complex, softening its militant edges. The early morning sun shone over their eastern peaks, casting ruby shadows that painted the escarpment scarlet.

Looking up at the glowing sky, Indy thought about Henry. As soldiers marched her family out to a heliport, she wondered whether he found what he was looking for and if he'd stay with his people. Or if he'd find his way back to Sawyer after learning more about where he came from. If he'd ever change his mind about who his 'people' are. *They* weren't going anywhere. They'd made that clear. She supposed Henry had time to figure out whether, after being on Earth for so long, he was more visitor or human.

Nearer to the heliport, Indy spotted Sawyer sitting with his parents in a military chopper parked on the blacktop and had to stop herself from running to him. At that exact moment, Sawyer glanced up. His back straightened as his face ignited, suddenly transformed by the relief that hijacked his eyes and mouth. Indy grinned at him and felt her jaw crack; it wasn't possible to smile any wider.

As Indy approached the chopper, the soldier walking beside her clasped her shoulder, speaking loudly over the whir of the slowly turning rotor. "It'll take you to the Santa Fe Airport. The rest of your friends have already been flown home. Take care, Orion," he winked. "I love your show. And I'm rooting for you."

Nodding her thanks, Indy made a beeline for the cargo hold, grasping Boo as another soldier helped her up into the tight compartment. He helped her mom and dad up, cramming them all together inside. Squeezed in beside Sawyer, Indy grabbed his hand, grateful for its feel when his fingers engulfed hers.

The helicopter lifted and banked left, sailing above the craggy mountains. They traveled toward Santa Fe silently and thank God because she was way too tired to try to make sense of the night, much less what it meant for her future. Quietly, she stared out the window, watching as they cruised over forested summits and long stretches of sharply peaked mountains, nervously white-knuckling Sawyer's palm until the chopper finally touched down on a private helipad at the Santa Fe Airport.

After the last twenty-four hours, landing almost seemed anti-climactic. Indy climbed out and straggled behind her parents, too exhausted to do much more than follow.

"India, do you have a moment?" Sawyer's mom stopped her just as they reached the row of idling Town Cars near a hangar. She motioned Indy away, pulling her aside. "I want to thank you. For helping Sawyer."

Indy searched her face. "You're welcome," she said softly.

"Sawyer is . . . *complicated*." His mom's voice sounded strained, but she followed it up with a meaningful smile. "You know him well, so I expect you've figured that out already. I have no idea what happened at Pigeon Ranch, but we're grateful you were with him and that he chose to come home. You've been good for him. And it's clear why."

Indy blushed, then hugged Sawyer's mom. When she let go, Sawyer was at her side. "What's going on here?"

"Your mom was just telling me how special you are."

"Yeah?"

"Yeah." Indy smiled. "And she's right."

Sawyer looked between them, winking at his mom before nodding toward the cars lined up on the tarmac. "Can I ride alone with India? Maybe you and Dad can ride with her parents?"

Sawyer's mom reached out and ran a hand over his cheek tenderly. "We have a lot to talk about, Sawyer. It's well past time. But if you promise to get home by dinner, I guess it's all right. As long as India's parents don't mind."

Sawyer hugged his mom hard, engulfing her tiny body. When they parted, he smiled at her shyly, brimming with realization. They knew. They'd probably always known. And they'd still loved him unconditionally.

Clasping Sawyer's hand, Indy got the go-ahead from her parents, then pulled him into one of the waiting Town Cars. Processing everything that'd happened would be a skullwank of epic proportions. But until she slept for like twenty weeks, it was pointless even to try. Right now, she just wanted to be as close to Sawyer as possible.

All shoulders and thighs, they clung to each other in the backseat as the car headed out onto the highway, driving under a dawn sky. Nearer to Indy's house, Sawyer leaned between the front two seats to get the driver's attention. "Do you mind if we stop at the overlook on Ridgetop Road for a few minutes?" he asked politely.

The driver slowed near the ridgeline above Indy's neighborhood, stopping at a dead end looking out over the city. A sliver of ruby sun peeked above the Sangre de Cristo Mountains, hanging over the Santa Fe Basin, and Indy marveled at how the light turned Santa Fe into a fiery wonderland. She opened her door and stepped out into the early morning air, thanking her lucky stars she got to see it. It wasn't the first time, but it was the best time, and something told her she'd remember the moment forever.

"How are you?" Sawyer asked, pulling her to him.

"Tired."

"I feel that." He tightened his arms around her. "I just wanted to make sure you're okay. I don't know about you, but they put me through the wringer."

"Yeah, me too." She stared up at him, visually tracing the worry lines etched across his usually smooth forehead. "But I stuck with our story. The Feds have no idea they're still here. Or that you have anything to do with Henry."

"They'll be watching me." His eyes sparkled. "And you. You know that, right?"

"Your people? Or mine?"

"Both." He tried to smile.

Sawyer toyed with Boo's leg, tapping his ratty foot against Indy's waist. She hadn't been able to let go of Boo since Sawyer handed him to her, as if their reunion absolved her of six years of questions and doubt, grounding her back in reality. Plus, she knew Boo's return was more than a token. It was a lifeline.

"We'll be okay," she reassured him.

Indy grimaced. The times she'd spent with Sawyer's people was slowly returning to her. Last night, and last week, and all the visits before that. All the years they'd taken her, and studied her, and relied on her to help them find Sawyer and Henry. The times they'd erased her memories; how she'd conveniently forgotten all the other nosebleeds and vomit-fests leading up to last night.

"Does it bother you?" he asked. "Knowing it's my people up there, plotting Earth's future?"

"Not the 'your people' part, no. I don't think they're evil. Just practical. The rest, though—it's a little scary. But we also have no idea what they'll decide. And whatever it is, it could also be hundreds of years from now."

He smiled warily. "Or tomorrow."

"You're the one who said if I can't change the future, I may as well enjoy the ride."

"No fair turning my words on me." Sawyer looked down at her. His eyes shone, crinkling at the corners as he leaned to kiss her. "But here's to a wild journey."

A cloud passed before the sun, casting shadows over the Santa Fe Basin. The last twinkling streetlights glittered for a second, and Indy turned to savor it. "At least they're rooting for us," she said softly.

One day, when the veil between Earth and the Etherverse finally thinned to a filament, and Sawyer's people had no choice, they'd arbitrate Earth's future. Judge, jury, and executioners. But they were also banking on people like her and Sawyer to persuade humans to get their asses in gear before it was too late. Sawyer's people *wanted* to think the best of humans. And ironically, by introducing her to Sawyer, even if not so intentionally, they'd taught her to start doing the same.

"It's all about True North," she told him.

"Helping people find their compass?"

She nodded forcefully and squeezed his hand, staring at him intently.

Sawyer held her gaze, swimming in it like always as if reading her mind. "Time to plot a revolution?"

Indy stood on her tiptoes and kissed his cheek. "I've got your back if you've got mine."

ACKNOWLEDGEMENTS

Writing acknowledgments is hard work. Since I reside in the land of 'too much information,' striking the perfect balance between sappy and genuine sometimes feels like it takes longer than writing a book. But since I've always tried to convey to my own YA crew that being yourself is the best self you can be, I'm just going to trust that you're okay with whatever side I land on. That said, thank *you*, first and foremost for reading this book. If even just one of you can't put it down, I've done my job. And also, your love and feedback keep me writing.

Many thanks to my incredible beta readers (and unofficial copy-editors) Greg Wagner, Susan Huber, Tamar Stein, and Stef Willen who gave me not just helpful, but incredibly thoughtful feedback. Thanks to my writing group for supporting me, believing in me, and listening to all my ideas these last few trying years, especially Patrick Lee. Your love and support are invaluable.

Thank you also to my people, some of whom I've already mentioned but also includes Carolyn Huber, Maria Virobik-Lee, Melissa Mendonca, Dondra Bowden, Margaret Marinoff, and Rachel Hopkins. Every writer needs a crew, and you're the best there is.

And a huge shout-out to Elaine at Illusion Publishing for being both awesome and talented and to Estella Vukovic for another incredible cover.

I also want to specially acknowledge everyone who has taken time out to review my books and share your posts on social media. The excitement and love you've shown my books online are both incredible and invaluable. I will forever appreciate you.

Finally, thank you to my family — my mom and dad Tamar and Abe, my spouse and confidant Greg, my too-hard-to-find-the-perfect-adjectives-to-describe-how-much-I-love-them kids Elijah, Gabriel, and Hubble (because dogs are family too), and my sister Libby Edelson, whom I always name toward the end of my acknowledgments, but only because I like saving the best for last. You are all truly the things that bring me the most joy and I couldn't possibly imagine doing any of this without you.